Mothers-To-Be

But they're unexpected pregnancies!

GW00393957

**Acclaim for Lynne Graham, Emma Darcy
and Leigh Michaels**

About Lynne Graham
"Lynne Graham's strong-willed, hard-loving
characters are the sensual stuff
dreams are made of."
—*Romantic Times*

About Emma Darcy
"Emma Darcy dishes up a spicy
reading experience."
—*Romantic Times*

About Leigh Michaels
"Leigh Michaels gives fans a wonderful
reading experience."
—*Romantic Times*

Mothers-To-Be

PRISONER OF PASSION
by
Lynne Graham

THE LAST GRAND PASSION
by
Emma Darcy

SAFE IN MY HEART
by
Leigh Michaels

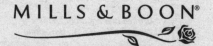

MILLS & BOON®

DID YOU PURCHASE THIS BOOK WITHOUT A COVER?

If you did, you should be aware it is **stolen property** as it was
reported *unsold and destroyed* by a retailer. Neither the author nor the
publisher has received any payment for this book.

*All the characters in this book have no existence outside the imagination
of the author, and have no relation whatsoever to anyone bearing the
same name or names. They are not even distantly inspired by any
individual known or unknown to the author, and all the incidents are
pure invention.*

*All Rights Reserved including the right of reproduction in whole or in part
in any form. This edition is published by arrangement with Harlequin
Enterprises II B.V. The text of this publication or any part thereof may
not be reproduced or transmitted in any form or by any means, electronic
or mechanical, including photocopying, recording, storage in an
information retrieval system, or otherwise, without the written
permission of the publisher.*

*This book is sold subject to the condition that it shall not, by way of trade
or otherwise, be lent, resold, hired out or otherwise circulated without the
prior consent of the publisher in any form of binding or cover other than
that in which it is published and without a similar condition including this
condition being imposed on the subsequent purchaser.*

*MILLS & BOON and MILLS & BOON with the Rose Device
are registered trademarks of the publisher.
Harlequin Mills & Boon Limited,
Eton House, 18-24 Paradise Road, Richmond, Surrey, TW9 1SR*

MOTHERS-TO-BE
© by Harlequin Enterprises II B.V., 1999

Prisoner of Passion, The Last Grand Passion and *Safe in My Heart* were
first published in Great Britain by Mills & Boon Limited
in separate, single volumes.

Prisoner of Passion © Lynne Graham 1996
The Last Grand Passion © Emma Darcy 1993
Safe in My Heart © Leigh Michaels 1993

ISBN 0 263 81543 9

05-9911

*Printed and bound in Spain
by Litografía Rosés S.A., Barcelona*

Lynne Graham was born in Northern Ireland and has been a keen Mills & Boon® reader since her teens. She is very happily married with an understanding husband, who has learned to cook since she started to write! Her three children keep her on her toes. She has a very large old English sheepdog, which knocks everything over, and two cats. When time allows, she is a keen gardener.

Lynne has been writing for Mills & Boon since 1987 and has now written over 25 books, which are loved by readers worldwide—she has had more than 10 million copies of her books in print, in many different languages.

PRISONER OF PASSION
by
Lynne Graham

CHAPTER ONE

HEADS turned when Bella walked down the street. Her rippling mane of Titian curls, her incredibly long legs and her outrageous hotchpotch of colourful clothes caught the eye. But it was her prowling, graceful stride and the light of vibrant energy in her face which made the attention linger. Bella always looked as if she knew exactly where she was going.

She lifted the public phone off the hook and punched in the number. 'Griff?'

'Bella, I'm so sorry…something's come up,' he groaned. 'I have to go back into the office.'

'But—' Her clear eyes froze as she heard a woman giggling somewhere in the background. Griff went on talking, although there was a similar catch of amusement in his voice. Apologising, he assured her that he would be in touch.

Five minutes later Bella was back in the wine bar with her friends.

'Where have you been?' Liz hissed, under cover of the animated conversation.

'Calling Griff…'

'You mean he's not on his way yet?'

Bella gave a careless shrug.

'He's let you down, hasn't he?' her friend said bluntly.

Bella didn't trust herself to speak. And the very last thing she needed right now was a lecture on the subject of Griff Atherton, who was everything Gramps had ever told her to look out for in a man but who was inexplicably as unreliable as they came, in spite of his good education, steady job and stable family background.

'You really know how to pick them,' Liz lamented. 'Why do you always latch on to the creeps?'

'He's not a creep.'

'It's your birthday. Where is he?'

Bella shed her battered cerise suede fringed jacket and crossed her legs below the feathered hem of her minuscule new chiffon skirt, covertly attempting to stretch it to a more reasonable length. Liz had bought the skirt for her birthday. It was far too short but she had to be seen to wear it at least this once.

'So what was Griff the Glib's excuse this time?'

'Wow, look at those wheels!' Bella exclaimed hurriedly, keen for a change of subject. She craned her neck to gaze out at the gleaming silver sports car drawing up outside the five-star hotel on the other side of the street. 'That's a Bugatti Supersport.'

'A what?' Obediently distracted, Liz peered without a lot of interest and then gasped. 'Look who's getting out of it! Now that is what I call—'

'Fabulous engineering.' Bella was eyeing the sleek lines of the powerful car, not the driver with his smouldering, dark good looks. Bella preferred blonds.

'I haven't heard Rico da Silva described in quite those terms before.'

'Who?'

'If you ever put your nose inside a serious newspaper, you'd recognise him too. He's absolutely gorgeous, isn't he?' Liz looked rapt. 'He's also single and loaded!'

'He has a beautiful set of wheels. Is he into motors?'

'He's an international financier. The local paper did a profile on him,' Liz told her. 'He owns a fabulous country estate just outside town. He spent millions renovating it.'

Bella grimaced. Finance…money…banks. She never went into a bank if she could help it, didn't even own a cheque book. People who wheeled and dealed in money and profit made her skin crawl. A faceless smoothie from

a bank had pushed Gramps' business to the wall and put
him into a premature grave.

'That's his current lady,' Liz murmured as a beautiful
blonde woman swathed in fur emerged from the hotel.

Tall, dark and handsome with the little woman. Bella
wasn't in the mood to be generous. They looked like some
impossibly perfect couple from a glossy magazine. His and
hers matching glamour. They had that aura of untoucha-
bility which only the seriously rich exuded. It was there
like a glass wall between them and the rest of the human
race. A clump of pedestrians stopped to let them pass in a
direct path to the Bugatti. They took it as their due.

'How the other half lives,' Liz sighed with unhidden
envy.

'Time we got this party off the ground!' Bella stood up,
spread a brilliantly bright smile round her assembled
friends, and switched into extrovert mode.

Dammit, where was the turn-off? Bella called herself a fool
for not staying the night with Liz as she had originally
planned, but Liz had been in the mood to preach and Bella
hadn't been in the mood to listen. Now it was three in the
morning. The roads were deserted. And somehow she had
got lost. *There* it was! Jumping on the brakes, Bella swung
into a frantic last-minute turn. As she made it a gigantic
yawn engulfed her taut facial muscles. As she emerged
from it, rubbing at her sleepy eyes, another car appeared
directly in the path of her headlights.

With a shriek of horror Bella barely had time to brace
herself before impact. The jolt of the crash shuddered
through her entire body, the sickening noise of buckling
metal almost deafening her. Then there was a terrible silence. Fast to react, Bella's first thought was for the other
driver. Her windscreen was smashed. She couldn't see a
thing. She lurched out of the Skoda on legs that felt like
jellied eels.

A hand clamped round her slim shoulder. 'Are you hurt?
Have you passengers?'

'No!' Taken aback by someone with even faster reactions than her own, Bella hovered in the biting wind tun-
nelling down the street as the powerful head and shoulders
ducked into the cluttered interior of her car, which more
closely resembled a travelling dustbin than a vehicle. Her
teeth chattered with shock, her aghast attention logged onto
the truly appalling amount of damage done to her car. The
whole bonnet was wrecked.

'You madman!' she burst out helplessly. 'What were you
doing on the wrong side of the road?'

The large presence straightened. Bella was not small and
she was wearing very high heels, but the male beside her
still towered above her. In the streetlight his hard, dark
features were as unyielding as hewn granite.

'What was I doing?' he repeated in a raw tone of disbelief, and this time she caught the foreign inflexion, the
thickness of an accent that was certainly not British.

'Did you forget we drive on the left here?' Bella asked
furiously.

'You stupid bitch…you're on a one-way street!' With
that he strode back to his own car.

A one-way street? About to open her mouth and loudly
disclaim that ridiculous assertion at the same time as she
asked him who the hell he thought he was calling a stupid
bitch, Bella looked back to the corner and saw the sign. A
one-way street. She had turned right into a one-way street
and not unnaturally had had a head-on collision. Devastated
by the realisation that the accident was entirely her fault,
Bella leant against the wing of the Skoda because her knees
were threatening to give way.

The other driver was lifting something out of his car. Oh,
dear God, what had she hit? For the first time she looked
at the other vehicle. It had a hideous *déjà vu* familiarity,
only it had looked considerably more pristine earlier. A

Bugatti. She had wrecked a Bugatti Supersport which retailed at somewhere around a quarter of a million pounds. She wanted to throw herself down on the road and scream like a banshee in torment. Her insurance premium would rocket into outer space after this…correction; she'd be lucky to *get* insurance. This wasn't her first accident, although it was certainly by far the worst. Dammit, what was the guy's name? Why, oh, why had she let her temper rip and called him a madman?

'What are you doing?' she demanded in a weak voice, moving forward.

He was lounging against his status-symbol car, which was not quite the status symbol it had been. And he had a mobile phone in his hand. Just her luck—a guy with a phone in his car!

'I am calling the police,' he imparted, with a decided edge of, And aren't you going to enjoy that? in his growling delivery.

'The p-police?' Bella stammered shrilly, plunged into further depths of unhidden horror. She turned as white as a sheet.

'Naturally. Why don't you get back into your vehicle and await their arrival?'

'Do we need the police?' she asked in a shaky voice, her heart sinking to the soles of her feet at the prospect of being arrested on a charge of careless driving.

'Of course we need the police.'

Bella took another desperate step forward. 'Please don't get the police!' she muttered frantically.

'I should imagine that you will be breathalysed.'

'I haven't been drinking. I just don't see the necessity to get the police!'

'I expect they already have more than a passing acquaintance with you.' Rico da Silva sent a glittering look of derision over her.

'Well, we wouldn't be complete strangers, let's put it that way,' Bella conceded, thinking back miserably to her earliest memories of what her travelling mother had called police harassment. No matter how hard she tried Bella had never lost that childhood terror of the uniformed men who had moved them on from their illegal camping grounds.

'I didn't think so. It's a hard life on the street,' he murmured, shooting her scantily clad, shivering figure an intent but unreadable glance. 'Heading home from the nightshift?'

What the hell was he talking about? Struggling to concentrate, she moved even closer. 'We could sort this out…just you and me, off the record,' she assured him in desperation, skimming an anxious glance across the street as another car passed by, slackened speed to have a good look at the wreckage, and then drove on. Any minute now a patrol car would be along.

'*Es verdad*?' Diamond-bright dark eyes scanned her beautiful, pleading face, his strong jaw line clenching hard as a long finger stabbed buttons on the mobile phone without her even being aware of it. 'I don't think so. In that one field alone I prefer amateurs.'

'Amateur what?' Bella returned in despair, deciding that *he* had definitely been drinking.

And then she heard the police answering the call, registered that he had already dialled, and allowed sheer panic to take over. Snaking out a hand, she grabbed at the phone. Lean fingers as compelling as steel cuffs closed round her wrist and jerked it ruthlessly down. She burst into floods of tears, her overtaxed emotions shooting to a typically explosive Bella climax and spilling over instantaneously.

'You bully!' she sobbed accusingly.

With a raw gasp of male fury, the background of the police telephonist's voice was abruptly silenced as if the man before her had cut the connection. 'You attacked me!' he grated.

'I just didn't want you to ring the police!' she slung back, on the brink of another howl. 'But go ahead! Have me arrested! I don't care; I'm past caring!'

'Stop making such a noise,' he growled. 'You're making an exhibition of yourself!'

'If I want to have hysterics, that's my business!' she asserted through her tears. 'What do you think *this* is going to do to my insurance?'

There was a short silence.

'You *have* insurance?'

'Of course I have insurance,' Bella mumbled, making an effort to collect herself and keeping a careful distance from him, since he had already proved that he was the aggressive type.

'Give me the details and sign a statement admitting fault and you can be on your way,' he drawled with unhidden relish.

Bella shot him an astonished glance. 'You mean it?'

'Sí…five more minutes in your company and I will understand why men murder. Not only that, I will be at the forefront of a campaign to bring in the death penalty for women drivers!' Rico da Silva intoned between clenched teeth.

Sexist pig. Smearing her non-waterproof mascara over her cheeks as she wiped at her wet face, Bella bit back the temptation to answer in kind. After all, he was going to be civilised. If he had smashed up *her* Bugatti she probably would have wanted blood too. Prepared to be generous, she still, however, gave a deliberate little rub to her wrist just to let him know that he might not have drawn blood but he might have inflicted bruises.

He planted a sheet of paper on the bonnet and handed her a pen.

'You write it; I'll sign it,' she proffered glumly.

'I want it to be in your handwriting.'

But he still stood over her and dictated what he wanted

her to write. She struggled with the big words he used, her rather basic spelling powers taxed beyond their limits.

'This is illiterate,' he remarked in a strained voice.

Bella's cheeks flamed scarlet. Her itinerant childhood had meant that she had very rarely attended a school. Gramps had changed all that when she had gone to live with him but somehow her spelling had never quite come up to scratch. Laziness and lack of interest, she conceded inwardly, for she possessed a formidable intelligence which she focused solely on the field of art. Spelling came a very poor second.

'But it's fine,' Rico da Silva added abruptly, suddenly folding it and stuffing it into the pocket of his dinner jacket.

Seeing him reach for his phone again, she gabbled the name of her insurance company in a rush.

'I'm ringing for a tow-truck for the cars,' he murmured, reading the reanimated fear on her expressive face.

'Oh... Thanks,' she muttered, turning her head and strolling away while he made the call, far more concerned with what it would cost to pay for the towing service. 'I'm sorry about your car. It was beautiful,' she sighed when he had stopped speaking.

'I'll call a cab for you.'

Bella bit out a rueful laugh. She lived in London, which was almost sixty miles away. The cab fare home would be a week's wages—maybe more. 'Forget it.'

'I will pay for it.'

She dealt him a disbelieving look. 'No way.'

'I insist.' He was digging a wallet out of his pocket with astonishing alacrity.

'I said no,' she reminded him flatly, embarrassed to death by the offer and hurriedly attempting to change the subject. 'Cold for May, isn't it?'

'Take the money!' he bit out with stinging impatience.

Bella frowned, hunching deeper into her battered jacket, one long, shapely thigh crossed over the other, her fantastic head of hair blowing back from her exotic features in the breeze. 'What's the matter with you? I have to wait for the tow-truck.'

'I'll wait for it,' he told her harshly.

'Look, it isn't my car...'

'What?' he raked at her.

'It belongs to this old man I live with. I only have the use of it,' Bella explained soothingly.

Narrowed dark eyes rested on her, his beautifully shaped mouth hardening, and she found herself staring at him, noticing the shape of his lips. It was the artist in her, she supposed abstractedly. He would be an interesting study to paint.

'How old is old?' Rico da Silva enquired, surprising her.

'As old as you feel.' Bella laughed in more like her usual manner. 'Hector says he feels fifty on a good day, seventy on a bad. I reckon he's about the latter.'

'And what are you?'

'Twenty-one...' she checked her watch '...and four and a half hours.'

'Yesterday was your birthday?'

'Lousy birthday,' she muttered, more to herself than him. 'I had to work.'

'It happens,' he said in a strained voice.

'And my boyfriend is two-timing me.' It just came out. She hadn't meant to say it. Maybe it was the effect of bravely smiling all evening and keeping her mouth shut with her friends.

'The pensioner?' He sounded even more strained.

It was the language barrier, she decided. How on earth could he imagine that she was dating a man old enough to be her grandfather?

'Not Hector—my boyfriend.'

'Maybe you should think of another occupation—something that keeps you home at night...although perhaps not,' he muttered half under his breath.

Had she told him that she was a waitress? She didn't remember doing so but she must have done. Screening another sleepy yawn, Bella sighed. 'I don't mind most of the time, although it's murder on my feet and it's very boring. Still, it pays the rent—'

'He charges you rent?'

'Of course he does…although not very much.' She yawned again, politely masking her mouth with a slender hand. 'He tried to claim for me as a housekeeper but the Inland Revenue weren't impressed. I'm not really very domestic but he wouldn't like it if I was. It's kind of hard to explain Hector to people…'

'Are you in the habit of telling complete strangers the most intimate details of your life?' Rico da Silva prompted in a tone of driven fascination.

Bella thought about it and then nodded, although she would have disputed his concept of 'intimate details'. Friends said, 'I told you so.' Strangers just listened and volunteered their own experiences. Not that the male standing next to her would. He was the secretive type, she decided. Still waters ran deep—dark and deep as hell with this one, she thought helplessly.

'You're a financier,' she remarked conversationally, thinking that what was good enough for the gander was good enough for the goose.

'How the hell do you know that?' he shot at her forbiddingly.

Bella gave him a startled look. 'I saw you earlier this evening and a friend told me who you were.'

'And then all of a sudden you crash into me. Two such coincidences in one night strain my credulity!' Rico da Silva shot at her.

'Pretty lousy luck, huh? If I'd done the cards this morning I probably wouldn't have got out of bed—'

'"The cards"?' he echoed.

'Tarot cards. Though mostly I steer clear of the temptation to tell my own fortune these days. Sometimes I think you're better not knowing what's ahead of you.'

'I do not believe in such a coincidence,' he stated afresh, staring down at her in a very intimidating fashion. 'It was your intent to meet me, *es verdad*?'

'You're a very uptight personality.' Bella shook her vibrant head. 'And a bit weird, to be frank—'

'*Weird*?' Rico da Silva roared. 'You think that I am weird?'

She raised her hands. 'Now just count to ten and back off, buster.'

'"Buster"?' he repeated, snatching in a hissing breath.

'Mr Silver...no, it wasn't that, was it?' She sighed.

'Rico...da...Silva,' he enunciated very slowly and carefully, as if he were talking to a complete idiot.

'Yeah, I knew it was something strange. I hate to tell you this but it *is* a little weird to imagine that a total stranger would crash into you *deliberately* to meet you,' Bella told him gently. 'I mean, I might have been killed.'

From beneath black lashes so long that they cast crescent shadows on his savage cheekbones, he cast her a glimmering glance. 'I have known women to take tremendous risks to make my acquaintance.'

'I wonder why?' she said, and then realised by the sudden, thundering silence that she had said it out loud instead of just thinking it. 'What I mean is...well, there's only one way of saying this, Mr da Silver—'

'Silva!' he slotted in rawly.

Uptight wasn't the word for it. This guy lived on the outer edge. On the brink of gently assuring him that he had met some very peculiar women, Bella was silenced briefly by the sight of the tow-truck surging up the street towards them.

'Talk about service!' she gasped. 'I thought we'd be here for hours!'

'Another half-hour of your relentless, mindless chatter and I would be—'

'More hyper than you already are? It's OK. I'm not offended,' she told him with a smile. 'You either love me or you hate me. But, for your own sake, get your blood pressure checked and take up something relaxing like gardening. Guys like you drop dead from heart attacks at forty-five.' Dragging her attention from the darkening colour of his cheekbones and the razor-slash effect of his incredulous gaze, Bella turned to gape at the arrival of a second tow-truck. 'Gosh…one each!'

With that, she rushed over to the Skoda, belatedly realising that she would need to clear the car out. She was kneeling on the driver's seat, poking around amongst the rubbish for stray items of clothing, letters, bills, her sketchpad and pencils, when his voice assailed her again from behind.

'I will expect you to pass on your insurance details to my secretary tomorrow. This is the number.'

Awkwardly she twisted round and reached out to grasp a gilded card and dig it into her pocket.

'If you don't call, I will inform the police—'

'Look, what are you trying to do—give me nightmares?' she exclaimed helplessly, clinging perilously to the steering wheel to lean out and look up at him. 'I am a law-abiding person.'

'To trust you goes against my every principle,' he admitted unapologetically.

'You wouldn't want me to lose my licence, would you?' Bella fixed enormous green eyes on him in reproach. 'It took me a lot of years to get that licence. The examiners used to draw lots for me and the one that got the short straw was *it*! I mean, we all have weaknesses and mine is in the driving department, but this is truly the very worst accident I have ever had and I am going to be much more careful in the future…cross my heart and hope to die—'

'Or shut up.'

'I beg your pardon?' She squinted up at him.

He extended his phone with an air of long-suffering hauteur. 'Ring your boyfriend to come and pick you up.'

'You've got to be kidding. He'd probably say his car had a flat tyre or something anyway,' she mused, returning to her frantic clean-up.

'There must be somebody you can contact!'

'At four in the morning to take me back to London?' And pigs might fly, her tone said.

'I am not giving you a lift!' he snapped in a whiplash response.

So he had been heading for London too. 'I wasn't aware I asked for one,' she hissed. 'Now why don't you just go away and leave me alone?'

'I am being foolish. No doubt you are accustomed to walking lonely streets at this hour of the night, *es verdad*? But it is hard for me to forget my natural instinct to behave as a gentleman—'

'I would have said you forgot it the minute I hit your car…but it's OK,' Bella continued sweetly. 'I didn't notice. I haven't got much experience of what you would probably call gentlemen. I cut my teeth on creeps.'

There was a fulminating silence.

'Make sure you make that call tomorrow.'

Bella scrambled out backwards with her bulging carrier bag, wondering why he was still hovering. Approaching the driver of the tow-truck, she told him to be sure to dump the Skoda at the *nearest* garage possible. Hopefully that would cut the cost. 'I can't pay you now,' she then said awkwardly. 'I haven't got enough money on me.'

'I will take care of it,' Rico da Silva announced glacially from behind her.

She grimaced and ignored him to ask the driver what it was going to cost. Her horror was unfeigned. 'I'm not asking you to *fix* it!' she protested in a shattered voice.

'I said I will pay the bill!' Rico da Silva blitzed.

Her temples were pounding like crazy. She just couldn't fight any more. Once again she nodded. Anything for a quiet life. She started to walk away. Her feet were killing her.

'Where are you going?'

'The bus station.' She glanced back at him with a frown of incomprehension, well aware that he liked her just about as much as she liked him, wondering why on earth it should matter to him how she intended to get home.

'*Madre de Dios*!' he ground out, skimming a furious hand of frustration through the air. 'There will be no buses until morning!'

'Morning's only a couple of hours away.'

'I'll give you a lift,' he bit out between clenched teeth.

'Forget it.'

'I said I will give you a lift, but only on one condition— you do not open your mouth!'

'I prefer the bus. It's more egalitarian. I'm allowed to breathe, you know, that sort of life-enhancing stuff called oxygen? I use up a lot of it, but thanks all the same.' And then she saw the limousine waiting by the kerb on the other side of the street and her sleepy green eyes widened to their fullest extent. She had assumed that he was catching a cab. But a lift in a real live limo... She just couldn't resist the offer. 'Mr da Silva?' she called abruptly.

'I thought you might change your mind,' he breathed, without turning his glossy dark head. 'I must be out of my mind to be doing this.'

'Doing what?'

'Give my chauffeur your address and then shut up,' he grated.

Bella climbed in and surveyed the opulent interior with unhidden fascination. 'Do you always travel...sorry, I forgot!'

The limo purred away from the kerb. Her companion

stabbed a button, and under the onslaught of her incredulous scrutiny a revolving drinks cabinet smoothly appeared. 'Wow,' she said, deeply impressed.

'Do you want a drink?' he asked shortly.

'No, thanks. My father was next door to being an alcoholic. Personally speaking, I wouldn't touch the stuff with a barge-pole!'

He expelled his breath in a hiss. She watched his hand still and then hover momentarily before he finally grasped the whisky bottle.

'I guess—'she began, and then sealed her mouth again as those black-as-night eyes hit on her with silencing effect.

'You guess what?' he finally gritted. 'Don't keep me in suspense!'

'I was going to say that we don't have a lot in common, do we? It's a bit like meeting an alien,' Bella mumbled, sleep catching up on her as she rested her heavy head back against the leather upholstery and closed her drooping eyelids. 'Except even the alien might have had a sense of humour...'

Someone was shaking her shoulder hard. She surfaced groggily, registered that she was lying face down on some kind of seat, then remembered and hauled herself upright into a sitting position.

'This cannot be where you live!' Rico da Silva vented with raw exasperation. 'Is this your idea of a joke?'

Bella focused on the familiar Georgian square of enormous, elegant terraced houses, which had been her home for the past year. 'Why should it be my idea of a joke?' She fumbled with the door-release mechanism but the door remained stubbornly closed.

'I should imagine that not one in a thousand hookers lives in a house worth millions!'

'Hookers'? He thought she was a hooker? He thought she sold her body for money? Aghast, Bella stared at him for several seemingly endless seconds, telling herself that she had somehow misunderstood him. 'You think I'm a prostitute?' she finally gasped, wide-eyed with rampant disbelief. 'How *dare* you? Let me out of this car right now!'

A winged ebony brow quirked. 'Are you saying now that you are not?'

'Of course I'm not!' Bella threw at him in violent outrage, belatedly understanding all of his peculiar utterances. 'I've never been so insulted in my life! You have a mind like a sewer—'

'You dress like one—'

'*Dress* like one?' Liz's wretched too short skirt! She wanted to scream.

'And you came on to me like a whore!' he condemned, without batting an eyelash.

'"Came on to" you?' Fit to be tied, Bella looked at him with splintering green eyes. '*Me*...come on to you? Are you crazy?'

'You offered yourself to me—'

'I *what*? You're a lunatic... Let me out of this car; I don't feel safe!' she shrieked. 'I should never have got into it in the first place. I knew you were weird!'

'Are you trying to tell me that I was mistaken?' His strong, dark features were fiercely clenched.

'How dare you think I would come on to you?' Bella spat at him like a bristling cat. 'I never go for dark men! Your car was at more risk than you were! And I may wear second-hand clothes, talk with an Essex accent and hardly be able to spell, but that doesn't mean that I don't have principles! It might interest you to know that I'm a virgin—'

He burst into spontaneous laughter. In fact he threw his dark head back and very nearly choked on his disbelief. Bella launched herself across the car at him in a rage and two strong hands snaked out and closed round her narrow forearms to hold her imprisoned mere inches from him and in devastating contact with every line of his leashed, powerful body.

'A virgin?' he queried in a shaking voice. 'Maybe not a whore…but definitely not a virgin.'

'Let go of me!'

For a split-second he stared down into her brilliant green eyes and something happened inside her—something that had never happened to Bella before; a tight clenched sensation jerked low in her stomach. It made the hair prickle at the back of her neck, the breath catch in her throat, every muscle draw taut. She looked back at him with dawning comprehension and horror, feeling the swell of her own breasts, the sudden, painful tightening of her nipples.

'So what *do* you do on the nightshift?' Rico da Silva probed in a purring undertone that set up a strange chain reaction down her spine.

Seriously shaken by the reaction of her own treacherous body, she remained mutinously silent.

'And where *does* Hector fit in?'

'Let go of me… I don't feel well,' Bella muttered tremulously, and it was true.

He searched her pallor, abruptly freeing her. His ebony brows had drawn together in a sudden frown. She had the strangest feeling that he was as disconcerted by his own behaviour as she had been.

'I'll talk to your secretary tomorrow,' she mumbled, her nerves strung so tightly that tension was a fevered pulsebeat through her entire body.

He pressed a button. The chauffeur climbed out and opened the door in the humming silence. Bella flew out like a cork ejected from a bottle and fled up the steps of the shabbiest house in the row. Inserting her key, she unlocked the front door, then rushed into the shelter of the dark house and rested back against the door like someone who had seen death at close quarters. Every sense on super-alert, she listened to the limo driving off before she breathed again.

Shock was still reverberating through her. She had felt so safe for so long. *That* had never happened to her before with a man. And then all of a sudden, when it was least expected, she had been gripped by the most dangerous drive in the entire human repertoire—sexual desire. But she was really proud of herself. Control and common sense had triumphed. She had run like a rabbit.

CHAPTER TWO

IN THE half-light Bella picked her way past the piled-up books and newspapers that littered every stair and headed up to the second floor and the privacy of her spacious, cluttered studio. She was still shaking like a leaf. So *that* was what it felt like! She lit the candle beside her bed, and slowly drew in a deep, sustaining breath. Well, thankfully she was extremely unlikely ever to see him again. There was no need to worry about temptation in that quarter. Even so, she was still shaken.

'I go with my feelings—that can never be wrong,' Cleo had once said loftily, supremely blind to the wreckage of disastrous relationships in her past. Her mother had been like a kamikaze pilot with men. Every creep within a hundred-mile radius had zeroed in on her, stopped a while and then moved on. But Cleo had kept on trying, regardless of the consequences to herself and her daughter, always convinced that the *next* one would be different. And Liz could have no idea just how much it scared Bella to be told that she suffered from a similar lack of judgement with the men in her life.

When she came downstairs later that morning Hector was shuffling about in his carpet slippers in the ancient kitchen. The gas bill had arrived. He was taking it as hard as he always did when a bill came through the letter box. There were the usual charged enquiries about how often she had used the oven and boiled the kettle. Hector Barsay's mission in life was to save money.

It was his one failing but, as Gramps had often said, everybody had their little idiosyncrasies, and those same little idiosyncrasies got a tighter hold the older you got.

Beneath his crusty, dismal manner Hector was kind. He had
a bunch of prosperous relatives just waiting for him to die
so that they could sell his house and make their fortunes.
None of them had visited since the time they had tried to
persuade him into an old folks' home and he had threatened
to leave them out of his will.

'I crashed the car last night,' Bella told him tautly.

'Again?' Hector cringed into his shabby layers of woolly
cardigans and she squirmed, guilt and shame engulfing her.

'It's not going to cost you anything!' she swore.

'I haven't got anything!' His faded blue eyes rolled in
his head at the very suggestion that his pocket might be
touched.

'That's what you have insurance for,' she told him in
consolation. 'Before you know it the Skoda will be back in
the garage as good as new.'

Back upstairs, she dug out her insurance details and
wrinkled her nose. The renewal hadn't yet been sent but
then they always took their time about that and, to be fair,
she had been a little late in sending on the money because
Hector had made her ring round half of London trying to
get a cheaper quote. When you had to do it from a phone
box, that took time.

She headed out for a phone. Hector insisted that his
phone was only to be used in an emergency. The girl at
the insurance company was chatty until Bella explained
about the accident. Then she went off the line for a while.

'I'm sorry, Miss Jennings,' she murmured on her return,
'but at the time of the accident you were not insured with
us—'

'What are you talking about?' Bella was aghast.

'Your premium should have arrived by Tuesday. Unfortunately it was two days late—'

'But surely—?'

'You were given an adequate period in which to respond
to the renewal notice.'

'But I—'

'We will be returning your premium in the post. The offer was not accepted within the stated period and we are entitled to withdraw it.'

Argument got Bella nowhere. Reeling with shock, she stood back to let the next person in the queue use the phone. From her pocket she removed the card that Rico da Silva had given her. How could she ring his secretary and tell her she had no insurance? Dear heaven, that was a criminal offence!

A Bugatti… In anguish she clutched at her hair, her stomach heaving. And what about the repair of Hector's Skoda? She would be in debt for the rest of her life. Maybe she would go to prison! Rico da Silva had that piece of paper on which she admitted turning the wrong way into a one-way street without due care and attention!

An hour later Bella was hanging over a reception desk and smiling her most pleading smile. 'Please…this is a matter of life and death!'

'Mr da Silva's secretary, Miss Ames, has no record of your name, Miss Jennings. You are wasting your time and mine,' the elegant receptionist said frigidly.

'But I've already explained that. He probably forgot about it, you know? He had a late night!' Bella appealed in despair.

'If you don't remove yourself from this desk I will be forced to call security.'

'At four this morning Rico told me to ring his secretary!' Bella exclaimed, shooting her last bolt.

Sudden silence fell in the busy foyer. Heads turned. The receptionist's eyes widened and were swiftly concealed by her lashes, faint colour burnishing her cheeks. 'Excuse me for a moment,' she said in a stilted voice.

Bella chewed anxiously at her lower lip and watched her retreat to the phone again; only, this time the conversation that took place was very low-key. She skimmed a hand down over her slim black Lycra skirt, adjusted her thin cotton fitted jacket and surveyed the scuffed toes of her fringed cowboy boots. A clump of suited men nearby were studying her as if she had just jumped naked out of a birthday cake.

But then it was that kind of building—a bank. Just being inside it gave her the heebie-jeebies. All marble pillars and polished floors and hushed voices. Sort of like a funeral parlour, she reflected miserably. And she didn't belong here. She remembered that time she had gone to plead Gramps' case and the executive had been so smooth and nice that she had thought she was actually getting somewhere. But double-talk had been created for places like this. The bank had still called in the debt and Gramps had lost everything.

'Miss Ames will see you,' the receptionist whispered out of the corner of her mouth. 'Take that lift in the corner.'

'How can I help you, Miss Jennings?' She was greeted by the svelte older woman as the lift doors opened on the top floor.

'I need to see Mr da Silva urgently.'

'I'm afraid that Mr da Silva is in a very important meeting and cannot be disturbed. Perhaps you would like to leave a message?'

'I'll wait.' Bella groaned. 'Maybe you could send a message in to him?'

'And what would you like this message to say?'

'Can I come in…like, go and sit down?'

The older woman stepped reluctantly aside.

Loan-sharking certainly paid. Bella took in her palatial surroundings without surprise. 'I'll write the message.'

A notepad was extended to her. Bella dashed off four words, ripped off the sheet, folded it five times into a tiny scrap and handed it over.

'Mr da Silva does not like to be disturbed.'

'He's going to like what I have to tell him even less,' Bella muttered, sprawling down on a sofa.

Miss Ames disappeared. The brunette at the desk watched her covertly as though she was afraid that she was about to pocket the crystal ashtray on the coffee-table. Two minutes later Miss Ames returned, all flushed and taut.

'Come this way, please…'

Bella strode up the corridor, hands stuck in her pockets, fingers curled round the pack of cigarettes that nerves had driven her to buy before she'd entered the bank.

'What the hell are you doing here?' Rico da Silva blazed across the width of the most enormous office she had ever seen. Her heels were sinking into the carpet.

She looked around her with unhidden curiosity and then back at him. He had to be about six feet four. Wide shoulders, narrow hips, long, lean legs. Michelangelo's *David* trapped in the clothing chains of convention. Navy pin-striped suit, boring white shirt, predictable navy tie—he probably put on a red one for Christmas and thought he was being really daring. He was looking her over as if she were a computer virus threatening to foul up the entire office network. She tilted her chin, and her gaze collided with glittering golden eyes…

He had really gorgeous eyes. In the streetlight she hadn't got the full effect. Eyes the colour of the setting sun, spectacularly noticeable in that hard-angled, bronzed face. Eyes that sizzled and burned. The key to the soul. There was a tiger in there fighting to get free—a sexual tiger, all teeth and claws and passion. On some primal level she could feel the unholy heat. Wow, this guy *wants* me, she registered in serious shock.

'I asked you what the hell you're doing here,' Rico repeated with leashed menace.

Bella dragged her distracted gaze from his, astonished to discover how hard it was to break that connection. Reddening, she went tense all over, embarrassed by her last crazy thought. 'I said it in my note.'

'And what exactly is "*We* have a problem" intended to denote? By the way, problem is spelt with an e, not an a,' he delivered, hitting her on her weakest flank.

'I'll try to remember that.' She studied her feet and then abruptly, cravenly yielded to temptation and dug out the cigarettes and matches. Never had she been more in need of the crutch she had abandoned the day she'd moved into Hector's house. She was just on the brink of lighting up when both the match and cigarette were snatched from her. Under her arrested gaze the cigarette was snapped in two and dropped in a waste-paper basket.

'A member of the hang-'em-high anti-smoking Reich?' Bella probed helplessly.

'What do you think?'

She felt that she had never needed a cigarette more. 'Just one…?' she begged.

'Don't be pathetic. It won't cut any ice with me,' he drawled, with a sardonic twist to his mouth. 'What is the problem?'

Bella swallowed hard and then breathed in deeply.

'You look guilty as sin,' Rico informed her grimly. 'And if my suspicions as to what has prompted this personal appearance prove correct I'm taking you straight to the police.'

The tip of her tongue slid out to moisten her dry lower lip. His lashes lowered. Hooded eyes, revealing a mere slit of gold, dropped to her mouth and lingered there. A buzzing tension entered the atmosphere. The silence vibrated.

As Bella laid her outdated insurance policy on the desk in front of him she felt as though she was moving in slow motion. 'Can I sit down?'

'May I sit down,' he corrected automatically. 'No.'

He scanned the document.

'You see, it only ran out Monday,' Bella pointed out, in

a wobbly plea for understanding. 'And I sent in the new premium and thought it was fine. But when I phoned the company this morning…'

The well-shaped, dark head lifted. Lancing golden eyes bit into her shrinking flesh. 'You were driving without insurance when you hit me—'

'Not intentionally!' Bella gasped, raising both hands, palms outward, in a gesture of sincerity. 'I had no idea. I thought I was covered. I'd sent off the money and I bet that if I hadn't had an accident they would have just accepted it and renewed my insur—'

'You're whining,' Rico cut in icily as he rose from behind his impressive desk.

'I'm not whining. I'm only trying to explain!' she protested.

'Point one—if you were not covered by insurance at the time of the accident the oversight was your responsibility. Yours, nobody else's,' he stressed with a glacial lack of compassion. 'Point two—in driving a car without insurance you were committing an offence—'

'But—'

'And point three—I most unwisely chose to let you go scot-free from the consequences of the offence you had *already* committed last night!'

'What offence…? Oh, the one-way street bit,' Bella muttered, hunching her narrow shoulders in self-defence. It was like being under physical attack. 'But that was an accident… It's not as though it was deliberate. Anyone can have an accident, can't they? I'm really sorry. I mean, I would do just about anything for it not to have happened, because now everything's in this horrible mess—'

'For you, not for me.' Rico sent her a hard, impassive look. 'When I inform my insurance company of this they will insist that I bring in the police and they will pursue you for the outstanding monies in a civil case.'

Bella went white and twisted her hands, moving from

one long, shapely leg on to the other with stork-like restiveness. 'Please don't get the police. Somehow I'll pay you back…I promise!' she swore unsteadily.

'Is Hector going to pay?'

Bella flinched. 'No,' she mumbled.

'I've already had a quote for the damage to my car.' He gave it to her. Bella watched the carpet tilt and rise as she fought off a sick attack of dizziness brought on by shock. 'Somehow I don't think that you can come up with that kind of cash.'

'Only in instalments.' And if I starved, lived rough and went naked, she added mentally, beginning to tremble. He had spelt out the cold, hard facts and her vague idea that they might somehow be able to come to an arrangement had bitten the dust fast. She couldn't expect him to pay for the repairs to the Bugatti and wait for twenty years for her to settle the debt. Intelligence told her that, but a numbing sense of terror was spreading through her by the second.

'Not acceptable. So therefore it goes through *on* the record with the police,' Rico da Silva informed her flatly.

Already she was backing away, knowing that she was about to break her most unbreakable rule and copy Cleo. She was going to run, pack a bag and leave London—go back to the old life where there were no names, no pack drill, little chance of being caught by the authorities. How had she ever got the idea that she could make it in this other world with all its rules and regulations?

'You're not leaving,' he warned her grimly.

'You can't keep me h-here!' Bella stammered fearfully. 'You can put the police on to me but you can't keep me here!'

'I call Security or I call the police. I'm not a fool. If you walk out of here you'll disappear. Maybe the police are already looking for you,' Rico da Silva suggested, studying her slender, quivering, white-faced figure with cool assessment. 'For some other offence?'

'I don't know what you're talking about!'

'You're terrified.' His shrewd gaze rested intently on her. 'A bit over the top for a charge of careless driving and doing so without insurance. If it's a first offence you'll be fined. However, if this is merely the latest in a line of other misdemeanours I can quite see why you wouldn't want the police brought in.'

In his mind she had already gone from being a lousy driver to being a persistent offender. She had met prejudice like that before. Her first year with Gramps had been hell outside the sanctuary of his home. Neighbours, teachers and classmates had been all too ready to point the finger at Bella when there had been a spate of thieving in school. Bella had never stolen anything in her life, but had the true culprit not been caught in the act she was well aware that everyone would have continued to believe her guilty.

With the last ounce of her pride she thrust her head high. 'I have a clean record!'

'*Excelente*. Then you will not throw a fit of hysterics when I take you to the police station.'

'*You*...take me to the p-police station?' The fire in her was doused, cold fear taking over.

'Tell me why you are so petrified of the police,' he invited, almost conversationally.

'None of your bloody business!'

His strikingly handsome features clenched. 'It's not my problem. I suggest we get this over with. I have a busy day ahead of me.'

'I'm not going to any police station with you!' Bella gasped strickenly. 'You'd have to knock me out and drag me by the hair!'

'Don't tempt me.' Rico da Silva sent a look of pure derision raking over her, his eloquent mouth compressing. 'And stop play-acting. I'm not impressed. You're no shrinking violet, *querida*. What you've got you flaunt!'

'Don't talk to me like that!'

'I took pity on you last night, but when you strolled in here today you made a very big mistake,' he asserted with cold emphasis. 'You thought all you had to do was flash those fabulous legs and the rest of that devastating body and I'd be willing to…shall we say…negotiate?'

'I didn't think that!' Bella objected in sick disbelief.

'*Sí*…yes, you did.' Rico vented a harsh laugh that chilled her. '*Dios mío*…you may not be able to spell anything above two syllables but you market flesh like a real professional. Hot and cold. I could have had you last night if I had wanted you. And I did want you. Just for a moment. There isn't a man in this building who wouldn't want you… You're an exceptionally beautiful young woman,' he conceded very drily. 'But I don't play around with whores. I never have and I never will.'

She was shattered by his view of her, could not begin to understand what she had done to arouse such brutal hostility. Nausea stirred in her stomach. She felt soiled. Apart from that final moment inside his limousine last night she had been totally unaware of him as a *man*, even as a very attractive man. She had made no attempt to attract him. She hadn't flirted or looked or done anything which could have warranted this attack on her.

Yet now he was calling her a whore again, clearly still convinced that she was at the very least promiscuous and the kind of woman who used her body like a bargaining counter in a tight corner. It was an image so far removed from reality that she told herself she should be laughing. But instead it hurt—it hurt like a knife inside her breast just the way it had hurt when the village had whispered about her behind her back all those years ago.

He closed a firm hand round her arm and propelled her out of his office towards the lift. Her dazed eyes caught the amazement on his secretary's face as she appeared in a doorway. Bella was too shocked to relocate her tongue before they were inside the lift.

'You're out of your mind,' she whispered, her temples thumping with tension.

'Tell it to the police.'

'You're not t-taking me to the police!' Panic set in again as she was recalled to the reality of his intentions. Like an animal suddenly finding herself in a trap, she whirled round, hands flailing against the stainless-steel walls as she sought escape.

He grabbed her with strong hands and settled her back against the wall.

'Let go of me!' she screamed, without warning running violently out of control. Fear was splintering through her in blinding waves. 'Let me go, you bastard!'

He pinned her carefully still with the superior weight and strength of his hard-muscled length. He spat something at her in Spanish, glaring down at her with incandescent eyes of gold and blatant incomprehension. 'I'm not going to hurt you. Why are you behaving like this? Calm down,' he bit out from between even white teeth.

'Let me go… *Let me go!*' she chanted wildly. '*Please!*'

'If I don't take you to the police I'll take you home.' Every muscle in his dark features rigid, he slung her a look of smouldering sexual appraisal which was flagrant enough to make her knees sag and her darkened eyes fill with an ocean of sheer shock. '*Sí*…and bed you like you've never been bedded before! I have never wanted anything as badly as I want you, and the knowledge that I can afford you doesn't help. It's a sick craving and I am not yielding to it,' he muttered roughly, so close now that she could feel his breath on her cheek as his dark head lowered, degree by mesmerising degree. 'And, if I did, you'd be sorry. Believe me, the police are the *soft* option…'

His voice seemed to be coming from miles away. There were so many other things stealing her attention—the heat of his body and the warm, oddly familiar scent of him, the pounding in her veins and the race of her heartbeat, the hot, tight, excitement clutching at her. These were sensations so new and so powerful that they imprisoned her.

His mouth crashed down on hers. Electric shock sizzled through every skin cell. Nothing that intense had ever happened to her before. His tongue stabbed between her lips and heat surged between her thighs. She quivered, letting him splay his hands intimately to the swell of her hips, lifting her to him, melding every inch of her screamingly willing body to the hungry threat of his. It still wasn't close enough to satisfy. A moan escaped huskily from the back of her throat—a curiously animal moan that she did not recognise as her own.

Abruptly he broke the connection. He broke it with such force, thrusting her back from him, that momentarily she slumped back against the cold wall, surveying him with unseeing eyes glazed by confusion. The lift doors suddenly glided back, letting in a rush of cold air, bringing her to her senses.

Every instinct Bella had was urging her to run. She took off through the doors, the blurred images of parked cars assailing her on all sides. A car park, an underground car park. Two large men were standing just beyond the lift, both of them moving forward, then hesitating, twin expressions of stunned incredulity freezing their faces.

'Get the hell out of here!' Rico da Silva roared at them.

'But Mr da Silva—?'

'*Out!*'

Seconds later Bella's run was concluded. She made it about halfway down the shadowy aisle of cars before she was intercepted by a hand hauling her back as if she were a rag doll. As he spun her round she kicked him in the shin, and would have kicked him somewhere that hurt even more if she had had the time to aim better.

'You pervert!' she sobbed with rage.

'You loved it,' he slung at her, grimacing with pain as he hauled her back to him with remorseless determination.

'Don't move… If you don't move, nobody will get hurt,' a completely strange male voice intoned flatly in a startling interruption.

'What the—?' As Rico's head spun round he fell silent, his entire body freezing with a tension that leapt through Bella as well like a lightning bolt.

Following the stilled path of his gaze, Bella looked in turn at the two men standing there. They were wearing black Balaclavas. Both of them had guns. Her jaw dropped, a sharp exhalation of air hissing from her.

'Keep quiet… Now back away from him slowly.' The taller one was addressing her. *Her*! Bella blinked, paralysed to the spot, unable to believe that the men weren't a figment of her imagination, and yet, on some sixth-sense level, accepting them, fearing them, sensing their cold menace. 'Move… What a clever girl you've been, getting rid of his guards, but frankly you're surplus to requirements. Is she worth anything to you?'

The scream just exploded from Bella. She didn't think about screaming, didn't even know it was coming. The noise just whooshed up out of her chest and flew from her strained mouth—a long, primal wail of terror. And the taller man flew at her, knocking her to the ground so hard that he drove the breath from her lungs and bruised every bone in her body. A large hand closed over her mouth and then something pricked her shoulder, making her gasp with pain…and she was plunging down into a frightening, suffocating tunnel of darkness.

CHAPTER THREE

BELLA was cold and sore. Her head was aching. Something was banging. It sounded like metal on metal—a brutal, crashing noise. Maybe it was inside her head. She had a horrible taste in her mouth and her throat hurt. Her arm was throbbing as well. She felt every sensation separately. Her brain was shrouded in a fog of disorientation. Thinking was an unbearable effort, but she willed her eyes to open.

Her dilated, still semi-drugged gaze fell on a blank wall. She moved her head and moaned with discomfort. She was lying on a bed—a hard, narrow bed. The unbearable banging stopped, but her ears were still so full of it that it was a while before she could actually hear. And then she heard footsteps.

'I was hoping you'd stay comatose. Then I wouldn't be tempted to kill you…'

The tangle of glorious hair moved and she turned over. 'Rico?' she said thickly.

'Why didn't I call Security? Why didn't I just ring the police?' Rico da Silva breathed in a driven undertone as he stared furiously down at her. 'Shall I tell you why? I let lust come between me and my wits. *Dios mío*…the one time in my life I stray off the straight and narrow I land the gypsy's curse and nearly get myself killed. If I come out of this alive I'm still going to take you to that police station! And, if there is any justice in the British legal system, you'll be locked up for ever!'

Her lashes fluttered during this invigorating speech. Then, slowly, jerkily, she pulled herself up onto her knees. 'What happened?' she mumbled weakly.

'I've been kidnapped.'

36

'Oh.' Incredibly it didn't mean anything to her until she remembered those final few minutes in the car park. The men, the guns, the violence. A wave of sick dizziness assailed her. 'Oh, dear God...' she said shakily.

Rico da Silva already looked so different. His jacket and tie had been discarded. His shirt was smeared with grime. His black hair was astonishingly curly, tousled out of its sleek, smooth style. 'No hysteria!' he warned with lethal brevity.

'You said...*you* have been kidnapped. But I'm here too.' Bella swung her legs down and slid slowly off the bed.

'I begged them to leave you behind. I told them you were so thick that you wouldn't be capable of assisting the police. I told them you were worthless...'

She thought about it. 'Thanks...I suppose you did your best.'

'Do you have a single, living brain cell?' Rico slashed at her without warning. 'Am I condemned to spend what may well be my last hours on this earth with a halfwit?'

Bella stiffened as though she had been struck. She was far from halfwitted. Indeed, she had an IQ rating which put her into the top two per cent of the population, but that was a fact she never shared. It tended either to intimidate or antagonise people.

Rico da Silva wanted an argument, she sensed. She understood that. He needed to hit out and she was the nearest quarry. Forgivingly she ignored him and concentrated on exploring their immediate environment and its peculiarities. She touched the wall. 'It's metal.'

'Be grateful. At least they gave us airholes.'

She wasn't listening. She scanned the bed, the single chair, the lit battery lamp. It was the only source of light. And she was used to the kind of light that came from paraffin, gas and batteries. She had grown up with it, sat in darkness when there was no money for replenishment. There was no window. She brushed past him to pass through the incongruous beaded curtain covering a doorway which his bulk had been obscuring.

In the dim light beyond she saw a gas-powered fridge, a small table, another chair, an old cupboard, and what looked like a tiny, old-fashioned stove heater connected by a flue to the metal roof. And then she glimpsed the door. She grabbed at the handle, suddenly frantic to see daylight, and was denied. The wooden partition concealed only a toilet and a sink. No windows—no windows anywhere. Her throat closed. She rammed down her panic and drew in a sustaining breath.

'What are we in?' she demanded starkly.

'A steel transport container. Most ingenious,' Rico explained without any emotion at all. 'I hope you're not claustrophobic.'

She never had been until now. Automatically she felt the cold metal walls, stood on tiptoe to touch the roof, felt the airholes he had mentioned, and a long, cold shudder of fear took her in its hold. 'It's like a metal tomb.'

'What time is it? My watch was smashed.'

Somehow that casual enquiry helped her to get a grip on herself. Moving back through the curtain into the other section, she peered down at her watch. 'Ten past seven.'

'Time to eat.'

'*Eat*?' Bella echoed shrilly. 'We've just been kidnapped and you want to eat? I want to get out of here!'

'And you think I don't?' Lean fingers gripped her taut shoulders as he yanked her forward. Grim dark eyes held hers. 'I've been conscious for two hours longer than you. I have been over every centimetre of every surface of this metal cell. But for the airholes it's solid steel. We have nothing here capable of cutting through solid steel,' he spelt out with cool, flat emphasis. 'Have you ever looked at the bolts on container doors? That is the only other option…'

She glanced past him to see the doors which were so closely shut that they were almost indistinguishable from the other walls. 'We'll never get through those either,' she mumbled sickly. 'People have died in these containers...suffocated, starved—'

'I have not the slightest intention of suffocating or starving,' Rico cut in with ruthless assurance. 'And, if one is permitted to take hope from appearances, neither have my kidnappers any such intention. Dead, I'm not worth a cent.'

'Ap-pearances?' she prompted jerkily.

'Someone's gone to a lot of trouble to plan this operation and take the minimum number of risks,' Rico pointed out. 'The necessities of life have been supplied. We have food and water. They have no immediate need to venture into further contact with us. They must be very confident we cannot escape. This leads me to believe that for the moment we are as safe as it is possible to be in such a situation.'

'S-safe?'

'I would feel more threatened if one of them was sitting in here with us,' Rico said drily. 'Or someone had come along to tell me to stop making such a racket when I was thumping the walls.'

'The noise—that was you,' she registered, shaking her head.

'I wanted to know if there was a guard out there...or even if it was possible to attract anyone's attention. But, this time, no joy.' His sculpted mouth tightened to a thin, hard line. 'However, we will keep on trying. There is always the chance that we could be heard at any time of the day or night.'

'Yes.' He was giving her something to hang on to—a slender hope. Bella nodded, almost sick with the nerves that were threatening her wavering composure. He had had the time and privacy supplied by her unconsciousness to come to terms with their situation. She had not had that time or that privacy. She was angry and scared to the same degree. Somebody had deprived her of the most basic of human rights—freedom. But even worse than that was the terror that in the end they might take her life as well.

'You hear that silence?' His nostrils flared as he flung his dark head back. 'Now we listen for some sound of humanity—traffic, a dog barking…anything.'

'These walls would act like double glazing, I bet. A friend of mine has just got new windows in and you can't hear the traffic through them…' Her voice trailed to a halt as she glimpsed Rico's arrested expression. 'Sorry, I sort of rattle on some—'

'Stop rattling,' he articulated with ruthless precision.

'You mentioned food?'

'In the fridge.'

'Enough for two?' she whispered as it suddenly dawned on her that his kidnappers could never have planned on having to imprison two people.

'We'll conserve it as far as possible. The same with the light. We have no idea how long we will be here,' he delivered smoothly.

The wild idea that in a strange way Rico da Silva was in his element occurred to her. It doused her urge to scream and shout uncontrollably. Pride kept her quiet. There he was, certainly tense but on the surface as cool as ice.

'Anybody could be forgiven for thinking that this has happened to you before!' she muttered with scantily leashed resentment.

'I have been prepared for this situation by professionals. Although I admit I did not expect to have to put what I learnt into action.'

Bella flashed through the beaded curtain and sank down on the chair by the table. Wrapping her hands together, she bowed her head. She just could not believe that this was happening to her. She just could not credit that she had been kidnapped. That was something that occurred to strangers in the headlines…and they didn't all come out alive! Her stomach heaved again.

'How rich are you, Rico?' she asked in a wobbly voice.

'Filthy rich.'

'Good.'

He had said that the kidnapping had been well organised. Hopefully they were not in the hands of maniacs. There would be a ransom demand and Rico's bank or his family or whatever, she thought vaguely, would pay up and they would be released just as soon as the money was handed over.

'Will they want money for me?' she muttered helplessly.

'I doubt it.'

She was worthless. His own assertion to the kidnappers drifted back to her. And she didn't know whether to be glad or sorry. She had been in the wrong place at the wrong time, an innocent bystander caught up in something that was nothing to do with her. And it was *his* fault. But for him she wouldn't have been in that car park! On the other hand, if anything happened to Rico—if, for instance, stress made him drop dead with a coronary—the kidnappers might just kill her to get rid of her. 'Surplus to requirements'… Nobody was going to pay for her release!

'Are you healthy?' she whispered.

'Very.'

In silent relief she nodded. But still she couldn't believe that it was real. Just twenty-four hours ago she had not even known that Rico da Silva walked this earth. Helplessly she pointed out to him that this time yesterday they had not even met.

'And wasn't ignorance bliss?'

'I don't see why you have to be so nasty!' Bella snapped. 'Personally I think I'm taking this very well. I've already been threatened and assaulted by you—'

'By *me*?' A lean hand thrust the beaded strands aside. Poised in the doorway, Rico surveyed her with incredulous, blazing golden eyes. The cool-as-ice impression was only on the surface, she registered. Beneath it lurked a deep well of near-murderous rage, rigorously suppressed and controlled.

'Yes, by you. Then I get thumped and drugged and kidnapped. I wouldn't have been there if it hadn't been for you!' she suddenly spat.

'And I wouldn't be here now if it wasn't for you.'

'I b-beg your pardon?'

Black lashes dropped, screening his piercing gaze. 'Forget I said that—'

'Oh, no, as you once said to me, don't keep me in suspense!' she shrieked.

'Cool down…and grow up,' Rico drawled in a soft tone that none the less stung like acid. 'How we got here is unimportant. The only item on our agenda now is survival.'

Bella studied the floor, tears burning at the back of her eyes. It was shock. She was still in shock. She wanted to ask him what he had meant just now. She wanted to know what had happened after she'd blanked out back in that car park. But she pinned her tremulous lips together instead.

'Let's eat.'

Eager to do something, she leapt off the chair and opened the fridge. It was bunged to the gills. Great, she thought for a split-second. Her next thought was entirely different. Dear God, how long were his kidnappers planning to keep them here? And, assuming that they hadn't added to the hoard when they'd realised that they had not one but two victims requiring sustenance, that was an enormous amount of food…most of which wouldn't keep that long even in a fridge—salad stuffs, cold meats, cheeses, milk, bread, butter. All perishable.

'There is a stock of tinned goods in the cupboard as well as extra lights and several batteries, plates and cutlery.'

'We could light another lamp—'

'We don't need it. Anything that we don't need we save,' he reminded her.

Bella burrowed into the cupboard, locating a tin of stew.

'If you light that stove, I could heat this on that little hot-plate.'

'There's no fuel.'

'We could smash up a chair or something,' Bella persisted, shivering.

'The ventilation in here is wholly inadequate. Fumes might not escape. We could be suffocated. The stove cannot be lit.'

The boss man had spoken. Bloody know-it-all! Her teeth ground together. It was freezing cold and it was likely to get considerably colder. He had a lot more clothes on than she had. And where the heck was she to sleep? One bed. Two dining chairs. A metal floor. Guess who would get the floor?

She found a bowl and peeled some leaves off a lettuce, before marching through to the sink which had the sole water supply. When she returned she stood at the cupboard, her back turned to him, washing the salad. And guess who gets to prepare the meal? she thought caustically.

She felt slightly foolish when she turned round to find that he already had two plates on the table, sparsely filled. The pieces of hacked cheese and the tomatoes complete with stalks made her mouth unexpectedly curve up into a grin. He was even less domesticated than she, but she liked him for making the effort.

'What happened after I got the needle in my arm?' she asked flatly as he reappeared with the second chair and she sat down.

An ebony brow quirked. 'Why talk about it?'

'Because *I* want to know!'

'I was afraid you would be shot when you screamed. The smaller one was very nervous. He was taking aim when the other one brought you down.'

Bella bit at her lower lip. 'I didn't mean to scream.'

'I suppose it was a natural response,' Rico conceded shortly, his mouth clenching.

But not a miscalculation that he would have been guilty of making, she gathered. He had been on all systems alert but in icy control. And for some reason he wasn't telling her the whole story. She sensed that. 'What did you do?'

'I deflected his aim,' Rico admitted.

'How?'

'By wrenching his arm.'

Perspiration broke out on her brow at the image which his admission evoked. 'You could have been killed!'

'I could not stand by and do nothing.'

'And then what happened?'

'There was a struggle and the other one struck me from behind. I remember nothing more. And when I came to I was in here and my watch was smashed,' he bit out.

'At least you weren't.' She dug up the courage to look up from her plate, her face flushed and troubled. 'Thanks for not standing by,' she muttered tightly.

'Don't thank me. What I did was foolish. He would not have fired that gun. His companion was in the way, probably already in the act of injecting you with the drug that knocked you out. Sometimes instinct betrays one badly,' he completed grimly.

He was denying the fact that he had saved her life. He didn't want her gratitude. But Bella was deeply impressed by his heroic lack of concern for his own safety. 'Instinct', he'd called it, depriving the act of anything personal. However, that did not change the fact that many men would have put themselves first sooner than risk their own life at the expense of someone who was little more than a stranger.

A stranger. Rico da Silva ought still to feel like a stranger to her, only he didn't any more. Shorn of the obvious trappings of his wealth, the male across the table was as human as she was. But she reminded herself how deceptive the situation in which they were now trapped was. They were stuck with each other. This uneasy intimacy between two people from radically different worlds had been enforced, not sought.

'If I hadn't been there, what would you have done?' she found herself asking.

'There is no profit in such conjecture.'

'You're a typical money man, aren't you?' Bella condemned helplessly. 'No such thing as answering a straight question!'

His strong features darkened. '*Estupendo*...then I'll give it to you straight. As you screamed I was about to activate the alarm on my watch. It would have alerted my bodyguards.'

'The alarm—it would have been that loud?'

Impatience tightened his mouth, hardened his narrowed gaze. 'It is a highly sophisticated device. The kidnappers would have heard nothing, but the signal emitted would have automatically activated an emergency alert on the radios my bodyguards carry.'

'And brought them running,' she filled in, dry mouthed. 'Some watch.'

'It would also have acted as a homing device once it was activated.'

'The marvels of technology,' Bella mumbled, regarding her lettuce with a fast disappearing appetite, unable to bring herself to meet his accusing gaze. It was her fault that his watch had been smashed, her fault that he hadn't got to activate the damned thing. 'You were wired like a bomb.'

'That went off like a damp squib.'

She fumbled to think of something to say in her own defence. 'There might have been a shoot-out if your guards had come rushing back.'

'They are too highly trained for such idiocy,' Rico retorted crushingly. 'In all likelihood they would have simply tracked me and followed without revealing their presence and risking my safety.'

Bella pushed away her plate. He was telling her that she

had wrecked his chances of escape. But for her persistence he would have continued to exercise restraint on that point. Rico da Silva was not the type to cry over spilt milk but, challenged beyond his tolerance threshold, he had given her what she'd asked for. And honesty had never been less welcome.

'Sorry really wouldn't cover it, would it?' she breathed jerkily.

'*No importa*… Who can tell what would have happened? A hundred things could have gone wrong,' he dismissed wryly. 'I bear my own share of responsibility for our plight. I dismissed my bodyguards. And had I not taken you down there you would not be here now. They were waiting for me. I have business lunches almost every day. As a potential target you are told to vary your schedule but lunch… lunch is difficult to vary—'

'I guess.' Bella was surprised by his sudden denial of her culpability.

Lustrous dark eyes glimmered in the dim light over her anxious face. '*Por Dios*… It is inexcusable that I should take my anger and frustration out on you. I owe you my apologies. I am not accustomed to this feeling of being powerless. I have always been aware that I could be the target for such a crime but I did not seriously believe that this could happen to me. Arrogance brings its own reward.'

'I don't see what you could have done to prevent it.' It was hard to drag her fascinated gaze from him. He was being so honest, so open. She had not expected that candour from a male as sophisticated and powerful as Rico da Silva. And the apology shook her rigid.

In her own way she saw that she had been as prejudiced as he was. She had not been prepared for the strength of will and purpose that he had revealed from the outset of their imprisonment. Survival was the only item on their agenda, he had said. He meant it; he would act on it. But what was really driving him crazy right now, she sensed, was the apparently foolproof setting in which their kidnappers had chosen to place them.

'Where do you think we are?'

'If they spent the time I was unconscious driving, we could be hundreds of miles from London. Then again, we could still be inside the city limits.' He shifted an expressive brown hand, his mouth tightening.

'But it's so quiet—'

'This container is set inside some sort of building. We are not outdoors. There is some kind of roof far above us. I was able to judge that through the airholes,' Rico supplied, acknowledging her surprise at his knowledge. 'There is very little light in the building. It could be a warehouse on an old industrial estate, miles from residential areas. On the other hand, it could equally well be a barn out in the depths of the country—'

'You've really thought about this.'

'I've had more time than you and more practice. International banking is cut-throat. Thinking on my feet comes naturally.'

Bella bent her vibrant head, amused by his assumption of mental superiority. He thought that she was thick just because her spelling was no great shakes. No doubt her second-hand clothing and her habit of chattering when she was nervous added to his prejudice. If he saw her paintings he might change his mind. Then again, he might not.

Hector didn't think she was ready for a first exhibition as yet. It had been Hector who had told her that she needed more time and more experience to develop as an artist before she even considered trying to show or sell her work. And Hector ought to have known what he was talking about. In the days before he had become a virtual recluse Hector Barsay had been a renowned international art critic, whose opinion had been sufficient to make or break many an artistic career.

'If we're inside a barn that probably means there's a

house close by!' Her sudden animation dimmed as quickly as it had arisen as she took that thought a step further and felt more threatened than ever by it. 'And if there is a house our jailers are probably inside it...' she whispered sickly.

'*Sí.*' He did not deny the possibility. 'But the environment they have chosen for us would suggest to me that they are equally likely to be miles away or even out of the country by now—'

'Out of the country...leaving us *here* trapped?' Bella had gone white.

'This was very carefully planned...all this,' Rico stressed again, indicating their surroundings. 'They did not employ gratuitous violence upon us—'

'I thought they were very violent.'

'They used drugs rather than brute force to subdue us. They might have stuck us in a basement somewhere and simply left us without food or any comfort,' he pointed out.

'Do you think they're terrorists?'

'I think not but I could be wrong. The nervous one did not strike me as a man used to having a gun in his hand. The other one was more professional, more confident... He was even enjoying himself.'

Bella's sensitive stomach churned. Unlike Rico she did not have the emotional distance to assess their captor's personalities.

'To take me in that car park was a challenge, and he was a man accustomed to danger. He enjoyed the risk. Possibly a former soldier or mercenary. He had fast reactions.'

'I'm scared,' she muttered in a small voice.

Disconcertingly he reached for her clenched hand where it rested on the table. His large hand briefly engulfed hers with very welcome warmth. 'Clearly *not* a halfwit,' he said with a self-mocking edge.

'The police will be scouring the countryside for us.' Endeavouring to cheer herself up, Bella thought for the very first time of the police not as a threat but as the strong arm of the law. Investigators, protectors, *rescuers*.

There was an odd little silence. She glanced across at Rico.

'*Sí...*' He was staring down into his glass of water.

'Leaving no stone unturned—a nationwide alert,' she continued, bolstering her nerves with conviction. 'It'll be on television and radio. Everyone will know about us and someone somewhere is sure to have seen something... Maybe a few someones.'

Tight-mouthed, Rico murmured, 'Tell me about Hector.'

Thrown by the abrupt change of subject, Bella echoed, 'Hector?'

'By now he will be aware of your disappearance.'

She thought about that and shook her head. 'Not yet. We don't keep tabs like that on each other.'

'You mean he is accustomed to you not always coming home at night?' Rico phrased abrasively.

'Everyone stays over with friends sometimes. And Hector's a very private person who believes in minding his own business. He has his own very set routines and I'm not a routine sort of person,' Bella admitted. 'We don't share mealtimes very often. When he asked me to move in—'

'And when was that?'

'A year ago.'

'Where did you meet him?'

'I've known Hector for ever.' Bella grinned. 'Well, since I was fourteen.'

'*Fourteen*?' Rico grated, his dark features rigid with a response that she couldn't quite read. It looked remarkably like distaste...but why should he react that way to such a harmless piece of information?

'Why not?' Bella frowned.

'If you see no reason why not, it is not for me to comment,' Rico returned thinly. 'Where were your parents?'

'I was living with my grandfather at the time.'

'And he did not protect you from this dirty old man?' he demanded with seething distaste.

Bella's mouth fell wide in astonishment. She sprang upright. 'Are you calling Hector a dirty old man?'

'This appears to come as a big revelation to you…but *sí*…yes. Such a relationship is an obscenity!'

Her green eyes fired, her temper exploding. 'You actually believe that Hector and I have a sexual relationship,' she realised in disgust. 'My God, you are stuffed full of prejudices about me! I'm sorry to disappoint your gutter assumptions, Mr da Silva, but Hector's nothing more than my landlord and a family friend—'

'A *family* friend?' Unperturbed by her anger, Rico surveyed her and merely continued to probe.

'Hector knew my father back in the sixties,' she volunteered with pronounced reluctance.

'When will he notice your absence?'

Bella drank down her glass of water, still trembling with bitter anger. 'I don't know. Not tonight anyway. He always goes to bed early and I'm often out all day. I don't always see him at breakfast. I also work shifts, and sometimes I do extra hours if I'm asked. By the way, I'm a waitress…I'm not out trawling the streets for men to sell my body to!' she hissed at him. 'What gives with you anyway? The fact that I'm out late at night and driving a beat-up car doesn't mean I'm a tart!'

Hooded dark eyes rested on her vibrant and passionately expressive face. His mouth quirked. 'You are quite correct. But you have a quite stunning quality of raw sexuality which tends to blunt the male perceptive powers. Your looks, your walk and the husky pitch of your voice,' he murmured softly, 'add to the confusion you create.'

Wide-eyed and bewildered, Bella stared back at him. He had delivered the assessment with the same distant coolness that an employer might use when he was discussing a potential employee with personnel management. But nobody had ever talked to Bella like that before—certainly not a man. A tide of pink illuminated her porcelain-fine skin.

'And I don't think you're half as aware of the havoc you wreak as I assumed you were, *querida*.' He thrust his empty plate away and rose. 'Now I think it's time I started trying to attract attention to us again.'

He left her standing there, uncertain, confused, anger and defensiveness still contributing to her feverish tension. The first crash of metal on metal made her flinch. He was hammering the container doors with what looked like a poker. The noise hit her in shock waves. But if someone heard them, came to investigate…? What were the chances? she wondered dully. If the kidnappers had really left them alone here, that signified a fair degree of confidence that their presence was unlikely to be discovered.

Clearing up the dishes, she discovered that a bone-deep exhaustion had settled on her without her even noticing. Rico was still banging the doors, vibrations running through the whole container like thunderclaps, hurting her ears, her teeth, her head. She withstood it, bracing herself. And then he stopped, releasing his pent-up breath in a hiss.

'I'll take a turn,' Bella proffered.

He swung round, his bronzed, startlingly handsome features and curling black hair damp with perspiration. 'No need. This is allowing me to work out my anger. And you look as though you're on the brink of collapse. Why don't you lie down for a while?'

'I can do my bit just like you can,' she insisted, hovering.

'You can do it tomorrow, or in the middle of the night. The noise will carry further then. If you fall asleep I'll wake you up,' he assured her.

She gave a rueful laugh. 'Sleep with that racket?'

'Try. We need to conserve our strength to stay alert.' From the shadows he studied her with slumbrous golden eyes and, astonishingly, for the first time since it had hap-

pened, she remembered that savage embrace in the lift—
the hard, hot hunger of his mouth on hers, the shatteringly
sexual feel of that lean, muscular form of his crushing her
to him.

'Yes,' she muttered, turning away, barely knowing what
she was saying, suddenly engulfed by a level of physical
awareness that she had never felt before, struggling to thrust
that intimate memory away again.

'You remind me of a marmalade cat,' he said abruptly.
'It's the hair.'

'I can see you slinking through the undergrowth, stalking
your prey.'

'I haven't heard that one before.' She forced a laugh and
vanished back through the curtain. At the sink she washed
her face and hands, dried herself on one of the two rough,
faded towels available, peered at the still wrapped toothbrush and paste. The kidnappers hadn't planned to make
Rico too uncomfortable. The conviction was soothing.

'Can we share a toothbrush?' she called in a lull in the
noise.

'If we can share a bed we can share a toothbrush,' Rico
murmured lazily.

But they were not going to share that bed. They would
take turns. Very democratic. Very sensible. One asleep, one
awake and alert. And always that background of deafening
noise. Thud, thud, crash, crash. It was impossible that anyone could fall asleep against that background. Having removed her boots and her tights in the kitchen section, Bella
walked back to the bed. Covertly undoing a couple of the
buttons on her fitted jacket, she slid below the blanket,
rested her head on the pillow, and turned away from him
towards the wall.

But still his image lingered behind her lowered eyelids,
stamped there like a cattle brand seared into her flesh. Involuntarily she remembered the kiss, relived the wildness
he had unleashed—from inside her, from inside him. Try-

ing to fly off the top of a tall building would have been less dangerous, less foolhardy. She shivered. The fire had simply taken over, burning out all self-control.

No man had ever made her feel like that. And she didn't ever want to feel like that again. Passion was greedy and mindless. Passion was lust, a purely physical thing which had no staying power. Bella knew that some people were lucky enough to find both love *and* passion in a lasting relationship but those people were in the minority. Many more mistook infatuation for love and then wondered why their feelings faded so quickly. But Bella knew the difference and knew what to guard against.

Both of her parents had been passionate people and neither Cleo nor Ivan had controlled that side of their nature. Neither of them had ever managed to sustain a stable relationship, not with each other and not with anybody else. Their love affairs had been volatile, short-lived and unfulfilling. Why? Because they had been greedy, impatient and always afraid that the grass might be greener with someone else.

Bella was determined not to fall into the same trap. Yes, she had needs and drives just like any other young, healthy woman, but she wanted to choose her life partner with her intellect, not with her body. It dawned on her that she had not thought of Griff in almost twenty-four hours. She was shaken. But then, it had been a frantic and worrying twenty-four hours, and Griff had hurt her, and no doubt she was already in the recovery phase. Bella's feelings shut down fast when she was disappointed or betrayed.

But she had been very fond of Griff. She had enjoyed his company, respected his intelligence and believed that his outlook and expectations of life matched her own. That, she had foolishly assumed, had been a sufficient basis on which to build a good relationship. Only it hadn't been enough for Griff. She had refused to go to bed with him in the absence of any deeper commitment on his part.

That giggle in the background on the phone had told her that he had been finding physical entertainment elsewhere. Griff had made his choice but she knew him well enough to know that he would still believe that he could string her along. But Bella wouldn't allow that. It was over. Griff was immature, clearly not yet ready to think in terms of permanence in spite of all the things he had said to the contrary.

That sorted out tidily in her mind, Bella contrived to do what she had not believed possible. She fell asleep. And she awakened to a situation that was entirely new to her.

She was lying on top of a living, breathing pillow. Her nostrils flared at the clean, soapy scent of warm male. Her breasts were crushed against a rough-haired chest, her cheek pillowed in the hollow of a smooth shoulder, and her pelvis was in direct contact with the thrust of a very masculine arousal. In the darkness her head flew up, her eyes wide with consternation.

CHAPTER FOUR

A HAND pressed her back down again. 'Go back to sleep,' Rico breathed tautly.

'Like hell I will!' Bella gasped in alarm, trying to rise but thwarted by the powerful arm wrapped around her hips.

'*Dios*! Relax,' he hissed with raw impatience.

'You've just got to be kidding! You're in bed with me!'

'*Madre de Dios*, it's four in the morning—'

'Time I got up and took my turn at thumping walls!'

Both arms closed round her. 'Forget it,' he groaned. 'It's the middle of the night. I need sleep. If you start, I won't get any.'

'I am not sharing this bed with you!'

'What do you think I am—a rapist?' he growled incredulously.

'How…do…I…know?' she fielded with growing fury. 'You're not wearing any clothes!'

'As I have only one set I refuse to go to bed in them. But I am *not* naked.' Closing his hand round one of hers, he thrust it down to the hard jut of his hips, splaying her fingers against the band of cloth there to prove his point.

Bella nearly went into orbit at the intimacy of the gesture. 'How dare you?' she screeched, snatching her hand back even though she hadn't been anywhere near the danger zone that she was already outrageously aware of.

He expelled his breath in a resonant hiss of exasperation. 'You are not that naïve. I am a man, lying in bed with a half-naked woman on top of me. I'm not a corpse, devoid of all sexual response. But I have no intention of making love to you.'

'I don't believe you!' she bit out, rigid as a stick of rock, holding her entire length taut in a fruitless endeavour to lessen the points of contact between them.

'I am fully in control of my sexual urges,' he extended grittily into her ear. 'But not my temper, I warn you.'

'I don't trust you,' she whispered back with venomous bite, infuriated by the position in which she found herself. 'I could fall asleep and you—'

'Oh, I do believe you would wake up if I touched you. I believe that I can safely say a woman has never slept through my attentions!'

'Don't be disgusting! Let me go!'

He gave vent to something rough and charged in Spanish and moved with an abruptness that took her completely by surprise. Suddenly she was flipped onto her back and Rico was lying above her instead, their positions reversed without warning. Before she could open her startled lips to demand an explanation he took her mouth in a surge of angry passion.

And what happened next she definitely wasn't prepared to deal with. As his tongue drove into the moist interior she had already accidentally opened to him she was seized by an explosive wave of excitement. It left her dizzy and stripped of every coherent thought. The intensity of her own response electrified her, opening up another world that was full of unbearable physical temptation. She returned the kiss with a kind of wondering innocence, arching her head back to deepen the pressure, involuntarily greedy and inviting more.

'*Por Dios…*' he groaned raggedly, his lean, hard body coming down into abrupt and abrasive contact with her yielding curves where, seconds earlier, he had held himself at a distance. 'I—'

Driven entirely by instinct, Bella speared her unsteady fingers into the thick silk of his hair and held him down to her, tracing the shape of his head in an exploratory caress. Touching had never felt so good, never felt so necessary.

Entrapped by the discovery and fired by the leaping, unfamiliar energy sizzling along her nerve-endings, she threw herself with natural generosity into the conflagration of their mouths' second meeting a split-second later.

Incredible heat rose from deep inside her, making her body shake and quiver with the sheer power of what she was feeling. He pulled her to him as he slid onto his side, his hand curving to the pouting thrust of one full breast, inadequately protected by the thin lace cup of her bra. And then the barrier was inexplicably no longer there, his fingers shaping her naked, sensitised flesh with an expertise that made her gasp. In the darkness she felt him move, and the yearning peak of one engorged nipple was brushed by the tip of his tongue and then engulfed by his mouth.

Bella moaned, and jerked as though she had been electrified. All she could hear was the rasp of her tortured breathing, the thunder of her heartbeat. Sensation so intense that it came close to torment had her in its grip. She was out of control, sensed it, felt it, *knew* it, and being out of control was something Bella never, ever allowed herself to be with a man. The shock of that realisation awakened her brain from its slumber, and in panic she wrenched herself free by rolling backwards.

'*No*!' she slung at him from between clenched teeth as she hit the hard floor with a force that hurt. Rolling over, feeling the nakedness of her back and breasts in dismayed confusion, she fumbled out blindly to feel the wall opposite the bed and sat there, hugging her knees and shivering as the light went on.

'*Madre de Dios…*' Rico hissed, studying her with incandescent golden eyes from the vantage point of the bed. 'What the hell are you playing at?'

'Please return my clothing to me.' She lowered her eyes and studied her raised knees, embarrassment and an unfamiliar self-loathing assailing her. But still she could see that strong-boned, hard face, brought alive by those astonishingly passionate eyes of his, the lithe, powerful symmetry of his bronzed, beautifully masculine body. Her nails dug into her skin in angry, fearful confusion as she fought to wipe out that unbelievably intense and detailed image.

Her jacket and her bra landed in a heap beside her bare toes. She skidded upright, twisting away from him, and dug her arms shakily into the sleeves of the jacket, ignoring the bra because *he* was watching her. She hadn't even noticed that he had removed both articles while she had been in his arms. It was a small point but somehow it underlined just how far her control and awareness had slipped and emphasised how complete had been his.

Smooth bastard, she reflected shakily, deciding that you couldn't know where you were with a guy possessed of that variety of sexual expertise. At least with the ones who grabbed and clutched you got fair warning of their intentions.

'You are behaving as though I attacked you,' he grated in a furious undertone.

'You started it, I finished it. Let's leave it there,' she muttered unsteadily, with her back still cravenly turned to him.

'I did not do *anything*—'

'That I didn't encourage you to do,' Bella completed in a grudging interruption. 'I know.'

There was a smouldering silence.

'If you acknowledge that—' and his accented drawl told her just how astonished he was that she had made that acknowledgement '—then why—?'

'My hormones are out of sync…or something.'

'*Qué dices*…?' Now he sounded slightly dazed.

Bella forced herself to turn around. It took courage. 'It's this situation…the proximity, the misleading intimacy, the tension we are both under,' she offered. 'I'm sorry I let it go so far but neither one of us can want to wake up in the morning trapped with a sleazy one-night stand we can't escape from—'

'"Sleazy"?' he echoed in disbelief.

'Listen, I am the girl whom just a few hours ago you believed to be shacked up with an old guy of seventy.' Having given the gentle reminder, Bella tilted her chin. 'And sex without emotional involvement or commitment is sleazy in my book. I don't know you well enough to say whether or not it would be in yours. But, if you're like most of the men I meet, you don't intellectualise much over taking sex where it's offered. You just *do* it and you don't have the sensitivity to feel bad about it.'

She gave a dismissive little shrug, the absorbing focus of his stunned scrutiny. 'But that's OK. I don't judge men on that. That's just the way nature programmed you to behave. Survival of the species and all that.'

His brilliant dark eyes shimmered, his facial muscles stiff with sudden hauteur, a faint but perceptible flush overlying his hard cheekbones. 'I did not emerge from the primordial soup within recent memory,' he gritted from between even white teeth.

'Only you don't think on your feet when you're in bed with a half-naked woman and feeling randy—'

'I refuse to believe I am hearing this!'

Bella lifted his jacket, which he had laid across the chair, and began to empty the pockets.

'What are you doing?' he murmured in a seriously taut tone, his accent thick.

'I'm going to use your jacket as a blanket for an hour and then maybe, when you've managed to drop off, I can take up the door-bashing again.'

'Don't be ridiculous. Come back to bed. I will not lay a finger on you,' he swore icily.

'It's not a very good idea for us to share that bed right now, Rico. Take it from me,' Bella muttered feelingly, 'it would just be asking for trouble.'

'If you are determined to treat me like some sort of lech—'

She cleared her throat awkwardly and mumbled, 'No, that's not what I'm trying to say. I'm simply trying to be sensible—'

'*Trust me!*' he bit out, with audible difficulty, anger and a whole host of other emotions she didn't recognise fracturing his diction.

'I'd like to…I'd really like to, but I don't trust me either,' she admitted in a stifled confession which she felt that, in all fairness, she owed him.

'You don't trust…? Ah.' A faint purr of complacency softened his drawl. 'I thought you didn't go for dark men?'

'There's an exception to every rule…but maybe Dracula could start looking appealing in this set-up.'

He sighed. 'I have never been so tired in my life. Come back to bed. I promise you…you will be safe as a nun handcuffed to a priest in captivity.'

Bella sent him a dubious glance. He had slumped back down again, black lashes fanned down on his cheekbones. Exhaustion emanated from every line of his long, muscular body. 'Go to sleep, Rico,' she whispered, a strange little arrow of tenderness piercing her. 'Just go to sleep.'

'I can't leave you on the floor…' he mumbled thickly.

'I've slept on a lot of floors in my time.' She sighed, thinking that no two individuals could have been more different.

She sat on the chair, wrapped in his jacket, watching him sleep. The exception to the rule, she reflected tautly. Well, you've been well and truly rocked off your smug perch this time, Bella.

She was locked in a container with the only male who had ever managed to penetrate her physical and mental defences. That scared her; that really did scare her.

Men flocked to Bella like bees round a honey pot but nine out of ten invariably wanted what she didn't want to give. Being a sex object was no compliment. Either she dated for fun and friendship or she quite cheerfully chose and dated a man who impressed her as having the kind of qualities she would like to find in a husband. There was nothing in between for Bella—no infatuations, no affairs, no regrets. She was determined not to give her heart unless she felt safe and secure.

And until now passion had left her alone and untouched by any inconvenient cravings. Saying no when lovemaking went beyond a certain boundary had never been a problem for her, and she had always sensibly ensured that she did not give any man the ammunition to accuse her of being a tease. Bella believed in being honest and fair with the opposite sex. It had not crossed her mind that some day a man might touch her and with every fibre of her being she might crave the passion he inspired inside her, and crave it with such intensity that she almost broke the rules she had lived by for so long.

Rico da Silva had taught her differently. He had shattered her control as easily as a child smashed an egg and with a similar lack of care or regard for the consequences. And did she blame him for that? Neither of them might emerge from this container alive, she thought, with a shiver of fear. When two people were attracted to each other and forced into such intimacy the act of sex might seem a very small thing to share in comparison to that hard reality…

But Bella was too conscious of her own vulnerability— this strange, new and scary vulnerability that she was feeling. Rico da Silva disturbed her more than any other male she had ever met. He was clever; he was strong; he was unexpectedly candid about his own emotions. And he also attracted her more violently than she had ever believed possible.

In the dim light she looked at him lying in the bed, and knew that lying in that bed with him would result in a conflagration of passion which she would find very difficult to handle. Yet she also knew that on some dark, deep level inside herself, unexplored until this moment, she wanted that passion very, very badly.

Why? Their situation, as she had told him? No, it was something more than that. He was so different from her. In every way. And that fact in itself fascinated her. Nowhere did they share anything in common—background, nationality, status, education, income, outlook.

Rico would have been quite capable of making love to her and forgetting her existence one second after he'd achieved the satisfaction of physical release. Rico was ruthless, single-minded, a sexual predator in this particular tight corner. Rico wouldn't have felt awkward over the breakfast-table. On his scale it would have been a minor event, unimportant when set against survival.

But Bella was not half as tough on the inside as she liked to pretend on the outside. Her outer shell of careless insouciance had been formed in the hard school of her childhood—with the slow, painful acceptance that her father didn't give a damn about her, and that her mother dragged her about in her wake not out of choice but out of necessity, because there was nobody else to take responsibility. And when one day the possession of that child, now grown to an awkward thirteen-year-old threatened to come between Cleo and her latest man Cleo had dumped her on her grandfather, who hadn't even known of her existence.

Bella had learnt not to let people get too close. She had learnt to protect her inner self from invasion. On the surface she was open, but inside herself she knew she told nobody anything which mattered. And now she could feel that reserve being threatened, her essential emotional distance coming under attack. Griff hadn't hurt her, Griff had disappointed her, but she had the horrible suspicion that Rico da Silva had the power to tear her inside out...

'*Por Dios*, what the hell are you doing?'

Bella jumped and unsealed her lips from the cold metal,

her shoulders and arms aching from the awkward stance she had repeatedly taken up over the past few hours. She teetered on the chair, her legs stiff, and she would have fallen if a pair of strong arms hadn't closed round her and lowered her down to the floor.

Rico was staring without comprehension at the line of tins, deprived of their labels, on the table. An incredulous frown was dug between his ebony brows as he abruptly noticed his open wallet, now emptied of the considerable amount of paper money that he had been carrying. One lean hand reached out and snatched at the single rolled banknote still lying there. He opened it up and read the message carefully printed on it.

'''Help. We're in the container''',' he said out loud.

'I took the labels off the tins and tore them up and wrote on them first,' she explained. 'Then I pushed them through the biggest airhole. Then I had to blow to make them move. I'm hoping that some of them made it down onto the ground, or that there's enough of a draught out there to take them off the roof. If anyone comes in they might notice them. That was when I thought of seeing what you had in your wallet—'

'*Had* being the operative word.' Rico studied her with intent, narrowed dark eyes.

'Sorry…but a rolled-up twenty-pound note is far more likely to be noticed than a torn piece of label off a tin,' she pointed out.

'*Sí*…' Still staring at her, he pushed long fingers somewhat unsteadily through his luxuriant hair and handed her the final note. Bella got back on the chair and posted it up into the world outside their prison. 'I should have thought of this…' he murmured tautly, gravely.

'You think you have the monopoly on ideas around here?' She laughed wryly. 'It's a far-out hope that someone will innocently walk in here, pick up one of those notes and release us—'

'But not impossible. It's a clever idea.'

'Not if the ground out there is already littered or covered with debris, but who knows?' Oddly embarrassed by his level of scrutiny, she turned away. 'What do you want for breakfast?'

'I think I owe you breakfast. You let me sleep for hours.' He caught her wrist to examine her watch and groaned in disbelief. 'It's after twelve…almost lunchtime! Why didn't you wake me?'

'Relax. I did a lot of poker-bashing on and off.' Bella flexed aching muscles, but she was horrendously conscious of those cool fingers still anchored to the tender inner skin of her wrist. 'You slept through it. You needed the rest. I think whatever drug they used on us was still pretty much in both our systems until we could sleep it off. Where did you find that poker anyway?'

'Stuffed behind the stove—an oversight on their part.' His oddly abbreviated speech was matched by the blatant intensity of his continuing appraisal. His lashes dipped, showing only a glimmer of a pure, glinting gold, and he breathed in almost jerkily.

Her mouth ran dry, her heartbeat accelerating in a sudden, alarming surge. The atmosphere was thick with explosive tension. It had come out of nowhere and inexplicably, although her brain screamed at her to move away, her feet were welded to the floor in front of him. She couldn't take her eyes off him. A pulse-beat of awareness vibrated between them. It was so powerful that it drained her of self-will.

'I've been thinking,' she said in a rather high-pitched voice, fighting for concentration, desperate to break the silence. 'It's more likely that we're in a warehouse than a barn. This container wasn't plumbed in with water just for us. Those fitments in there have been *in situ* for years. This place has been used maybe as an office…or some sort of permanent site hut, I reckon… What do you think?' By the time she reached the end of that question she was spitting out words so fast that they ran into each other.

He wasn't listening. He muttered something rough and yet soft in Spanish, and just as suddenly reached for her. As possessed by that terrifying strong need to physically connect as he was, Bella made no demur. Lost in the slumbrous demand of his golden gaze, she was mindless. He took her mouth with a hunger that burned like flames of fire over her unprotected skin.

And yet she craved that fire, needed that fire as she needed oxygen to live. Her hands gripped his broad shoulders, loving the heat of his flesh through the fine shirt. She pushed against him as he crushed her to him, her breasts flattened to the hard wall of his chest, already heavy with a sensitivity and an anticipation which he alone had taught her to feel. Her body remembered him with every newly awakened sense.

His mouth on hers was a source of unbearable pleasure. She was inflamed by it, driven with incredible speed to a pitch of desire strong enough to make her legs tremble and offer only the most fragile support. Every stab of his tongue intensified the drowning excitement that was fast claiming her. She kissed him back with an intensity of response that utterly controlled her, her hands sliding under his unbuttoned shirt, smoothing wonderingly over the flexing muscles of the satin-smooth skin of his back.

He dragged his lips from hers with a fevered imprecation and looked down at her, his breathing roughly audible. Hot golden eyes raked her flushed, vibrant face, and he set her free with an abruptness that felt like an amputation. Bella was less able to pull back from the extraordinary power he could exert over her. Every time it happened it was a revelation, and, instead of it strengthening her resistance, she found herself further weakened by the repetition.

Rico lounged back against the edge of the table, tension screaming from every poised angle of him. He appraised her with fiercely narrowed eyes, his sensual mouth compressed in a hard line. He looked like a pirate, his jaw-line obscured by a blue shadow of dark stubble. Her own skin was tingling from that abrasive contact. She raised a shaky hand to her reddened lips, feeling as though she had been branded, feeling as though she would never, ever be the same again.

'I can keep my hands off you,' he asserted with almost ferocious bite.

No, you can't and the knowledge is killing you. Bella read in his clear eyes the frustration, the anger he couldn't hide. This was a male accustomed to calling every shot, staying in control, never leaping before he looked. She remembered the tidiness of his desk and the incredulity with which he had emerged from the cluttered chaos of the interior of the Skoda that first night. Rico was one of those very organised and disciplined individuals who very rarely made an uncalculated move...and she threw him off balance and he didn't like that one bit more than she did.

'This will not happen again,' he drawled flatly.

'I know...you don't want to seem like a snob but I'm really *not* your type,' she remarked brittlely. 'And you're not my type either. Let's leave it at that.'

His teeth clenched. 'I am not a snob!'

'You just like to think that everyone's your equal from the safe cocoon of your bloody great limousine? Now you know that you don't think that, Rico. You're rich and you're successful and you probably come from a rich, priveleged family. You have power and financial clout. You probably get a lot of respect and an equal amount of grovelling flattery and servility. You're bound to have a good opinion of yourself. And you definitely don't expect to be attracted to an Essex girl who writes illiterate prose!'

'*Basta...enough*!' he slashed back at her rawly. 'How can you talk like this?'

'And that bothers you even more, doesn't it? People don't say stuff like that right out where you come from.' Bella treated him to a grim little smile, her beautiful face cynically set, masking the pain she was feeling. 'But what the hell...? I'm not about to change myself for your benefit!'

'You don't know what you're talking about.' He sent her a glittering glance that was alight with impatience and anger. 'I drew back because I had no other choice. I cannot protect you. Even if you are on the Pill you have no supply with you. I could get you pregnant, and that is a risk that neither of us can want!'

The blood drained from her face, leaving her pale, and then abruptly her skin flamed again with a stupid embarrassment she couldn't help. Hurriedly she turned away from him, shaken that he could reason so coolly about an unlikely possibility, the mere mention of which infuriated her. Did no woman ever say no to Rico da Silva? Did he think he was irresistible? Did he really imagine that she would have been foolish enough to let matters proceed to the point where the risk of pregnancy could have become a consideration?

'It wasn't going to go that far, believe me!'

'I wish I had your confidence—'

'All I did was let you kiss me, for heaven's sake! That doesn't mean I was about to jump into bed with you!' she hissed, slamming into the fridge, unwilling to look at him because she was so outraged by his assumption that she was easily available should he choose to exert sufficient persuasion.

'Keep quiet. Talking about it doesn't help,' he breathed in a sudden, savage undertone that brutally ruptured the heavy silence, sentencing her to nervous paralysis. 'I ache to have you...*Santa María*, I am in torment. I want to rip your clothes off and fall on you like an animal, and in all my adult life I have never been so challenged to retain control and consider consequences!'

Bella straightened and slowly turned. Rico glowered back at her, the raw reality of what he was telling her etched in the ferocious set of his dark, startlingly handsome features.

'And if you did not want me the problem would not be there. I would never touch a woman without her consent,' he continued forcefully. 'But every time you look at me I see the same hunger in you.'

'I—'

'Do not deny it,' he cut in grimly. 'And that we should be distracted by such primitive instincts when our very lives are at risk outrages my intelligence!'

'It's the fact that we're trapped here,' she muttered, shattered by his candour, devastated by the manner in which he was still looking at her, and shamefully lost in a colourful image of him ripping her clothes off and her liking it. Dear God, what was happening to her? What was happening to them both?

'*No digas disparates!*'

'In English?'

'Don't talk rubbish.' He flashed her an exasperated glance, his beautifully shaped mouth twisting. 'I felt exactly the same way in my office. Why do you think I was so determined to take you to the police?'

'I had to be punished for attracting you? Are you a sadist or something?'

'Since I met you I have been *crazy*!' he raked back at her in a sudden explosion of raw, passionate resentment. 'I don't know myself any more!'

Swinging on his heel, he strode through the beaded curtain. A second later she heard the fiery assault of the poker on the container doors and couldn't help smiling to herself. Rico was as disconcerted by the attraction between them as she was. That made her feel less threatened and more in control. Neither of them wanted anything to happen. Between them they ought to be capable of behaving like civilised adults and observing proper boundaries in spite of this horribly intimate and suffocating prison.

But, dear heaven, when he threw off the ice-cool front and let the tiger roar, she thought distractedly, Rico was quite shockingly volatile—yet another trait she ran a mile from in men. Only then did it cross her mind that she found the same trait astonishingly, paradoxically attractive when Rico revealed it. The sheer elemental physicality and passion which he suppressed and controlled with cold intellect fascinated her.

She made sandwiches for lunch—no sense in letting the bread go stale. Rico sank down on the other side of the table, his every graceful movement catching her attention. She averted her eyes to her glass of milk. 'Do you have a family out there worrying about you?' she asked abruptly.

'My parents are dead. I have an older sister, who's married with a family, but she lives in Spain.'

'I imagine the police will have carried the news that far by now.' Bella sighed.

Rico seemed to hesitate. '*Sí...*'

He reverted to his own language only when tense. No doubt he was disturbed by the idea of his sister's current state of terror on his behalf.

'Are you close?'

'Yes.'

Bella was determined to keep on talking. Maybe conversation would keep other, far more dangerous undertones at bay. 'You're Spanish, aren't you?'

'My father was Portuguese but my mother was Spanish. I grew up in Andalusia.'

'Rich?'

'Rich,' he conceded almost apologetically.

Involuntarily she glanced up and collided with a posi-

tively dazzling half-smile that gave her a seductive glimpse
of another Rico entirely—a Rico with a sense of humour
and considerable charm. That smile made her feel curiously
light-headed. 'What were your parents like? Distant?'

'Not at all.' He looked surprised by the suggestion. 'We
were a happy family but I was born late in their lives. My
father died when I was a teenager, my mother a couple of
years ago—'

'So what age are you?'

'Thirty-two...far too old for you,' he murmured in unwelcome addition.

'Look, we're not going to talk about things like that!'
Bella snapped, emerald-green eyes flashing reproach and
reproof. 'You're an...Aquarius...right?'

Rico frowned. 'Ah...astrology. *Sí.*'

'We should avoid each other like the plague,' she told
him morosely. 'It's a combustible combination.'

'I do not require a horoscope to know that, *gatita*,' he
returned with dark satire. 'So tell me about your background.'

'Forget it. It would give you indigestion.'

'I would like to know. Who were your parents?'

Bella stiffened. Of course he didn't mean 'who' in the
worldly sense. He certainly wouldn't be expecting to hear
a name that he might recognise. She lifted her vibrant head,
her sultry mouth compressing. 'My father was Ivan
Sinclair.'

His winged ebony brows drew together in unconcealed
surprise. 'The artist?'

'My mother was one of his models. They had an affair.
I was the result.' She wondered why she had told him
something that she usually kept very much to herself.

His dark visage was set in uninformative lines. 'There
was no marriage?'

'Ivan didn't believe in marriage. He visited Cleo on and
off for a while after I was born but that eventually ground

to a halt,' she admitted. 'I didn't see him again until I was thirteen. And my mother initiated that meeting. She wanted him to take charge of me… It was a really stupid idea…'

The silence stretched and then Rico murmured, 'What happened?'

'Nothing much.' With a jerky shrug she got up and began to clear the table. 'He was furious at being put on the spot. He accused her of trying to blackmail him, even tried to say I wasn't his… He was quite pathetic actually. He was no hero.'

'He had a lot of talent.'

'But, let's face it, he was much better known as a drunk and a womaniser.' Bella stated the obvious for him.

'Scarcely a suitable guardian for a thirteen-year-old. Why did your mother even consider such an arrangement?'

She turned back to him, her beautiful face strong and her expression clear. 'She had a lover who didn't want a kid hanging around,' she said bluntly. 'But her visit to Ivan wasn't a total disappointment. He coughed up some cash to get rid of us; she bought a new van and dumped me with my grandfather instead.'

An ebony brow quirked. 'A new van?'

'My mother was a traveller. She wasn't born to the life, but then few are.' Bella sighed. 'She left home when she was eighteen. She was a hippie. Gramps said she was wild. He threw her out after an argument and then regretted it, but he didn't see her again until she showed up with me twenty-odd years later. She was only involved with Ivan for a couple of years and then she met some guy with a lorry and took to the road—'

'For how long…until you were thirteen?'

She nodded.

'But you must have settled somewhere at some stage?'

'Never for longer than a month.'

'What about your education?'

She smiled. 'I started that at thirteen.'

'It must have been an appalling life.' Rico frowned at her, his consternation palpable.

'I didn't know anything else. Sometimes it was fun.' But her expressive eyes shadowed. She was thinking of the hunger and the cold and the wet, the lack of hygiene and privacy, the raw hostility of their reception everywhere they went. Travellers were not welcome visitors in any locality.

'Time I bashed the poker,' she announced abruptly, suddenly bewildered and alarmed by the extent to which she had allowed him to draw her out. She never told people about that old life if she could help it, and could not understand why she had revealed so much to him. It was none of his business.

She strode down to the container doors and lifted the poker. She had only struck the metal a few times when another sound broke through in startling, shattering response—a series of sharp, zinging thuds. The poker fell from her nerveless fingers. She spun round, heard Rico behind her, then they were suddenly plunged into darkness and he was dragging her down on the bed. 'Keep quiet,' he urged in a raw breath of warning.

'*But*—' Had he gone crazy? Someone was out there—someone who could open those doors and set them free!

'Those were bullets.' Rico's hands framed her cheekbones in the darkness and she fell back, sick and weak with terror.

CHAPTER FIVE

THERE was a loud thud up on the roof. Bella shivered violently as she heard the unmistakable sound of feet walking up and down above them. Nausea filled her stomach. Somebody laughed. There was a roaring in her eardrums. Her heart threatened to burst from her ribcage. For just a little while she had managed to close out the fear but now it was back with a vengeance.

Rico rolled over, pinning her body almost protectively beneath his. She could feel the splintering tension coursing through him and abruptly she closed her arms around him, needing that reassuring contact with every fibre of her being. She felt so small, so frighteningly powerless. They were caught like rats in a trap, wholly at the mercy of their captors.

Her breath rasped in her aching throat as there was another thud, then nothing. The silence dragged past on leaden feet until it seemed to thunder in her straining ears.

'He's gone,' Rico grated.

'How do you know? He could be standing out th-there just waiting for us to make more noise…and then he might come in!' she gasped strickenly.

'I doubt it. I suspect he was only checking on us…but for the moment we keep quiet.'

'Bastard,' Bella mumbled, still shaking like a leaf in a high wind, her face buried in the hollow between his shoulder and his throat. Her nostrils flared on the warm, musky scent of him, already so reassuringly familiar. 'You imagine you're coping and then…then they take that away and remind you how it really is!'

'The ransom will be paid, no questions asked—'

'But maybe the police won't allow that!'

'The police are unlikely to be actively involved at this stage.'

'*What*?' In the darkness her dazed eyes flew wide.

Rico shifted and switched on the light where it sat on the chair by the bed. 'My bank will pay up. The police will stand back at this early stage. That is standard procedure. Publicity could be our death warrant. Scared kidnappers get more dangerous…'

Bella met his shimmering gold eyes, absorbed the wry, apologetic curve of his mouth as he released her from his weight and coiled back from her. He had allowed her to believe that the police were out there searching for them because that had appeared to keep up her spirits. 'Oh, God…' she whispered shakily as reality sank in.

'*Lo siento, gatita*…I'm sorry.'

'I guess if that's the best approach…'

'At the highest level the police will certainly have been informed of the kidnapping,' Rico asserted. 'But I would imagine that at this point they are merely waiting to see how the situation develops.'

'And if what you euphemistically call "the situation" develops into tragedy, then they'll be more actively involved!' Bella could not resist saying.

His jaw-line clenched. 'Don't talk like that!'

'You want me to maintain a positive outlook when we're stuck here like sitting ducks inside a metal tomb with some maniac taking pot-shots at us for fun?' A shrill, hysterical edge had entered her voice.

'Every occurrence increases our knowledge of the environment outside,' Rico intoned, staring her down with icy night-dark eyes.

'I beg your pardon?' she said incredulously.

'We're wasting time and energy with that poker,' he imparted with grim emphasis. 'He would not have fired that

gun at this hour of the day had there been the remotest
chance of anyone hearing the gunshots.'

'Oh…Rico…that is *so* comforting to know!' she spat
back in helpless disbelief.

'I do not think that our lives are in any immediate danger,' he grated.

'You also thought that our kidnappers might be out of
the country!'

'*Por Dios*…pull yourself together! This far you have
acted with commendable courage.'

Bella could feel her control unravelling as fast and as
inescapably as a cotton reel of thread thrown down a steep
hill. 'Not quite what you expected from me, I gather. Well,
I'd appreciate it more if you showed a little human sensitivity, instead of acting like Mr Macho all the time…even
when we're in the middle of a nightmare!' Her voice rose
steeply on the last words, fractured by the sob choking her
throat.

'I don't think you'd appreciate it if I was sitting here
paralysed with fear!'

The sobs she was frantically struggling to suppress over-
came her. She bowed her head, ashamed of the weakness,
and wrapped her arms round herself. Tears streamed down
her cheeks. He touched her damp chin with a not quite
steady forefinger and then, with a muttered, vicious imprecation, reached for her, unpeeling her arms and hauling her
close.

She needed that contact. She needed that warmth… She
needed *him*. Caught up in the charge of an explosive surge
of feeling, she pressed her mouth feverishly to the angular
curve of his stubbled jaw-line.

She felt him tense but there was an unstoppable flood of
emotion suddenly churning about inside her. Her hands slid
up, her fingers shyly splaying across his blunt cheekbones
in a wondering caress. As she held him she looked at him
with darkened green eyes full of new self-knowledge and

a kind of helpless joy that was insanity, but which she couldn't help. Her feelings were so intense that they consumed her.

'I don't trust myself this close,' Rico breathed roughly.

'Trust your instincts,' she whispered, and she dropped her hands, then hesitated in a momentary agony of uncertainty before her fingers found the buttons on her jacket and began to release them.

'Bella...'

Her pale skin burned under the golden flare of his arrested gaze, but the driving need to give, to share, was far more powerful than the fleeting recall of her own sexual inexperience.

'This is just you and me,' she reasoned in a breath of sound as the jacket slid off her shoulders, her slender form quivering with sudden awareness of her own daring. 'And this is what I want.'

Every poised inch of his lithe, powerful length exuded the raw force of his tension. Bella looked bravely back at him, still clothed, but naked to the world as she had never before allowed herself to be. It was a risk she had to take, a leap of faith, and even though she knew that she might regret her own unquestioning generosity she also knew that she would regret it for the rest of her life if she simply hid behind her own insecurities.

'Sí...' He moved with an abruptness then that shattered her—reaching for her, dragging her into his arms, every restraint overpowered by the hunger which blazed in incandescent gold from his fierce gaze. 'No regrets?'

He wanted a passport to freedom before he even touched her. Pain trammelled through her. She might have turned away then, devastated by the reality of how little he offered and too proud to take on such terms, but he closed his mouth in devouring passion over hers and the ability to be rational was violently torn from her.

He invaded the moist interior of her mouth, his probing

tongue a raw, masculine imitation of an infinitely more intimate penetration. She trembled, every physical sense leaping into automatic response. Control was wrested from her without remorse. He unleashed the turbulent force of his desire on her and she drowned mindlessly in the tidal wave of her own shock. It was no slow, gentle seduction which took account of her innocence.

'You're a witch, *querida*…' Rico groaned. 'I am no saint to resist such enticement.'

'Enticement'? Some faint shred of reasoning absorbed the word, shrank from it. But he took her mouth again, made love to it, enveloped her in the staggering surge of her own helpless excitement. He lifted his dark head and she opened her heavy eyes. He had bared her breasts. The pale mounds rose in shameless supplication to his heated appraisal.

'You are so beautiful.' He cupped her sensitive flesh with firm hands, his smouldering golden scrutiny raking over her as a flush of pink crept up over her cheekbones.

He bent his head. She watched him, shameless in the grip of her own anticipation and yet so afraid that in some sense she might not meet his expectations.

The tip of his tongue skidded down the valley between her breasts before circling the engorged thrust of one pink nipple. She gasped, her lashes sweeping down, her back arching. Thought was suspended. The erotic tug of his mouth on the sensitised buds was unbearably erotic. Her hands rose of their own volition and speared into his hair, caressing him, holding him to her as the sweet torment of her own arousal plunged her into ever deeper response. In all her life she had never dreamt that such pleasure existed.

She was so hot that she couldn't stay still. His fingers smoothed over the quivering tautness of her stomach and located the tangle of curls at the junction of her thighs. Her whole body jerked, out of control. Her breath rasped dry in her throat, her thighs parting in a spasm of intolerable need. He laughed softly and covered her mouth again, teasing this time, nibbling and tormenting with devastating expertise.

Instinctively she moved against him, her hips rising. He explored the damp, silken warmth at the very heart of her, every expert caress making her sob with the crazed heat of that intimate pleasure. Lost in the depths of an extraordinary passion, she was at the peak of an intense excitement, tortured by the desperate ache of unfulfilment.

He shifted over her then, ravishing her swollen lips one more time, and then, abruptly, he drew her up to him with impatient hands and plunged inside her. She hadn't expected the pain that tore at her as he entered her. Her shocked eyes flew wide and she bit her tongue so hard that she tasted blood in her mouth.

'*Madre de Dios*!' Shattered golden eyes held hers, and then his teeth clenched as the momentum of his own desire made him drive deeper still, his swollen shaft forging a path through the tender tissue that had sought to deny him.

'That hurts!' Bella panted.

With a sharp intake of breath he stilled, and long fingers knotted painfully into her tumbled hair. 'I didn't *know*!'

She saw the anger and the shock etching his bronzed features into rigidity and she could not bear the sight. If he turned from her now he would never come back to her again. She knew that as clearly as though he had spoken and she fought it with her instincts, reaching up, touching his sensual mouth with the soft promise of hers, refusing to let him go.

'Rico…'

And it was done. In the circle of her arms he trembled, far less in control than he had sought to pretend. His rigidity broke, his body surging against hers again in a rhythm as old and as relentless as time. With a stifled groan of earthy satisfaction he completed his possession of that place which had once been hers alone.

The pain had gone as though it had never been. Renewed heat flooded her as he thrust into her again, fast and deep, his hands sinking beneath her hips to press back her thighs. She gasped as he moved inside her and enforced the pace to a level of shattering, driving intensity. Her heartbeat thundered, her pulses madly accelerated. She was controlled, dominated, excited to a pitch beyond her belief. When she went over the edge into the tumultuous, shuddering pleasure of release she cried out his name as if it were a talisman in the swirling darkness that blocked out everything else in the world.

Except his withdrawal. It could not block out that. Within seconds of that climax Rico dragged himself free of her arms. The shock of that abrupt severance was immense. Bella opened dazed eyes and focused on him. 'What's wrong?'

'*Qué pasa*? ''What's wrong?''' Rico sliced the repetition back at her with stinging derision. 'You dare to ask me what's wrong?'

It was like a bucket of cold water on sunburn. Bella sat up, every lingering and pleasurable sensation stolen from her. With a shaking hand she drew the blanket over her. But Rico stood there, unashamedly naked, every taut line of his magnificently masculine body exuding fury.

She had never felt more agonisingly confused. She would not have given herself without love. And with the people she loved Bella was a giver of unparalleled generosity. She asked for nothing in return. But *did* she love him?

'I don't know what's wrong.' She couldn't yet think straight and opted for honesty, searching his hard, dark features with a pain concealed by the veil of her lashes.

'What's your game? What do you want from me? What was that sweet little seduction scene angled at?' he demanded with raw hostility. 'Had I known I was to be the first I would not have touched you!'

'I think that was my choice to make,' Bella muttered, lowering her head, the sting of tears furiously blinked back.

'*Por Dios*…it was certainly not mine! I believed I was making love to an equal partner. I do not sleep with virgins,' he said darkly, with a positively vicious bite.

'I told you I was—'

'But you were aware that I did not believe you. If there's one thing you don't look it's *innocent*!' he condemned. 'And innocent in thought and deed you're not. Tell me now…what is this likely to cost me?'

'C-*cost* you?' she repeated blankly.

'The honey trap and then the price,' he drawled with chilling menace. 'I've been down that path before. This scenario has a deeply sordid familiarity for me. If you're the fertile type I expect I'll be supporting you for the next decade and a half at the very least!'

Every icy word fell like a whiplash on her exposed back. Bella was appalled. He had made love to her with incredible passion, and now he was rejecting both that passion and her with a brutality that paralysed her. 'Rico…?'

'I warn you now…I will not marry you,' he imparted with icy emphasis. 'I will never marry again.'

Again? He had already been married? Even in the midst of her turmoil Bella was struck by that unexpected revelation.

'So, if you are cherishing some pitiful fantasy of Cinderella catching her prince, let me assure you that even a pregnancy wouldn't persuade me to make that ultimate sacrifice!'

Bella sucked in badly needed air to fill her seemingly squashed lungs. She studied her tightly clenched hands. 'You're not my prince, Rico. Relax,' she whispered painfully. 'Learn to enjoy life as the toad who didn't deserve to be kissed and transformed. This particular Cinderella doesn't believe in fairy tales.'

He expelled his breath in an audible hiss. She sensed that

whatever he had expected from her it hadn't been that. In that sense they were equal. She had been thrown violently off balance by his accusations. Where she had given, he saw deliberate enticement. Where she had expected nothing, he demanded to know the cost. It was impossible to believe that mere minutes ago they had been as intimately close as a man and a woman could be. For when Bella had trustingly dropped all her defences Rico had raised his with a savage hostility which took her breath away. And her pride revolted against the image he had formed of her.

'Why, then? Why did you give yourself to me?'

In a sudden movement Bella scrabbled for her clothes where they lay about the bed. A deep, sustaining anger made her hands tremble. Well, you lived and you learnt. There was no surer truth, it seemed. She had been a fool to expose herself to such an extent to a male who understood her about as well as he might understand an alien being. Where emotions were concerned she was dealing with a male so impenetrably thick that he ought to be locked up for his own safety, she thought furiously.

'Bella…?' he pressed harshly.

'I wanted you! Lust…what else?' Magnificent green eyes flashing, she shot him a look of vibrant derision, unperturbed by his sudden stillness and the freezing of his strong features. 'There was no hidden agenda.'

He stared at her, forbidding dark eyes, fringed by lush ebony lashes, nailed to her with mesmeric intensity. His sensual mouth compressed into a cold, hard line.

'I thought that might shut you up.' Bella let loose a not quite steady laugh as she pulled on her jacket and rummaged beneath the blanket to haul up her skirt. 'Lust is OK for you but not for me, right? Did you think I was about to delicately beat about the bush like your fancy ladyfriends?' she hissed. 'Or did you fondly imagine that I was going to tell you I had fallen madly in love with you and just couldn't help myself? Get real, Rico!'

With that final, ringing statement Bella sprang out of bed and strode through the beaded curtain. She turned on the water full force at the sink and leant back against the door, trembling on legs that briefly didn't feel strong enough to keep her upright. Love grabs you by the throat when you least expect it and rips the heart out of you, she thought sickly. I don't *want* this…I don't *need* these feelings!

Stripping off, she began to wash the scent of him off her body with slow deliberation. It had been a mistake and she wasn't too proud to admit to mistakes. Sometimes you played and you lost. Sometimes you made a fool of yourself. That was life. But as long as you hung on to your pride and your integrity you would recover. That was life too.

A knock sounded on the door. Bella said something very rude and was then ashamed of herself. The use of bad language was childishly offensive. But, for the first time in a lot of years, her thoughts and emotions were in real chaos. She hurt. The shock of that pain sliced through her, sharp, piercing and inescapable. She had only to think of the manner in which she had thrown herself at him and she felt sick with humiliation.

Rico and she didn't fit, didn't suit in any way. They lived in different worlds. Had fate been kind they would never even have met. They didn't have a thing in common. Rico was an ambitious, ruthless, fully paid-up member of the workaholic financial fraternity. He didn't have a creative bone in his body.

For heaven's sake, this was a guy who wore pinstriped suits, kept his desk tidy, thought of precautions against pregnancy in the midst of stormy passion! He maintained a rigorous leash on every spontaneous impulse. Her virginity had not been a gift, it had been a threat to him! How could she possibly think that she had fallen in love with someone like that? She studied herself, wide-eyed, in the mirror, searching for signs of incipient insanity.

Where had her intelligence gone over the past hour? *Of course* it wasn't love! Their imprisonment had twisted and confused her emotional responses, magnifying them into something they were not. When those bullets had hit the container she had been terrified and Rico had been protective. The release from that terrible tension had sent her emotions into overload. He had offered her comfort and warmth and she had been so grateful for his presence and in such mental turmoil that she had wildly misinterpreted her own feelings.

Really, Bella…is that why you recklessly gave away the virginity you were saving for your future husband? She paled, crushing that inner voice. But right through her teens Bella had been indoctrinated by her grandfather's moral standards. It had been an education. Cleo had had an 'anything goes' outlook on the morality front. But her lifestyle hadn't made her happy.

Bitterly aware of that reality, Bella had decided that the field of sexual experimentation was not for her. If she loved someone and he loved her, and a future together was on the cards, that would have been different. But passion without love… That had been the biggest 'do not' in Bella's rulebook. And she had just broken that rule. Received her just deserts in record time too, she acknowledged on another wave of pain.

Rico had illuminated another light when she emerged. What had happened to conservation? she wondered nastily. But then she saw him standing in the shadows by the curtain and her ability to be sharp and critical momentarily deserted her. She was assailed by a blinding urge to rush back into his arms and that terrified her. It was as though there were two people inside her—one trying to be sensible, one racing out of control on an emotional roller coaster. What the heck was the matter with her? Rico looked as dangerous as a prowling predator and she had already found out the hard way that she bled when he clawed.

'I believe that I have misjudged you,' he conceded in his silky, accented drawl which trickled down her sensitive spinal column like the caress of rich velvet.

'Forget it. I already have.' But her nervous antenna went on to instant red alert.

The level of physical awareness splintering through the atmosphere between them shattered her. Instead of fading with satiation, as she had naïvely assumed they would, the sexual vibrations had merely intensified. Bella went into restive retreat. She turned away to the fridge, her skin heating, her brain suddenly a wasteland awash with a devastating wave of unbelievably unwelcome erotic imagery. Her body ached and burned with the memory of that wild passion.

'Lust works for me as well,' Rico murmured in a purring undertone.

Her lashes fluttered. She froze halfway into the fridge, certain that he couldn't have said that. 'I don't want to talk about it,' she mumbled, intimate recollection having vanquished her defences.

'Don't be coy, *gatita*. It doesn't suit you.'

Her cheeks burning fierily, Bella straightened. 'Look, I made a mistake, and not one I intend to repeat…' She had forced herself to look at him and her voice trailed away as she registered that his attention was no longer directed at her.

Reaching for the light, Rico took an abrupt stride forward and held it above the stove, his glittering gaze fixed on some point above her. '*Infierno!*' he breathed.

Dazedly Bella watched him set aside the light at speed and reach up to touch the surface of the roof round the metal flue of the chimney. 'What is it?' she demanded.

'Get me the poker!'

'But—?' Meeting the whiplash effect of his impatience, Bella moved to oblige.

Grasping the poker, he swung it up against the roof. A

piece of something like plaster or cement broke away and fell to the floor. 'What are you doing?' she gasped.

But as he struck the roof again and more debris flew down, sending up a cloud of dust which made her cough, she realised exactly what he was doing. When the flue for the stove had been put in a hole had naturally been cut and, for simplicity's sake, not a circular one. A rectangle of metal had been removed. She could dimly see the edges exposed and her momentary excitement faded.

'They welded it back in after cutting it to take the flue.'

'That isn't steel!' Rico gritted. 'And it's only spot-welded. It'll come out!'

With punishing force he rammed the poker up against the insert, which buckled under the blow. Her heart in her mouth, Bella watched him batter it until it came loose, and then plant two powerful hands round the flue. The upper section lifted away and dim light filtered in. With a powerful push Rico rammed the section upwards, slamming it out onto the roof to clear the aperture he had exposed.

Bella's fingernails, which had been biting into her palms, bit even harder. Acid tears hit the back of her eyes as she looked up. 'It isn't big enough to take either of us!'

Rico surveyed her with raw determination. 'With a little help from me it'll take you,' he asserted.

Awkwardly she climbed up onto the top of the stove and raised her head through the aperture, her eyes flying up and down and around the rafters, the sheet-iron roof above the rusting hulk of an old tractor lying in the corner. 'We're in a barn,' she whispered.

'*Santa María!*' Rico slashed from below her in raw disbelief. 'You're not up there to see the scenery!'

Before she could react a pair of hands closed round her thighs and forced her upwards, not even giving her time to hunch her shoulders. Her collision with the edges of the rough metal hurt and she uttered a stifled shriek to which he paid no attention at all. He simply lifted her again, and this time she automatically curved her shoulders in and she went through, snaking out her hands to brace herself in amazement on the roof. With his help she hauled herself through the rest of the way.

'Now get me out of here!' Rico urged from below, as if he was afraid that she might go off and paint her nails or something and forget about him.

Her heart thudding like a wild creature's, perspiration beading her upper lip, she lowered herself down off the roof, hitting the rough ground below hard enough to jar her ankle-bones painfully. In a stumbling run she raced round to the doors. If they were locked—dear God, if they were locked...

For the next few frantic minutes it crossed her mind more than once that they might as well have been as she pushed and hauled and thrust with all her might, sweat rolling off her as she struggled to drive back the bolts, and all the time Rico was shouting at her from inside.

'Shut up!' she screamed, pausing to get her breath back.

It took her another ten minutes and he didn't shut up. As the bolts finally gave that final, necessary inch Bella slumped back winded on the dirty ground, as wrung out as a limp dish rag. Rico strode out and the first thing he did, which she found quite inconceivable, was to close the doors again and force the bolts back with an ease that made her hate him.

With a powerful hand he hauled her upright and dragged her towards the rickety barn doors.

'Suppose *they* are out there?' she hissed.

Rico, his dark features alight with savage determination, shot her a silencing glance. He pushed the barn door back slowly and she tried to duck under his arm to see what was beyond. Rain was lashing down in sheets outside.

'Come on...skulking here isn't going to get us any-where,' he asserted.

She sidled out after him, paradoxically appalled by the

emptiness she saw all around them. A derelict stone cottage lay off to one side, and in every other direction all she could see was the rough moorland edging the muddy track that ran down the hill. There was no sign of life anywhere.

'Now what?'

The wind and the rain made a truly ghastly combination as they raced down the lane. Rico hauled her relentlessly in his wake and she forced herself onward, fearfully aware that they were not safe until they could transport themselves some distance from their prison. They reached a road, not a very wide one—the sort of road which might see a vehicle maybe once a day, she thought hysterically.

'I'm so cold,' she gasped, soaked to the skin and shivering.

'Moving will keep you warm.' Shimmering dark eyes appraised her. His mouth tightened. He wrenched off his jacket and held it out to her.

Bella gave him a startled glance before she dug her numbed arms into the sleeves. 'Now *you'll* freeze,' she muttered guiltily.

'The subtle difference between a creep and a gentleman—the creep stays warm,' he drawled from between clenched teeth. 'We have to find shelter. It'll be dark soon.'

The road twisted and curved downhill for what felt like miles, and at the foot of that hill met yet another narrow road. Without any other options they kept on heading down. The rain slackened off but both of them were so wet that it made little difference. When they finally rounded a corner and saw a dim light at the top of a rough track Bella thought it was a mirage. Every muscle in her body ached by that stage and her steps were clumsy and wildly uncoordinated. Even speaking was too much of an effort. She stopped, staggering like a drunk.

Rico put a strong arm around her and propelled her towards the track. Later she couldn't recall climbing that final hill. A dog circled them, barking fit to wake the dead. A light went on, blinding her, and she came to a halt and swayed.

'Come on,' Rico pressed, and he was already almost carrying her.

She tried—she really did try—but in all her life she had never been so tired. Her legs simply folded beneath her, her head swimming, and she sank down into the thick, welcoming darkness behind her eyelids without a murmur.

'Wake up…'

Bella surfaced, cocooned in wonderful warmth, a fleecy blanket against her cheek. Her eyes opened and focused on the logs crackling in the grate several feet from her, and then landed on Rico, who had crouched down to block her view of the fire. She searched his starkly handsome features with softened green eyes. A helpless smile curved her lips.

'You look wonderful.' Her voice was slurred, sounding as though it was coming from miles away, and with immense effort she freed a hand from the blanket and reached out to him, curving her palm against his blue-shadowed jaw-line. 'But you need a shave.'

'*Muchas gracias, querida mia.*' She connected with his brilliant golden eyes and her heart turned right over. He caught her hand in his and pressed his mouth almost reverentially to the centre of her palm. 'You scared me,' he muttered roughly.

He sprang upright again and moved out of her view. It was still too much of an effort to turn her head. She heard another voice, female, elderly, somewhere behind her. Rico said something about a phone, and the lady was talking nineteen to the dozen about food and hot baths and him needing to change out of his clothes *right this minute*, stressing the fact with the kind of gentle but steely authority which reminded Bella very much of one of her former schoolteachers.

She drifted off again then, curiously uninterested in her

unfamiliar surroundings, content merely with the warmth and the feeling of security. Time had no meaning until Rico reappeared. He bent down and swept her up off the sofa. 'You can have a bath now that you have warmed up sufficiently,' he informed her.

That struck Bella as hilariously funny. She giggled.

'By the sound of it you're feeling better.' An elderly woman with a stern but smiling face looked down at her where she lay nestled in perfect relaxation against Rico's broad chest. 'Some day you'll be able to tell your grandchildren that you almost died of exposure on your honeymoon. That should provoke a few interesting questions.'

'Honeymoon?' Bella whispered blankly as Rico carried her up a flight of stairs.

He set her down on a chair in a large, old-fashioned bathroom and peeled her out of the blanket. She was dismayed to discover that she was wearing not a stitch of clothing, but before she could react to the startling discovery he had lifted her up and settled her down into a massive Victorian bath filled with deliciously hot water.

'Honeymoon?' she said again.

'I thought it best not to tell the truth. I said that we had got lost and our car had broken down. Mrs Warwick is a widow living alone. This is a remote place. I wished to minimise any fears she might have about opening her doors so generously and trustingly to complete strangers who look far from respectable.' As he talked he was stripping off his clothes.

Bella's cheeks warmed to a temperature that had little to do with the bath water. Smooth brown shoulders gave way to a muscular torso sprinkled with curling black hair that arrowed down into an intriguingly silky furrow over his flat stomach and then... Embarrassed, she glanced away, but still she saw him before her—the lean, angular hips, the long, powerful thighs, the sleeping promise of his manhood in a nest of ebony curls.

'You were wearing a ring on your right hand. When I was undressing you downstairs I slid it onto your wedding finger.'

Belatedly she noticed the ring. 'It was my grand-mother's.'

'Move over…'

'*Rico*!' Bella twisted her head round and skidded forward towards the taps in a rush, water sloshing noisily every-where as he simply stepped into the bath behind her. 'Lord, you're cold!' she gasped, all of a quiver as a pair of long, icy thighs closed round her hips from behind. 'Sorry, I should've thought. I'll get out!'

As she began to get up he reached for her and pulled her back, bringing her down on top of him, anchoring both arms round her. Above her head he laughed sonorously as she went from rigid to trembling and back again. 'You have so much to learn, *gatita mia*. I shall enjoy teaching you.'

Bella squinted frantically down at the hands firmly cup-ping the pouting thrust of her breasts and blushed. Beneath his palms she could feel her nipples swelling and tightening in shameless, instantaneous response. 'Rico…?'

'I have informed my chief executive, Kenway, of our whereabouts. I also spoke to the police. Thanks to Mrs Warwick, I was able to give the exact location of the barn,' he imparted with sudden harshness. 'They will stake it out and wait until those bastards come back to check on us again. They will walk into a trap just as we did in that car park. The police will be waiting for them.'

The icy chill in his voice made her shiver. All Bella had thought about was freedom—the luxury of the fire and the bath, the wonderful release from fear to *safety*. Her world had not yet expanded beyond those things. The intensity of her relief and her continuing exhaustion had combined to blunt and blur her reasoning powers. Rico, she noted, was not similarly affected. He was already grimly anticipating their kidnappers' capture and punishment.

'Had they asked for a ransom?'

'*Sí*…and the agreed arrangements will continue so that they do not become suspicious. Kenway has been in constant touch with Hector Barsay on your behalf. He will inform him of your release—'

'How did they know who I was?' A yawn was creeping up on her. She was lying naked in a bath with a man and she was ready to fall asleep, so complete was her relaxation. She couldn't believe it.

'My chauffeur knew your address,' he reminded her. 'Had he not, the police might have suspected that you had something to do with the kidnapping.'

'Me?' It barely penetrated. Her eyelids felt as if someone had attached weights to them, but she wasn't so far gone that she was not aware that Rico's lean, hard length was reacting far more energetically to her proximity. But she didn't tense, only smiled sleepily. There was something so wonderfully reassuring about being that close to Rico.

'You're falling asleep,' he groaned with more than a hint of incredulity.

She wanted to remind him that she had been up since half past four in the morning, battering doors, posting 'help' notes through the container roof, while he had slept until noon, but she couldn't find the energy. And he seemed to understand for he sat up and pulled her with him, and a minute later she was wrapped in a fleecy towel. Like a child she stood there, dead on her feet, while he patted her dry and pulled something over her head— something crisp and cotton and clean-smelling.

And then she was sinking into a warm bed without even caring how she had got there, sighing with pleasure as every limb relaxed. Voices spoke over her head. The smell of food briefly flared her nostrils but even that couldn't push back the sleep enclosing her.

In the darkness, a long time later, Bella shifted against a warm, hard body and curved instinctively closer, her hand splaying over a hair-roughened chest, her cheek resting against a smooth shoulder. 'Rico,' she breathed sleepily in instant recognition combined with instant contentment, and she would have drifted away again had he not tangled a hand in the mane of her tumbled hair, tipped her mouth up and kissed her.

It was like coming alive when you thought you were dead. Every skin-cell suddenly flamed into red-hot life, a kind of frantic, feverish hunger possessing her. Her response was so intense that it swallowed her alive.

'Rico…' She gasped again as he pinned her to the mattress beneath him and kissed her breathless, his mouth, hard, hungry, hot, exciting her beyond bearing.

He freed her and wrenched the nightdress off. In the darkness there was no warning before his mouth closed round the engorged bud of one swelling breast. The sensation hit her with stunning effect. Her neck extended in an arch, a stifled moan torn from her when she felt the erotic brush of his teeth and his tongue as he pulled on her taut nipples. And there was no time for anything, not a single thought, nothing but the raw, driving intensity of need screaming through her veins.

His lips skimmed a tormenting path over the quivering muscles of her belly, his hands parting her thighs, and then he was doing something…something so intimate that she tensed in sudden alarm before the power of simple sensation tore her every inhibition away. And then she was lost again in a hot, swirling fire, conscious of nothing but the incredible, torturous excitement roaring mindlessly out of her control as he employed the same technique on the most sensitive flesh of all.

She was at screaming-point when he moved over her, every shred of physical awareness centred on the ache of emptiness between her thighs. And then he thrust into her and she moaned and arched in one taut movement, her body clenching on a pleasure so intense that she was utterly possessed by it. Her fingers raked down his back in reaction and her teeth nipped at the strong brown column of his throat in instinctive revenge for the ragged laugh he gave vent to.

After that there was nothing but the long, pulsing drive for satisfaction. It went on and on and on. She hit the heights fast, unable to rein back the flood of release, but he didn't stop. She had barely hit ground level again before the frantic climb back up began, and in all her life she had never felt so controlled, never dreamt she could enjoy that reality so much. And when the second climax whooshed up inside her she was wiped out.

He shuddered above her, every muscle clenching taut, and she put her arms round him, happiness flooding through her like a rejuvenating drug. There was only one thought in her mind as she sank back into sleep. She would never let go of him again.

CHAPTER SIX

'SOME more tea, Mrs da Silva?'

Out of the corner of her eye Bella noticed Rico tense just as he had the last time their hostess had addressed her as his wife. 'Please call me Bella,' she said tightly, politely refusing the offer of a refill for her cup.

Rico had wakened her when he was already dressed. That had been her first shock. Shaven, his shirt immaculately clean—thanks, no doubt, to Mrs Warwick's ministrations—his tie reinstated and his exquisitely expensive suit pressed and only a little limp from yesterday's soaking, this was not Rico as she remembered him during their captivity—it was Rico the intimidating international financier she had faced at the bank.

'A car will pick us up at eight. We will make our statements to the police as soon as possible,' he had murmured smoothly before leaving her alone to rise and dress.

Her attention had fallen on the nightgown which had been discarded on the carpet the night before, and suddenly Bella had felt as though she was dying inside. How *could* she have made love with him again? The fevered, driving passion of the night haunted her now. He had a bruise from her teeth a half-inch above his collar and it seemed to scream at her like a badge of public shame every time she looked at him.

In the dark he was one hundred per cent sexual predator and she was one hundred per cent victim of her own wanton nature. Recalling that she had been all over him like a rash afterwards only intensified her sense of humiliation. There was a new distance between them and it wasn't coming from her side of the fence. Rico had an aloof quality that he hadn't had the night before. It had been there from the first moment she'd set eyes on him again.

And she understood, wished she didn't, wished she were wrong, but knew she was right. The *real* world was about to reclaim them again. Their time together in that container had been time outside the real world. Now they were back to being the people they really were. He was Rico da Silva, rich, influential financier...and she was Bella Jennings, an illegitimate waitress who wanted to be an artist but who might never make the grade. The gulf was enormous and Rico had been the first to recall it.

Her inner turmoil was so intense that it threatened to swallow her alive. Suddenly she was wallowing in terrifying confusion, not knowing what she felt, not knowing what she thought. Involuntarily she collided with the dark density of Rico's flashing gaze and her heart stopped beating altogether. Was it possible that he was enduring the same conflict?

But then she watched him smoothly turn his dark head and speak calmly to Mrs Warwick, and her heart beat again and sank simultaneously. Rico was in control. Rico knew exactly what he was thinking and feeling. Confusion and Rico da Silva were not a credible combination. Why had he made love to her again last night? Why had he pounced and moved in when she had been half-asleep, her every defence mechanism at rest?

P for predator, P for passionate, P for prey. Her stomach heaved. He was a very virile male. When he wanted sex he was used to taking it. She had just been a willing female body in the bed and, as he had once reminded her, he was not a corpse, devoid of all sexual response. And if he was now wishing that he hadn't bothered, she had no doubt that he had the cold will to ensure that she didn't form any silly ideas about their possibly having embarked on a continuing relationship.

The four-wheel drive that picked them up arrived early,

hastening their departure from the farmhouse. Two men were seated in front. They hadn't even reached the end of the lane before she realised that they were policemen driving an unmarked car—a chief superintendent and an inspector, no less. The taut questions came flying within seconds.

Every time a question came in her direction Rico stepped in to answer it for her. In another mood, in another situation and with other companions, Bella would have roundly objected. But right now she felt detached from everything, everybody…Rico and the police included…and she didn't care—she really didn't care—if sitting there in silence, letting him do the talking for her, made her look like the dumbest cluck of all time.

Her mind had already leapt forward to the parting of the ways ahead. Her thoughts stayed there, frozen in intense shock at the image of forthcoming loss and departure that unexpectedly tore at her.

'Miss Jennings?' a voice said loudly.

Dredged from her inner conflict, Bella jerked and flinched, and found herself staring wordlessly at the older man in the passenger seat, who had turned round and was studying her intently. 'Sorry, I—'

A hand suddenly closed tightly round hers where it lay clenched on the seat. 'Bella's still in shock,' Rico delivered with chilling bite, and 'leave her alone' was writ large in his assertion.

Shaken by that hand on hers and that cold intonation, Bella saw the senior policeman's gaze drop and linger on their linked hands, and abruptly a tide of burning colour flushed her cheeks. 'I'm fine,' she said tremulously, shielding her eyes with her lashes.

'We do require some form of statement from Miss Jennings. Of course, I understand what a devastating experience this must have been.' Even so, there was the merest edge of wry amusement in the older man's voice and she knew then that he knew that, whatever their relationship might have been before they had ended up in that container, it was now one of intimacy, and that stifled her natural effervescence even more. She did *not* want anyone else to be aware of what she could barely deal with herself. She snaked her fingers free of Rico's, denying herself that warmth although every treacherous sense longed to maintain it.

There was a town not many miles from the farmhouse, complete with police station. They were practically smuggled into the building through a rear entrance.

'Can't hold the Press off much longer, though,' the chief superintendent sighed.

'The *Press*?' Bella gasped.

'They'll be down on us like vultures the minute they know we're free,' Rico drawled flatly.

'They could blow the whole bloody show,' the inspector chipped in bitterly as they were hustled into a small, bare interviewing room which made Bella feel more claustrophobic than she had ever felt in the container.

'The Press know about us?' she whispered dazedly.

'We have their agreement to hold off on printing a word, but *now*…well, let's say there's a risk of a leak before we get a proper chance at catching those b-blighters.' He selected the word grimly.

'Miss Jennings will be staying at my estate,' Rico volunteered without any expression at all. 'My staff are trustworthy.'

'*Her* story has got to be worth a quarter of a mill flat, even at a conservative estimate,' the inspector muttered with cold cynicism. 'I hope you know what you're doing.'

She heard the senior policeman's slight intake of breath, knew the inspector was all at sea as to what he had said wrong. And several lowering realisations hit Bella very hard all at once. The police *already* knew all about her—her background, the accident through which she had met

Rico, her unarguable poverty. Even as a victim she had been investigated, possibly just to make sure that she was *indeed* a victim… Rico's remark in the bath the previous night—about her being a suspect—returned to haunt her.

And clearly in the inspector's biased view she was exactly the kind of woman who was likely to jump on some tabloid bandwagon and tell all for a price.

'Bella's not going to talk.'

Glancing up, she met Rico's brilliant golden gaze, aimed at her like a stranglehold and a gag. That look spoke not of faith but of threat. If you talk I'll personally throttle you, that look said. Her cup of humiliation ran right over there and then. She looked away, her facial muscles locking tight, an acrid sting burning her eyelids. 'O ye of little faith', she reflected, in more pain than she could have believed possible and sick to the heart from it.

Did he really think that he was in danger of waking up some morning soon to a kiss-and-tell revelation about their lovemaking in captivity? Her stomach churned. After all they had gone through together he still distrusted her. So maybe she wasn't a whore, but she could still be a greedy little gold-digger, it seemed! And *this* was the male that every hateful instinct urged her to cling to and stay with?

That was when she knew it was over between them— absolutely, finally and conclusively over, regardless of what she did or did not feel for Rico da Silva.

'Of course she's not about to talk.' The older policeman patted her shoulder in reassurance as he tactfully angled her down into a chair, and she had the bitter pleasure of appreciating that a man who had met her only an hour ago already knew and understood more about her than Rico did.

She answered questions like an automaton. Inside herself she just wanted to die behind her forced smiles, but torture wouldn't have wrung an ounce of her true feelings from her. Pride… Thank the Lord it was there for her when she most needed it. Rico watched her like a hawk throughout, as if he were programmed to probe that uncharacteristic complete emotional withdrawal of hers. But she really didn't credit him with that much sensitivity.

The noisy clatter of rotor blades stole through her self-imposed inner wall, her darkened green eyes briefly revealing her turmoil as she frowned.

'Mr da Silva's helicopter landing in the car park,' the chief super revealed. 'I'll take you wherever you want to go, Miss Jennings. I'm heading back to London.'

'Bella's coming with me,' Rico murmured drily without a single shade of doubt.

Without looking at him, so grateful to the older man that she could have grabbed his hand and kissed it, Bella sprang upright. 'Thanks, but I have friends I can go to…friends I want to be with,' she muttered abruptly.

'Perhaps you could leave us alone for a moment?' Rico suggested smoothly to their companions.

'I'll be waiting outside,' the chief super told her, with a wry smile. And then the door closed, sealing them into the privacy which she would have done any craven thing to avoid, but which her intelligence told her had to be faced.

'What the hell are you playing at?' Rico enquired harshly. 'Of course you're coming with me!'

She had to force herself to look at him again. She had to know, before she walked away, that she was making the only possible decision…and yet she already knew that, and loathed herself for being weak enough to require further proof. 'I'm not going to talk to the Press,' she said stiffly.

The faintest hint of dark colour accentuated the angular slant of his hard cheekbones. His hooded dark eyes were nailed to her, however, without any perceptible emotion at all. He made no comment on her reassurance. His sensual mouth twisted. 'I want you to come with me.'

'Why? The party's over…don't you think?' Behind her mocking grin she felt like somebody handing a murderer a knife.

'But I don't mind if the band plays on…for a while,' he murmured, coolly careful to conclude with that candour.

He had used the knife without compunction. It was sex, nothing else. That was all he wanted—a temporary affair in the privacy of his home, with the added security of knowing that she couldn't talk to the Press while he was around. Neat, tidy, every necessity covered, sexual and otherwise…so much Rico's stamp that she wanted to shout and scream and claw him.

But she didn't. She used her talons to hang on like grim death to her pride instead. 'I don't think so.' Turning, unable to meet his sharp appraisal any longer, she began moving towards the door.

'You're as hot for me as I am for you, *gatita*…and I won't make you a better offer,' he warned with silken insolence.

Her spine stiffened. She spun back, unable to let that go unchallenged. 'So what? You think that matters to me?' she demanded shakily.

'I want you in my bed.' The admission might have been wrenched by force from him. His strong face was hard and taut, his eyes as dark as black ice, biting into her almost accusingly.

Bella gave vent to an edgy laugh. 'I'm sure you've got no shortage of willing replacements!'

'And what if you're pregnant?'

Bella paled but her magnificent eyes flashed at him. 'Highly unlikely…it was the wrong time,' she told him brittlely as she made for the door again, really desperate this time to escape.

'Then allow me.' He reached the door ahead of her and swung it wide. 'Look after yourself,' he murmured drily as she preceded him into the corridor. And then he was gone, striding past her in the direction of the rear exit.

On cotton-wool legs she wandered down to the window and stood there, watching him walk out and spring into the waiting helicopter. Well, that was that, she told herself. The feeling that she had been cut in half without an anaesthetic would wear off. She was not, could not be, in love with a creep like that. Fear had somehow made her emotions centre on him. She had become disgustingly dependent, weak and vulnerable, but now that the whole ghastly experience was over she would swiftly recover and return to normal.

'A self-contained bastard, isn't he?'

Her head flipped round, her every feeling exposed. And the chief super placed a supportive arm round her and wafted her out to his car. He asked her where she wanted to go and then handed her a box of tissues. Sorry, he had four adult daughters, he told her ruefully; couldn't help reading her like a book. He had seen her paintings, he told her. Fabulous, out of this world, he added almost shyly. Was there the slightest chance that she would sell one?

And that cracked her shell as nothing else could have done. The tears flooded out, and she got dug into the tissues with the agonised acknowledgement that this stranger, this kind, clever man whom she barely knew, knew so much more about her than the arrogant, hateful swine she had stupidly, recklessly gone to bed with!

It was a long drive down to Liz's country cottage. With Liz she knew she was always welcome and she knew that Liz would keep her mouth shut. And she even knew where her friend kept her spare key—under the second tub of pansies to the left of the back door. The policeman was appalled, but to her he didn't feel like a policeman any more. He had become Maurice during the drive.

'I'll stay until your friend gets home,' he told her.

'I want to be on my own.'

He studied her and then sighed. 'If he asks where—?'

'No!' she interrupted, with helpless force.

'I'll keep you in touch with developments,' he asserted, and took his leave with a touching reluctance to leave her alone.

Liz wouldn't be back until far later than she had admitted to him. This was her night with the art club. She dined in town those nights and went straight to the college for her class. Liz was an accountant, several years Bella's senior, who painted great, vibrant canvases of the flowers she loved and enjoyed a lucrative sideline from their sales. She joked that her clients would be unnerved by that flamboyant side to her nature and only ever signed her creations with her initials.

Gramps had enrolled Bella in the art club long before she'd attended art college at seventeen. She had been the youngest in the class and had had no training whatsoever, but from her first visit the instructor had been excited by what he'd called her 'raw talent'. More worried than pleased by his enthusiasm, her grandfather had got in touch with Hector through the medium of one of Cleo's fleeting visits. It had been Hector who had advised them on what art college and which course, Hector who had taken charge of her artistic development.

She made a dive for Liz's phone, suddenly desperate to hear Hector's querulous but familiar voice.

'I was worried sick when those nosy policemen landed on the doorstep,' he complained furiously, making her smile. 'And I don't want any blasted reporters following them!'

'I'll stay here until the fuss blows over. I'll ring the restaurant and tell them I'm sick,' she muttered, speaking her thoughts out loud on the subject of her job.

'That Griff character has been calling too. Give him a ring,' Hector advised irritably, and then added as an afterthought, 'You didn't damage your hands, did you?'

'Just my heart.'

'I beg your pardon?'

'Never mind. I'll keep in touch.'

'Phone calls cost a fortune,' he reminded her in dismay.

'The Royal Mail is expensive but considerably cheaper in comparison.'

She came off the phone and laughed until she cried. Through her tears she picked up Liz's sketch-pad and began to draw, her agile fingers moving at speed over the paper. Only when she registered what she was drawing did she stop. With a choking sensation in her throat she looked down sickly at the slashing lines of Rico's impassive face as she had last seen him.

She threw the pad aside, in more turmoil than ever. She would work through this, get her feet pinned back down hard to ground level and gather her common sense if it killed her! After all, a week ago she hadn't even known Rico da Silva walked the same earth. But he *didn't*, she reflected with sudden fierce anger; he didn't walk the same earth at all.

'I feel like an idiot…a total, absolute idiot!' Griff complained for the third time. 'Every one of my partners is sniggering behind his hands. So what *did* happen in that blasted container between the two of you? I have a right to know!'

'The same way I have the right to know who was with you the night of my birthday?' As soon as she said it she regretted it. Griff was very handsome but suddenly, betrayed by his fair skin, he looked like a guilty beetroot that had been stabbed unexpectedly in the back by a pickle fork.

'Well, I…I don't know what you're talking about! I was working that night.'

He lied so badly that she was embarrassed for him. Why was he being so possessive all of a sudden? Why was it that even an unfaithful man suddenly hung on like grim death when he sensed that you were ready to break it off? It crossed her mind that Rico hadn't hung on…Rico had been off like an Olympic sprinter… Only good manners had made him let her out of the door in front of him.

'OK.' Griff heaved a constricted sigh. 'Guilty…but it was only a flirtation… I was tempted, that's all. Unforgivable, I know, on your birthday—'

'Don't you think that date was subconsciously chosen to hurt most?'

He looked blankly back at her. She was too clever for him, could practically tell him what he was about to say before he parted his lips, and whatever had been between them had evaporated entirely on her side. She decided to let him off the hook.

'Look, it doesn't matter, does it? We're finished. Good *friends* still, I hope,' she stressed gently. 'But that's all, Griff.'

'I didn't sleep with her!' He startled her by surging across Liz's tiny lounge with an amount of emotion she would never have expected from a male usually so cool and controlled. 'And I'm sorry; I'll never do it again,' he swore, grasping both her hands.

He *had* slept with that other woman. She could tell, but it was not her place, after what had happened with Rico, to stand in pious judgement.

'Let's go out to dinner somewhere very public,' he urged tautly. 'You have to come out of hiding some time. Da Silva's "no comment" is beginning to fall pretty hard on my ears! You're my girlfriend, for God's sake, but all that trash in the tabloids and your disappearance is giving everyone the idea…well, that you've got something to be ashamed of!'

Liz walked into the tiny bedroom where she was changing. 'You're going *out* with him?'

'It seems that I owe it to him to help him save face with his colleagues in the office.'

'He never said that, surely?'

'I don't think he even realises that that is what he said. I'll pack. It's time I went home anyway.' A rueful smile curved Bella's lips. 'Thanks for having me, but I've got to face the music sooner or later. Not that I'm expecting to be mobbed. I'm old news since our kidnappers were caught. There won't be much interest now until the case reaches court,' she pointed out.

'Don't you believe it... You've got a price on your head whether you like it or not! And the longer you keep quiet about your *ordeal*,' Liz said grimly, 'the more outrageous become the tabloid fantasies. You'd be better off issuing a statement.'

Bella sat silently in Griff's BMW as it transported her back to London. The more questions he asked about Rico the tenser she became. Why the heck couldn't he just take the hint and shut up?

It had been three weeks since she had been dropped by the chief superintendent at her friend's cottage. Hector had packed a case for her and Liz had collected it covertly from his back door, because the Press had been encamped at the front continuously during those first days after her captors' arrest. She had twice been collected and smuggled into a central London police station where the evidence against their kidnappers was being carefully stockpiled. But all that was over, bar the court case.

Only now did she wonder if it would ever be over. The Press had ferreted into her past and published *everything*—her colourful parentage, her cursory education, her artistic talent. It seemed to her that everyone she had ever known in life had talked about her to the tabloids—Gramps' neighbours, fellow students at the college, her tutor, former boyfriends—bitter and otherwise. 'Frigid', had said one; 'wild', had said another. I'M STILL IN LOVE WITH HER, had screamed the headline given by an ex she barely recalled from six months ago.

She didn't recognize the *femme fatale* the tabloids had depicted her as. Her every piece of privacy had been ripped from her resistant body. She had been invaded, raped in print and twisted into something she was not, and as far as she could see there was not a damn thing she could do about it!

'*Here*?' Bella gasped when she realised where Griff was planning that they should dine. 'You'll be broke for six months!'

'Will you keep your voice down?' he hissed at her, paling to the same shade as his brand-new dinner jacket. 'I can well afford to splash out occasionally.'

Only he had never splashed out for her benefit before. Griff might have earned a very healthy crust as a partner in a busy legal firm but he was careful with his cash. Was he celebrating something—a more than usually lucrative divorce?

The head waiter looked at her with recognition. She threw her slim shoulders back and smoothed her elbow-high black gloves up her arms. Her figure-hugging black velvet dress could mercifully hold its own in any company. A seventies designer original, the colour spectacular against her wealth of vibrant Titian hair and creamy skin, its deceptively simple cut made the most of her lithe, female shape and fabulous legs.

Their table was right in the very centre of the crowded dining room. 'Are we celebrating something?' Bella whispered, maddeningly conscious of heads turning in their direction. Surely not all these beautiful people read the same rubbishy tabloids?

'I hope so.' Griff gave her a wide, self-satisfied smile as their menus arrived and he ordered wine in execrable French.

'I don't drink,' she reminded him.

He leant almost confidingly closer. 'I believe you'll break that rule tonight.'

Just as she was on the brink of questioning the peculiarity of his behaviour, Bella's attention was stolen. Griff could have stood up and stripped and she wouldn't have noticed. Rico da Silva was in the act of taking a seat at a table about fifteen feet away. She froze, her heartbeat slowing to a dulled thud as if she was being forced to witness a disaster. And, inside herself, indeed she was…

For three endless weeks Bella had rationalised away every single feeling that Rico had inspired in her. She had blamed fear, propinquity, hysteria and her own repressed sexuality. She had lost weight, endured sleepless nights and stubbornly considered herself cured of emotions that she refused to rate higher than the level of an adolescent infatuation.

But at the same second as her shocked gaze located him and everyone else in the room vanished from her awareness, her so-called cure came apart at the seams. A hunger so intense that it was agonising clawed at her. Her mesmerised eyes roved from his dark head to the soles of his hand-made shoes and back up again. Worst of all, she couldn't stop herself from doing it.

'Your wine…' Griff prodded her fingers with the glass at the same instant as Rico's dark, restive gaze landed on her. Bella watched his hard, bronzed face tauten with something that looked very much like savage disbelief, and hurriedly she tore her dazed scrutiny from him. She fumbled for the wine and drank the whole glass down in one go.

'I do realise that you haven't indulged before,' Griff reproved, 'but one is supposed to enjoy the bouquet.'

The waiter was already refilling her glass.

'Now…' Griff dealt her an expectant look.

'Now what?'

Belatedly she noticed the ring glittering in the palm which he was extending to her. 'What do you want me to do with that?' she muttered helplessly.

'I am asking you to marry me,' he told her smugly, reaching for her hand.

'You're what?'

Everything happened at once. A camera flash went off

somewhere near by. The head waiter looked shattered. A man in a dinner jacket, clasping a camera, raced past... 'Thanks mate!' he tossed back, apparently at Griff, as he headed for the exit fast.

'I'm sure you won't mind if we join you.'

Open-mouthed, Bella stared incredulously as Rico, appearing out of nowhere, cooly pulled out one of the two vacant chairs at their table for the exquisite blonde who was hovering with an air of unease beside him.

'Sophie Ingram, this is Bella. Bella, meet Sophie. Since we are the cynosure for every eye in the room, we might as well join up, *es verdad*?'

'*Es verdad* nothing!' Bella hissed, recovering her tongue. 'I do not wish to share a table with you. You're butting in where you are not wanted—'

'Bella, *please*,' Griff intervened in a shocked whisper.

'If you whisper at Bella you'll make her shout,' Rico murmured flatly, sinking down into the seat beside her and signalling to the hovering head waiter with an imperious movement of one hand. 'Now, you are Griff Atherton... Does she accidentally call you Biff from time to time? I ask because when we first met it took Bella four attempts to even recall my name.'

'Shut up!' she bit out from between clenched teeth.

'Bella, please,' Griff said again. 'Mr da Silva and Miss Ingram are very welcome.'

'Of course we're welcome,' Rico drawled with lancing satire, shooting Griff a look of unconcealed derision.

Bella reached for her glass and drained it for a second time all in one go.

'I'm very sorry about this,' Sophie murmured, openly studying the engagement ring still lying on the linen cloth in front of Bella.

'Wedding bells...' Rico laughed sardonically.

'If you don't shut up and back off,' Bella spat in a shaking undertone, 'I'm going to hit you with that bottle!'

'That would be a first.' Incandescent golden eyes challenged her, his strong mouth twisting. 'Another first. But not one half as enjoyable as the last we shared.'

'Excuse me.' It took immense restraint but Bella shakily reached for her bag and rose from the table.

She reached the cloackroom only seconds before Sophie. She spun from the sink her green eyes swimming with tears. The blonde gave her a wry glance. 'If I could do to Rico what you can do, I wouldn't be crying over it.'

'I don't know what you're talking about,' Bella said in a stifled voice.

'You're so young.' Sophie sighed, studying her averted profile. 'I came to bitch but I can't. It isn't your fault he's about to dump me—he never stays with anyone longer than a couple of months. I'm past my sell-by date and frankly I've had enough. Rico has been like a stranger since the kidnapping—'

'Has he?' Bella looked up, all damp eyes and helpless curiosity.

'He's all yours.' Sophie was extracting several items from her beautiful beaded bag. 'The card that opens the city apartment, the keys for the main house on the Winterwood estate and the keys for the Porsche. He told me to keep it…but I don't think I earned that size of pay-off.'

'I don't want them!' Bella exclaimed in horror as the items were thrust into her hand.

'You're planning to marry Biff or whatever his name is?'

'Well, no, but—'

'Save Rico the trouble of getting extras cut,' Sophie said very drily.

'You've got it all wrong—'

'Good luck. You'll need it. He's anti-love, anti-commitment and anti-marriage. Sensational divorces leave scars,' she murmured tightly, turning to the door. 'It's just a pity that Rico doesn't appreciate that he's not the only one ever to have been hurt!'

Bella was left holding the keys. Sophie had shattered her. She was one very strong lady…one very generous lady. After all, had it once occurred to Bella whilst in that container that she was playing around with another woman's man? *Not once.* Maybe she hadn't wanted to recall seeing Rico with Sophie that very first night, emerging from that hotel, climbing into the Bugatti. Suddenly Bella, who prided herself on her principles, saw that she had sacrificed more than one with Rico, and whether it was fair or otherwise she hated him for reducing her to that level.

Head high, she walked back to the table, as beautiful and as remote as a moving statue. Without looking once at Rico, she dropped the keys and the card in front of him. 'I want to go home, Griff.'

'*Hasta la vista, gatita,*' Rico drawled smoothly.

CHAPTER SEVEN

IT HAD taken quite some time for Griff to unload her paintings and possessions from the BMW. He was in an astonishingly good mood. Rico had known the way to Griff's heart. He had promised to recommend him to one of his friends, who was currently enduring the horrors of a broken marriage.

'And once I get *those* kinds of people coming to me for advice,' Griff bored on, 'I'll be offered a senior partnership.'

'Marvellous.' Had he always been this boring, this predictable? She felt awful even thinking that, but couldn't wait to escape.

'It could bring our wedding forward by a year or two—'

'Say that again?' she practically whispered.

Griff gravely outlined his agenda for their future—a three-year engagement, her discovery as an artist to facilitate the expense, marriage only when they had left no stone of possible incompatibility unturned and explored. It was so very sensible that she wanted to tear her hair out, for this was a man whom a few short weeks ago she had believed she would marry, should he ask.

Without warning she belatedly recalled the photographer who had shouted his thanks to Griff before he'd taken off. 'Why did that man with the camera thank you?'

Griff frowned. 'I told him we would be there.'

'You did *what*? Were you also aware that Rico would be there?'

'It's his favourite watering-hole, I understand, and I was delighted when he showed up and joined us. It was unfortunate that his date chose to take off early, but there'll be no more undesirable publicity once our engagement is announced in print, complete with photo,' Griff pointed out with pride, blind to the gathering rage and disbelief in Bella's face, he was so patently pleased with himself.

'But I didn't say *yes*!' she hissed.

He took a step back, flinching from her venom.

'The answer is no. I don't want to marry you. Not only are you unfaithful, you are stingy. You pocketed the ring again... You just couldn't bring yourself to part with it!' she reminded him witheringly.

'How dare you call me stingy?'

'And you can take that announcement right back out of the paper again, because I'd sooner starve than be married to a stingy, manipulative man who is more concerned with his image at the office than with me!' Thrusting him bodily out of the dingy hall, Bella slammed the door on him before he had the chance to snap his dropped jaw closed again.

She perched on the step one up from the bottom of the stairs. She was waiting for Rico. He would come. She knew it in her bones. And she was all shaken up just thinking about it. A man who bought women the same way he bought his shirts. Sophie had ripped the scales from her stupid eyes. Anti-love, anti-commitment and anti-marriage. How could she have fallen in love with a man like that?

For it was love. She could no longer lie to herself. Seeing Rico again tonight had torn her apart but it had also made her face the truth. She had fallen violently in love with a man who bonded with women on an immoral basis of keys and gifts of expensive cars, a male who might have remarkable staying power in bed—her cheeks burned—but whose staying power in relationships was abysmal. *Two* months? Even Bella allowed men to last longer than two months...most of the time, she adjusted. Griff had lasted three, but then he worked a lot of overtime, she conceded absently.

And what about the sensational divorce? She should have

asked Liz about Rico's failed marriage. It was strange that there had been no mention of it in the papers. Liz was a walking encyclopaedia on celebrity lives and scandals. But then maybe Liz hadn't known, or maybe Liz had just been too good a friend to mention Rico when Bella had gone to such ridiculous lengths to avoid referring to him herself. Poor Liz. She must have used superglue to keep her lips sealed on all the questions she'd been dying to ask!

The mechanical Edwardian doorbell shrilled and made her jump. She unlocked the door.

'You should have a chain on,' Rico grated, striding in. 'Why is this place in total darkness?'

'Hector doesn't like electricity bills!'

Thrusting arrogantly past her, Rico skimmed a hand along the wall, and abruptly the great chandelier above blazed into light. Bella had never seen it illuminated before and she stared up, wondering how it would look without the cobwebs. There was a strangled moan from the landing above.

'Switch that off!' Hector urged in horror. 'Are you trying to ruin me? Have you any idea how many watts that burns?'

'Switch it off, for heaven's sake…before he has a heart attack!'

Rico stared up at the thin figure wrapped in the ragged wool robe and mounted the stairs. 'Mr Barsay…I am Rico da Silva.' He extended a lean hand with awesome cool.

Hector pressed his hand to his palpitating chest instead. 'Switch off that light!' he pleaded.

'I'll pay for it,' Rico drawled smoothly, tugging out his wallet and extracting a crisp note. 'I'm reduced to a shuddering wreck by darkness after my experience in that container. My nerves couldn't stand the strain.'

'Bella has candles—'

'Not enough.' Rico pressed the note apologetically into Hector's trembling hand. 'And I do understand what a struggle it is for you to survive in this house.'

There was no subject dearer to Hector's heart. He managed a brave smile while surreptitiously pocketing the money. '*Hector*!' Bella moaned in embarrassment.

'Women don't understand these things,' Rico sighed.

'I don't like visitors,' Hector snorted. 'But you can stay.' And off he went.

Bella raced upstairs.

'Where do you hang out?' Rico enquired, shooting an incredulous glance over the peeling walls and general air of decay surrounding him. 'In the attic with the bats? No wonder you're off the wall, *gatita*. He's as nutty as a fruit-cake.'

'How dare you?' she said, her teeth gritted. 'He can't help being poor—'

'*Poor*?' Rico burst out laughing. 'He could buy and sell everyone else in this street! He has a solid-gold investment portfolio that keeps on raking in the cash year after year.'

'I don't believe you—'

'He has just about everyone fooled but I checked him out. Hector Barsay is stinking rich and he never parts with a penny if he can help it. Charities know not to knock on this door.'

'You've mixed him up with someone else...you must have done!'

'Where's your lair?'

Stiff-backed, she mounted the second flight of stairs ahead of him and reluctantly pushed open the door. He reached for the light switch.

'There's no bulb,' she said with pleasure, and then abruptly she recalled her paintings and spun round. 'We'll go downstairs.'

'I wouldn't dream of it. I've always wanted to see a starving artist's garret. Where's the flea-ridden straw pallet and the mousetraps?' he enquired, lifting the solid-silver candelabra by her bed and using the matches sitting beside it. '*Madre de Dios*...' he breathed, surveying the bare room with an emotion akin to incredulous fascination. 'You will think you have entered paradise when I take you home with me!'

'You're not taking me anywhere, Rico.' She folded her arms. In the flickering light from the candles he was a dark silhouette in bronze and black—lithe and sleek and as graceful as a jungle cat. Her mouth went dry.

'Even if you can't paint anything other than blobs in primary colours I'll be your patron,' Rico said smoothly. 'And you deserve that I say that to you. I've learnt more about you in the papers than you ever deigned to tell me.'

She flushed. 'And that should tell you something—'

'That you like to dramatise...that you like to play games?' He shot the demand at her in fast, fluent French. 'You may not attach too much importance to spelling but you speak French, German, Italian and Russian like a native, I believe.'

She tensed even more, her mouth tightening. 'You shouldn't believe everything you read—'

'Do you or don't you?' he raked at her in German.

'OK...OK...guilty as charged!'

'You described yourself to me as a waitress—'

'I'm not ashamed of being a waitress—'

'But you could have been a rocket scientist if you'd wanted to be! Your teachers said you were brilliant—'

'A slight exaggeration—'

'But bone-idle academically and fixated on art...and I have this awful suspicion that you can't paint for peanuts,' Rico bit out harshly. 'Hector's the father you never had and you would very much like to walk in your lousy father's footsteps!'

Bella had turned white. She hadn't expected such a forceful attack as this. Rico was so angry. Why? Did he think that she had made a fool of him? Was she supposed to have reeled off a boastful list of her abilities for his benefit? 'Clever clogs', the other kids had whispered nastily behind her back when she had been at school. Bella had learnt the hard way that it was easier to be average than gifted.

'Biff thinks you're as thick as the proverbial plank; can't understand why the papers are making up so many ridiculous lies,' Rico derided.

'His name is Griff and he does not think I'm thick—'

'"Exquisite on the eye, dizzy as a dodo," he told me cheerfully. He would run a mile if he knew that you were capable of out-thinking, out-guessing and out-plotting his every move!'

Bella compressed her lips. 'What are you doing here?'

'You were waiting for me,' he reminded her smoothly, surveying her with smouldering golden eyes that burned wherever they touched. 'When I saw you in that restaurant I wanted to put my hands round your throat and squeeze hard. Where the hell have you been for the past three weeks? Why the hell did Chief Superintendent Nazenby treat me like a convicted criminal who was dangerous to women and refuse to divulge your whereabouts?'

Bella went pink and managed a jerky shrug. 'It didn't occur to me that you'd ask.'

'This is not Biff you are talking to…this is *Rico*,' he growled, moving forward, his handsome face as hard as iron. 'And I can scent female deviousness a mile away. I offended your pride at the police station, and you removed yourself from my radius to let me learn to appreciate you in your absence. Then magically you reappeared in my favourite restaurant with another man—a man all primed and ready to propose holy matrimony with *me* as an audience!'

'You conceited jerk!' Bella slung at him in disbelief. 'You actually think I would sink to that level to try and trap you?'

'*Sí…*' He threw her a seething look of condemnation. 'I might respect you more if you simply admitted how calculating you are!'

'How did you get through the front door with an ego that size?'

'My apologies if I did not rise to your expectation of me throwing a jealous scene! I am not the jealous type.'

'I'll believe you…thousands wouldn't,' she responded sweetly, recognising with a kind of savage pleasure that he had indeed been jealous, and ready to thank him even more sweetly for bringing it to her notice. 'You were rude to me, rude to poor Sophie, and rude to Griff, although it probably went over his head. I don't know what I did to earn that… And as for Sophie, my heart went out to her—'

'What heart?' Rico slashed back viciously. '*Por Dios*…to see you sitting there holding hands with *him*! You got exactly the reaction you expected—'

'I didn't know you would be there!' But she knew that she was talking to a brick wall. Rico was convinced that she had set him up. Griff had set them both up, but Rico would not believe that. Why? Because Griff had been so polite that Rico had written him off as a lame brain. But Griff would never have risked offending someone as powerful and rich as Rico da Silva.

'I want to see these famous paintings, not one of which has ever been sold,' Rico derided, heading for the pile of canvases stacked along the entire length of the spacious room, 'but which Nazenby considers works of pure genius… *Infierno*! He probably couldn't tell an old master from a Picasso!'

'No!' Bella planted herself squarely in his path.

'And what happened to your terror of the police force? I did everything within my power to support you at that police station,' Rico reminded her rawly, setting her out of his path with one imperious hand. 'And now Nazenby talks about you as though you're part of his family!'

'Face that container and you can face anything. I'd kept up the fear out of habit… *No*, Rico!'

'I want to see them. You live with Hector Barsay and,

unless old age has mellowed him, you have to be accustomed to criticism.'

'Why is it so important for you to see them?' she wailed in distress.

'Why is it so important for you to prevent me?'

'They're private,' she muttered tightly.

'An artist whose every work is private—how thought-provoking,' he drawled nastily, flipping back the first canvas.

'Hector says I'm not ready to be shown yet. He thinks my interpretation needs a lot more work...more maturity,' she proffered unsteadily, voicing her supposed flaws in advance.

The silence went on and on. She clutched her hands together, as nervous as someone watching her children jay-walking across an accident black spot. Rico shone the candelabra on about half a dozen, slowly moving from one to the next. Nothing could be read from the taut lines of his dark features. Expelling his breath, he straightened, but he was still studying an oil of children playing in the mud round a lorry.

'You paint your childhood,' he breathed tautly.

'Not all the time.'

'Hector is not only a miser, he's a liar. He wants to hold onto you, *es verdad*? His own discovery. He can't let you go. He hid away from that world out there years ago, and if he encourages you to exhibit he knows he'll lose you!' Rico sent her a shimmering glance, his expressive mouth compressed into a strangely bloodless line. 'You have extraordinary talent and you cannot possibly require someone like me to tell you that.'

'You like them?'

He set the candelabra back by the bed and stood there, watching her with hooded dark eyes. 'I'm in shock and you know it. Why are you working as a waitress?'

'It pays the rent. I paint in daylight, work at night. I get fabulous tips—'

'I can imagine.'

'The hours suit me.'

'Biff told me you were a catering supervisor, not a waitress—'

Spontaneously, Bella laughed. 'He would say that!'

'With me you'll be what you are—an artist—'

Bella stilled. 'I won't be with you, Rico. Never again,' she swore shakily.

'No more games, *gatita mia*.' He strolled fluidly across the bare boards. Even the way he moved, the effortless grace of that lithe, powerful body, shook her to her very depths. He took out his wallet and extracted a cheque.

'Where did you get this money?'

When Liz had collected her clothes she had also collected the one valuable possession Bella had—a small oil of her mother, painted by her father. Liz had taken it to a top art gallery and sold it for her. She would have made more at auction but she had been desperate to dissolve what she'd seen as her last tie to Rico and settle the debt. The canvas had fetched enough to cover the repairs to the Bugatti and the Skoda.

'That's my business.'

'What did you do?' he asked, indulgently amused. 'Tell Hector you were about to be dragged off to prison?'

'It was my debt. *I* paid it without anyone else's assistance,' she stressed proudly.

'I don't want it. In fact, I refuse to accept it.' Rico tore the cheque in two and let the pieces fall like a statement of intent between them.

'I'll just have to get another one…' In bewilderment she stared at him. 'That was your money—'

'Lovers don't have debts between them,' he purred lazily. 'And if you hadn't smashed up the Bugatti I would never have met you. In retrospect it seems a very small price to pay for the amount of pleasure you've given me.'

Feeling the atmosphere thicken, Bella took a jerky step in retreat. 'Less than a month ago you were going to take me to the police—'

'No... I changed my mind in the lift on the way down to the car park...I was taking you home instead,' Rico drawled with rueful amusement.

'I wouldn't have gone! And would you really have done that to Sophie?'

A winged brow elevated. 'What would it have had to do with her?'

Bella threw him a look of distaste. 'She was living with you at the time...or did you think I hadn't worked that out yet?'

'Sophie had keys for convenience. She never lived with me. I haven't shared a roof with a woman in the past decade. Live-in relationships can get very messy and possessive—'

'And with a two-month limit on your interest it really wouldn't be worth the effort?'

'You're talking to *me* about track records?' Rico threw back his dark head and laughed with a forbidding lack of humour. 'What about yours?'

'*Mine*?'

'You are one flighty lady if one half of what I read is true, *gatita mia*.'

'I am not flighty—'

'No...I'll clip your wings, chain you to the bed when I'm out, take you with me when I go abroad, employ only ugly old men.' He watched her with mesmeric intensity and then he smiled—a brilliant smile of unconcealed triumph. 'Then again, I'm really not that worried. Out of all those men I was the only one you slept with, *es verdad*?'

Outraged by the blazing confidence with which he surveyed her, she said, 'That wasn't how you felt at the time.'

'I'd never made love to a virgin before. You took me by storm.' Rico spread his smooth brown hands with expressive amusement. 'I had to escape to fully appreciate what an enormous compliment it was to be selected out of a cast of thousands to make the grade.'

'I think it's time you left.'

'Only if you come home with me. Don't bother packing. I'll send someone over to clear this place tomorrow.'

Her nails cut purple crescents into her palms. 'Are you asking me to live with you?' she whispered tightly.

He winced. 'Do you have to be so precise? I suggest we spend a month together and take it from there.'

'You said live-in relationships get messy and possessive,' Bella reminded him doggedly.

'That is a risk I'm prepared to take—'

'Briefly,' she inserted, thinking of the month he had designated. Not much of a risk at all.

'—to have you in my bed again,' he completed shortly.

'And that is all you want?'

A spasm of raw impatience flashed across his set features. 'The generation gap, *es verdad*? Have you ever heard of subtlety? *Infierno*…what the hell am I doing here?'

'When you only came to insult me? I'm wondering too.'

He glowered at her in disbelief. 'How have I insulted you?'

Bella was starting to shake with rage and reaction, much of which, she acknowledged, stemmed from bitter disappointment. 'You offer me a month's trial in your bed as if you're some sultan talking to a little harem slave and you don't think that's an insult?' she spat with unashamed contempt.

Rico merely shrugged and looked levelly back at her. 'What have you got to lose—Biff and the ring he put back in his pocket?' he mocked.

'Maybe…'

'I won't ever offer you a ring, *gatita mia*. If that is your goal, settle for your tame little solicitor and suburbia,' he advised, his lip curling.

Inside herself she ached. Had she had the faintest suspicion that Rico cared for her, she might have settled for the month's trial in the hope that it might develop into something more. That awareness shamed her. How many rules did you break before you began to hate yourself? Every rule she broke as far as Rico was concerned shaved away her self-respect, and without her pride she would be weak. She was an all-or-nothing person.

'Since you've been so frank, I'll match you.' She walked away, working up the courage to do so, her beautiful face deeply troubled, tiny little shivers of high-wire tension rippling through her. 'I grew up with instability, with my mother's love affairs, her broken hearts, her depressions, her humiliations. I will not live like that. I saw how you treated Sophie tonight—'

'Sophie and I were not lovers.'

Bella stared at him in shock.

'Sophie acted as my hostess. We probably would have become intimate,' he admitted, 'but then you and I were kidnapped and everything changed.'

'Everything changed'. Yes, everything had changed for Bella too. Within the space of less than thirty-six hours the entire course of her life had been altered. Bonds had been formed, emotions unleashed and her every desperate attempt to put the clock back had failed.

'It was over before it ever began between Sophie and me. This evening she invited herself,' Rico revealed grimly.

'Even so, you didn't give a damn about her!' Bella accused, recalling his complete detachment from the other woman, knowing that there would be a day when she would earn a similar lack of interest. 'I'm worth more than that.'

'You should have kept that in mind, *querida*...before you offered yourself to me. That was your value, not mine.'

Bella flinched as though she had been struck. She was

in love with a total, irredeemable swine. Cleo's bad taste paled beside this demonstration of raw masculine arrogance. She refused to lower herself to the same level.

She thrust her head high. 'I won't do it. I need more.'

'You want marriage.' Rico dealt her a look of supreme derision, but at the back of that derision lurked a simmering pool of explosive rage. 'I said I wanted you. I didn't say I was down on my knees and certifiably insane!'

'I didn't say I wanted marriage!' she gasped strickenly.

'You don't need to. You could spell it out in fireworks above my bank and it would be less obvious than what I see in your face!' he bit out with sudden viciousness as he strode forward and closed hard hands round her forearms before she could retreat. 'I was right all along. You had your price all right. But it's not a price I would even contemplate, and you have to be bloody naïve to imagine that I would be that desperate!'

'I never mentioned marriage!'

'In the next breath you were about to mention children, no doubt,' he scorned. '*Madre de Dios…*'

'I *love* them!' Bella flung at him, losing her head. 'I also want a large fluffy dog and a cat and a pony for them. So take yourself off, Rico! Go find a bimbo to audition for the honour of sharing your precious bed! And if she amuses herself on the side with your gardener or one of your security men you will only be getting what you deserve!'

'*Por Dios*…you may have an IQ higher than my credit rating but you are unhinged.' Rico swore furiously. 'No normal woman would speak like this to me!'

'I'm ashamed I ever let you touch me. I'll be scrubbing myself clean for a month!' she shouted back. 'How dare you come here into my home and talk to me as if I'm some sort of glorified whore? Was I going to get a Porsche as well?'

'Driving lessons,' he raked down at her, his dark head

lowering. 'Putting you behind the wheel of a Porsche would be like putting an arsonist in a barn!'

'Don't you dare!' she warned, shaking like a leaf as the scent of him washed over her, as the taut, muscular angles of his hard body met in direct collision with hers.

'You're gasping for it too.'

He kissed her and the world fell away and everything else soared to an ungovernable height of excitement. He closed his arms around her so tightly that she couldn't breathe, but she didn't want to breathe. Dizzy and disorientated, she clung to him, lost in the devastating plunge into passion, her heart racing, her pulses throbbing, every muscle taut with a hunger that dominated and controlled. Heat surged into her loins, making her thighs tremble against the aroused thrust of his manhood. He swept her up in his arms and then dropped her on the ancient feather mattress from a height.

'You're a pushover, *querida*.' He stared down at her, his hard-boned features grim and derisive. 'And you will crawl for that month's trial before I am finished with you!' he stated chillingly.

'Push off, you bastard!' Bella shrieked, her voice cracking.

'And you will stop using language like that,' he hissed in outrage. 'If you want me to treat you like a lady, talk like one!'

'You wouldn't recognise a lady if you fell over one!' she sobbed, out of control with rage and self-loathing. 'I hate you, Rico!'

The door closed. She thumped the pillow with clenched fists. She hadn't buckled. She had been tempted but she hadn't buckled, hadn't surrendered. Why then didn't she feel better? Why had the sound of that door closing filled her with dread? But she knew why, didn't she? He had left her alone again and, for a charged instant, she didn't believe that she could bear the emptiness that stretched ahead without him.

CHAPTER EIGHT

'"A COMPLETE gentleman",' the journalist repeated woodenly, disappointment emanating from her in waves. It might have been an exclusive interview but the content was not of the salacious variety guaranteed to titillate.

'Absolutely,' Bella stressed.

The woman coughed. 'I understand there was only one bed—'

'Mr da Silva slept on the floor.'

'*Mr*? You mean you didn't even get on first-name terms?'

'I *think* of him as Mr da Silva,' Bella muttered.

The brunette sighed. 'He's so gorgeous... He looks so...sexy.'

'Looks can be deceptive.'

'He sounds about as exciting as cold porridge.'

'He did take his jacket off and give it to me to keep me warm when we were escaping!' Bella rushed to assert, fearful that she had overdone her efforts to silence press speculation.

Hector was sitting in the kitchen over a cup of tea.

'The paparazzi will vanish tomorrow when that interview is published,' Bella told him with forced cheer. 'The phone will stop ringing and the doorstep will be clear again. Our lives will return to normal.'

'You should never talk to journalists. They twist things,' he warned her.

125

Bella cleared her throat and surveyed him reflectively.
'Rico said you were stinking rich...'

Hector choked on his tea. She had to bang him on the
back. It was five minutes before he stopped spluttering.

'Absolute rubbish!' he swore weakly.

'But maybe you have a few savings...just for a rainy
day?'

He looked distinctly cornered and shifty. 'It's possible.'

'And maybe you could afford to put on a few lights now
and then. If you have a fall in the dark at your age,' Bella
pointed out gently, 'it could be serious. Gramps was never
the same after *his* tumble down the stairs. The shock took
an awful lot out of him. And then there's the candles,
Hector. They're a fire hazard.'

'I'll think it over,' he muttered, looking grey at the grim
pictures she had painted. 'You're not thinking of moving
out, are you?'

'Where on earth would I go?' she laughed, seeing his
fear.

Hector sighed. 'I meant to say to you last night but I fell
asleep... I used to know da Silva's father, João. He had a
tremendous art collection. Old money, of course. Shame
the son made such an idiot of himself, but then young people do...'

Bella frowned at him and then sat down opposite.
'You're talking about Rico?'

'I was living in Spain then. Must be easily ten years ago,'
he mused. 'His divorce case was plastered all over the
newspapers out there. He had married some totally unsuit-
able female. She was an actress or some such thing. She
had a string of lovers. There was a young child involved
as well—'

'A child?' she broke in helplessly.

'It wasn't his child. I remember feeling very sorry for

the family, and particularly for the boy, having all that dirty washing dragged out. Ghastly.' Hector shook his head expressively, shooting her a troubled glance. 'Not an experience I should think he came through unscathed. These days he seems to have more of a reputation as a womaniser.'

Bella was shaken by what Hector had told her. A failed marriage she was already aware of but *this* was something else entirely. 'The Press went over my life with a fine-tooth comb…how come they didn't pick up on his marriage?'

'It happened in a different country. He's just been lucky.'

She lay in bed that night mulling the bare facts over. By the sound of it Rico had been badly burnt. And at what age—twenty-one? He couldn't have been much older. The same age as she was now. But Rico might well have been far more vulnerable. Growing up in a rich, privileged and happy family did not necessarily prepare you very well for the darker side of life and the people who used and abused you. In fact money had probably made him more of a target.

He had told her so much but she just hadn't been listening carefully enough. That very first day, when he had quite unreasonably accused her of flaunting herself and trading on her looks, he had also called his attraction to her 'a sick craving'. Right from the outset Rico had fought to deny that attraction. Heavens, did she remind him of his ex-wife? She recalled his preoccupation with the possibility of consequences… 'The honey trap and then the price'… Had it been a shotgun wedding?

Whatever the circumstances, Rico had been betrayed and humiliated, and just thinking about that made Bella's heart go out to him. She was a soft touch. She couldn't help it. Her fury with him from the night before evaporated. For all she knew the suggestion that she *live* with him for a month—an invitation that he had denied ever offering to any other woman—had been a courageous stab at what had felt like a mega-commitment on his part.

On the other hand, it could equally well have been a deeply basic indication of how highly he valued the sexual passion they had shared. Beneath those beautifully tailored suits lurked one very passionate male, no matter how hard he tried to hide it. And he did have a sense of humour. Anyone who could handle Hector without batting an eyelash deserved applause.

He wasn't remotely intimidated by her intelligence either and even in a rage he had been capable of eating his own words and admiring her paintings. He even fitted Gramps' yardstick of eligibility—good education, stable family background, steady employment. And she loved him. It was a shame that he had gone ballistic when she'd mentioned the large fluffy dog, the cat and the pony. Rico did not want children. Still, you couldn't have everything.

And right at this moment you have *nothing*, she reminded herself in exasperation.

Griff rang her mid-morning the next day. 'Bella…it would have been kinder to hit the guy with the bottle in the restaurant!'

'What are you talking about?'

'Your exclusive interview…priceless, absolutely priceless. Let's do lunch tomorrow. You really should be wearing my ring. It was too late to stop the announcement and I know you didn't mean what you said,' he asserted.

Bella dropped the phone as though she had been burnt. Half an hour later she was standing in a newsagent's, learning that Hector had spoken truly when he'd said that you shouldn't talk to journalists. Rico had been labelled as a boring stuffed shirt, a male so inflated with his own importance that he hadn't even allowed her to call him by his Christian name, the implication being that he was a raging snob. There wasn't even a mention of his taking his jacket off…probably because it might have made him sound human.

Bella cringed, cursing her own stupidity. She checked her watch. She had agreed to work a rare lunchtime shift at the restaurant. In her break she would get on the phone and apologise to him. It had never crossed her mind that anyone could turn their ordeal into sheer comedy, or that so unjust a picture might be drawn. If she had been able to choose a fellow victim out of a million names, she would have chosen Rico every time… She could have wept.

Gaston's was choked to the gills with customers. Serious foodies ate there, studying the yard-long menu with blissful intensity. Bella was loaded with empty plates when she noticed a curious lull in the level of quiet conversation. She turned her head, saw Rico and simply froze.

'What were you paid for that character assassination?' he blazed at her down the length of the entire dining room.

Her staggered gaze clung to him. The tiger had escaped again. Rico in a rage. He strode across the floor in two long, lithe strides, indifferent to the turning heads, the buzz of conjecture. '*How much?*' he breathed in a tone that quivered with fierce emotion.

There was a look of savage betrayal in his brilliant dark eyes. She couldn't bear it. It cut her to pieces. She forgot she was holding the plates. They dropped with an almighty crash. She barely noticed. 'Nothing…'

'You hate me that much?' he shot at her from between clenched teeth.

'No…no,' she whispered, on the brink of tears, appalled

that he had taken it so badly, making the worst possible interpretation of that foolish interview.

'I do not appreciate being lampooned in print. It was a pack of lies!' he condemned with raw distaste.

'All I was trying to do was get rid of the reporters…they were upsetting Hector,' Bella muttered frantically.

'And regrettably we're everywhere you look,' a wry voice added from a nearby table in what just might have been a friendly warning.

Exhaling his breath in a sudden hiss, Rico surveyed her, his dark gaze chillingly cold. In the space of a moment he had switched from seething rage to black ice, his strong face clenched hard, his mouth twisting. 'I had you taped from the beginning. No pay, no play…*es verdad*?' he murmured in a derisive undertone.

She had never played poker but she caught his drift. Her cheeks burned. Her lashes swept up on her anguished eyes. 'It's not like that…'

'It's over,' Rico drawled with lethal finality, and swung away.

Every skin-cell in her body vibrating with raw tension, Bella watched him stride towards the exit. And she knew that if she let him go she would never see him again. Her nervous paralysis gave. Tearing the chintzy apron from round her waist, she flung her hovering boss a look of apology and took off after Rico.

He was already climbing into the limousine waiting by the kerb. As she raced across the pavement he stilled and straightened, one lean hand planted on the door. Glittering dark eyes hit her in near physical assault. 'What now?' he demanded.

'I'll play…I mean—' gritting her teeth, cursing her fair skin as it heated, she sealed her lips again and sucked in oxygen '—I'll move in with you.'

His gaze narrowed, sliced even deeper into hers, tension tautening his set features. 'You surprise me—'

'Well, you'd better not surprise *me*,' she warned fiercely. 'You'd better treat me right!'

Sudden vibrant amusement banished his stasis. He reached for her in one supple movement and pulled her to him, his hands splaying across the swell of her hips as he looked down at her. 'You won't regret it, I promise you,' he assured her huskily.

'If you don't shift this car you're going to get a ticket,' she muttered, her heartbeat thundering in her ears as her gaze collided dizzily with his smouldering golden eyes.

But he lowered his head to hers, one hand skimming up her back to wind into her tumbling hair. Their lips met slowly, almost hesitantly, and she trembled, the amount of emotion she was holding back flooding through her in powerful waves. With a ragged groan he forced her closer and took her mouth with a sudden, explosive hunger that made the ground fall away beneath her feet. Her hands closed round him convulsively, holding him to her. And she knew then that when the time came to walk away it would rip her apart.

The limo got a ticket before it rejoined the slow-moving traffic. Bella looked at Rico, every pulse still racing, her heart pounding. It was the first time in her life that she had made a decision that already felt like a foregone conclusion.

A part of her feared the devastating strength of what he could make her feel. Reason hadn't powered her change of heart. She had reacted on instinct and she was still in shock because of it. He had walked away from her. It had cut her in two, forced her into compromise. But she was painfully aware that she was entering the relationship with needs and expectations that Rico might not be able to meet.

'I'm flying to Tokyo in the morning for a three-day conference. You can come with me,' he murmured smoothly.

And Rico might also have needs and expectations that she might not be able to meet, Bella registered abruptly. She wasn't some little bimbo, ready to drop everything to become a twenty-four-hour handmaiden, programmed to serve with a smile and satisfy every masculine demand.

'I'll be working—'

'*Por Dios*!' he gritted in disbelief. 'Waiting tables?'

'After the number of plates I broke and my departure at the busiest hour of the day, you can forget that,' she said ruefully. 'No. I'll concentrate on my painting for a while.'

'Then you can come to Tokyo,' he asserted forcefully.

'And what am I going to do with myself all day while you do whatever you do at the conference?'

'Shop,' he retorted impatiently.

'I am not that heavily into shopping, Rico.'

'Naturally I will be paying the bills.'

'When I said that I would move in with you I somehow missed out on the fact that you planned to pay me for my services.' Bella shot him a furious look. 'I am not going to be a kept woman!'

Rico treated her to a fulminating stare, visibly hanging onto his temper. 'I was not aware that I used that designation.'

'You didn't need to,' she said tightly.

'*Basta*…so I go alone! Leave it there!' he ground out with raw bite, patently dissatisfied and antagonised by her response.

He just doesn't know any better, she told herself painfully. He was accustomed to having his own way with her sex. Sophie hadn't been offered a Porsche for acting as his hostess alone. He might not have slept with her but it had been a pay-off. She hadn't earned it, the blonde had said bluntly. Bella's nostrils flared with distaste. If Rico knew what was good for him, he would keep the financial aspect out of their relationship. Bella might not be rich but she considered herself his equal on every other level.

'Where are we going?' she asked abruptly.

'My estate…I'm taking you home with me.' Rico's mouth compressed. 'Don't tell me…you have an objection to that as well?'

'If you want to rescue a stray, try Battersea Dog's Home!'

'What the hell is the matter with you?' he suddenly exploded.

'I just don't like being taken over as if I'm some sort of cypher!' She swallowed hard, feeling the dismaying sting of tears in her eyes. 'Look…this—'

'Maybe now that you appreciate that the dog, the cat and the pony will be neither required nor appropriate you're having second thoughts!' he grated in a tense undertone.

'I seriously doubt that I'll be with you long enough for it to become a pressing problem!' Bella was angered and embarrassed at having her own words thrown back in her face.

He went rigid, his jaw-line squaring. 'Don't miscalculate and make it one.'

Bella paled. 'I wouldn't do something like that!' She was shocked by the suggestion that he thought she might.

Abruptly Rico muttered an imprecation and released his breath. 'How can I even say that to you after the risks we ran a few weeks ago?' he murmured drily. 'Let us face facts; we are fortunate indeed that you are not now pregnant.'

Bella bent her head, suppressing an urge to tell him that she was only now expecting the confirmation that their passion was to have no further consequences. Why worry him unnecessarily? It wasn't as if *she* was worried that that confirmation would not arrive. It was extremely unlikely that conception could have taken place at that time of her cycle, she reminded herself, and it was precisely because of that unlikelihood that she had not allowed herself to spend the past three weeks anxiously fretting.

'Becoming a father is not one of your ambitions, I take it.'

'No, definitely not on my agenda. A complication I will happily do without.' His bronzed face was shuttered, taut. 'How did we get onto this subject?'

'You started it.'

'Come here…' With a slightly twisted smile, he stretched out both hands and drew her closer. 'If this feels like a big step to you, *gatita*, it feels just as big to me,' he confided almost harshly, studying her from beneath thick ebony lashes. 'If I get it wrong sometimes, try to make allowances.'

Her tension evaporated. He hadn't found it easy to make that admission and she loved him all the more for making it. Asking her to live with him had been a very real commitment on his terms, she registered, a relieved feeling of contentment enclosing her, smoothing over the ragged edges of her nerves.

'You've been trying to take me home with you ever since you met me,' she whispered.

'With a notable lack of success,' Rico murmured thickly, tugging her relentlessly across the space that still separated them, dark eyes firing gold.

'But you're very persistent.'

'And if I say please…?'

'The world's your oyster,' Bella affirmed, barely able to think straight that close to him.

He linked his arms around her but he tilted his head back,

narrowly appraising her. 'You have stars in your eyes, *gatita*. That worries me.'

'You have a fear of being trapped. That worries me even more.'

'Why did you talk to the Press?' he enquired flatly, ignoring her sally.

'I told you why. I just wanted to bring it all to an end. And I thought that if I made it clear that nothing happened between us they would leave me alone—'

'So you lied.'

'I could hardly tell the truth!' But she flushed, her eyes troubled, her mouth faintly mutinous. 'OK...I lied.'

'Don't ever do it again. Don't lie to me and don't lie about me,' Rico told her with level emphasis. 'In fact don't talk about me at all. What is between us is private.'

'I know that!'

'This one time I give you the benefit of the doubt and I forgive you.'

'What's that supposed to mean?'

He surveyed her with cynical dark eyes. 'Bella...I'm not a fool. I can add two and two. Less than forty-eight hours ago you handed me a cheque for a considerable sum of money. Today the article appeared. Obviously you were paid for that interview.'

She sprang back from him in consternation. 'That money came from the sale of a painting!'

Rico elevated an ebony brow, clearly unimpressed. 'I don't have you on a pedestal, *gatita*. So you don't need to worry about falling off one. I don't expect perfection but I do expect honesty. Who would pay that much for the work of an unknown artist?'

'It wasn't one of *my* paintings!' she flared back at him, both angered and hurt by his lack of trust in her. She would not even have considered accepting money for talking

about him to the Press. 'It was one Ivan did of my
mother—'

'*Qué dices*?' Rico interrupted, abruptly jerking up out of
his lounging position, his attention fully arrested.

'And, before you ask me why I didn't think of selling it
that day I came to the bank to tell you I had no insurance,
I'll tell you why,' Bella said tightly. 'I forgot about it. I've
had it all my life. It didn't occur to me until a few weeks
ago that it was a valuable asset which could be sold.'

His incandescent golden eyes bored into her. 'You sold
a painting of your mother by your father…to pay me back?
Are you crazy?' he launched at her.

Bella blinked at him in bewilderment. 'What else could
I do?'

'Where was it sold?' he demanded.

'What does that matter?'

'*Where*?'

She told him.

'If it's already been sold, you'll only have yourself to
thank!' he shot at her furiously after he had instructed his
chauffeur to head for the art gallery. '*Por Dios*…you don't
need to take lessons on how to make me feel bad!'

'I owed you money. It had to be repaid somehow.'

'We were lovers! What do you think I am?' he blazed
back at her. 'A debt collector?'

'You are in banking,' she retorted helplessly, infuriated
by the reaction she was receiving. Selling that painting had
been a considerable sacrifice and she resented the assurance
that it had been an unnecessary one. 'And if you think that
I was content to believe that just because we had briefly
shared a bed I no longer needed to worry about the fact
that I owed you thousands of pounds you don't know me
at all! I also had to cover the repairs to Hector's Skoda—'

Rico said something incredibly rude about the Skoda.

'We don't all slink about in status-symbol cars!' Bella hissed. 'Why did you tell your driver to go to the art gallery?'

'If the painting's still there, naturally I will buy it back for you.'

'You buy that painting, it's *yours*,' Bella warned him fiercely.

She sat in the car fuming while he was in the art gallery, having flatly refused to accompany him. If he hadn't been so damned suspicious and cynical, he would never have known where she'd got the money from! A debt was a debt. She didn't want it written off. Maybe the money didn't mean much to Rico but it was the principle that mattered.

He swung back into the car and he wasn't empty-handed. He settled the small canvas on her lap. 'Here...take Mummy back,' he said very drily.

Bella squinted down at Cleo's familiar features. Her throat ached but she was stubborn. 'I told you I wouldn't accept it.'

'*Madre de Dios*...' Rico bit out with raw impatience. 'I could shake you until your teeth rattle!'

'What did you pay for it?'

Grudgingly he told her.

'They saw you coming. You were ripped off. It isn't one of Ivan's best.'

Rico stabbed a button and the window beside him purred down. 'I'll just chuck it out, then, shall I?'

A lean hand closed with purpose round the frame. Involuntarily Bella's gaze clashed with smouldering golden eyes and she gaped. 'You'd do it, wouldn't you?' Her fingers curved protectively round the disputed article.

'You drive me crazy sometimes.' He slung her a fulminating glance and buzzed up the window again.

And sometimes he shook her rigid. He *would* have

thrown it out. He had called her bluff and Bella was not
accustomed to having her bluff called. She had finally met
her match in temper and tenacity. For the first time she was
in a relationship where she was not the dominating partner.

'Are you planning to pay me rent?' Rico enquired
smoothly.

'Don't be ridiculous!'

'But I sense that money promises to be a bone of contention. If we were married would you feel like this?'

'Of course not,' she said, and then wished she hadn't.

'Illuminating… Clearly I have to suffer for not offering
that band of gold,' he murmured sardonically.

She ignored the crack about the wedding ring, barely
trusting herself to speak.

'Shut up, Rico…'

'Maybe I should,' he conceded silkily. 'Maybe this is
one of those times when you need to make allowances for
me.'

Bella was seething. She gritted her teeth.

'This promises to be a deeply challenging relationship.
I'm used to having my own way,' he volunteered unapologetically.

'Tell me something I don't know.'

Silence fell. She got lost in her own thoughts. She studied Cleo with far less judgemental eyes than usual. 'I go
with my feelings,' her mother had said. And that was exactly what Bella was doing with Rico, had done with Rico
even in that wretched container when they'd first made
love. No wonder that emotion-driven surrender had filled
her with turmoil. Bella always liked to know where she
was going. She liked important things cut and dried. But
now she had a future in front of her that was a giant unknown.

She surfaced from her introspection as the limousine

purred through tall, electronic gates and up a long, winding drive—the Winterwood estate, she gathered, scanning the great sweep of landscaped parkland with curious eyes. In the early summer sunlight of late afternoon the setting was idyllic.

'Do you like the country?'

Bella shrugged a narrow shoulder, struggling not to gape as a vast ancestral pile in stone swam into view round the next bend. It was a magnificent house, designed with all the grace and understated elegance of the eighteenth century. The limousine swept up onto the gravelled frontage and even the soft crunch of the wheels somehow sounded filthy rich. She moistened suddenly dry lips, quite overpowered. What the heck was she doing here with him?

She was wearing a denim skirt with a carefully frayed hem and a T-shirt. She had no make-up on. Her hair was all mussed—*his* fault. And there he was, immaculate as usual, all sleek and sophisticated in a pearl-grey suit that fitted like a glove and screamed expensive tailoring. They were the original odd couple. If she lost him at a party, she would be thrown out as a gatecrasher.

The chauffeur opened the door. Bella stepped out, feeling more and more as though she had stepped into *Brideshead Revisited*. And then she saw the rosebeds and grimaced.

'What's wrong?' He sounded incredibly anxious, as if he was primed to her every move and change of expression.

'Rico, roses are supposed to riot, not march in lines like soldiers. That looks like council planting at its worst.' Then she flushed. 'Sorry, that wasn't very polite of me.'

He smiled at her. 'I don't expect you to be polite—'

'Thanks for the vote of confidence.'

'What I meant was...' he placed an arm around her narrow back '...you just say what you think. It's a very unusual trait in the world I move in—'

'Sure, you know loads of dreadful people who have tact and good manners!'

'I like your honesty. It disconcerts me from time to time,' he murmured, 'but I find it very attractive.'

'Why are you being so *nice* all of a sudden?' she asked suspiciously.

'This is going to be your home. I want you to relax here, not behave like a guest,' he asserted.

'I thought I was only here to visit for a month.'

'*Bella*!' he grated.

'Sorry, was I being disconcerting?' She chewed at her lower lip. 'But you know you have to be up front about things like that. At the end of the month we put our cards on the table and if it's not working out—'

'We try harder,' he slotted in fiercely.

Bella had been about to conclude that she would move out with no hard feelings...at least, none that she would show.

An elderly little man in a dark suit was awaiting them below the imposing pillared entrance. 'Good evening, Mr da Silva...madam.'

Bella very nearly went off into whoops of laughter. Dear God, he had a butler, a real *live* butler! Her mouth wobbled.

'This is Miss Jennings, Haversham.'

'Miss Jennings.'

'H-Haversham,' she acknowledged, her face frozen as she fought back her giggles.

Rico walked her into a huge, echoing, tiled hall. She felt like someone on a National Trust tour—a member of the paying public, programmed to gawp. She trembled and reckoned that she was winning until a voice said from behind them, 'And what time would you like dinner to be served, sir?'

That was it. Bella went off into gales of laughter. 'Sorry!'

she gasped, bending over and hugging her aching ribs as amusement bubbled out of her convulsed throat.

'Seven,' Rico told his butler in a strained tone. 'Are you going to share this joke?' he asked as the stately footsteps of Haversham retreated.

'Definitely not. You wouldn't appreciate it.' Wiping her damp eyes, Bella pulled herself together with difficulty.

'Try me.'

'I thought butlers died out around half a century ago.'

'Haversham came with the house,' Rico told her very seriously, as if he was excusing himself for possessing one of a dying breed.

Bella shook her head, vibrant hair flying like flames round her shoulders. 'Rico…this is another world for me.'

'And you don't like what you've seen of it?'

She grinned. 'No, I'm fascinated.'

'Would you like me to show you around?'

Standing there in the stray patch of sunlight arrowing through a tall sash-window, he looked so good that she couldn't take her eyes off him. Six feet four inches of spectacular masculinity. Visually she adored every extravagantly gorgeous inch of him, her heart accelerating like a racing car screeching round a bend at a hundred-plus miles an hour. She felt her breasts stir and swell inside the cups of her bra, helplessly struggled to fight the electric tension that was wantonly taking her over.

'Bella…' he murmured unsteadily, his shimmering golden eyes suddenly hotly pinned to her.

Emboldened by the discovery that he could look helpless too, Bella smiled, all female. 'Turned very coy all of a sudden, haven't you?'

There was nothing coy about the manner in which he grabbed her, and there was nothing cool about the manner in which he kissed her breathless halfway up the fabulous staircase. She wound her arms round his neck and let him carry her. She wasn't sure that her own legs were up to the feat.

He kicked the door shut on a wonderfully elegant bed-room, decorated in eau-de-Nil with accents of pale gold. He brought her down on the canopied bed and she laughed again, a slim hand stretching up to flick playfully at an exquisite hand-made tassel. 'Who did your decorating?'

'My sister, Elena.'

'She has style…but only a sister would have put you in a room this feminine.' She kicked off her shoes.

'You look incredibly beautiful,' he breathed, his gaze roaming intently over her as he came down on the bed beside her.

Bella reached out and caught his silk tie, drawing him down to her, drowning in the slumbrous glow of his eyes. Their mouths connected, clung, and she went weak, letting her head fall back again. He followed her down, prising her lips apart with the tip of his tongue, ravishing the moist interior that she opened to him with a ragged groan.

She pulled his jacket off, tore at his tie, and as he fought his way out of his shirt let her palms smooth up over the warm, hard wall of his muscular chest, her fingertips teas-ing at the dark whorls of hair in her path. With an earthy growl he brushed her hands away, thrust her T-shirt up and found her breasts.

It was her turn to gasp and quiver as his expert fingers pushed up her bra and tugged at her engorged nipples. Her back arched in a blinding wave of intolerable excitement.

'You have the most exquisite breasts,' he breathed, graz-ing her swollen lower lip with his teeth. 'So sensitive…'

His dark head swooped and seized a rose-pink bud. Her blood pressure rocketed sky-high. She dug her hands into his hair, driven nearly mindless with the hot, drugging pleasure. She went out of control without a murmur, her heart slamming against her ribcage, every nerve-ending raw with sensation.

He ran a hand up the length of one slim thigh, ruthlessly wrenching her skirt out of his path. Their mouths met again in a torturously hungry mating, and she was shaking, trembling, her hips shifting upwards in a primitive rhythm, all consciousness centred and driven by the erotic brush of his fingers skating over the taut triangle of cloth still dividing her from him.

She burned and panted for breath as he tugged the briefs away and discovered the damp, hot secret of her desire. Intolerable excitement held her in its grip. Suddenly he was pushing her back, shifting over her, unexpectedly stilling when she was poised with anticipation on the furthest edge, every nerve ready to scream with frustration.

'Don't stop!' she gasped.

She felt his hands, roughly impatient on her thighs, and then, with a suddenness that stole her breath away, he thrust into her hard and deeply. An ecstatic cry escaped her, wanton in the depth of need it expressed. She stretched up, kissing his throat, licking the salt from his skin, adoring him. But he pushed her back, arching over her like a primitive god, demanding absolute control, thrusting harder and faster, filling her again and again with the driving force of his manhood. The tension exploded inside her and she jerked like a doll under him, her teeth clenching, a wild, excited cry torn from her as the waves of violent pleasure engulfed her.

Lying shattered and winded in the circle of his arms, listening to the ragged edge of his breathing, she was conscious of a surge of love so intense that it hurt. She rubbed her cheek sensuously against his sweat-dampened shoulder.

'*Dios*...we didn't even get our clothes off.' Rico

stretched luxuriantly against her. 'I planned a romantic dinner, champagne—'

She wrinkled her nose. 'Predictable.'

'Life is not very predictable around you,' he conceded lazily, and withdrew from her.

Belatedly she understood that pause before he'd possessed her. He had been protecting her. Birth control. She brushed a hand abstractedly over her breasts, conscious of a slight ache that was new to her experience. It had translated into an intense sensitivity when he'd touched her... She tensed, the sudden memory of a pregnant friend complaining about the soreness of her breasts flying through her head, jolting her. No, next door to impossible, she christened the fear which followed. Any day now she would know that she was all right. With determination she pushed the concern back out of her mind.

Without warning, strong hands settled beneath her as Rico scooped her up into his arms. 'Why so serious?' he murmured curiously.

'Me...*serious*?' Bella forced a laugh, emerald-green eyes fastening on him, cold fear burrowing up momentarily inside her. 'I was miles away.'

'I want you here,' he told her, setting her down in the beautiful *en suite* bathroom and peeling her T-shirt off.

She reddened. 'I can take my own clothes off.'

'I want to take them off.'

'You think I'm a doll or something?'

'It's an excuse to keep my hands on you,' he breathed. 'And right now I would settle for any excuse.'

Her gaze colliding with lustrous dark eyes, she stretched up and linked her hands round his strong brown throat. She felt dizzy with happiness, and generous. 'You don't need an excuse,' she whispered with all the natural warmth that lay at the core of her temperament.

'Tomorrow will come too soon. Tokyo…' Rico murmured. 'I'll send Kenway in my place—just this once.'

And then he covered her mouth with erotic precision, his hands buried in her hair. It was a long time before they made it into the shower.

CHAPTER NINE

'THEY belong to my sister. They should fit.'

Bella surveyed the riding gear with concealed amusement. 'I could wear my jeans.'

'You'll feel more comfortable in these. Jeans can be very constricting,' Rico informed her.

'You're planning for me to look impressive round your stables?' She looked at him with mockery.

'I intend to teach you how to ride.'

Of course, far be it from Rico to ask if she could already ride. He specialised in making assumptions. But then it was encouraging that he should want her to share a pastime which he obviously enjoyed. Obediently sliding into the borrowed outfit, she watched him out of the corner of her eye and wondered where the past two days had gone. Time was already slipping through her fingers like sand.

They hadn't made it down for dinner that first night. They had picnicked like starving adolescents at the kitchen table in the early hours. The next morning she had insisted on going up to London to see Hector and supervise the removal of her possessions. She had wanted to leave her paintings behind but that had provoked an argument, so she had given way. Rico had already had a room cleared for her to use a studio. Filled with natural light, it was an artist's dream, and if there was such a thing as inspiration, she reflected wryly, Winterwood would surely provide it.

Although not according to Hector. Bella's cheeks flushed as she recalled his reaction to her chosen change of abode. He had been shocked, unhappy and dismayed. In all fairness, what other response could she have expected? Hector was of a different generation. But seeing his disappointment in her had upset her.

'If he cared about you he'd want to marry you,' he had told her sternly, and she had bitten her lip and refused to argue. Only time would tell whether Rico cared or not.

'Come closer.' Rico beckoned with an imperious hand. 'Horses sense fear. It makes them nervous.'

'You think I'm afraid?'

'Why else would you be standing so far back?' Arrogantly he took her hand and showed her how to become acquainted with the velvet-nosed bay mare that was shuffling restively on the cobbles while a groom saddled her up. 'Sheba's a little fresh. I'll put you on her in the paddock…on a leading rein.'

'Gosh…it looks a long way up,' Bella twittered, striving to look scared.

'I'll be with you. You'll be fine. *Dios*…I told him I wouldn't be riding,' he bit out impatiently, only then noticing that the other groom had already tacked up the glossy grey stallion on the other side of the yard.

And I told him you would be, she thought. Grasping Sheba's reins, Bella planted a foot in the stirrup and mounted up in one smooth movement.

Halfway across the yard Rico swung back. 'Bella!' he yelled, clearly thinking that she was being recklessly daring to impress.

'Last one over the fence is a wimp!' she called over her shoulder.

Sheba was fresh all right. Given her head, she took off like a bullet out of a gun, racing for the fence. Bella gloried in the wind tearing at her hair and the speed. It was over a year since she had been on a horse. She heard the thunder of pursuit and grinned. Next time Rico would *ask* whether

or not she could do something before he *told* her she was
going to learn.

Sheba sailed over the fence like a champion and galloped
across the rolling parkland. Rico's stallion thundered past
and was reined in on a rise beside a clump of massive oak
trees. Sheba was slowing down by then. Bella let her trot
the last hundred yards.

Two long strides carried Rico to her side as she slid
down off the mare's back.

'Sorry…but I couldn't resist it.' Her spontaneous smile
lit up her whole face as she turned to him.

Her smile lurched and died as Rico closed angry hands
round her forearms. 'Don't ever get on one of my horses
again without a hard hat!' he seethed down at her.

'I never wear a hat.'

'You will… If you don't, you don't ride,' he spelt out
flatly, pale beneath his golden skin. 'And only an idiot
would jump a fence like that on a strange mount!'

'Or an idiot who asked the groom first how she performed. He told me she jumped like she was on springs.'
Bella looked up at him, into still grim dark eyes, and
groaned. 'I gave you a fright. I'm sorry.'

'Where did you learn to ride?'

'Well, not in a paddock on a leading rein.' She threw
herself down on the lush grass and turned her face into the
sunlight. 'Cleo had friends we sometimes stayed with. They
had horses. I was crazy about them. And Gramps kept stables—'

'Stables?'

'Boarding, riding lessons, all that sort of stuff.' She
linked her hands round her raised knees and stared down
the rolling slope into the distance. 'The business went bust
when I was nineteen. He broke a hip while I was at college.
He could've asked me to come home but he didn't. By the

time I realised how bad things were the bank was calling in his loan. All he needed was a little more time but they pushed him to the wall.'

'I gather you tried to persuade the bank otherwise.'

'A waste of my breath.' Bella grimaced. 'And when the horses had to be sold Gramps just gave up. He didn't own the stables. He had to move out into a council house in the village. It killed him.'

'Why do you blame yourself?'

Bella tensed, unprepared for someone saying out loud what she had often thought. 'I could've stopped it happening.'

'How?'

'I could've run the place for him until he got back on his feet.'

'But he obviously didn't want you to drop out of college, *gatita*. And what business experience did you have? Why blame yourself when you lost your home as well?'

'Fiddlesticks,' she said, with a wry curve to her expressive mouth. 'A little tub of an elderly Shetland pony called Fiddlesticks. I was more upset about him being sold. Silly really—I mean, he was only a pet. I was far too big to ride him.'

Rico tugged her back against his chest. '*Dios*…loath as I am to admit it when you have been showing off, you're a terrific rider.' His breath stirred her hair, the familiar scent of him blissfully enveloping her.

She felt at peace in Rico's arms and that worried her. At peace was the last thing she ought to have felt around him. This was an interlude for him. It wouldn't last. He didn't even want it to last. He wanted a passionate affair and an open door to freedom at the end of it. No strings, no complications, no recriminations. He had made that resoundingly clear.

She felt mean and she acted accordingly. 'Tell me about your ex-wife.'

The strong muscles in his arms drew taut. 'What do you want to know?'

'Her name…that would be a start.'

'Margarita.'

'And then maybe you could tell me why you're so bitter,' she dared.

'I am not bitter.'

'Do I remind you of her?'

'Not at all. She was small, black-haired, blue-eyed.'

'Beautiful?'

'Stunning.'

'You could ease up on the superlatives if you like,' she told him. 'So how did you meet?'

'A nightclub. She was an actress but I had no idea how ambitious she was. In fact I never really knew her at all,' he admitted flatly. 'I was twenty, she was two years older. I didn't know the difference between love and sexual obsession. At that age *everything* feels so intense. When she told me she was pregnant I married her.'

'Yes,' she whispered softly.

'Once he was born, Margarita dropped any pretence of wishing to be a mother and went back to the film world,' he said drily. 'I tried very hard to make the marriage work. Everyone had told me I was making a mistake. I was determined to prove them wrong…and I trusted her.

'Even when I found her in bed with another man I didn't realise that he was one of many. She would have slept with anyone capable of furthering her career. She was drunk that night. She told me how many others there had been. The next morning she moved out and moved in with her producer. I instigated the divorce…'

'What else could you have done?' Bella leant her head

back against him, understanding all that he had left unsaid. He had been used, kicked in the teeth and dumped. She waited for him to mention the little boy again, realised that he hadn't even referred to him by name, and also that he had not told her that that child had not been his.

'Margarita made it a battle, and she revelled in the publicity until it turned on her,' he drawled. 'Her career nosedived after the divorce. Nobody came out of it happy.'

Had he still been in love with his ex-wife? His grim intonation suggested regret to Bella. Regret for what? She wanted to probe deeper but resisted the temptation. She knew that she would drag it all out of him eventually. But now, she sensed, was not the time.

'But I learnt a lot from Margarita,' Rico murmured with satire.

Nothing good, Bella thought. He didn't trust women. He was always looking for ulterior motives. He didn't believe in permanence. And marriage for him had been a destructive trap from which he had gained nothing. But one truth he had spoken. He had said that he wasn't bitter and on that count she believed him. He had come to terms with that part of his past.

Why, then, did she sense that there was a whole lot missing from what he was telling her? He had glossed over the subject of the child. But then he wasn't that fussed about kids anyway, was he? In a marriage as bad as that, and as short-lived, it might well have been a relief not to be linked to his ex-wife by a tie as unbreakable as that of a child.

'What did you learn?'

He settled back on the lush meadow grass and looked down at her, scanning her vibrant face with glittering dark eyes. 'That I don't have to get married to enjoy myself. That what we have here, now, is far more exciting than being welded together by an empty contract full of prom-

ises destined to be broken. If we stay together it will be a
free and uncomplicated choice—'

'Nothing's that uncomplicated.'

'Trust me…I trust you,' he breathed, lowering his dark
head. 'I know you took a risk on me. I know this wasn't
your dream. This has to be the first time in my life that a
woman hasn't wanted anything from me but myself.'

'And I'm only after your body, so you can feel safe.'

With an appreciative grin he slid a hard thigh between
hers, pinning her in place, studying her slumbrously from
beneath the thick veil of his black lashes. 'When you look
at me like that you fill me with uncontrollable lust, *gatita
mia*.'

'But then that doesn't take much,' she muttered, dizzily
drowning in his intent gaze as he shifted fluidly against her,
letting her feel the hard thrust of his arousal.

Bella was down at the stableyard one morning when she
was told that a visitor was waiting to see her. Returning to
the house, she stilled in the doorway of her studio, taut
with disbelief at the sight of a complete stranger calmly
leafing through her paintings. 'What are you doing?' she
demanded sharply. 'Who are you?'

The man straightened, seemingly unaware of his offence,
and crossed the room. He extended a polite hand. 'Dai
Matheison…Rico asked me to pay you a visit next time I
was in the area.'

Rico had asked him? Bella's face froze. 'The Matheison
Gallery, right?' she murmured, mentioning the prestigious
gallery with distinct coolness.

'Try not to hold it against me.' Shrewd blue eyes read
her taut facial muscles.

'Rico didn't tell me you were coming.' She wanted to
leap up and down with sheer rage and embarrassment. How

dared Rico humiliate her like this? Unknown artists did not receive personal visits from the owner of the Matheison Gallery.

'Between you, me and the gatepost,' Dai Matheison said drily, 'I didn't want to. But if what I have so far managed to see is a sample of your work Rico did us both a favour. I'm doing an exhibition in late September. I'm willing to include you if you're interested.'

Her teeth gritted. 'Thank you but I don't think—'

'Rico may be a friend, but don't insult me by assuming that I would issue such an invitation on that basis alone,' he cut in smoothly. 'If I didn't think you were worthy of my gallery's reputation, Miss Jennings, God Himself would not persuade me otherwise.'

Bella reddened, sharply disconcerted. 'I—'

He handed her a card. 'Call me if you're interested and don't leave it too late. I need an answer soon.'

'Mr Matheison, I'm sorry—'

'Not half as sorry as I am.' He smiled with rueful amusement. 'I was looking forward to shooting Rico down in flames. But after what I've seen here I shall have to grit my teeth and say, Thank you for the tip. You're even more talented than he said you were.'

He was gone before she could gather her wits again. In one explosive stride she reached the nearest phone and dialled Rico's private number.

'Did you remember to call the caterers?' he asked straight off, reminding her about the party he was planning to hold in a fortnight's time.

'*Yes*. Dai Matheison has just been here!'

There was a moment of silence.

'And?' he responded calmly.

'And nothing, Rico! How dare you do that to me?'

'I have other contacts.'

'Stuff your bloody contacts!' she hissed. 'If you must know, he's willing to show me, but that's not the point—'

'That was exactly the point,' Rico interrupted with unhidden satisfaction.

'You had no right to interfere.'

'You and your giant insecurity complex were likely to avoid the issue into the next century,' he informed her. 'So I took care of it for you.'

His lack of remorse only inflamed her more. In all her life she had rarely felt so mortified as Rico had made her feel. 'You humiliated me,' she condemned shakily. 'And if you can't see that, then there's not a lot of hope for us!'

'Be brief, Bella,' he sighed, refusing to take her seriously. 'I have two diplomats waiting to see me.'

'I make my own breaks. I don't need you to pull the strings for me. Dai Matheison didn't want to come here. He thought he was coming to see your little bimbo's etchings—'

'Now he knows differently,' Rico returned with exasperated unconcern. 'Tell me, is there a point to this howling melodrama? You should be grateful I had that amount of faith in you. I told you I'd be your patron—'

'You just can't accept what I give!' she accused in stark distress. 'You're not happy unless you think you're paying for what I do in bed!'

'Bella, no man in his right mind would pay for this. I'll call you from Edinburgh.' The assurance was icy cold. The phone went dead.

Throwing herself face down on a sofa, she burst into floods of tears, shocking herself. She felt out of control, desperately hurt, desperately confused.

They had been together for three and a half wonderfully happy weeks. But sometimes she got scared; sometimes she admitted to herself that temperamentally she was not cut out for a relationship in which she could not say openly, honestly, I love you. She guarded her tongue more and more. It had become harder to keep up the free-and-easy sallies that demanded nothing, asked for no reassurance, never mentioned the future. And all of a sudden Bella knew that she was facing up to the reality of their relationship.

Rico didn't want any more from her. He wanted her passion, not her love. She felt like somebody squeezed into a box that was becoming suffocating. Holding her emotions back didn't come naturally to her. The longer she held them in, the more dangerous they felt. On the surface everything was fine but underneath she was always waiting for the ice to crack and plunge her into the icy water of disaster.

She rubbed absently at her aching breasts and then realised what she was doing. What on earth was wrong with the stupid things? Maybe it was the weight she was putting on—too many regular meals, too much rich food. It was time she went to a doctor. But look on the bright side, she reflected; at least you weren't pregnant. Not that she had had much literal proof to the contrary, but a few tiny spots of that very light period had released her from her growing anxiety.

As she sprang upright a wave of dizziness left her lightheaded. Stress, she decided. Rico was bad for her nerves. Stupid of her to start a row on the phone, though, especially when he wouldn't be coming home until tomorrow. But then she had had every right to be angry. Rico had no right to ride roughshod over her wishes. Maybe he was keen to make her more socially acceptable, she thought bitterly. His live-in partner, the artist…no longer an undiscovered talent.

Face it, she conceded abruptly, you're really hurt that he didn't invite you to Edinburgh. It was so ridiculous too. Couldn't she bear him to be out of her sight for even twenty-four hours? But whereas three and a half weeks ago, feeling as she did now, she would have cheerfully and spontaneously invited herself along the same period had reduced her ability to be that bold. Being careful was inhibiting. She snatched up a piece of charcoal and her sketch-pad and drew a caricature of Rico, complete with grinning bimbo on his arm, festooned in jewellery that resembled chains.

So they had had a fight. Fights were not infrequent, she had to admit. How had she ever thought they had nothing in common? Her mouth twisted. Both of them were stubborn, quick-tempered and bossy. But neither of them was prone to holding spite. They were both crazy about horses and they spent an awful lot of time together without ever getting bored. It had been like a honeymoon—two people wrapped up in each other to the exclusion of the rest of the world. She would keep that thought to herself. She was well aware that he was throwing the party to introduce her to his friends.

Late that afternoon Haversham announced a second visitor. Bella looked up from the magazine she had been somewhat sleepily studying and was astonished to see Griff bearing down on her.

'Getting in here is like getting into Fort Knox,' he complained grimly. 'And as for getting the phone number...forget it. That is highly confidential information!'

Bella stood up with a frown. 'What are you doing here?'

'I'm not here by choice.' He sighed. 'Look, if Hector had had a note of the phone number I wouldn't be here—'

'Hector?'

'My boss is Hector's solicitor.' He reminded her of the connection through which they had met. 'I'm afraid the old boy's had a heart attack.'

Bella stared at him in mute horror and swayed sickly.

'Steady on.' Griff pushed her back down on the seat she

had vacated. 'You're really fond of the old buzzard,' he muttered in surprise. 'He's not dead but he's not too good from what I understand.'

Afterwards Bella could never recall that drive to London with Griff. She spent the whole journey spinning between awful guilt and simple prayer. Had it been her decision to live with Rico which had prompted this? She had only seen Hector twice since then and he had still been trying to persuade her to leave Rico.

'He *is* seventy-eight,' the sister in Intensive Care told her quietly. 'If he's still with us in the morning, he has a chance.'

'I thought he was only about seventy,' Bella mumbled thickly through her tears.

'You can sit with him for a while. You're the only person he asked for.'

'I'll wait out here,' Griff said resignedly.

She had forgotten about him. Awkwardly she turned to thank him for driving her to the hospital. 'But don't wait for me. I won't leave until…well, until I see how it goes,' she completed tautly.

Hector looked so frail, so shrunken lying in the railed bed. She covered his hand with hers, willed him to feel her presence, and sat there, gripped by the awareness that she had been far closer to Hector than she had ever been to her grandfather. Hector had understood her in a way her mother's father never had.

In the early evening Hector's solicitor, Mr Harvey, arrived. He gave her the keys to the house and mentioned, with a cloaked look, that if Hector made it out of Intensive Care he would be moved to a private room, and then to a convalescent home. Those were Hector's wishes as laid down by him in the event of serious illness.

'He'll hate that.' Bella sighed, refusing to believe that

Hector would not live to see those wishes carried out. 'What about his relatives? Why aren't they here?'

'Hector didn't want them told,' the solicitor admitted. 'But I have informed them. They said that they would keep in touch with the situation by phone.'

It was a very long night. Around dawn Hector opened his eyes on Bella and smiled. Then, after weakly squeezing her hand, he drifted away again. She bought herself breakfast in the cafeteria.

She needed sleep. Accepting that reality, she caught a bus back to Hector's house. She was in the act of wearily climbing the steps when a hand came out of nowhere and snatched the key from her grasp. She spun round.

'Rico!' she gasped in consternation, pressing a hand to her palpitating heart. 'What a fright you gave me!'

He unlocked the door, pushed it back and thrust her inside. Slamming it, he rested back against it and released his breath in a hiss. His eyes were slivers of raw gold condemnation in his dark, set face. 'You little bitch,' he muttered raggedly.

'I beg your pardon?' Reeling with exhaustion and shock at his sudden appearance, Bella slumped down on the stairs and focused on him with dazed eyes.

'*Por qué*…why?' he slammed at her with unhidden savagery.

She could feel the violence in him, coiled up tight like a cobra ready to strike. He was struggling to contain it, on the edge. Her brain was moving in slow motion, could not yet comprehend what on earth was the matter with him. 'Rico…I—'

'Don't try to lie to me!' he grated with vicious bite. 'You've been out all night. You're still wearing the clothes you had on at breakfast yesterday. *Madre de Dios*, I trusted you, I actually trusted you! But I make one wrong move and you react like a whore—'

'A whore?' She framed the words with the greatest of difficulty, scrutinising him with wide, incredulous eyes.

Outraged by her lack of response, Rico reached for her with hard hands and hauled her upright. 'You thought I wouldn't find out, *es verdad*?' he seethed down at her in a blaze of fury, his diction destroyed by the thickness of his accent. 'You would've told me that you came up to see Hector and stayed the night here. If I hadn't seen you coming back this morning I wouldn't have known that you had been with Atherton all night!'

The penny finally dropped with Bella. Her stomach heaved with nausea. 'The butler talked,' she said with heavy irony. 'He told you that I left Winterwood with Griff.'

As Rico released her with a vicious burst of Spanish she slumped back down again, feeling really ill. That Rico could believe for one second that she could be that treacherous, that disloyal and that *cheap* filled her with shrinking distaste.

When she spoke it was more like talking to herself than to Rico. 'I meant to phone last night and leave a message for you but I was so upset that I forgot. It didn't even occur to me that you would distrust me to this extent…that you *could*… Dear God.' Bella groaned, staggering upright on a wave of nausea more powerful than any she had yet managed to ride out and heading blindly for the sanctuary of the downstairs cloakroom, 'I've been sleeping with a stranger…

'''I kiss'd thee ere I kill'd thee,''' she mumbled in a daze as she yanked open the door. '''He was a gentleman on whom I built An absolute trust.'''

. '*Othello* and *Macbeth*,' Rico growled in incredulous recognition. His bewilderment and frustration unconcealed, he simply stood there glowering at her. The phone started ringing. Neither of them paid it any heed.

To the accompaniment of the phone shrilling, Bella just managed to shut the door before she was horribly sick. As someone who had always rejoiced in an iron digestive system, she was shaken by her own bodily weakness. Afterwards she clung to the sink and rinsed her mouth out. At least the phone had finally stopped.

The door opened. 'Go away,' she said thickly.

'The phone,' Rico breathed tautly. 'It's some cousin of Hector's. He wants to know what hospital Hector's in... He's waiting for an answer.'

Bella swallowed hard and gave the answer, then listened dully to him concluding the call.

'How bad is it?' Rico murmured even more tautly. '*Dios*, you look terrible—'

He was a quick study. Reasoning had returned, suggesting the real explanation for her overnight absence. Bella wished that the call hadn't come. She would have left Rico to stew in his own vile assumptions. He didn't deserve to be let off the hook this quickly and this easily. This was the male she had sacrificed her dreams for, the male she had burnt her rulebook over...and where had it got her? Maybe exactly where she deserved to be.

'Bella, Hector's *not*...?'

'No, he's still hanging in there.' As she spoke he attempted to curve an arm round her. Jerking dizzily away and grabbing hold of the banister, she gasped, 'Leave me alone!'

Ignoring her demand, Rico closed his arms round her from behind. 'Forgive me,' he said tightly.

She was too physically weak to fight him. 'Why can't you just go? I've been at the hospital all night and I'm not in the mood for you or any of this… It's probably my fault he's in there in the first place!' she completed with a stifled sob, her hand flying up to her wobbling mouth.

'It couldn't possibly be your fault.'

'He was upset when I moved in with you!' she slung at him shakily.

She heard him expel his breath.

'Oh, just go away,' she mumbled, barely able to stand, she felt so faint.

'I'm not leaving you like this. I'll take you back to my apartment—'

'I'm staying here.'

Rico swept her up into his arms. 'You're not well. You can't stay here alone. You should be in bed.'

'Someone should be here to answer the phone—'

'Not you in the condition you're in,' Rico spelt out.

He carried her out to the limo and there was nothing she could do to prevent him. All her concentration was bent on holding back the sick wooziness that was afflicting her. She would be all right once she had a couple of hours' sleep but she could not understand why her body was letting her down so badly. Had she caught some bug? Worse, could she have put Hector at risk by sitting with him? She had never felt so drained in her entire life.

When they reached the spacious apartment Bella crawled straight into bed. She had nothing to wear. Rico produced a silk pyjama jacket which she donned in silence. He said that he had called a doctor—a friend of his in the private sector—who had consulting rooms just down the street. Dully she nodded, relieved to notice that her nausea was beginning to recede.

'Maybe it was something you ate,' Rico suggested stiltedly.

She said nothing.

He sank down on the foot of the bed, searching her pinched profile. 'Bella…we'd had a row,' he reminded her in a tense undertone. 'When I heard you'd gone off with Atherton naturally I was disturbed.'

'The senior partner in Griff's firm is Hector's solicitor. He put Griff in charge of informing me about Hector's heart attack. Griff had to drive all the way down to Winterwood because he couldn't find out the phone number.'

'How could I have known of that connection?'

'It doesn't matter. I haven't given you any grounds for thinking that I would behave like a tart,' she muttered tightly. 'I'm not your ex-wife and I won't take the heat for her.'

'I made a mistake,' he acknowledged tautly.

Bella felt horribly confused. Deep down inside she knew that she was going to forgive him but somehow she just couldn't bring herself to tell him that yet.

Loving someone who did not love you was an unrewarding road to humiliation, she reflected miserably. His distrust had bitten deep, hurting her badly at a moment when she was already struggling to cope. With Rico she had no defensive shell, and part of her deeply resented that vulnerability. She wanted to make him suffer and she was ashamed of that fact. How could you try to punish someone for not loving you?

'Two mistakes,' Rico adjusted flatly in the continuing silence. 'I shouldn't have asked Dai to call. But it seemed such a waste—all those fabulous paintings piling up. I'm proud of what you can do with that brush.'

His weight left the mattress. Bella curved her face into the pillow, tears stinging her eyes. What a bitch she was! She was in the act of stretching out a forgiving hand when she heard the door open, the murmur of an unfamiliar voice. The doctor had arrived.

He told her to call him George. He had one of those wonderfully round faces which instilled good cheer. Rico had barely left the room when Bella found herself sitting up and reeling off her symptoms with the subdued irritation of someone who was rarely ill. She submitted to an examination and answered one or two questions which struck her as highly irrelevant when she was suffering from a stomach disorder. But no doubt George knew his business better than she did.

'You're pregnant,' he finally delivered very quietly.

Bella changed her mind about him knowing his business. 'No way,' she told him, with a forced laugh at such an insane diagnosis.

'Bella, I'm a consultant gynaecologist,' he returned gently. 'And if I'm wrong I ought to be back in medical school. First pregnancies in particular carry unmistakable signs. You are at least two months pregnant.'

'But I had a—' she began jerkily.

He explained that sometimes what he described as a partially suppressed period could occur. Bella went into cold shock while he talked to her about not pushing herself too hard and taking proper rest.

'Don't tell him!' she begged abruptly.

He reminded her of patient confidentiality and she apologised, so shattered by what he had told her that she could hardly think straight. He paused at the door, clearly troubled by her reaction.

'Bella, Rico's very fond of children. You should see him with mine,' he said ruefully.

So Rico liked other people's children. What did that mean? Feeling weak, she lay down again. Her hand slid down unsteadily to her still flat stomach. She struggled to accept that there was a baby growing inside her—a baby

conceived weeks ago while she had been convincing herself
that no such conception *could* take place.

She had been as foolishly naïve as an uninformed teenager, she realised. There was no such thing as a fail-safe
time to make love. There was always a risk. And Rico had
ironically been far more concerned by the possibility than
she had been…probably because it was the very last thing
he wanted to happen.

The door opened.

'George was very cagey,' Rico said impatiently.

'It's just a stupid stomach upset—probably that breakfast
I ate at the hospital,' Bella volunteered, and forced herself
to turn over and meet his enquiring gaze. 'I'm glad it
wasn't anything that could have put Hector at risk of in-
fection. Now all I want to do is sleep.'

Just looking at Rico suddenly tore her heart in two. She
searched his strong, dark face, read the relief there, and
knew she deserved an Oscar for her performance—but then
it was wonderful what fear could do. It sharpened the wits
and in the short term chose deception over honesty. She
wasn't ready yet to share such devastating news, was already wondering how she would ever bring herself to share
it.

'I'll go back to the hospital in the afternoon,' she added,
dropping her head back down on the pillow as if she were
too exhausted to stay awake.

She closed her eyes, knowing that it would take a miracle
for sleep to overcome her now. For it was over—she and
Rico—over, finished, *destroyed*. Fate had had the last laugh
of all. Secure in the belief that there was no question of
her being pregnant, Rico had been brutally frank. A baby
was a complication he did not want. She told herself that
she was lucky to know his true feelings on the subject. Who

could tell how he might have felt forced to react if she had discovered that she was pregnant a month ago?

Certainly he wouldn't have felt disposed to offer marriage, but he might well have felt that sensitivity demanded that he conceal just how appalled he was by the news. She didn't want pretences like that between them. Honesty was always the best policy, but oh, God, how it could hurt sometimes…

She drove back the pain consuming her, calling herself a coward. Their affair would have burnt out on his side anyway sooner or later. Now it would just happen sooner and she would be the one to make the break. She had no choice.

Just as Cleo had once made Bella welcome—a child unplanned and unsupported by any man—Bella would do the same for *her* child. It was that simple. But she felt horribly guilty. How could she have been so reckless? Whenever she had thought of becoming a mother she had always believed that the event would take place within a stable, loving relationship.

By three in the afternoon Bella was up again under her own steam. Incredibly she had dozed off. She showered and changed into the fresh clothes which she had flung into an overnight bag the previous day at Winterwood. Physically she felt much better but inside herself she felt dead.

She had woken up with the knowledge of what she had to do. Break it off, finish it…get it over with! Hector's illness and her argument with Rico, which now seemed so pitifully unimportant, had supplied a natural break. When she came back from the hospital this evening she would tell him.

Since she had assumed that he was back at the bank, it was a shock when Rico strode out of the drawing room as she was heading for the hall. She froze, shielding her startled eyes with her lashes.

'You were in the shower when I came to wake you up. How do you feel?'

'Fine now,' she said stiffly.

'I've ordered a light meal for you.'

'Thanks, but I'm—'

'Bella, be sensible.' He pressed her into the dining room where a place for one was already laid at the gleaming table. 'You have to try to eat something. Hector's fine, by the way. You don't need to rush.'

His manservant appeared out of nowhere and a beautifully cooked omelette was slid in front of her. Her hands trembled as she reached out for the knife and fork. 'I thought you'd be at the bank,' she said once the man had gone.

'I took the afternoon off.'

She couldn't eat; she just couldn't eat. She replaced the cutlery again, studied the table with anguished eyes and then cleared her throat. 'You remember we decided on seeing how it went for a month?' she whispered in a rush. 'Well, it's not working for me any more and I think you must feel—'

'Eat before I force-feed you,' Rico broke in, as if he were talking to a difficult child.

Bella stood up and backed away from the table. 'Rico, listen to me,' she muttered tightly, crossing her arms and turning away from him, unable to stay still. 'This is nothing to do with those stupid arguments we had…please believe that. But sometimes a crisis makes you see more clearly—'

'You're so blind right now, *gatita*,' Rico interposed in the same indulgent tone, 'that you'd fall over your own feet. Our relationship has nothing to do with Hector's heart attack.'

'That isn't what I was going to say!' she protested, in so much turmoil that she couldn't even keep her voice steady. Involuntarily her look clashed with steady dark eyes and she hurriedly averted her gaze again. 'The point is... The point is,' she repeated doggedly, 'that two months ago we were kidnapped, and in the grip of that trauma sex got involved and—'

'Sex got involved the first time I laid eyes on you,' he proffered without shame. 'The trauma of being kidnapped had nothing to do with it.'

Bella ignored that. She didn't trust herself to look at him, couldn't afford to be tempted. 'What I realise now is that we sort of became dependent on each other in that container, and I don't want to be dependent any more. I want my freedom back.'

'I might be more impressed if you looked me in the face and told me that,' he drawled with derision.

Bella looked up, blocked him out, a terrible pain scything through her. 'It's over. I'm sorry but that's the way it is.'

'You are one lousy liar,' Rico said grimly, crossing the room in one long, menacing stride. 'What the hell is going on here?'

Before he could reach her Bella dived for the door. In seconds she was out of the apartment and into the mercifully waiting lift. She made it out onto the busy street at speed. Sobs were tearing at her convulsing throat. She dashed her hand across her streaming eyes, devastated by the force of her emotions. Then she drew in a deep, slow breath and walked on down the street.

CHAPTER TEN

AN HOUR later Bella was sitting by Hector's bedside with the fixed expression of someone in shock and striving to hide it. He had already been moved out of Intensive Care and into a private room. But while she had been asleep at the apartment Rico had visited him.

'Absolute nonsense for you to think my dicky heart had anything to do with your love life,' Hector was telling her in reproof. 'I had an attack three years ago, as you very well know. As for you and Rico…well, times have changed and he seems very fond of you—'

'Fond of me?'

'Why else would he invite me to Winterwood to convalesce?'

'He's done what?' she squeaked, shattered by the news.

'I must say I'm really looking forward to seeing the house again.' He sighed fondly. 'When it belonged to the Cliffords in the fifties I was a regular visitor there—'

'But I thought you were planning on a convalescent home?'

'Rico told me what that would cost.' Weak as he was, Hector all but shuddered in recollection.

'How clever…I mean, how *conscientious* of him to have found out for you,' she managed with the greatest difficulty. 'But I could look after you at home if you like.'

'Not with that showing at the Matheison Gallery coming up. I wouldn't dream of it.'

Bella's nails dug into her palms like talons. Ten minutes with Hector had sent her from utter despondency to sheer rage. Rico had trussed her up like a goose ready for the oven! Perfectly well aware that their relationship was in deep water, he had ensured that it would be virtually impossible for her to move out. Hector was positively looking forward to a break in the country which would cost him not a penny and where he would be waited on hand and foot.

How could she now announce that she had broken up with Rico? That was no longer the news which she had innocently imagined would cheer Hector up. Indeed, she had the hideous suspicion that Hector, who liked very few people, had decided to make an exception of Rico.

As he drifted off to sleep he was mumbling about what ingenious ideas Rico had on the enthralling subject of reducing expenditure and making the most of a small income. Fit to be tied, Bella stalked out of the room.

She found Rico standing in the small waiting area at the end of the corridor. He watched her striding towards him with supreme cool.

'You devious toe-rag!' she launched at him from ten feet away.

'"A slippery and subtle knave,"' Rico murmured smoothly.

'Don't you dare quote Shakespeare at me!' she hissed in fury. 'How could you use an old man like that…how *could* you?'

'If you don't lower your voice, I shall treat you exactly as if you were the child you are choosing to emulate,' he drawled in a whiplash tone. 'Now take a deep breath and calm down…*right now*.'

Her outraged eyes shimmered. She buttoned her mouth shut, not trusting herself to speak. She wanted to slap him and he knew it and he wasn't impressed. Flinging her a grim glance, he stood back for her to enter the waiting lift.

'We'll talk in the car,' he told her.

Bella shot into the back seat of the limousine like a spitting cat, temper still blazing through her. 'How dare—?'

'Be silent,' Rico said sharply. 'You cannot make accusations of that variety and expect to get away with it. Hector Barsay may not be a blood relative but you are very attached to him. Since he was also a friend of my late father's for many years, I naturally felt that I should visit him.'

Gritting her teeth, she studied her tightly clenched hands. So far, so good, but there was no way he could explain himself out of what he had done during that visit.

'When I saw him earlier you were sulking—'

'I do not sulk—'

'You sulk,' Rico assured her. 'We had had an argument, but when I went to that hospital I had no idea that when I returned to the apartment you would announce that our relationship was at an end.'

Bella swallowed hard. It was a point she had to concede.

'Hector doesn't want to go to a home where he will be surrounded by strangers. He also misses you a great deal. That I should offer him hospitality was a natural progression from those facts. At Winterwood he will have every comfort but he will also have the privacy which is so important to him.'

'All right, I'm sorry,' Bella muttered from between clenched teeth. 'But where does that leave us now?'

'You appear to have already made that decision,' Rico retorted drily. 'I gather you didn't tell him the truth?'

'How could I?' she demanded fiercely.

'Especially when you would have looked a little stupid when I'd told him that you were staying put.'

She looked at him for the first time. 'I beg your pardon?'

Hooded dark eyes rested intently on her. 'You've been crying. Your nose is still pink.'

'Thank you so much for telling me,' she mumbled in a wobbly voice, suddenly feeling tearful again and ready to scream at the hormonal upheaval of pregnancy. Of course, that was what was the matter with her.

'We're going back to Winterwood,' he informed her.

'I'm going back to Hector's house.'

'I have the keys. I'm not giving them to you until you calm down.'

'I am perfectly calm,' Bella bit out furiously. 'Give me those keys! I don't know what I'm going to do when Hector comes out of hospital but that has to be a few weeks away and I'll deal with it then!'

'You're not getting those keys.'

'And you call *me* childish?'

But he didn't answer her. Her throat was thick with clogged tears. Defensively she turned her head away again. In a sense this was all her own fault. Back at the apartment she had not been prepared to face Rico. She had not had time to work out what she needed to say to sound convincing.

In short, she had made a mess of telling him that their relationship was over—so great a mess that he thought that she was simply being pathetically immature and vindictive over that argument in spite of his apologies. He did not believe that she really wanted to break off their affair.

And, since the truth was that she *didn't*, it really wasn't that surprising that Rico should think that way. Walking away from the man she loved demanded a degree of detachment and acting ability which Bella now acknowledged she did not possess. It was going to take lies to convince Rico that she had meant what she said. Maybe she ought to tell him that she had realised yesterday that she still had feelings for Griff…or maybe she should just tell him the truth.

No, not yet, she decided tautly. That would be a truth more easily dealt with when they were no longer together.

As she headed for the stairs in the echoing hall at Winterwood Rico murmured, 'I expect you to come down to dinner.'

Bella almost exploded. He had tied her up in knots with Hector, forced her to return to Winterwood and he was withholding the keys to Hector's house. He had been treating her like a fractious toddler on the brink of a temper tantrum from the minute she'd walked out of Hector's room!

She spun round. 'Tough!'

'It'll be Haversham's turn to laugh if I have to carry you downstairs,' Rico warned her.

'You wouldn't dare.' But she knew he would, knew she could push him so far and no further. Biting her tongue, green eyes blazing, Bella looked back at him, thwarted.

'Don't wear that figure-hugging black velvet dress,' he murmured softly. 'I don't like it.'

'I'll wear whatever the hell I want!'

And from the minute Bella got out of the shower she knew it would be that dress which she put on. Only, the zip proved oddly reluctant to go up. When she finally got it up and turned to look in the mirror she realised why. Her breasts now foamed over the straining neckline like overripe fruits. She looked down at them in horror and attempted to squash them down again. It was a pointless exercise. Until that moment she really hadn't appreciated just how much her shape had already changed.

Coming down the staircase in a relentlessly shapeless floral dress which had been a fashion accident, Bella found herself wondering why Rico had told her *not* to wear that black dress. He had only ever seen her in it twice and the second time, weeks ago, he had told her she looked stunning in it.

He was waiting for her in the drawing room. Tall, dark and spectacularly handsome, he surveyed her entrance. Her heart skipped a beat; her mouth went dry. In mute misery she swerved her attention off him again.

'That dress looks like a maternity outfit,' he drawled.

Bella flinched and spilt some of the sherry which Haversham always served her before dinner and which she had yet to drink. But, since the same thought about the dress had occurred to her, she thought nothing of the remark. She contrived a shrug and said, 'It's comfortable.'

'Allow me to get you another drink,' Rico said.

'No, I'm not really— Oh, dinner!' she exclaimed with relief, rising to her feet as Haversham appeared.

Since she was really hungry, she was on the second course before it crossed her mind that it was time to bite the bullet and convince Rico that their affair was over. So far the meal had been unusually silent. And that, now that she actually thought about it, was strange. Rico was not, as a rule, someone who quietly smouldered. Rico did not suffer in silence. Yet, in spite of emitting hostile vibrations into the steadily thickening atmosphere between them, he had barely opened his mouth.

'Why are you so quiet?'

He sent her a glimmering smile which made her feel uncomfortable. 'I wanted to see you eat a decent meal.'

'Like the condemned man?' Bella looked across the table at him and steeled herself. 'I'm afraid I wasn't very honest with you this afternoon…'

He tautened perceptibly. His narrowed dark eyes rested on her with grim intensity. He drained his glass of wine

and set it down without taking his attention from her once.
'I am aware of that fact.'

For some peculiar reason Bella felt as though the dining-
table between them had just become a bank manager's
desk, with her playing the role of debtor asking for a loan
that was about to be refused. There was just something so
cold and businesslike about Rico's attitude.

'Well, I owe you the truth,' she told him.

'You do,' he agreed.

'I've realised that I still have feelings for Griff,' she muttered, and she didn't need to pretend to feel guilty saying
that; she *did* feel guilty.

The silence stretched like a rubber band pulled to break-
ing-point. Then Rico's strong face clenched, his sensual
mouth flattening into a bloodless line. 'To employ your
jargon...tough!'

Bella gave him a dazed look, wildly disconcerted by such
a response.

'Why don't you tell me the *rest* of the truth?' he invited
softly, only there was something innately menacing about
that tone.

'I don't know what you're talking about.'

'Maybe you could tell me why you're not wearing your
black dress...or why you've sworn off alcohol again?' Rico
invited. 'Or why one of my closest friends can't meet my
eyes when I ask him a perfectly reasonable question?'

Bella had turned pale.

'Or how about why you're developing a bosom worthy
of a *Playboy* centrefold?'

'How dare you?' she gasped, unable to dredge anything
more riveting from a brain in the deep freeze of turmoil.
He couldn't possibly have guessed, she told herself frantically; he couldn't possibly have!

Rico vented a harsh laugh and thrust his plate away.

'You're pregnant…and all I want to know now is *how* pregnant?'

In a wave of pain Bella bowed her head.

'George didn't tell me but when you got up out of that bed and told me we were finished *you* told me,' Rico spelt out. 'I can add two and two. So tell me, when did this happy event take place?'

'When we were kidnapped—'

'So now I discover *why* you suddenly agreed to move in with me!' he shot at her.

'I didn't know until today!' she protested, shocked that he could think that.

'And with the best will in the world how am I supposed to believe that?' he breathed, sounding almost weary.

'Because it's the truth.'

'For someone who prides herself on telling the truth, and who gives an outstanding impression of always delivering it, you tell a lot of lies!'

A sob was trapped in her throat. Why, oh, why hadn't she had the wit to tell him this afternoon as soon as she'd found out? But she knew why. This was the very scene she had sought to avoid and it was tearing her apart. She had believed that a few weeks or months down the line, when they had already split up, she would have been able to handle his bitter reaction a lot more easily. But in avoiding the issue she had only made Rico more suspicious.

The tip of her tongue stole out to moisten her dry lips. She lifted her vibrant head. 'I can't blame you for thinking that, but I just wasn't ready to face this yet. I was as shocked as you are and I knew how you would feel—'

'*Por Dios*, you have not a clue how I feel!' he raked back at her.

Bella forced herself to explain why she had assumed that she was not pregnant, and at that moment did not much care whether Rico believed her or not. They had both taken that risk two months earlier, and if the first time their love-making had been prompted by her, the second time Rico had been the guilty party. The responsibility cut both ways.

'And what are your plans now—a termination?' he demanded abruptly.

She looked back at him in horror.

'I had to ask,' he murmured tautly, and oddly enough her unspoken rejection of such an option seemed to remove much of the strain stamped into his bronzed features. 'I was afraid that that was your intention.'

'No,' she confirmed, decidedly knocked off balance by his reaction because deep down inside she had been equally afraid that that might have been *his* intention.

'I would not have allowed that,' Rico added, just in case she hadn't got the message.

'And I wouldn't have considered it,' she asserted tightly.

'We will get married as soon as possible.'

Bella very nearly fell off her chair. Wide-eyed, she stared back at him, refusing to believe that he had simply murmured that statement as if it almost went without saying that they should now get married, as if any other response to their predicament was not even to be considered.

Rico dealt her shocked face a look of granite-hard determination untinged by any amusement. 'I intend to have full legal rights over this child.'

Bella unglued her tongue from the roof of her mouth. Just minutes ago he had told her that she didn't have a clue how he felt about her being pregnant. Now she was tasting the literal truth of that assurance. 'But—'

'Let's go into the drawing room,' he suggested drily, rising fluidly from his seat. 'I doubt that either of us is likely to eat any more tonight.'

Once there, Bella sank down into an armchair. 'How can

you talk about marriage?' she whispered helplessly. 'I thought you didn't even like children—'

'When did I ever say that?'

'You said you had no desire to become a father.'

'Naturally not…outside marriage,' he stressed.

She was shaken by the simplicity of that clarification.

'As it happens, I am very fond of children,' he breathed tautly as he poured himself a brandy. 'But children make you vulnerable. I had a son once and I lost him again. It was an experience I did not wish to repeat.'

'I'm not sure I understand.' He was talking about the child he had had with his ex-wife.

'His name was Carlos.' Rico sent her a brooding look, his tension palpable. 'And to this day I do not know whether or not he was my child. But it really didn't matter because when he was born I believed he was and I loved him,' he proffered tightly. 'He was the only good thing to come out of a rotten marriage, the only reason I tried so hard to make the marriage work.

'Margarita didn't give a damn about him. He was simply the means by which she married money. But when it came to the divorce he was also the means by which she hoped to achieve a very large settlement.'

All at once Bella was seeing how wildly off-centre her own assumptions had been. 'I wish you had told me this sooner.'

'When Margarita moved out she took Carlos with her. She expected me to buy him back,' he muttered harshly, his jaw clenching. 'But she wanted more than I could afford to pay *then*. When I didn't pay up she lost her head and told everyone that he wasn't mine anyway—'

'How could she do that to you?' Bella whispered.

'The reality was that she didn't know whether he was or not. I had not been her only lover at the time of his conception. Her claim threw the custody battle into chaos, causing a delay in the giving of the judge's decision. Tests had to be carried out. Carlos remained with Margarita and...' he hesitated and gave an almost clumsy shrug '...one day when she was partying he fell into a swimming pool and drowned.'

'Oh, God,' Bella mumbled in shock.

'He was eighteen months old,' Rico revealed curtly. 'And she wasn't fit to have the charge of him. She had had a row with his nanny and sacked her the day before. He didn't have a hope in hell.'

'I'm so sorry.' She swallowed back the tears that were threatening and watched the carpet swim instead. She was appalled by what he had told her.

'And I swore I would never have another child because losing Carlos was the toughest challenge I have ever had to face.' His facial muscles locked, he downed his brandy in one. 'But be assured that now you carry my baby inside you *everything* changes...'

'Yes.' Her head was aching from the tension he had induced.

'We do the very best we can for that baby,' he informed her with sudden savage ferocity. 'And I will not allow you to walk away as Margarita did and take that child from me! He or she is as much mine as yours...and the sooner you accept that reality the better!'

'I don't want to walk away,' Bella said thickly just as the door closed. She looked up. Rico had gone. She flew to her feet and went after him, but by the time she realised that he had left the house and not just gone into another room he had already driven off.

She was distraught and yet part of her wanted to kick him for not telling her about Carlos sooner. It wasn't her fault that she had made a series of false suppositions on the subject of how he felt about children, it was *his*. Yet she understood why he hadn't told her as well. Understandably, talking about that tragedy really upset him. Dear God, what an evil bitch he had married, she thought helplessly.

At first she planned to sit up and wait for him and explain how she had misunderstood. But then she began to go back over all that Rico had said. Marriage hadn't been on his agenda because he hadn't wanted to risk having another child with any woman. Once bitten, twice shy. But the fact that a baby was actually on the way had completely altered his attitude.

And he wasn't worried about losing *her*, was he? It was a bitter irony. Rico was more worried about losing control of the new life in her womb! No wonder he had relaxed when he'd realised there was to be no threat of a termination. Rico, whether he realised it or not, could not *wait* to get his paws on her baby! He was even prepared to marry her to ensure that he had greater legal rights!

She went up to bed, deeply shaken and deeply hurt. She was distressed by what he had told her about Carlos but never in her entire life had she felt more rejected. Regardless of the fact that Rico really seemed to want their child, he seemed to have pitched their relationship right out the window. And she just couldn't comprehend why it was happening that way.

He woke her up coming to bed. It was some unholy hour of the morning and he was humming under his breath. She couldn't believe it. Her teeth clenched. And when, ten seconds after he got into bed, a pair of arms reached for her she presented him with a back as welcoming as Everest in a blizzard.

'I asked you to marry me. I thought you'd be pleased,' he murmured without any expression at all.

Bella shot upright as if he had stabbed her with a knife. 'Why the hell would I be pleased?'

'It *is* what you wanted at the beginning.'

'I wised up!' she screeched.

A lamp was switched on. 'Calm down,' he instructed. 'How do you think that baby feels listening to you scream?'

'It's listening to you too…being totally, hatefully objectionable!' she sobbed, her every worst fear about the exact nature of her value to him now confirmed.

He enclosed her in his arms. She did her stick of rock impression.

'Bella…' he said tautly. 'I was under a lot of strain earlier. I felt incredibly confused. I was scared that you *were* pregnant…and then scared that you might *not* be! But by the time I was cracking open the champagne with George…' Bella froze in absolute disbelief at this revelation of how he had passed his time away from her '…I realised how extraordinarily happy I feel about this baby,' he delivered with positive fervour, in the tone of someone who believed that he was telling her exactly what she wanted to hear.

'You've been *celebrating* with my doctor?' Bella enunciated in a voice which shook.

'Naturally we did not discuss you either medically or personally,' Rico assured her.

'You *toad*!' she spat.

Rico dropped his air of insouciance and compressed his lips, his glittering golden eyes splintering into hers. 'Do you really think he'll still want you when you tell him you're pregnant?'

'Who?' Bella looked blank.

'*Who*?' Rico echoed, cuttingly incredulous.

Comprehension assailed her. A heady tide of pink washed over her complexion. Somehow, in all the turmoil of the evening, she had forgotten telling him that lie about Griff. Since it now seemed pointless to continue it, she muttered, 'I made that up—'

'*Qué dices?*'

'About Griff…that was a little white lie—'

'"A *little* white lie"?' Rico thundered, springing out of bed. '*Madre de Dios*…you tell me you're in love with another man and you call that "a little white lie"?'

'I had to give you a reason for leaving!' Bella protested.

'So if you are not pining for Biff why *were* you leaving?' he slung at her with a positively feral snarl as he began to get dressed.

'Because of the baby.' Bella gave him an 'are you stupid?' look of angry reproof. 'I thought you wouldn't want it…I thought it would be the worst news you had ever heard—'

'And when was I going to hear this news?' he roared at her.

'Some time after we'd split up…when the subject wasn't so emotive.'

Rico sent her a glimmering glance of disbelief.

'When it felt less…personal,' she floundered in desperation.

His disbelief was magnified.

'Does that really make sense to you, *gatita*?' he enquired gently.

Reluctantly she shook her head. In retrospect it didn't make sense. Finding out that she was pregnant had made her panic. She had not been thinking clearly about what she was doing. 'I guess I was running away. I couldn't work up the courage to tell you something I thought you didn't want to hear.'

'And that was my fault?'

Bella shrugged. 'You didn't want to be trapped into marriage again. That's fine.' She took a deep breath. 'But I don't want to marry you on that same basis, Rico. Even though both of us were reckless—'

'I'm never reckless, *gatita*. I knew the risk and I accepted it. I should have known then that there was something special between us…'

Bella winced. 'Rico, you would tell me just about anything to persuade me to marry you. I can understand that but—' A hand had closed round her arm. Rico was pulling her out of bed. 'What are you doing?'

'I want to show you something.'

'It's four o'clock in the morning!'

But he wasn't listening to her. He thrust her robe at her and tossed her mules across to her. 'Come on.'

'Where?'

'You'll see.' Impatiently he propelled her out of the bedroom and downstairs.

When he climbed into the Bugatti outside she hissed, 'I'm not dressed!'

'We're not leaving the estate.'

He drove down the lane that ran from the stable block out to the fields. At the end of it he parked, leaving the headlights on, and walked over to the fence. Thoroughly exasperated by now, Bella leapt out and followed.

'Keep your eyes peeled for something vaguely animate that reminds you of a very tatty, small, moving hearth rug.'

A shape ambled out of the darkness, attracted by the light.

'I located him five days ago,' Rico murmured. 'He hasn't been very well looked after but the vet says he'll be fine once he's groomed and fattened up.'

Bella was already striving to climb the fence, somewhat hampered by her flowing nightwear. Rico lifted her over.

'Fiddlesticks,' she whispered shakily, and then surged over the grass to the Shetland pony.

Ten minutes later she was wiping at her eyes, genuinely overcome not just by the reunion with the little pony she had never thought to see again but by the fact that Rico had gone to so much trouble to trace him and give him back to her.

Rico swung her back over the fence. She slid back into the car, still in a happy daze.

'I planned to get a dog and a cat to go with him,' he murmured very tautly. 'And I was also planning to present the three of them to you before the party.'

'Dog…cat…party?' Bella mumbled in helpless repetition.

'You told me that you loved children and wanted a large fluffy dog, a cat and a pony for them,' Rico reminded her stiffly. 'Well, I was ready to supply them.'

She went rigid, understanding finally sinking in. Rico was telling her that at least a week ago he had been ready to give her what he believed she wanted. And all of a sudden, instead of being touched and pleased by the gesture, she felt like screaming. She wanted him to *love* her, not drag her out to a field in the middle of the night and offer her a menagerie!

He dug something from his pocket and handed it to her. 'This is a sample of the invitations I was having printed. It was going to be an engagement party…a surprise,' he breathed in a harsh undertone. 'I took a lot for granted, *es verdad*?'

Bella was reading the invitation, her heartbeat accelerating. Long before he'd known about the baby Rico had intended to ask her to marry him. She sniffed, her eyes stinging. The fear that he only wanted to marry her because of their child was for ever vanquished.

Rico released his breath in a hiss in the continuing silence, seeming not to appreciate that she was stunned by sheer shock. He drove back to the house and switched off the engine. 'Until you told me you wanted to leave me I thought you loved me...'

'I do,' Bella said distractedly.

'Then why the blazes are you sitting there in silence?' he roared at her without warning.

'Sh-shock,' she proffered shakily.

He groaned something in Spanish and brushed her hair back from her cheekbone with a not quite steady hand. 'I was terrified of losing you. When you said you wanted out I saw my whole world falling apart. There was nothing I would not have done to keep you. And I seemed to have no hold on you but the baby.'

'And you were prepared to use that—'

'Sí... I never thought that I could love anyone the way I love you.'

Bella threw her head back, her green eyes clinging to the blaze of his possessive golden gaze. 'I fell in love with you in the container.'

Rico cursed as he collided with the gearstick in his attempt to drag her into his arms. Bella giggled and climbed out of the car, watching him make it round the bonnet to her in record time. He swept her up into his arms and kissed her passionately as he carried her back into the house.

Between kisses he talked all the way up the stairs. 'When you collapsed outside the farmhouse I was like a man possessed. I knew I was in love...or that I thought I was in love. But I had no idea that you felt the same way. You are so different from every other woman I know. I was afraid to tell you how I felt in case you laughed...'

'I wouldn't have laughed,' Bella whispered, all choked up from realising that he was vulnerable too.

'I am eleven years older. I feared that you might become bored with me.'

'No chance.'

'I couldn't take my eyes off you the first time I saw you. You didn't even *notice*,' he complained.

'Rico, try being poor and smashing up a Bugatti. I was in shock, and then you started calling the police—'

'And you fell asleep in the limo…as if I wasn't there!'

'Strikes me your ego needed a little challenge.' She dropped her voice an octave and boomed in mocking mimicry, '"I have known women to take tremendous risks to make my acquaintance." What do they do—abseil down the walls of the bank and kick their way in through the windows?' She giggled.

Rico lowered her onto the bed. 'You might as well have done. You came into my life and turned it upside-down. You fascinate me.'

'You fascinate me too.' She reached up to him, found his mouth again and yanked him down to her.

They made love slowly, luxuriating in every sweet sensation.

'Am I allowed to buy you things now?' he asked afterwards. 'Festoon you with jewellery?'

'I want a Porsche,' Bella said out of sheer badness.

His black lashes dropped over his too expressive eyes, but his sudden tension said it all for him. 'No problem. You pass an advanced driving test and I'll buy you one.'

'Just you wait,' Bella told him.

Bella watched Rico swing their daughter up in his arms as he came through the hall. Jenny wrapped her little arms round his throat in a death grip and hugged him, making excitable 'da-da' sounds. He had clearly been affectionately attacked by their wolfhound before he'd even got in the door: there was a large, muddy paw-print on his jacket. Bella grinned as he looked up and their eyes connected over Jenny's dark, curly head—smug green into slightly tense gold.

'You passed…?'

'I passed.'

'Congratulations,' It sounded rather forced. He couldn't help it. The thought of her in a Porsche, empowered by an advanced driving test or otherwise, still brought him out in a cold sweat, she assumed.

Having put Jenny down for a nap, she suggested, 'I'll take you for a spin, shall I?'

'You've already bought it?' Rico breathed, looking shattered.

'It's in the garage.'

Hector was out for his evening stroll down the drive. He waved. Rico had bought his London house for their use and renovated it. The court case which had put their kidnappers into prison was thankfully long behind them now and Hector had decided to rent a cottage on the estate.

When he wasn't playing honorary grandpa for Jenny's benefit, he was fully occupied with thinking up economies for Rico to make at Winterwood. And Rico would listen with that little smile of his and marvel that he had never had such ideas himself. It was just one of the reasons why Bella loved him so much.

Rico peered into the garage with a fixed smile which quickly fell away. 'That's a Volvo estate!'

'I never wanted a Porsche. I'm not that fond of speed,' Bella said gently. 'And this is much more practical for a working artist with a child.'

'You never wanted a Porsche…but you made me jump through all the hoops pretending you did!' Rico was now struggling to look angry, she gathered, instead of painfully relieved.

She reached for his silk tie and tugged him towards her with all the provocativeness of a very confident woman. 'I like to keep you on your toes, Mr da Silva.'

'*Dios mío*, you are not joking,' he growled thickly, crushing her into his arms and kissing her breathless, passion blazing up between them just as it always did. 'And fortunately for you I find it irresistible, because, having phoned Haversham to ascertain your success, at lunchtime I went out and bought you a Porsche.'

Bella's jaw dropped.

'Just think of the mileage Hector is going to get out of conspicuous consumerism like this!' Rico suddenly said, laughing.

Initially a French/English teacher, **Emma Darcy** changed careers to computer programming before marriage and motherhood settled her into a community life. Creative urges were channelled into oil-painting, pottery, designing and overseeing the construction and decorating of two homes, all in the midst of keeping up with three lively sons and the very social life of her businessman husband, Frank. Very much a people person and always interested in relationships, she finds the world of romance fiction a happy one and the challenge of creating her own cast of characters very addictive. She enjoys travelling and her experiences often find their way into her books.

Emma Darcy lives on a country property in New South Wales, Australia. She has been successfully writing for Mills & Boon® since 1983, and has since written more than 60 novels, which have been published worldwide.

THE LAST GRAND PASSION

by

EMMA DARCY

CHAPTER ONE

"DON'T YOU *WANT* TO GET married, Anne?"

Anne Tolliver cast an exasperated look at her youngest sister. Did *every* member of her family have to ask that question at *every* opportunity?

Jenny was not looking at her, nor at the sketches strewn across the desk. She was admiring her engagement ring, jiggling her fingers so that light sparkled off the facets of the diamond. It was all too obvious marriage was the only thing on Jenny's mind. Which was natural enough with her wedding barely four months away.

Anne's irritation melted into bleak loneliness as she remembered what she had been like at twenty-one. So madly in love...a head full of romantic dreams...all coming to nothing. Worse than nothing. It had been seven years since Thady Riordan had walked out of her life, but the memory of how she had felt with him still had the power to make any other man less than right for her.

Young as she was then, she had sensed the dark passions in his soul, the reaching out for something that she wanted to provide. Why he had chosen not to take what she had offered Anne still did not understand. It was well after he had returned to England that she began to understand there was far more to Thady Riordan than she had imagined.

When she had known him Thady had been a script writer, working on a joint British and Australian production for television, a mini series that was being partly shot at the studios where Anne worked as a wardrobe assistant.

Barely a year after Thady had left her, his first play was a highly acclaimed hit on the London stage. It had been followed by others, two of which had been made into films.

His plays were stark and compelling revelations of human relationships. The depth and breadth of the knowledge behind them was both fascinating and disturbing. There were people comparing Thady Riordan to Tennessee Williams or Eugene O'Neill.

To Anne's mind, Thady stood alone. No other playwright exposed the folly and tragedy of human existence with such savagery and depth of feeling, laying bare the isolation and loneliness in every beating heart. Anne knew that inner loneliness only too well.

At least she had a career to keep her life busy and interesting. Her gaze drifted to the other end of her workroom. There on the bench along the wall sat the miniature stage sets she had built while experimenting with the production design for Thady Riordan's latest play.

So far it was her most prestigious job. The play had opened to great reviews two weeks ago, and the plaudits she received for her work should help to make her name in the theatrical world. Unfortunately that world was rather limited in Australia. She had to take work where and when she could get it, and it was scarce at the moment.

Which was just as well, she supposed, since she had promised to do the dresses for Jenny's wedding. She returned her attention to her sister, whose pretty vivacious face still wore a rapt expression. The diamond ring had caught a beam of sunlight from the window behind them.

"Jenny, I do need you to concentrate on all the details today if we're to get everything organised and made in good time," Anne gently reminded her.

"Sorry, Anne. I was just thinking…oh, never mind. What's next?"

"Are you happy with the jade silk taffeta for the bridesmaids?"

"Oh, yes! The girls are going to adore those dresses," Jenny enthused. "I don't know how you come up with such wonderful ideas."

"Costume design is my job," Anne stated dryly. "Among other things."

Jenny's face suddenly creased with uncertainty. "Anne, you don't mind not being one of my bridesmaids, do you?"

"Of course not."

"I felt awful about not asking you, but Mum said—" Her mouth twisted into a grimace as she pulled herself back from blurting out an embarrassing truth that could only hurt.

"It's all right," Anne hastily assured her.

She didn't have to wonder what her mother had said. She knew. "Three times a bridesmaid, never a bride." For Anne to fill that role again would undoubtedly tempt fate, since she had stood up for her other two younger sisters when they were married.

In fact Anne was relieved not to be involved in the wedding party. It would be enough to simply stand back and enjoy the whole production from a distance. Perhaps then she wouldn't be continually pestered with the question of when *she* was going to get married.

"It will be more fun for you to have your friends around you," she said, smiling to ease Jenny's concern.

Her sister heaved a big sigh. "I guess so. Though I still feel sorry that you won't be in my wedding photograph. Liz and Kate have you in theirs."

Both were framed for posterity and sitting in pride of place along the mantelpiece in her mother's living room. "I'm sure you'll look so beautiful that no-one will bother looking at anyone else," Anne assured the bride-to-be.

And after Jenny's photograph was added to the mantelpiece, their mother would undoubtedly use it as an even more pointed reminder that her oldest daughter was still on the shelf.

It could be argued that getting three out of four daughters married off was something of an achievement in these liberated times, but Anne doubted her mother would appreciate that argument. The women's liberation movement had passed Leonie Tolliver by. It was her entrenched opinion that a career, no matter how successful, was no substitute for marriage.

To Anne, a career was more fulfilling and rewarding than drifting along without any goals whatsoever, apart from waiting for a marriageable man to make her a housewife and mother. And if he then turned out to be the wrong man... Anne shuddered at the consequences.

"You didn't answer my question," Jenny remarked.

"What question?"

"About not wanting to get married."

"Don't you think I get enough of that question from Mum?" Anne demanded in a dry drawl.

It was meant to cut the subject dead, once and for all. But it didn't. Curiosity and concern gleamed in Jenny's bright brown eyes. "But what's going to happen to you if you never get married?"

"What *I* choose to happen," Anne said decisively.

"You must have been in love at least a couple of times, Anne," Jenny argued. "You *are* twenty-eight...."

"Which isn't exactly over the hill," Anne mocked.

Jenny flushed. "I didn't mean you were old. You've got a great figure and the kind of face that looks good even without make-up. Sexy hair..."

"*Sexy* hair?" Anne laughed, tugging at the untidy strands that had escaped from the loosely wound knot at the top of her head.

"Men like long hair. Especially when it's thick and soft and shiny and touchable like yours."

"You obviously have expert knowledge," Anne teased, reaching over to stroke Jenny's blonde bob.

Jenny sighed her exasperation. "I'm serious, Anne.

There must have been guys attracted to you over the years.''

''I wasn't attracted to them,'' she replied lightly.

''What about Tom Colby?''

Anne felt her face tightening. She could never think of that dreadful self-delusion without pain. If Tom had not looked like Thady, if she had not felt so lonely… But neither of those excuses lessened her guilt where Tom was concerned.

''I wasn't in love with him,'' she stated flatly.

''Then why did you have an affair with him?''

''Because I was curious and I thought I was in love.'' She forced a dismissive smile. ''Maybe I'm not as lucky as you, Jenny. It didn't work out.''

The big brown eyes softened with compassion. ''Were you terribly hurt, Anne?''

''I'd really prefer not to talk about it.''

''You shouldn't let it sour you off all men.''

''It doesn't. I wish you and your Brian every happiness in the world,'' she said with fervent sincerity.

''I want you to be happy, too,'' came the equally fervent response. ''What would you consider the right man for you, Anne?''

The telephone rang.

Anne was grateful for the interruption. This personal probing by her sister had gone far enough. She was reaching for the receiver when Jenny suddenly jumped to her feet in a flutter.

''It'll probably be Brian wanting to know if everything is okay,'' she babbled as she skipped around the desk. ''In fact, I'm certain it's Brian.''

Anne withdrew her outstretched hand, allowing Jenny to snatch up the receiver.

''Oh, Brian!'' she gushed. ''I'm so glad you called. The bridesmaids' dresses are fabulous. We're just about to start on—'' She stopped.

Anne looked up in idle interest, wondering what amazing piece of news Brian was relating to distract Jenny from her present obsession.

Jenny's face was flushed with embarrassment. "Oh, I'm sorry. Wrong person," she gabbled, then gave a nervous little laugh as she cupped her hand over the receiver and looked at Anne. "It's for you."

"Who is it?"

"It's a bad line. I don't know. I think it's Roy somebody or somebody Roy."

Anne didn't know anybody of that name. Maybe someone with a job proposal.

"Annelise Tolliver." It was her full name, her professional name.

"It's Thady, Anne. Thady Riordan."

The soft Irish lilt sent prickles down Anne's spine. Her heart stopped dead. Her head whirled with incredulity and doubts, yet there was no mistaking that voice, and not even seven years had dimmed its effect on her.

Seven years!

And not one word from him since he had walked away from her and pursued his own purpose on the other side of the world.

Why had he remembered her now? What possible purpose could he have in calling, speaking to her as though the long separation had never been?

"Anne? Am I calling at an inconvenient time?"

Her eyes focused on the clock. Eleven twenty-four. She wondered what time it was in London. Her mind was incapable of calculating the difference. Nine...ten hours. Backwards or forwards? It didn't matter anyway. She tried to compose herself. Somehow she made her tongue work.

"The time is fine. You surprised me. A call from you is hardly a daily occurrence, Thady."

"Anne, I saw the play last night," he said quietly. "I saw what you had done with it."

What *she* had done!

For a moment her head pounded dizzily as the meaning of what he was telling her hammered through her mind. Thady couldn't be calling from England. Not if he had seen *her* work on his play. He had to be in Australia, right here in Sydney! The distance between them suddenly dwindled into nothing.

Into the dead silence Thady's voice spoke again, soft, intimate, promising. "I'm in Sydney, Anne. I want to see you."

His words triggered a turmoil of hopes, fears and wild desires. Anne tried to steady herself, to be sensible. Thady hadn't called her *before* he saw the play. His interest in seeing her had been prompted by her work. She would be an absolute fool to think it could be anything else.

"I'd like that, Thady," she said, trying her utmost to sound as calm and collected as a professional person should in such circumstances. Yet a deeply primitive need for his approval prompted her to ask, "Did my production design fit your vision of the play?"

"More so than I could ever have imagined, Anne," he said with the caressing warmth that used to curl her toes. It still did. "I can't stop thinking about it. I want to see you, talk to you about it. Can you meet me for lunch?"

She was supposed to be spending the day with Jenny, going through the sketches, finalising details. But surely Jenny would understand how important this was to her. She could say it was important business. Vitally important. Which it was.

"Or dinner tonight?" Thady pressed.

No, she thought wildly. She couldn't bear to lose one minute of being with him. He might be flying back to England tomorrow. Anything might happen to prevent their meeting between now and tonight. She couldn't, wouldn't risk postponing the time.

"I can make it to lunch," she said decisively.

Jenny started waving her hands and pulling faces at her, but Thady was on the line, talking to her, and nothing else mattered.

"I'm at the Park Hyatt. Right next to the harbour bridge. Could you join me here? Or if you'd like to suggest somewhere else…"

"No. That's fine."

"What time suits you?"

She needed time to get ready, time to get there. "One o'clock?"

"One o'clock," he confirmed. "I'll look forward to it, Anne. Thank you."

That was it. An invitation and an acceptance. No "How are you?" No "What have you been doing all these years?" But there would be time for that when they met, Anne argued to herself. Or did he only care about what she had done for his play?

Seven years and no word from him. Seven years, during which he had been publicly connected to several beautiful women. Anne had seen photographs in the celebrity sections of women's magazines. Thady Riordan with Lady So-and-so, successful young playwright being lionised by London society. Thady Riordan with leading actress. Thady Riordan with scintillating socialite. But he hadn't married any of them, Anne fiercely reminded herself.

"What's the matter with you, Anne?"

Jenny's sharp tone and question snapped her attention to her sister. "Nothing," she mumbled. The wall clock read eleven twenty-seven. Three minutes for the world to turn.

"You make an appointment for lunch when we're supposed to be spending the day together," Jenny reminded her. "Then you sit there with glazed eyes. You're still holding the phone, you know. So what's going on?"

The mixture of accusation and concern brought a wry smile to Anne's lips. "Sorry, Jenny. I guess I was in shock. That was Thady Riordan on the phone."

Jenny's eyes widened. "You mean the guy who wrote the play you just did?"

"The same. He's over here from England and he wants to meet me. It's a professional opportunity I can't miss, Jenny."

"Wow! Go for it, Anne! We can do this stuff tomorrow." Her eyes glittered with excitement at the idea of her sister meeting an international celebrity. "From the photos I've seen of him he's a gorgeous hunk. What are you going to wear?"

"I don't know. I need to be alone to think about this, Jenny. Do you mind?"

"No, that's okay! I'll hop off now. I hope it works out great for you, Anne."

"Thanks, Jenny. Come around tomorrow and we'll finish working on these sketches."

"Sure!" She was already on her way out when a last thought struck her. "Wear your hair down, Anne. It's sexy."

Sexy!

It hadn't been sexy seven years ago, Anne thought with grim irony. Not sexy enough to draw Thady into any more than a few gentle kisses. What had he felt for her then? He had to have been attracted to her. Had he thought she was too young for him? Too young and inexperienced for any deep involvement?

Well, she wasn't so young and inexperienced now, Anne thought as she headed for her bathroom. This was a chance to find out the answers to all the questions that had haunted her over the years, a chance to settle what she felt about Thady Riordan once and for all.

Was it the dream of a young heart?

Or was it a passion that would never die?

Anne was aware of her pulse quickening as she tossed off her clothes. Stay calm, she told herself fiercely. Having showered, dressed, and groomed to her professional best,

Anne surveyed her appearance with critical eyes, trying to assess what Thady would see.

The cream linen suit skimmed the curves of her figure with enough style to be feminine without being overtly sexy. Her stockings matched the taupe silk blouse, very much the in-fashion colour at the moment. Her cream high heels and handbag featured a touch of gold, which her gold ear studs and the fine gold chains around her neck picked up.

She had brushed her long, thick, honey-coloured hair into a soft dip above one ear before looping it into a loosely wound knot at the top of her head. It was an elegant, sophisticated style that accentuated her long, graceful neck. The make-up she had applied lent a light sheen to her smooth skin, subtly highlighted her darkly lashed amber eyes and outlined the full feminine curve of her lips.

She looked good.

She didn't look twenty-one any more.

Thady Riordan wanted to see the woman she was now. Anne had come a long way from the tumble-haired, scattily dressed wardrobe assistant who had briefly caught his attention. Anne knew there was no going back to that young woman with her head full of dreams. The mirror reflected an experienced, confident woman.

Thady Riordan was about to meet Annelise Tolliver.

CHAPTER TWO

THE TAXI RIDE from her home at Paddington to the Park Hyatt at Campbell's Cove took a bare twenty minutes. Anne needed every second of it to settle her composure. It was precisely one o'clock as she stepped out of the cab.

The roar of a train crossing the harbour bridge startled her, and the doorman quickly ushered her into the hotel which was completely sound-proofed. The sudden quiet emphasised the elegance of the decor.

An expanse of highly polished tiled floor swept to a magnificent view of the opera house through the long windows on the other side of the room. Wonderful floral arrangements graced tall vases and urns, forming splashes of exotic luxury. The reception desk was a period piece, its simplicity statement enough no bustle occurred in this hotel.

Unobtrusively a number of staff in smart black suits waited patiently to give any service or courtesy. Anne wondered if she should notify the receptionist of her arrival, but even as she considered it, her eye caught movement from the seating area to the right of the entrance.

She turned her head and there he was, the man who had held her heart captive from their first meeting so many years ago. He was already on his feet and moving steadily, resolutely towards her.

Their eyes locked, simmering green and golden amber. Anne breathed in deeply to counteract the sudden surge of excitement that was almost panic. Her heart seemed to be beating much faster, creating a drumming effect in her ears.

Her mind instructed her to move forward to greet him, but her feet didn't receive the message. They stood riveted to the floor as her eyes absorbed the physical presence of Thady Riordan.

Recognition had been instant, yet he was different from her memory of him, different from her dreams of him. Disturbingly different. She tried to pinpoint what it was, because she felt the difference coming from him, causing her to react physically in a way she never had.

Her skin was prickling, tightening, all over her body. She was acutely aware of her femininity, the silk of her blouse skimming the soft swell of her breasts, the close fit of her skirt around her hips, the bareness of her thighs above her stockings.

Something had changed. But what?

His physique looked the same. He was well over medium height but not overly tall. The grey suit he wore displayed the strong breadth of his shoulders and the muscularity of his thighs. Perhaps there was an added hardness to his face, a hollowness in his cheeks that threw his bone structure into gaunt relief.

It was a strongly chiselled face with a high, wide forehead, angular jaw line, prominent nose and clean-cut chin. The contrast of soft hair, a riot of black curls flopping across his forehead and tumbling over his ears and collar, gave him an untamed look that was compellingly attractive.

Was it his eyes that were different? She remembered them as dark fathomless green eyes, deeply set and shadowed by thick black lashes. Eyes filled with gentle humour when he smiled. He was smiling now, a whimsical little smile that accentuated the sensuality of his wide, full-lipped mouth, a mouth that Anne knew could weave magical feelings inside her.

There was something more powerful, more dominant about the way he walked towards her. Ready to take and do whatever he willed. Did success engender that in people? Did wealth? It was in his eyes. No trace of gentleness. They were hard and determined. Perhaps even…yes, ruthless.

A convulsive shiver ran down Anne's spine. What did he want of her? Her mind reasoned that he couldn't take anything unless she let him, but her body was registering a terrible vulnerability to this man, whatever he had become.

He was more handsome than any memory or photograph could ever capture and retain. As he came to a halt in front her, Anne noticed the fine quality of his suit, his white silk shirt and silk designer tie, the obvious trappings of success. She had looked past the clothes to see the man, but logic argued that the clothes were now part of the man, a part she had never known.

"You remember me?" he asked in a voice that was barely audible.

Anne jerked her gaze up from the brilliantly coloured tie. She remonstrated with herself to pull herself together and be a bit professional. Her imagination was running riot.

"Thady," she acknowledged in a fair semblance of a matter-of-fact tone.

"You've grown more beautiful, Anne."

His eyes said desirable. Intensely and immediately desirable.

"You've grown more handsome," she replied, the words tripping off her tongue without any sensible thought at all.

His smile took on an ironic curl. "You never married."

"No. It seems we're two of a kind."

There was a quick flitter of expressions, speculation, relief, then a settling into satisfaction. "That was what I thought last night," he said softly. "Someone in tune with me. It was an exciting revelation to see how well you understood what I'd written, Anne. To know we share the same passions."

He paused, then added almost carelessly, "There's no-one you're attached to at the present moment?"

Resentment washed through Anne, sobering her stupidly infatuated response to him. After all these years, and after what he had done and hadn't done, did he really think he could walk back into her life, just like that?

She had never fully admitted to herself how deeply in love she had been with Thady Riordan. But this was not the man she had loved. Not even remotely. That Thady had made her feel like Cinderella every time she had gone out with him. As though she were beautiful and precious and very special to him. This Thady was making her feel like… Whatever it was, it was deeply disturbing.

"As it happens, I'm not attached to anyone at present," she stated coolly. "But I didn't come here to discuss my private life, Thady. I thought you wanted to talk about my work on your play."

He raised a challenging eyebrow. "You think our work doesn't reflect our private lives, Anne?"

"Not all of it!"

"That's why I want to know all that's happened to you. How you've come to where you are now."

Smooth as silk he was, primed to pounce whichever way she moved. The aura of kindness and giving he had once worn was totally gone.

"I doubt we could fit in seven years of my life over lunch," she said with a touch of bitterness.

"The time it takes means nothing to me."

That was a lie. It *had* to be a lie. "What brought you back to Australia, Thady?" she tossed at him.

"Memories," he said in the soft Irish lilt that played havoc with her nervous system.

Anne steeled herself against this further lie. If he had a treasure chest of memories of her, it had taken a hell of a long time for him to open it!

"There were no memories worth keeping," she asserted,

rejecting the idea that what they had once shared meant anything to her. "At least there were none for me," she added to completely smash that insultingly facile approach from him.

A bittersweet smile curved his lips. He lifted a hand to her face. A feather-light touch stroked down her cheek, her throat, shoulder, arm. "Then perhaps we can make new memories, Anne. Ones you won't want to dismiss so easily."

All the reasonable logic in Anne's mind flew into chaos, her emotions twisting into utter turmoil. She had not expected such directness. For whatever reason, Thady Riordan had decided he wanted her, and he could have her.

His fingers closed around her arm, pressing a seductive possessiveness. Heat radiated from his touch, infiltrating her entire body. Her stomach contracted in a clutch of sheer physical desire. Thady Riordan had lived in her mind for so long. And she *could* have him now if she wanted.

What would it be like to know all she had never had with him? To have the kind of intimacy she had craved? To lie in his arms and make love? But was this man capable of love?

He was not the Thady she remembered. He was more the man who had written the plays. Dark and dangerous, emanating a frightening flow of hidden undercurrents.

"What do you want from me, Thady?" she blurted, desperately wishing she could read his mind.

"Nothing you can't freely give, Anne."

"What does that mean?" Her eyes sharply challenged his claim.

Determination glittered back. "What do you want most in the world, Anne?"

It had been *him* up until a few moments ago.

Anne decided to let him think that ambition was her highest priority. She lifted her chin in defiance. "The most important thing in the world to me is my career."

It jolted him. His hand slid away from her arm. The flesh on his face seemed to tighten. His lips thinned. The warmth in the green eyes glittered into a chilling cynicism.

"Then I'll give you that," he said, still undeterred from having whatever he thought she could give him.

That jolted Anne. Of course it was possible with his connections and influence to open paths for her that she could never forge herself, but to use that power to cold-bloodedly bribe her into his bed was the last action she would ever have expected from him.

"Why, Thady? What's in it for you?" she asked, inwardly pleading for some understanding of why he was treating her like this. "What do you get out of it?"

His eyes emptied of all expression. "I've arranged for lunch to be served in my suite. Shall we go there and discuss the matter?"

The thought of being alone with him in his suite sent a quiver of fear through Anne. So many emotions warred through her that she knew intuitively that such a move could only bring her grief.

Yet pride insisted that she appear totally unmoved by this arrangement. Pride insisted that she see this encounter with Thady Riordan through to its absolute end, whatever that entailed. Only then might she be able to cut herself free of all the years of yearning for what might have been.

"And after lunch, Thady…what happens then?" Her eyes derided his obvious purpose for getting her alone with him.

"Why, Anne," he drawled lightly, "what happens after lunch is entirely up to you."

A mocking little smile lingered on his lips as he linked her arm to his and drew her towards the elevator. She didn't resist. Although she felt sickened to her soul, she could not tear herself free of him. Not yet. Perhaps not ever.

Anne had the miserable feeling that they had both lost what they had most wanted. Yet they were both tied to whatever happened next.

CHAPTER THREE

ANNE'S LEGS WERE trembling by the time they reached the door to his suite. When Thady withdrew the support of his arm to open the door, a sudden pause in her heartbeat made her sway. It lasted only an instant before she managed to recover herself, yet when Thady turned to usher her inside, something about her caused him to hesitate.

Whether she looked pale or feverish, Anne had no idea. There was a flicker of pain or regret in his eyes, perhaps the memory of a different time, a different place, a different person. It was gone so quickly Anne wasn't sure she saw it. His face reflected set determination for the here and now.

"Be my guest," he said as he gestured for Anne to enter ahead of him.

"As long as that's all I am," she returned with pointed irony, then pushed her legs forward and past him with as much dignity as she could muster.

It was a spacious, plush apartment. The walls were angled in such a way that they made niched areas for the dining setting, a lounge suite and a king-size bed with all of its convenient facilities. Floor-to-ceiling glass gave a spectacular view of the harbour, and the curtains were pulled back to make a point of it.

She heard the door close and kept on walking towards the view. "You do yourself proud these days, Thady," she remarked, feeling absurdly conscious of the bed and even more conscious of his eyes following her.

"I can afford it now."

"Do you favour water views?" she prattled on, words spilling out to break her tense awareness of his physical presence behind her.

"Yes."

"Different from the old days when we slummed it together, isn't it?"

"Yes. It's different."

"Do you enjoy it more?" she quietly asked.

As stupidly impossible as it was, she yearned for him to say that nothing was more enjoyable than the time they had shared, the simple fun they'd had, the walks and talks and the easy laughter between them.

He made no reply. His silence chewed up Anne's memories as effectively as a kitchen disposal unit. She stared out at the water, deriding herself for asking the question in the first place. Wasn't wealth always better than poverty?

She heard the rattle of ice, the popping of a cork, the fizz of champagne as it was poured into glasses. The fizz of success, she thought sourly, which he had shared with other women.

He came to stand beside her, handed her a glass of champagne. He lifted his in a toast. "To Annelise Tolliver and her career."

She forced herself to look up at him with a bland smile. "Thank you, Thady." Then, unable to contain her seething bitterness, she added, "Do you make good on your promises? Or are they as false as your interest in me once was?"

His eyes seemed to go flat, opaque. "I was interested, Anne."

"You left without saying goodbye."

"If we'd met again we would have become lovers," he stated as a matter of fact.

"Was that so bad?"

"Yes," he replied simply. "Yes, at that time it would have been bad."

"But it's not so bad to become lovers now."

"That's correct. It's not so bad now."

"How very reassuring," she drawled, hating him for his decisions. No consultation. No discussion. Only what he wanted. She raised her glass in a toast to him. "To good and bad," she said with brittle mockery. "May the bad sometimes win."

They both sipped the champagne. Anne had to fight against choking on hers. She wished she hadn't brought up the past. She couldn't deny she would have been his lover for the taking at almost any time they'd been together. The mutual acknowledgement shamed her.

She could feel Thady brooding, looking intently at her. He exuded a magnetism that her body responded to whether she liked it or not. Every breath she took seemed full of him, as though the air itself was permeated with the powerful pull of his physical presence.

"Do you ever feel lonely with your career, Anne?" he asked softly. "Don't you want more than that?"

He knew where to strike. Where to twist the knife. But the same knife was in her hands. She lifted her eyes and hurled her knowledge at him.

"Everyone suffers moments of loneliness at times, Thady, with or without a career. Isn't that what you write in your plays? Utter and total loneliness? Loneliness so extreme that no person should ever experience it."

His fingers were on her lips, silencing her, in a motion so swift that it caught Anne by surprise. His eyes had turned to a greenish-black. His brow furrowed. Anne sensed that what she'd said was some unacceptable violation of his private world.

Just as suddenly his mood changed. His eyes gathered a

lighter gleam that mocked her attempt at hurting him. He lifted his hand away, palm out in a gesture implying he had nothing to hide.

"That's why I'm always alone," he said matter-of-factly. "I write what I know. I write what I feel. I know loneliness best. That is my life, Anne. My constant companion."

"Not exactly *constant*," she flashed at him, remembering her heartache over the glamorous women who had starred in his life. "Your affairs with various *companions* have fed the gossip columns around the world."

One eyebrow rose in derisive challenge. "Do you believe everything you read?"

"Are you denying that you've been attached to an array of beautiful women?"

"There was no affair. Not in the sense you mean."

"What was there, then?"

"Publicity."

"You don't expect me to believe that?" Anne scoffed.

He shrugged. "Believe what you please."

"Sure! You live like a monk in a monastery."

"When I want to."

"And all those highly desirable women were left disappointed."

"They meant nothing to me."

"You remained totally celibate?" She couldn't believe it. Not from the kind of man he was showing her today.

"I'm a man with normal urges," he bit out.

"So you did—"

"Yes, I did," he snapped. A dark torment suddenly swirled from his eyes. "But only after you took up with Tom Colby."

Anne's jealous anger froze into shock. The mad triumph of having forced Thady into his admission was completely shattered. Had she lost Thady because of Tom? But how could that be? It didn't make any sense.

"What do you know about Tom?" she cried in anguish.

"Enough to know I want what *he* had."

CHAPTER FOUR

ANNE COULD FEEL the blood draining from her face. Shock upon shock trembled through her. Thady knew about her relationship with Tom Colby. He hadn't touched any other woman until after he knew. Or so he said. And the vehement possessiveness in his voice just now...wanting what she had given Tom...

Thady could have had that and more if he hadn't left her. She had loved *him*. Only him. And she hadn't met Tom Colby until three years after Thady had gone from her life. And then she had deceived herself into believing Tom was just like Thady.

She lifted pained eyes to the man who had twice led her into a deep personal hell. "If you wanted me, why didn't you come back?"

His mouth twisted. His eyes simmered with soft mockery. "I couldn't belong in your dreams, Anne."

"What dreams?"

"Getting married, having children, the happy ever after. When I heard about Tom Colby, I hoped he'd give you everything you wanted."

"How altruistic of you, Thady. Caring so much about my needs. Playing God on my behalf."

He flinched.

Anne drove on savagely, wanting to hurt as he had hurt her by arrogantly judging that he knew best for both of them. "Did it make you feel less of a failure when you thought my dreams were being answered?"

"A failure?" He gave a harsh, derisive laugh. "Because I don't fit into the nice neat slot that you consider acceptable?" His bitter amusement faded into a grim smile as he quoted from *Hamlet*. "There are more things in heaven and earth, Anne, than are dreamt of in your philosophy."

"And *you* know all about them," she taunted, smarting at his condescension.

"Enough not to wish them on anyone else." His eyes bored into hers with certain knowledge. "But you're learning about the downside of life, aren't you, Anne? You're learning about loneliness, aren't you? Your work on my play was not all skilful artistry. You *knew* what it was about. You created from what you *knew*. Was Tom Colby responsible for that?"

You were the one responsible, she wanted to say, but she bit the words back. He would never appreciate how much she had felt for him, how deep it had gone. Yet she must have touched something in him for there to have been no interest in any other woman until he knew she had been taken.

Perhaps it was because he hadn't had sex with her, the fruit he had forbidden himself, the sweet young dreamer he'd turned his back on out of some core of decency.

"How did you hear about Tom?" she asked.

"From Alex Korbett."

Alex, her boss at the time. Anne had learnt a lot about production design under Alex's tutoring. She remembered his trip to England. He hadn't mentioned seeing Thady Riordan. There was no reason he should. He had been full of talk about what was being done in the theatres over there, which was their common interest.

No doubt his meeting with Thady had been totally incidental. There would have been a chat about mutual acquaintances in Australia. Alex loved to gossip about people. As soon as her name had come up he would have prattled away about her involvement with Tom.

"Did you love him, Anne?"

She stared hopelessly into his eyes.

"I answered your questions," he reminded her softly.

She dragged out the truth. A truth of which she was ashamed, but the truth nevertheless. "No. I didn't love him."

"But you gave yourself to him."

"Completely."

That was the truth, too, as far as it went. She supposed Thady considered that it gave him free licence to go after a loveless affair with her since she had done what she had done. After all, here she was, still unmarried, a self-declared career woman who owned to no other dreams.

"Was it out of loneliness?" he asked.

Out of need, she thought despairingly. The need to be loved. The need to be loved as she had imagined Thady would have loved her. But she couldn't tell him that. It was even more shaming, and far too revealing. He didn't love her. He only wanted her. Free and clear of dreams.

"Perhaps I have the normal urges of a woman, Thady," she answered dryly.

Satisfaction gleamed in his eyes. "In that case," he said easily, "we're equals."

He lifted a hand and gently laid his fingertips on her cheek. She felt the skin beneath his touch burn, felt a quiver of weakness run through the muscles of her legs, felt her heart leap into chaotic pounding. Half of her wanted to back away, but the other half wavered on a knife-edge of curiosity and anticipation. The pull was still there, no matter what had been said or done.

Not for one moment did his eyes move from hers, mesmerising in their relentless purpose as he trailed his fingers over the smooth curve of her cheek, along her jaw line, down her throat to the gold chains, which he slowly traced around to the nape of her neck.

"You feel the same way I do, Anne," he murmured, his voice husky with desire. "The wanting each other never died, did it? The moment I looked at you, you looked at me, I knew it was still there for us."

Did it all come down to this? she agonised in silent torment. All the pain, the grief, the loneliness, the wanting? Just two bodies coming together to satisfy an animal instinct?

Her stomach churned between excitement and revulsion. The knowing caress of the erotic spots around the nape of her neck was almost hypnotic. Cats purred for this, she thought, feeling a thrum of sensation spreading through her nerve ends.

Thady's fingers drifted up to the pins that secured her hair. "Your hair is so beautiful. Far too beautiful to be pinned away."

It was what Tom used to say. Tom, who had believed he loved her, at least for a time. But there was no love coming from the man who was touching her, arousing responses in her, wanting her to give what she had given Tom in his place.

A sense of terrible betrayal ripped through Anne. She twisted away from Thady's seductive touch, out of his reach, barely aware of what she was doing, where she was going. She felt sick to her very soul at all the deceptions that were played for the appeasement of physical desire.

Her eyes fell on the bed. She walked towards it, gripped by a wild urge to wreak vengeance on the man who had reduced her love to sex.

Every person destroys best the thing they love the most, she thought savagely, and the feelings Thady had aroused in her made Anne hell-bent on destruction. He shouldn't be able to do that to her. It wasn't fair. It wasn't right. The power he still had over her needed to be smashed once and for all.

He wouldn't be ending it this time. She would. Once and for all. She'd reduce everything she'd ever felt for him to dead ashes so there could be no possible comeback from him. Ever again!

Memories! She would give him memories. Memories he'd carry with him for the rest of his life. The innocent dreamer had come of age, all right! She had no illusions left at all.

Anne set her handbag and the glass of champagne on the bedside table and wheeled around to face him, her eyes burning with fiery contempt.

"You don't have to dress it up, Thady. You don't have to play pretend. You want me? You can have me. At no cost to yourself. You can save your pretty compliments for other women."

She struck a provocative, flaunting pose as she took off her suit coat and dropped it on the floor. "Come and get it, Thady," she invited silkily. "Take what you want. Have what Tom had."

The stunned look on his face gave her a fierce but grim satisfaction.

"Do you have a thing about hair, Thady?" she taunted, reaching up to remove her hairpins. "Does it excite you in some special way?"

His face tightened as though she had hit him. Two red slashes appeared high on his cheekbones. Violent anger, no doubt, that any woman could treat his approach to love-making with such disdain.

Anne didn't care what he thought any more. Didn't care if he did nothing or said nothing. The need for total destruction rolled relentlessly through her mind.

She freed her hair from its constriction, raked her fingers through the thick coil, then shook her head, making the long tresses spill around her shoulders.

"Is that better? More to your liking, Thady? You prefer the sensual, accessible look in your women?"

His mouth thinned into a grimace of painful distaste but he didn't look away. His eyes were glued to her.

Anne unbuttoned her blouse, drew it off her arms, dropped it on the floor. She felt a primitive thrill of triumph when Thady's gaze fell to the soft swell of her breasts above the lacy line of her petticoat. The glass he held tipped, spilling champagne onto his fingers. He seemed not to notice.

"Stop it," he said thickly.

"You started it, Thady. I'm simply delivering what you asked for. What you wanted."

"For God's sake, Anne! Not like this."

"You prefer to pretend, do you, Thady? Do you think that is in better taste?" She unzipped her skirt and slid it down over her hips. "Why don't you come over here and start undressing? Or would that be too *equal* for you?"

She stepped out of her skirt with cool disdain while the rage inside her burnt more fiercely. The scourge of seven years' desertion, then his wanting sex with her on the first day back, drove her onwards.

"Anne." It was a strained plea.

"Am I spoiling it for you?" she railed bitterly at him. "Would you rather have something less direct? Do tell me if it's sensuality that turns you on, Thady. The feel of silk and lace…"

She ran her hands up the slippery fabric of her petticoat

and cupped her breasts. "Should I leave my underwear on for you?"

"I told you to stop it, Anne!" Hoarse vehemence.

She kicked off her shoes and turned towards the bed, meaning to set her foot on it while she rolled down her stocking. The shattering of glass halted her in mid-action.

"I said stop it!"

At the harsh command, she jerked her head towards the man who had given it. He was no longer holding a glass of champagne. His hands were fiercely clenched at his sides. His chest was heaving. His eyes blazed with warring passions.

A cold, deadly calm settled over Anne's inner rage. "Something wrong, Thady?"

He exploded into movement as though her taunt had released a compressed spring inside him. "*What* made you like this? *Who* did this to you?" The questions burst from his lips as he covered the short distance between them. He grabbed her arms, fingers biting deep as he shook her. "Was it Tom Colby?"

The mad irony of the questions snapped something inside Anne's head. Her brittle control fell apart. Her voice shook with outrage. "Don't you dare blame Tom for this. I was a person to him. Not just a…" She choked on a welling lump of other emotions. Tears spurted into her eyes.

"If it wasn't Tom Colby, then who was it?"

It was you, you who did this to me, her mind screamed at him. But somehow she couldn't bring herself to say the damning words.

"Anne, tell me who it was who hurt you so badly."

She began to tremble with reaction. What had she done? "It's better if you don't know," she choked out.

"Why?"

Tears overflowed, spilling down her cheeks. The constriction in her throat made speech impossible. She shook her head.

"Anne…"

With a tortured groan he wrapped his arms around her and crushed her to the solid warmth of his body, rocking her as though she were a child who needed the security of being held. He rubbed her back, stroked her hair, every touch imparting an agonised caring that plunged Anne into utter confusion. Was it for *her?* Or was it simply compassion for another person in distress?

All she really knew was how good it felt with him holding her like this. It was so easy to rest her head on his shoulder, to close her eyes and simply give herself to his keeping. She wasn't sure if the trembling weakness inside her was a reaction to what had gone before or a response to what was happening now. Somehow it didn't seem to matter.

It didn't bother her when Thady started trailing soft kisses over her hair. They were warm, gentle, conjuring up memories of how it had been with Thady in the past. She sighed in contentment. She felt his chest expand, felt a shudder run through him. Then his hand slid down to the pit of her back, lower, and she felt the beginning of his arousal.

Before she could even think what she should do about it, he wrenched himself away from her, stepping back, holding her at arm's length. "Get dressed!" he commanded gruffly, his face tight with strain, his eyes sick with wanting.

"Thady…" It was a plea for understanding, but sheer confusion prevented any clarity of thought.

"For God's sake! I'm only human, Anne! Cover yourself up before I—" He made a sound of aversion and spun away, striding forcefully towards the dining setting on the far side of the room.

She watched him go to the bar. He yanked the top off a bottle of whisky, splashed some into a glass. The hand that lifted the glass to his lips was trembling. He took a few quick gulps, shook his head, drank the rest in one fell swoop.

"The door over there leads to a bathroom. Help yourself to whatever you need," he said in a deadly monotone, not turning around to look at her.

There was a rigid finality in the stiffness of his back. Thady would not have her now, no matter what she said or did. She had achieved what she set out to achieve. She had given him memories that hurt. And it was indeed ended...with cold ashes.

She felt like the living dead as she went about getting dressed. She took her handbag and hairpins into the bathroom for the final tidy up. When she emerged, her professional appearance intact again, there was no glow of anticipation in her amber eyes. She knew, with a burrowing sense of loss, that there was nothing to anticipate.

Thady was standing where she had stood before, staring out at the harbour view. She doubted that he was seeing any more than she had. He had an intensely alone air that suggested a complete and utter detachment from the world around him.

"I'm sorry." The words spilled from Anne's lips without any conscious thought of why she should apologise to him.

He turned. There was a haunted look in his eyes that twisted her heart. His mouth moved stiffly into a wry little smile.

"Nothing for you to be sorry about. You simply proved what I've known all along. I'm the wrong man for you."

"Then why did you pursue it?"

He shrugged. "A man can fool himself. When he wants to enough."

She shook her head. "I don't understand you, Thady."

"I don't pretend to understand myself."

It was a glib reply. When her eyes flatly challenged it, a violent distaste twisted across his face.

"Let it go, Anne," he commanded harshly, then made a visible effort to recover a calm composure. He waved towards the dining table, where everything was set for their lunch. "Will you have something to eat now?"

"No, thank you." To stay and eat anything in these circumstances was utterly impossible. Anne knew the invitation was only a bridging politeness. "There's nothing more to be said or done, Thady. I'll go now."

He didn't argue. It was finished, and it was too much a strain on both of them to keep raking over dead ashes.

"I'll see you to a taxi," he offered.

"No. I'd rather you didn't." She fought the stupid tears that were pricking her eyes. "I'll let myself out. Goodbye, Thady."

"La comedia e finita," he quoted softly.

They were the bitter words spoken by the tragic clown at the end of the opera *I Pagliacci,* when his beloved wife lay dead by his own hand.

Destroying what he had most loved.

Did Thady understand what she had set out to do? Or was he referring to what he'd done himself?

Anne stared at him for one further moment, but whichever way the line was read, it was the truth. The play was finished. It was time to ring the curtain down, the cue for her exit from Thady Riordan's life.

She left without another word, closing the door on all that might have been. Yet Anne knew, with a sense of deadly inevitability, that she would be picking over the debris of this day for the rest of her life.

CHAPTER FIVE

ANNE FELT TOTALLY NUMB on the way home. She saw nothing, heard nothing, felt nothing. Like a robot, she automatically registered the necessary movements to get from one place to another. It wasn't until she was inside her small terrace house at Paddington that the numbness started to wear off.

The act of removing her clothes set off the first intense reaction—shivering, as though the temperature had suddenly dropped by twenty degrees. Despite her warmest tracksuit and a heavy woollen jumper, she could do nothing to stop the tremors.

She went downstairs to her workroom in the basement. It was air-conditioned to the same moderate temperature all year round, a necessity for comfortable working conditions because the large below-ground room was freezing in winter and like an oven in summer.

She sat down at her desk and listlessly leafed through the sketches for Jenny's wedding party. She was incapable of concentrating on any detail. Her gaze kept drifting to the miniature sets for Thady's play, and her mind fought vainly against bursts of emotional turmoil.

Any kind of involvement with Thady Riordan could not have led anywhere good, she told herself over and over again. That was evident from all that had happened. It was an absurd waste of time thinking about it. Yet Anne could not help feeling that these self-assurances were very hollow.

We share the same passions. The words kept tormenting her no matter how hard she tried to dismiss them. Thady's manner had led her into thinking that he only had sex on his mind, but maybe he had meant a whole range of sharing. The way they thought. The way they worked. A mutual understanding that took away the loneliness they both felt, that went far beyond a togetherness in bed.

Although bed was certainly part of it.

And marriage certainly wasn't.

Thady had flatly stated that he didn't belong in her dreams. He had undoubtedly thought she had given up on them because of her affair with Tom. Such an interpretation was way off the mark.

The truth of the matter was, she had never meant to have an *affair* with Tom Colby. She had simply drifted into it, anticipating the dream of marriage and children and being happy ever after. The illusion that such dreams were possible with Tom was quickly and painfully shattered.

If Thady had been proposing a more serious affair than the strictly sexual encounters he had apparently conducted with those other women, it still fell far short of what Anne wanted. And it was insulting that he should think she would accept it, particularly on the first day of meeting again. It demonstrated the kind of attitude she despised—that a "used" woman was available for sex.

She had definitely done the right thing to cut it dead, although she shuddered with horror every time she remembered how she had gone about it. But it was Thady who had degraded her before she had degraded herself in that mad strip-show. All the same, she was intensely relieved he hadn't followed through on it. She would be hating herself even more now.

Yet maybe that would have been better than brooding over the caring he had shown, the things he had said that indicated she was special to him, at least more special than any other woman over the last seven years. Or had he lied to soften her up, to ease himself over the hump of seven years' desertion?

The room gradually grew darker, the telephone jarring Anne out of her agonising introspection. She stared at the receiver as though it were a coiled snake, ready to strike with deadly venom should she move to touch it. Then a burst of irritation at her paralysed state drove her to snatch it up. Life went on, she fiercely berated herself. It had gone on after Thady Riordan had left her seven years ago, and it would go on now.

"Anne, it's Jenny. How did it go with Thady Riordan?"

The mention of his name was like a stab to the heart, but Anne schooled herself to strain all emotion from her voice. "We met. We talked. It was an experience to remember. That's all." The irony of that truth would be completely lost on her youngest sister.

"Oh!" The sound of disappointment. "Nothing's going to come of it? Not even for your career?"

"Not that I know of."

A big sigh from Jenny. "What a waste! I was hoping to hear some good news."

"Sorry. Clouds with silver linings don't happen very often."

"Maybe you don't look for them," Jenny muttered. "Anyhow, I called to tell you that Brian will drop me at your place on his way to football tomorrow. That'll be after lunch. Okay?"

"Okay. See you then."

The mention of lunch reminded Anne that she hadn't eaten anything since morning. The thought of food had no appeal but she went up to the kitchen and made herself an omelette. It slid down her throat easily enough, although it didn't sit well on her stomach. Sick with nervous exhaustion, she decided. Feeling a desperate need to be finished with this day, she took a sleeping tablet and went to bed.

If anything, Anne felt even more wretched the next day. The night had been a torment of memories. Thady's eyes haunted her dreams of need, loneliness and deep, dark passions.

It was a relief to wake to the morning light of Saturday even though she felt like a limp wrung-out rag. It was also some comfort to know that she would have her sister's company for some of the day. Besides, the inevitable talk about Jenny's wedding would be a continual and salutory reminder to Anne that Thady Riordan's needs and loneliness and desires fell short of wanting a wife.

At one o'clock, Brian Clark, Jenny's devoted fiancé, delivered Anne's youngest sister to her door. Brian was a pleasant young man, a master bricklayer by trade, with the tanned skin and physique that went with his outdoors way of life. He had all the confidence of a twenty-four-year-old who knew where he was going and what he wanted.

He and Jenny swapped a few teasing remarks before he kissed her goodbye and left to go to the football match with his friends. Observing the young couple together, Anne couldn't help wondering if there was a time for such confidence in making a future together, a time that was already past for her. Even though she was only twenty-eight, they made her feel old.

It was obvious that Brian thought the world of Jenny, and there was certainly no doubt that Jenny thought Brian was the answer to all her dreams. Once he had gone, she chattered non-stop about him while Anne made coffee in the kitchen.

Anne could not repress a little stab of envy. To be so happy, to be so in love, to be so sure her love was returned, how good it must feel! Jenny's pretty face was alight with it, her brown eyes sparkling, her skin glowing, her mouth wreathed in continual smiles. Even when she complained that her bouncy blonde hair wasn't growing fast enough for the style she wanted for her wedding, she was unable to look displeased about it.

Once they were settled at Anne's desk in the basement workroom, Jenny's bubbly happiness was entirely focused on the sketches for the wedding dress. She was thrilled with everything Anne set in front of her, her delight increasing with the discussion of detail, choice of fabric, type of veil, accessories.

By mid-afternoon they were going over the designs once more, working out cost estimates. Anne had the contacts to get the fabrics at wholesale prices and she was calculating the total cost for the wedding dress when the door chimes rang.

"Would you get that please, Jenny?" she asked distractedly.

Jenny was up and gone in a flash while Anne concentrated on working out precise figures. It vaguely occurred to her that it was probably Brian returned from his football match. She took no notice of the interruption until she heard Jenny's voice say, "Come this way, please."

She looked up.

Jenny was leading a visitor down the stairs to the basement. The person behind her wore shoes and trousers that could only belong to a man. Each step revealed more about him. He wore a grey suit. A huge bunch of spring flowers rested on the crook of one arm. Curly black hair tumbled over his collar.

Anne's heart clenched as he reached the foot of the staircase. He was the last person in the world she expected to see. When he turned, his gaze swept directly to where she sat at her desk. His eyes caught hers, compelling in their darkly intimate search for a response that would not turn him away.

Anne sat like a stone, incapable of doing anything but staring at him.

Thady Riordan had once more walked into her life.

CHAPTER SIX

"IT'S MR. RIORDAN, ANNE. Mr. *Thady* Riordan," Jenny announced, excitement bubbling through her voice. She was innocently enjoying the impact of his unexpected visit on Anne, and was clearly anticipating a show of pleasure.

It did not come.

In reply to her sister, Anne simply said, "Thank you, Jenny."

The flat words belied the whirling storm in her mind, the irrepressible ache of hope in her heart, the despair of knowing there was no possible future to be forged from this meeting.

Yesterday had seen to that. Tom Colby had seen to that. And so had Thady Riordan. So why had he come? What could he possibly hope to gain from seeing her again?

He walked towards her, the arc of tension between them tightening with each step. Anne was vaguely aware that Jenny held back, apparently sensitive to an atmosphere that totally excluded her. Thady didn't attempt a smile. Nor did he bother with any facile words for social ease. His face was set in tight determination, his shoulders straight, his whole bearing one of resolute purpose, and his eyes burned with the resolution to carry that purpose forward no matter what the odds and what the cost.

Anne remained totally still, waiting, watching, silently agonising over all that had happened between them. A treacherous little hope kept whispering that this was another chance, that maybe this time…

"I hope you don't mind my coming here, Anne," Thady said softly. "I wanted to say a final goodbye to you. I'll be flying back to London in the morning."

Any last possible hope crumbled. "Hasn't everything been said, Thady?"

"No." He shook his head as he advanced the last few steps to the other side of her desk. "I couldn't leave without apologising. Without saying how sorry I am that I've hurt you. Without doing something to restore what I've taken from you. Without asking for your forgiveness."

"You didn't take anything from me. You don't need my forgiveness," she retorted fiercely, denying her need for the love he would never give her and hating the memory of what he had offered her and she had offered him.

He laid the massed array of flowers on the desk in front of her with the slow deliberation of a petitioner laying an offering on a church altar. His fingers trailed gently over the vibrantly coloured petals of daffodils and poppies. His gaze lifted from them to look at her with pained regret.

"Words do not always express what the heart feels. I wanted to give you these flowers to remind you that even after the most bitter winter, spring does come. I didn't mean to hurt you as I did, Anne. I was anxious, overeager, too wrapped up in my own needs. I'm deeply sorry for the blind selfishness that drove me to pursue something that was always going to be destructive to you."

He paused, seemed to take stock of himself and the situation. His mouth curved, but not into a smile. Rather reminiscent of the light and sweetness they had both known so many years ago. "I always thought of you as spring. That was the time of year we spent together. I guess I want to think that spring can come again for you, with all its warm promise of something new and beautiful.''

Anne was both moved and deeply hurt by this farewell gesture. It was the hurt that rose uppermost and spilled from her tongue. "Lovely words, Thady, but that's all they are. Words!'' The need to challenge all he had done to her broke into voice, harsh and insistent. "Tell me why spring can't come for you?''

A bleak weariness, colourless and infinite, dragged over his face. "There are some things that no power on earth can change, Anne.'' His mouth twisted sardonically. "What I can do is strictly limited to what is within my power to do.''

"Like leaving me to my fate," Anne mocked. She felt a burst of bitter anger against this further emotion-tearing intrusion into her life. "Why pretend you care about what I feel, Thady? Why did you bother coming back to Australia? Why the hell did you bother coming here today?''

Suddenly she was on her feet and sweeping the flowers from her desk with a swing of her arm that sent Jenny's sketches fluttering after them. "I don't want your guilty conscience!''

"Anne!'' Jenny's shocked gasp and move forward was a jolting reminder of her presence.

"Stay out of this, Jenny," Anne commanded through clenched teeth. Some self-protective instinct urged she keep Jenny nearby, yet Anne could not bear any overt interference in this last confrontation.

"That's all this is, isn't it?'' she raged on at Thady, her amber eyes blazing in savage accusation. "I made you feel bad yesterday, and you didn't like it. So before you flew off out of *my* life, back to *your* life in London, you wanted to make yourself feel better and you wanted me to feel worse.''

His head jerked in an anguished negative, but he made no other move. His face had gone deadly pale but seemed to have tightened in its resolution. "No," he answered quietly. "What I feel doesn't matter and never has."

She couldn't bear the sadness and gentleness in his eyes. It accused her of not understanding him, and all her tortured emotions twisted into a desperate need to know the truth. "Did you ever care about me?"

"Yes."

"Tell me one thing you ever did that showed you really cared about me!"

"Anne…" Something dreadful warred across his face. He lifted a hand in appeal, dropped it, then half-turned away.

"You can't tell me one thing, can you? It's all been a pose to get what you want. Whatever that is. I don't understand you. I never have. I never will. I want to forget you, forget you ever existed." She gave a harsh laugh. "What a marvellous sense of freedom you must feel, Thady, that you can afford to fly around the world for a one-night stand!"

He spun to face her, his eyes searing hers with naked need. "I wanted to be with you. I wanted you to be with me." His voice shook with passion. Then his hands sliced a violent dismissal. "What I did was wrong. I know I was wrong. But don't say I haven't cared, Anne. I've always cared."

He saw her blank disbelief.

It goaded him into a further passionate declaration. "I gave you the career you wanted. It was the one dream that I could do something about."

She shook her head in fierce denial. "I got to where I am on my own. You had nothing to do with it, Thady. Nothing!"

"Contacts are everything in this business, Anne. You know that. Without—"

"Alex Korbett saw my production design for *Godspell*. He offered me a job because I had the kind of talent and skills he was looking for. He saw that for himself. It had nothing to do with you."

"What was Alex Korbett doing at a show put on by an amateur musical theatre group, Anne? Why do you imagine he was there to see your work, to see your talent, to see your skill?"

Anne froze. She remembered how she had thought it an amazing and incredible stroke of luck at the time. She had involved herself with amateur theatre ever since her school days, always on the production side of things. She had been very proud of her work on *Godspell*, and she had asked Thady to the opening night. He had been enthusiastic about it. It had been a wonderful night together.

It had also been their last night together. Although she hadn't known it then. She remembered how she had bubbled over with excitement because of the marvellous response from the audience. She remembered Thady looking at her in a different way, and she had thought it meant a breakthrough in their friendship, that he was seeing her more as an equal, that he wouldn't hold back from her any more.

She had been so hopelessly wrong. He did more than hold back. He left Australia without saying goodbye, without seeing her again.

"You told Alex Korbett about me before you went away?" she choked out.

"I pressed Alex to take you on as his assistant. I used all the influence I could bring to bear on him. I bribed him with a case of his favourite champagne to go and see your

Godspell. I offered to pay your wages for a trial period of a year.''

''You paid him?'' she cried in pained protest.

''Alex wasn't looking for an assistant, Anne. He didn't need one.''

It was all fixed, Anne thought dully. What she had achieved was worthless. The miracle that had started her in her career had been no miracle at all. Alex Korbett attending the last night of the show, coming backstage to find her, introducing himself, giving her his card, offering her a job as his assistant…everything arranged and paid for by Thady Riordan.

''So what you're telling me…all I've achieved is owing to your intervention on my behalf,'' she forced out, feeling so sick she could barely keep standing.

''No. You did it on your own merits, Anne. I merely gave you the opportunity.''

''How can I ever be sure of that now?''

''Because you've proved your talent over and over again. You were better than anyone could ever have anticipated. That was why Alex made a point of coming to see me when he was in London. It was simply to tell me all about you, what had happened to you, the exciting prospects he had held out for you. He also gave me back the money I'd paid him. And two cases of champagne.''

She felt numb all over. What had possessed Thady to do what he had done? ''I suppose…I should thank you.''

''It was the least I could do for you in the circumstances.''

Her eyes raked his in her naked need for the truth. ''A consolation prize for losing the lover I wanted?''

''Anne…'' He looked sick. ''It wouldn't have worked out. Not then.'' He grimaced. ''Not ever.''

"Then what was yesterday about, Thady? Getting something back for all I owed you?"

He shook his head tiredly. "If you want to believe that of me, then do so. But you need have no fear that you'll ever be asked for such *payment* again."

"The *final* goodbye," she muttered, more to herself than him.

"Yes," he affirmed, his voice a low, gravelly rasp. "I need to get on with writing again." He dragged in a deep breath and continued in a more controlled tone. "You asked why I bothered coming back to Australia. It was to see your production design for my play."

He drew an envelope from the inner breast pocket of his suit coat and laid it on the desk in front of Anne. "This is a fax of a contract drawn up by my solicitors in London. It came through early this morning. If you sign it as an interim measure until the original arrives, it will give you the right to the stage design of all future productions of my plays, no matter where they are performed in the world."

Anne felt the blood draining from her face as she stared at the envelope that promised to make her name in production design all around the world. Thady was not merely opening a door of opportunity, he was ensuring her career in a way that guaranteed success at a level she had never dreamed of.

Her mind ran over all the implications. Her heart screamed its protest at how inexorably she would be tied to Thady Riordan if she signed. He would always be part of her life, even though they might never meet again.

"I can't accept—"

"It's for my benefit, Anne, not yours," he argued softly. "Having seen what you can do, I don't want anyone else working on my plays."

"No. It's worth a small fortune. It's too much—"

"It's worth a small fortune to me to have my plays presented as you alone can present them. There's no favour involved in this. It's strictly a professional decision, Anne. I want the best. You are the best."

She dragged her gaze up to his and met only a steadfast resolve.

"You won't be dealing with me in any shape or form," he assured her. "My agent will handle all business details. As it happens, my next play is ready to go into production, so you'll need to be in London by the end of next week. I've written down everything you need to know once you get there. The contacts I've already set up for you—"

"Thady, you can't—"

"Yes, I can. It's done, Anne. There's an airline ticket for you in the envelope. Also the keys to a flat in Knightsbridge. The lease has over two years to run so there's no worry for you about where to stay."

"It's too much," she protested in painful confusion.

"You told me that the most important thing in your life is your career," he reminded her with relentless purpose. Then his voice softened. "Don't let what I did yesterday influence you against taking this up, Anne. There are no strings attached to it. The contract is watertight. Sign it. And show the theatre-going world what Annelise Tolliver can do."

Her eyes filled with tears as she looked at him with all the unfulfilled yearning in her soul. Pride didn't matter any more. He was making himself unreachable, and this was the last she would ever see of him. The green eyes with their dark hidden passions. The strong face that would always be stamped in her memory. The softness of the tumbling black curls. The tenderness she had known from him.

His lashes swept down, veiling whatever he was feeling as he reached into his pocket again and brought out a little box wrapped in gold paper. He laid it on top of the envelope.

"A small gift," he said huskily. "I hope, sometime in the future…years from now…you might look at something I gave you and remember me kindly."

His eyes seared hers before he turned and strode away from her. He was leaving. Leaving forever. And Anne's whole body reacted in violent protest. She had to speak, had to stop him.

"Thady, wait."

He paused. His back stiffened. He resumed walking away from her.

"Don't go," she pleaded.

He reached the foot of the staircase.

"Is it your need to write that makes you do these things to me?" she cried, grasping at any straw in her need to understand him.

He paused again, longer this time, his hands clenching and unclenching as he seemed to grope for an answer. "Yes," he said simply, barely audible.

"Are you then totally selfish, Thady Riordan?" she hurled at him, fighting his retreat from her every inch of the way.

His back was still turned to her. She saw his shoulders heave as he sucked in a deep breath. His hand curled around the newel post, knuckles gleaming white. "Yes. Totally selfish," he said harshly. "I have my destiny to fulfil, just as you have yours. It's best that you think of it that way."

"Don't tell me what's best for me!" Anne retorted fiercely. "You don't know what's best for me!"

He started up the stairs, ignoring her claim, not looking at her.

"Don't go," she begged. "Not yet."

His head turned. His eyes raked her face and body with a raw desire that made her flesh prickle with heat. "I could not repress my *sexual* feelings," he said bitterly. "You remind me all too earnestly that I'm the kind of man you don't want any part of."

"What if I do want what you want?" she answered recklessly.

"You don't, Anne. And I could not bear a repetition of yesterday."

She had no answer to that. The memory throbbed between them in all its bitter horror.

"I *must* go, Anne," Thady said quietly. "There is no more I can do for you."

There was not so much as a further fleeting glance from him as he moved swiftly up the stairs. She caught only a glimpse of grimly set features. Then he was gone. Having done all he could for her. Having made his final goodbye.

A convulsive shiver ran through Anne, followed by an unnerving attack of trembling. She sank onto her chair. She stared at the envelope and the little gold box on top of it. She reached out and touched them, wanting, needing to feel something of Thady in them. But they were cold and lifeless.

Tears welled in her eyes, and she did not have the strength to force them back or blink them away. She buried her face in her hands and wept, her heart pouring out its grief for all that had been taken beyond her reach.

CHAPTER SEVEN

A GENTLE TOUCH on her hair jerked Anne out of her heart-broken misery. She looked up to find Jenny standing beside her. Jenny, whose presence she had completely forgotten. The realisation that her younger sister had witnessed everything was another agonising truth to absorb. With an anguished moan she dropped her head back into her hands.

"Leave me, please," she sobbed. "I want to be alone."

Her sister's hand went on softly stroking, trying to impart loving comfort. "Anne, I can't leave you like this. Please…I want to help."

"Nothing can help." It was a cry of bottomless despair.

"Don't say that, Anne. I can't bear it. And I'm sure it can be made right."

Jenny's arm came around her shoulders, giving her a tight hug. They had never been a demonstrative family. They all knew what they felt but they rarely showed it. Somehow Jenny's demonstration of love and concern made Anne feel worse. She had always been the one to give love and consolation to her younger sisters. To have Jenny, the youngest of all, doing this for her only pointed out more clearly the hopelessness of her case.

"It can't be made right, Jenny," she choked out.

"Why not?"

"Because Thady wants what Tom Colby had with me. And I gave Tom Colby nothing but pain. I couldn't love him the way he wanted to be loved."

"But that was because you still loved Thady Riordan, Anne. Love is the most tearing, blinding, passionate emotion...."

"Thady doesn't want my love. He wants...only what he wants."

"No. He does want your love, Anne. It half-killed him to walk away from you."

"You don't understand."

"I do. Brian and I have had our fights, our disagreements. Everyone does."

"Not like this."

"Anne, you have to accept that the person you love isn't perfect. No-one is. You have to accept Thady as he is. I think you've tried to shut him out because he didn't fulfil your expectations when you wanted him to. You've made a habit of shutting us all out."

"I don't shut you out." She raised pained, tear-laden eyes. "If you ever needed me for anything..."

"You gave it to us," Jenny finished for her. "All of us. And we love you for it. But, Anne, that's not the same as letting us into *your* life. You let us think all that mattered to you was your career. But that's not true, is it?"

"Oh, Jenny! That's all there is for me. That's all I've got left."

"Anne, it's so obvious now," Jenny said softly, sadly. "*He's* the only man you ever loved. *He's* why you've never married. All these years of lonely heartache... You never gave a hint of it. You never let us help you."

Anne shook her head wearily. "There was no point."

"I suddenly feel we haven't known you. That you're a stranger."

"Nothing's changed." Anne released a deep sigh, mopped up her tears and lifted her head, looking at Jenny with bleak resignation. "Nothing is going to change. I'm a career woman. That *is* it, Jenny. That's all I've got."

Jenny looked at her with sympathy and deeply anxious concern. "Because of Thady."

Anne gave a harsh, mirthless laugh. "Without Thady, I'd never have got started." Dully she reached out and picked up the envelope he had left behind. "And now he's lifting me to the heights. All I have to do is sign his contract."

"I think Thady Riordan loves you, Anne."

The painful constriction in her chest seemed to tighten. "I don't know what he feels for me, Jenny. It's not what Brian feels for you."

"People are passionate because they care, Anne. Thady is passionate about you, and Brian is passionate about me. They both care for us very deeply."

"Thady cares about his writing. That's what he cares about most."

Jenny moved to take Anne's hand and press it hard, compelling her attention. Deep conviction was in her voice. "You're wrong, Anne. You didn't see his face when you asked if it was his writing that made him do what he has to you. I saw his face. I saw what was written on it. It was pure agony. He was lying to you, Anne."

"Why should he lie?" Anne shook her head in mocking dismissal of Jenny's contention. "He left me the same as he did before. Except this time he said goodbye. And he said he would never see me again."

"He didn't want to leave," Jenny retorted. "He made himself do it. He was lying about being totally selfish, too. I'm as sure of that as I have been of anything in my life. If he hadn't had his back turned to you, if you'd seen his face, Anne, you'd know that what I'm saying is true."

"Why? Why would he do such a thing?"

"I don't know. Perhaps..." Jenny frowned and shook her head. "That may be too fanciful."

"Tell me!"

"Have you ever thought he may be protecting you?"

"From what? What do I need protection from?"

"I'm not sure," Jenny said slowly. "Maybe..."

"Yes?"

Jenny searched her eyes anxiously. "Could it be that he's protecting you from something within himself? Something he knows he can't change, not even for you?"

The wrong man...some things no power on earth can change...

"But he could have tried to explain," Anne reasoned.

Why couldn't he have appealed to her understanding instead of making judgments? How was she supposed to overlook such a basic failure in communication? He didn't care enough about her. He couldn't. And yet why had he done all he'd done for her?

"He's not selfish, Anne," Jenny said, as though picking up on Anne's thoughts. "How can he be selfish when he cared enough to start you in your career? And this contract. You may be the best, but I bet he would have given it to you anyway."

Anne dragged in a deep breath, trying to relieve the awful tightness in her chest. She looked down the room to the miniature stage sets on the workbench. Thady's destiny. And hers. Tied together, but somehow always apart.

"Whatever Thady feels for me, Jenny, believe you me, it's not the kind of love that leads to marriage."

"I don't know. I can't answer that."

Anne heard the caring anguish in Jenny's voice, but there was no escaping the truth. "He wants sex with me."

"For God's sake, Anne! Is there something wrong with

that? Isn't it natural when two people feel deeply about each other?''

I wanted to be with you. I wanted you to be with me....

Thady's words haunted her. But for how long would he want that? He had said straight out that whatever they had together would ultimately be destructive to her. He believed that. He truly believed it was best for her that he stay right out of her life. Although he wasn't out of her life, and never would be, except in the physical sense. If she signed the contract it would bond them all the closer, even though she would never see him again.

''What happened yesterday?'' Jenny asked quietly. ''Or is that too intrusive a question?''

Anne turned to her, bitter ashes in her mouth. ''He gave me a proposition. I threw it back in his face. A proposition, Jenny, not a proposal. And he made it clear that that was all he would ever offer me.''

Jenny winced in sympathy, reached out and tenderly stroked Anne's hair from her face. ''He might change his mind if you give him another chance.''

Anne shook her head. ''It's not so simple, Jenny. You don't know how it was. And I could never explain it.''

''I don't know what went on between you and Thady yesterday, but I know what I saw today, Anne. That man cares for you. *Really* cares for you.''

Jenny stepped back and began slowly picking up the flowers and papers that were strewn across the floor. ''You can say it's none of my business,'' she continued quietly, ''but I want to see you happy, Anne. Like you used to be when you were my age. I don't want to see you eating your heart out. Anything would be better than that.''

''Jenny, I tried to stop him from leaving,'' Anne muttered defeatedly. ''He's made up his mind. There's no turning the clock back.''

"You can turn it forward."

"You don't know Thady. He retreats inside himself where no-one can reach him."

"Whatever barriers he's been putting up between you, I can tell you this—they were cracking all over the place this afternoon. He's like a dam, and that dam was about ready to burst."

Jenny straightened up, laid the papers and the flowers on the desk and eyed Anne with a very adult look of measured calculation. "What have you got to lose? You don't want any other man. If he's the only one for you, why not go to him and give him another chance? He's not leaving for London until tomorrow."

Tears blurred Anne's eyes again.

"Oh, Anne…" Jenny flung her arms around her and rubbed her cheek affectionately over Anne's bent head. "I want everything to be right for you. The way it is for me and Brian. It's not impossible, is it?"

Thady had already done what he believed was right for her. It was too late to turn that decision into something else. They had both acknowledged that yesterday. Thady had confirmed it beyond any doubt today. The final goodbye was *final*. If she went to him now, she'd be asking him to do something he felt was wrong.

The door chimes rang.

"That will be Brian," Jenny said.

Anne caught her hand as Jenny began to withdraw her arms. She pressed it with compelling urgency. "Please don't invite him in, Jenny. Leave with him. I'm not up to…to socialising."

"I could tell him to come back later."

"No. I don't want…" She twisted around to appeal to her sister. "Jenny, please don't talk about this to the family. I can bear it alone. I can't… I'd hate for them to know. I'd rather them think I have my—'' she forced a wobbly smile ''—my brilliant career.''

''If that's what you want, Anne.''

''Thank you, Jenny. I'll ring you on Monday night about the dresses.''

''It's not urgent. It's not important if...'' Her face reflected anxious concern. ''Will you consider what I said about Thady, Anne? I truly think he loves you. If you opened up and told him...''

''I'll think about it,'' Anne said dully, not wanting to invite further argument.

Jenny leaned down and kissed her cheek. ''Remember we love you,'' she murmured. ''You've always been special to me, Anne. Whatever you decide, that will be the right decision, and I'll always love you.''

Anne could make no reply. She blundered to her feet, blindly reaching out to embrace her little sister and hug her close.

The door chimes rang again.

She stroked Jenny's silky blonde hair, the baby of the family, the sweet natural one who had always taken it on trust that everybody loved her. ''Go,'' Anne whispered. ''Go and be happy with the man you love.''

Jenny drew back. They exchanged wobbly smiles. Anne watched her sister run up the stairs. Then she sank onto her chair.

In front of her on the desk were Thady's gifts—the little gold box, the envelope containing her future career, the keys to a flat in London and the massed array of spring flowers. She reached out and gently trailed her fingers over the soft fragrant petals. *The warm promise of something new and beautiful.*

But there were no promises from Thady.

Only offerings.

A gift so that she might remember him kindly.

A contract to further her career.

And whatever was meant by *sharing the same passions*.

Slowly Anne gathered up the flowers and carried them upstairs to the kitchen. She filled a plastic bucket with water, then set the flowers in it. Into every life some rain must fall, she thought. Rain to let the flowers grow.

She hoped the sun would shine on Jenny on her wedding day. For herself, it didn't matter so much anymore.

The thought came to her that she would rather have rain with Thady than all the sunshine in the world on her own. And who knew what flowers might grow in that rain? Brief. Ephemeral. But like so many of the transient things in life, those flowers could be the most beautiful of all. She could try keeping them alive. Why not? Any kind of life with him had to be better than the emotional winter she faced without him.

With her mind working feverishly over how best to change Thady's mind, Anne headed for the bathroom. She needed to take a shower. She needed to wash her hair, her beautiful hair....

CHAPTER EIGHT

ANNE KNOCKED on the door to Thady's suite at the Park Hyatt. Her knuckles echoed the resounding thud of her heart. In her other hand she held the envelope and the little gold box, ready for Thady to see that they remained unopened. She had her speech rehearsed. She was ready. But when her knock was not answered, the words were dispersed by fear.

She stared at the door, which remained shut to her. Was she locked out of Thady's life forever? Was she too late? Had he already left the hotel?

She knocked again. Harder. Longer. Louder.

The door opened.

He wore one of the thick white bathrobes the hotel supplied to guests. His face was half turned aside. Apparently he was expecting to admit a maid. His demeanour was one of complete disinterest with the world in general. Anne saw his body instantly stiffen at the sight of her. A tense wariness wiped the weariness from his face.

"May I come in?" She spoke the words out of conventional politeness. The door was open. Before he could think of saying anything or denying her entry, Anne brushed straight past him, putting him between her and the door, swiftly and decisively gaining the space she needed to feel safe inside his domain.

"I needed to see you again, Thady," she rushed on, talking fast to claim his attention. "There are a number of things about the contract I need to get straight with you."

She heard the door closing behind her. Her sense of relief at this initial acceptance was so intense she began to shake.

"What things, Anne?"

The terseness, even cynicism in his voice told her he wanted this over and done with as fast as possible. She took a deep breath, struggling for the control she needed to get through this ordeal with him, to convince him she meant what she said. Her heart had leapt into a chaotic rhythm. She forced her legs to walk a few more steps into the lounge area of the suite before she turned to face him.

He stood in the small passageway to the door, obviously intent on cutting this visit to the minimum necessities. The grim set of his face made him look older than his thirty-four years. The green eyes were narrowed to dark slits.

He did not look at the luxuriant fall of her honey-brown hair flowing softly over her shoulders. She might have been wearing rags for what little notice he took of her rich gold cashmere sweater and brown velvet slacks. He appeared totally unaware of the manner in which they clung sensually to all the feminine curves of her body. She had a sense of him deliberately blocking out her sexuality, reducing his vision to a narrow tunnel that saw only a problem to be solved and eliminated.

Anne fiercely repressed all the doubts and fears that tore at her resolution. This was the last chance, the only opportunity she would ever get. She had to seize it. She saw his gaze drop to the envelope and the little gold box she held out to him, saw him frown over the fact that neither had been opened.

"It's no good, Thady," she started softly. "I don't want to work on your plays without talking to you and seeing you. I need to see you and talk to you. I need to be with you.''

''No, you don't, Anne,'' he replied decisively. ''You can manage quite superbly without any input from me. This last production design you did—''

''Was sheer hell for me!'' she cut in, silencing him with her vehemence. ''It was a constant living reminder of what I didn't have. I don't want to have known you briefly. I don't want to remember you kindly. I *need* to have you in my life. I want to be with you. I want to know you. And taking these things from you—''

She tossed his contract and gift onto the nearest armchair. ''I can't do it. They'd only make the wanting worse. Because they'd keep reminding me of all I don't have. I *need* you, Thady.''

For a moment there was stunned disbelief on his face.

''Ever since you left me seven years ago, my life has been empty,'' Anne continued, her voice trembling with the force of her emotion. ''I filled it with the career you gave me. I don't know if you've ever met Tom Colby. He's like you in many superficial ways. I fooled myself into thinking I was in love with him. Simply because you weren't there, Thady.''

''No.'' It was little more than a breath of denial coming from lips that had gone bone dry.

Tears sprang into her eyes. Words kept spilling from her lips. ''I caused Tom pain through no fault of his own. He couldn't fill your shoes. I caused myself pain. Perhaps I even caused you pain. I'm sorry. Sorry for everything I did.''

''Anne.'' He lifted his hand in some tortured appeal. A haunted look came into his eyes. ''For God's sake! Say that isn't true.''

''You don't have to love me, Thady,'' she rushed on,

hearing the desperation creeping into her voice. She was unable to suppress it. "As long as you care a little about me. And I'm not just a woman you need to use occasionally."

"God, no! No!" He shook his head in anguished protest at the revelations that were pouring from her. "Don't say it was because of me. I tried... I left before it went too far."

"What's too far, Thady?"

"Nothing happened between us."

"Too much had happened. Too much that was unforgettable to me."

"No!" His hand sliced the air as though he was warding off what she was pressing on him. "I can still hurt you, Anne. It's hard enough that I can't be what you want me to be."

"I don't want you to be anything but what you are, Thady. I swear that I'll never try to change what you are," Anne pleaded, afraid of losing this encounter, afraid of losing him. "Please. Can't we share things together like we used to?"

He sent a searing look over her body as his mouth twisted into a savage mockery of what she was suggesting.

"I meant for us to be lovers, as well," she added, urgently correcting what she had just said. "I meant it to be that way seven years ago, and I mean it now."

He slowly lifted his gaze to hers, challenging her desire with the rawness of reality. "You think I could take you after yesterday? That I'm an animal with no conscience at all about hurting you, Anne?"

"I want you to take me," she answered simply. "That's part of being in love. It's only natural. I want to share everything that is possible between us, Thady. As man and woman. As lovers. As friends. As professionals working together for the same purpose. To create things. To achieve. Couldn't we try that, Thady?''

He stared at her as though he were seeing her for the first time. His chest rose and fell quickly as though he needed all the oxygen he could get to clear his mind, to see more clearly.

''And yesterday?'' he asked hoarsely.

''I was expressing my hurt, my grief, my anger because you left me and didn't seem to care.''

He was deciding whether it was *right* or not, Anne thought with a surge of panic. It drove her to move towards him. She held out her hands to him, appealing, offering, inviting.

''You showed me you did care this afternoon, Thady. If you care for me, please don't shut me out. I *need* you. I'm so lonely…so desperate. I *need* you so much.''

Whatever thoughts Thady Riordan had were obliterated by that last despairing cry. His arms opened to accept her, to take her into his embrace. She had said the words that overrode everything else in his life. He could not deny her need.

CHAPTER NINE

RELIEF FLOODED THROUGH Anne as Thady enfolded her in his arms. His body emanated strength. It promised that for however long she was with him like this, there would be no loneliness.

She pressed closer, resting her head against the angle of his neck and shoulder. She listened to the pulsing thud of his heart. His arms tightened around her. His breathing seemed to intensify, becoming deeper, faster. His head brushed against her hair, her beautiful hair, and she felt the warmth of his breath as he trailed his lips over it.

"I'm home," she whispered.

"Yes," he replied huskily.

His tongue traced the outer rim of her ear. He moved one arm down to cement her body against his, then increased the intimacy of their closeness by straddling his legs against her thighs, holding her within the power of his strong masculinity.

"There's no going back from here, Anne."

"I know."

He planted deep, passionate kisses on her neck. She slid a hand up to the open V of his bathrobe, pushed the heavy cloth aside. His flesh was firm and smooth and hot. His shoulder bunched with tense muscle. His hair was a soft tangle of silk. She pressed her lips to the throbbing artery in his throat.

He made a low, guttural sound. A hand swiftly curled

around her chin, tilting her head back. His mouth was on hers, his lips moving quickly, persuasively, possessively over hers, pressing for all she would give him.

She surrendered to the craving she felt in every ounce of his body, the rising tension and excitement. As she welcomed the deepening of his kiss, she moved her arms around the top of his shoulders, caressing his neck, revelling in the joy of loving freely, with Thady wanting her, Thady loving her.

She felt the thickness and hardness of his arousal and moved her body sensuously, the seductive call and response of lover to lover. Her head was spinning from lack of air, but that felt right, too, not belonging to herself anymore, whirling into sensation.

Thady's mouth broke away from hers, taking deep, hoarse breaths, his chest heaving. She could feel the rigidity of the muscles in his neck and shoulders, in his stomach and thighs. He picked her up in his arms.

He walked around the suite, carrying her with him, pausing when it suited his purpose. "Turn out the light," he softly commanded at each stop. And while she extended her arm to the switch he indicated with a nod of his head, he kissed her, completely and passionately, sometimes moving straight to the next light switch, sometimes lingering to increase the sensuality of their togetherness.

He came to the last glowing lamp upon the table near the window. "Turn out the light." And while his mouth found hers, her arm extended sightlessly to do what she was bid.

She found the button and pressed it. Darkness cloaked them in a private, intensely intimate world. She thought Thady would take her to the bed, but he didn't. He set her on her feet, not releasing her from the intimacy of the kiss.

He straightened up with her, perfectly balanced, helping her to balance with his strength.

Their bodies came together and she felt him tremble, perhaps from exertion or from having his control overcome by unbearable excitement, or both. She clung more tightly to him, running her hands urgently over his body, trying to soothe his tremors. A moan of longing came from his throat. He kissed her with a devouring passion that seemed only to increase the spasms of rippling muscles.

It was the most wonderful thing Anne had ever experienced. She broke away from the pressure of his need, gasping out a plea for his sake. "I want you now, Thady. I want you now."

It seemed to affect him, to steady him. "No." He dragged in a deep breath, shook his head. He stepped aside, reached out for something. Behind her the curtains swished open. "I want you to have everything, Anne," he said softly. "Everything I *can* give you."

He turned her to face the beautiful vista of the harbour, the lights of the city, the shimmering reflections of the water. His arms slid around her waist, gently pulling her against him. He had discarded the bathrobe, and the feel of his warm nakedness burnt through her clothes, exciting a sexual awareness that quivered inward.

"The mystery of the night," he murmured, his mouth grazing erotically over her hair. "So much that is ephemeral, but behind it, the hidden depths of eternity stretching out to the end of time. And we stand here together, live warmth, defying the cold loneliness of all the dark spaces." His hands glided up to caress the soft swell of her breasts. "Earth has nothing more beautiful to offer."

Anne knew intuitively that he didn't mean the night. He meant the sharing, she with him, he with her.

He gathered up the cashmere sweater and the silk cam-

isole she had worn underneath it. She swayed as he lifted
the garments over her head and dropped them on the floor.
He caught her to him, his hands taking total possession of
her breasts as he pressed her bared back to the muscled
breadth of his chest, naked skin to skin, hot, vibrant.

Instinctively Anne lifted her hands to cover his, holding
them in place over her heart as she leaned her head to one
side, then the other, revelling in the passionate rain of
Thady's kisses down her neck and across her shoulders, in
the sensuous rub of his aroused state against the soft curves
of her bottom. Then his hands slid from under hers,
dropped to the fastening of her velvet slacks. He snapped
it open, undid the zipper. With a smooth action that collected her panties as well, he eased the fabric over her hips,
down her thighs, fingers softly stroking the material down.

She stepped out of her shoes, lifted her feet free of the
clothes and stood trembling with anticipation as Thady
trailed feather-light fingers up her legs, behind her knees,
the soft inner flesh of her thighs, the erogenous zones below
her hipbones. Her stomach contracted in spasms of excitement as she felt him straighten up behind her.

Again his arms encircled her, pulling her back against
him, but the intimacy of his embrace was immeasurably
heightened as she felt the hardness of his manhood slide
between her thighs, stirring a range of sensations that
flooded through her in rippling waves.

There was something intensely primeval in facing the
night like that, totally naked, locked in a world of their
own, yet looking out at the shifting waves of the harbour,
the lights that glowed for other people, the stars of the
universe, the darkness beyond. Wrapped within the shelter
of Thady's arms, anchored between his legs, rocking to the
rhythm of his exquisite stroking.

Anne wanted to see his face, his eyes. It wasn't enough

to feel him with her. She needed to know. An image flashed into her mind of Eve reaching for the apple from the Tree of Knowledge, the serpent coiled there ready to strike. It was wrong to question, she told herself. She had to accept. That was what she had said to Thady, that she would accept whatever he was. No turning back from here.

But the brief perturbation of mind had made her heart beat faster. He felt it. As though he knew what she wanted he withdrew from her, turned her around, held her away from him so they could gaze upon each other. In the dim light thrown from beyond the window she could see the brooding intentness with which he looked at her, as though measuring her meaning to him.

"Thady..." His name broke from her lips in a whisper of yearning.

"It's all right," he assured her huskily. "I want the magic of this moment stored in my memory forever. The reality of you as a woman."

He began touching her with mesmerising softness, running his fingertips over her face, down her throat, across her shoulders, tracing the line of her arms to her fingertips, then up again to begin another journey of discovery. Her skin leapt with sensitivity, but the thrill of his touch held her totally captivated. He caressed every inch of her body, moving her to his will.

Only when he bent to kiss the tips of her breasts was the spell he had cast on her broken enough for her to lift her arms and touch him. It seemed right, imperative, to cradle his head there, to make him feel as precious to her as he had made her feel to him. Yet there was a tingling weakness in her arms that robbed her of any power to keep him in her hold. Her fingers slid through the thick curls of his hair as he lowered his head to trail warm kisses over her stomach.

Then he was kneeling in front of her, pleasuring with his touch, his tongue, his lips, searching out and drawing on the very essence of her femininity. Never in her life had Anne imagined anything like this. She arched against the glass of the window as his mouth moved from side to side, his tongue sometimes darting, sometimes caressing, sometimes evoking almost violent sensations. She could bear no more. The need for some final, more complete appeasement racked her entire body. Her fingers raked through his hair, tugging, pulling him up to her in blind, frantic urgency.

He rose, his manhood surging into her with a vibrant pulsation that made her knees collapse. He caught her to him, lifting her, supporting her as he filled her with his own engorged need, and their bodies became one, flesh to flesh in an orgasmic joining that went far, far beyond any simple togetherness.

Somehow Anne found the strength to lock her legs around him as he carried her to the bed. The movement was exquisitely sensational. The rapid heaving of his chest against her breasts created another delicious rhythm of sensitivity. Then the sight of him leaning over her as he knelt on the bed, arranging pillows for her, positioning her to his need, so dominantly powerful in cradling her body against his.

She could feel herself opening further and further to him, welcoming, flowing around him, releasing him only to draw him into more and more sublime intimacy. She felt his muscles spasm, out of control, heard him cry out in agonised pleasure as the ultimate tension of climax gripped him. His whole body convulsed at the final release of all he had held back in giving everything he could to her, but this gift of himself provided the greatest fulfilment.

A sweet flood of warmth permeated Anne's entire body, and even when Thady took her with him to lie on their sides, they stayed locked together, and the flood rolled on and on in rippling waves. It was so beautiful she wanted to keep capturing it, prolonging it. Instinctively she arched away to an angle that allowed her to move in a voluptuous roll around their togetherness.

Her body hummed to an exquisite sexuality that Thady played on, stroking her, fondling her breasts, shaping them to his mouth, drawing on them with a hard sucking that had her writhing with pleasure. Somehow he knew what she wanted, what she needed, intuitively accommodating her every movement, sliding his body against hers, inciting the continuation of intense sensation.

She felt him grow hard again, filling her with the throb of his wanting for more. He pulled her on top of him, his hands feasting on her womanly curves, his mouth claiming her breasts. Anne was filled with a wild need to take him, possess him, submerge herself in nothing but pure woman instinct, pleasuring herself and the man she loved.

If it was madness, it was a madness Thady shared with her and fed to the extremes of experience, leading her to other positions, encouraging and inciting her to feel all there was to feel in the physical intimacies they could take with each other. There were no inhibitions, nothing that was forbidden.

It was as though they were driven to know, to have, to take all they had missed out on in the years apart, as though they only had tonight and there was no tomorrow. The sense of wanting everything now was utterly compelling. There were no questions. Only responses. Every response was a passionate yes, a sensual, sighing, exultant, triumphant, soothing, satisfying yes, and ultimately an exhausted yes.

They lay in each other's arms, Thady slowly caressing away the aching inner glow of so much sustained excitement, soothing her into blissful relaxation. Then they slept, stirred and aroused the desire to make love again, to live once more in each other, and again their bodies tuned to a harmony that neither wanted to end.

There were times when Anne woke and wondered if this was a dream, but she had only to touch Thady and she was once more submerged in the warm and wonderful reality of him.

They did not talk. Implicit in every kiss and caress was an acceptance of each other that transcended words, and that acceptance erased all the loneliness they had known.

For now.

And that was all that mattered throughout this night of sharing.

CHAPTER TEN

ANNE WOKE TO LIGHT. The early morning sun was streaking the horizon with fingers of pink and gold. The water of the harbour was a pale glitter waiting for the deep azure blue of the day sky to soak in its colour.

Anne didn't feel tired, although she should have. The broken and intermittent night of sleep should have left her feeling exhausted; instead she felt more vibrantly alive than anytime in her life.

Thady lay behind her, one arm serving as a pillow for her head, the other holding her close to him, his hand resting lightly on her breast. She wriggled her toes against the top of his feet, felt his leg slide sensually over her own, rubbing against the softness of her thighs.

She felt Thady stir, knew that he was awake beside her, looking through the window at what was undoubtedly one of the most beautiful vistas in the world.

"A new day," she murmured, more to herself than to him.

His hand curled possessively around her breast and his leg trapped hers more firmly, his body instinctively asserting its hold on her as he answered, "A new life."

The past was done with, Anne thought exultantly. This *was* the beginning of a new life for them. Together. "What are you going to do today, Thady?" she asked, smiling, knowing what his reply would be.

He didn't answer straight away, but that didn't fray

Anne's confidence. The way he was holding her was answer enough that he had no intention of letting her go anywhere without him. She snuggled her bottom and back
more firmly against him, revelling in the security that his
strong possessiveness imparted.

She thought of all that had happened in the past nine
hours. Until last night, her experience of lovemaking was
extremely limited. She had thought of it mainly as two
bodies coming together, driven by biological urges. That
was how she had felt it to be with Tom Colby. Now she
understood that making love was an art form of intimacy
and bonding and sharing, an intimacy so deep that once
experienced would never let people pull apart.

"Today," said Thady, "I'm cancelling my flight to London. I'll wait and help you get ready to leave with me.
We'll go together. If that suits you."

Anne's smile grew more serene. She had known it
couldn't be any other way. Not after last night. "I couldn't
think of anything better," she said.

"Do you feel hungry?"

"Ravenous."

"I'll order breakfast."

He rolled away from her to pick up the telephone. Anne
turned, compelled to keep him in sight, in touch. She ran
her hand lightly over the firm muscles of his shoulders and
back. He had a beautiful physique. She loved the lines of
his taut, cheeky bottom. Somehow it was the perfect contrast to the strength of his upper body and the virile power
of his thighs.

She drew tantalising little patterns with her fingertips,
mischievously enjoying Thady's reactions as he tried to
give the breakfast order.

The receiver crashed down. Thady spun to Anne, caught
her hands and pinned them down, leaning over her, playing

the role of dominant male. Except that the green eyes were dancing with pleasure from her teasing.

"You are a very wicked woman," he declared, his voice unashamedly lacking in censure.

"Let he who is free from defects, cast the first stone," she retorted archly.

He laughed, his whole face illuminated with inner joy. Anne had always thought him handsome, but in that moment it seemed to her that Thady Riordan had to be the most beautiful man in the world. She felt her heart turn over.

"I think I need a shave," he said, releasing one of her hands to feel the stubble around his jaw. "Yes, definitely a shave." The green eyes twinkled with sheer devilment as his mouth moved into a tantalising curve. "I wouldn't want to put you off because I wasn't as perfect for you as I can possibly be."

He bounded off the bed and strode across the room to where he had dropped his bathrobe the night before. Anne hitched herself up on the pillows to watch him. He moved with an arrogant grace that reminded her very forcefully of how he had orchestrated all that had happened from the time he had first accepted what she wanted with him.

For one stomach-churning moment Anne wondered how many women had known him like this. Then she determinedly squashed the thought. He had told her all those other women had been meaningless to him. He had come back to Australia for her because she was special to him. He cared about her. So this was different. They were lovers in the true sense of the word. After last night, it couldn't be anything else.

He picked up the bathrobe and pulled it on. He gathered up her clothes from the floor near the window. He was turning toward her when something made him pause. She saw him frown at one of the armchairs. Then he leaned over and picked up the little gold box she had tossed away as something she didn't want from him.

"You didn't open my gift to you." He brought it to her, an indulgent smile on his lips, a sparkle of anticipation in his eyes. "You have no excuse not to accept it now."

She flashed him a smile of courteous curiosity and started pulling apart the fancy ribbon bow, teasing Thady with a show of nonchalance. She would, of course, express delight and surprise and wonder at his marvellous gift when she got to it. But in reality, whatever the gift was, it was irrelevant now. Thady had given himself to her. That was the only gift that was important.

She unwrapped the gold paper and found a black velvet box. Jewellery, she thought. Men always gave jewellery to their women. It was probably part of their genetic pattern. Still maintaining an outward air of nonchalance, Anne sprang the catch and opened the lid.

She froze with shock when she saw what lay within. Into her stunned mind slid Thady's words of yesterday. *Years from now you might look at something I gave you and remember me kindly.*

Her heart clenched painfully at the cruelty of his kindness. Not that she thought Thady meant to be cruel, but such a gift made certain that the giver would be totally unforgettable. Such a gift would keep the memory of him alive forever. Impossible for any other man of Anne's acquaintance to match it.

She managed to tear her eyes from what had to be worth a king's ransom. There was something almost obscene about the extravagance of this gesture from him. It had to be wrong. Grossly wrong. She swung her head violently from side to side. "No, Thady. It's too much. You shouldn't have done this."

He sat down beside her. He cupped her face in his hands to still her nervous agitation. The green eyes bored through the emotional confusion in hers, blazing their own conviction of what was right to him and searing away any need to object to his generosity.

"I want to see them on you, Anne. I want to see if they suit you. I had them specially designed for you at De Mestres in Brussels. Please put them on."

Specially designed for her before he came back to Australia to press his claim on her. Was this how he handled his relationships with women, buying them designer jewellery beforehand? Anne swallowed to clear the tightness from her throat. She fought to keep the pain out of her eyes as she questioned his intentions.

"You meant to use them? To persuade me?"

"No." He frowned and shook his head in decisive denial. "They were for you. No matter what happened between us."

He had already proved that, Anne reminded herself. Yet her heart still recoiled from accepting them as she stared down at the perfectly matched diamond earrings. They were designed as small flowers, yet the diamonds in the petals were larger than the diamond in Jenny's engagement ring, and the centre stone of each earring was far larger than any she had ever seen, utterly dazzling in their clarity and brilliance.

It was the kind of gift that a man gave to a highly prized mistress, and she would have given anything for the box to have contained a simple little ring that promised a lifelong commitment. Despite having accepted that their relationship was not to be on those terms, it still hurt to think that Thady would never ask her to be his wife. All the more so after last night. Yet she had promised not to try to change the kind of man he was.

"Don't you like them?" Thady asked, concern and disappointment threading through the soft caring in his voice.

"Of course I do. Who wouldn't? They're the most fabulous earrings I've ever seen," Anne replied truthfully, yet still she didn't want to accept them.

"Then please put them on, Anne."

Denying him this would only stir rejection between them, Anne argued to herself. The desire to please him, to be in harmony with him again overrode her deep-seated reservations. She lay the box on the bed and with nervously fumbling fingers removed the gold studs she had put in her earlobes yesterday. She set them on the bedside table, then turned her attention to Thady's gift, conscious of him watching and waiting for her to complete his bidding.

She forced herself to meet his eyes as she fastened first one, then the other earring to her lobes. She saw twinkling anticipation glow into intense satisfaction when she finally lowered her hands. His gaze roved slowly over her face, down her throat to the tangled mass of her hair falling over her shoulders, then to her breasts still bared for his pleasure.

Anne felt her nipples stiffen. She couldn't help it. What Thady was thinking was clearly written on his face: *My woman.* While into her mind crept the awful thought, *Bought and paid for.*

"You look so beautiful," he murmured huskily.

She forced a bright smile. "I'm glad you think so."

He laughed, his face aglow with happy satisfaction. "Come. I'll show you," he said, rising to his feet and taking her hands to pull her up with him.

He led her to a mirror and stood behind her, trailing his fingers through her hair to fan it out away from her ears. The diamond flowers flashed with a myriad facets of glittering light, making her look a very expensive and classy lady, even in her naked and unkempt state.

"They're perfect for you," Thady said in decisive triumph. "And you enhance them."

The material and unimportant things in life, Anne thought, and felt relief when a knock on the door saved her from having to find an appropriate answer.

"That will be breakfast," Thady said, turning away to open the door. "There's another robe in the bathroom."

Anne took temporary refuge in the bathroom, suddenly hating the situation she was in. It was not only the suite's butler coming in, seeing that Thady Riordan had a woman with him. The diamond earrings somehow made the whole scene unsavoury. They seemed to scream that she and Thady were not equal lovers.

She could accept that there was to be no marriage, but she couldn't accept him giving her more than she could give him. It had to be a complementary relationship, with respect on both sides. She couldn't bear it to be any other way.

Anne washed and tidied up her appearance as best she could, wishing she could tear off the diamonds but knowing she couldn't yet. It would raise questions she didn't want to answer. Later on she could say they didn't suit the clothes she had to put on to leave the hotel.

Other excuses ran through her mind. They were to be reserved for a special occasion. She didn't know what that occasion would be, but she knew intuitively that if it didn't arise, she would never wear the diamond flowers again. Thady might feel right about them, but she didn't, and while she didn't want to hurt Thady by rejecting the gift he had specially chosen for her, until she could feel right about it, the earrings would remain in the black velvet box.

Breakfast was all set out for her when she emerged from the bathroom. The butler had been dismissed and Thady obviously took pleasure in seeing that Anne was served with everything she wanted. It was easy to relax and enjoy their new togetherness. Their awareness of each other seemed to sharpen their appetites, making everything taste better than it ever had before.

They discussed how to settle Anne's commitments in Australia. There was packing to be done, the terrace house to be put into the hands of an agent for subletting, personal effects to be put into storage or left with her mother or Jenny.

Apart from settling her own business, Anne also had to organise the dressmaking for Jenny's wedding before she left. A promise was a promise, and Anne was not about to let her youngest sister down.

There were also telephone calls to be made, informing people of her departure from the country, not only to business connections, but family and friends. All in all, Anne figured she could be ready to leave by the end of the week.

In that calculation she completely underestimated the driving force that Thady brought to bear on the situation. Having taken on a new life, he lived it to the full, driven by a seemingly inexhaustable passion to eke the most out of every moment. Not only was he an exciting, creative and inventive lover, he also threw himself into being totally supportive and caring of Anne's needs. It took only three days to finalise all her preparations for her departure to England with Thady.

So accustomed was she to doing everything for herself, Anne felt oddly swamped by Thady's constant attention and consideration for her. Their relationship was so different from what she had experienced with Tom Colby. Far more intense, far more intimate.

She had the feeling of not being herself any more. She learnt an entirely new appreciation of the word "couple." She didn't move or think or feel without Thady being an inextricable part of the moving and thinking and feeling. It both exhilarated and frightened her. Having had nothing from him for so long, it now seemed that so much couldn't possibly last.

This underlying fear made her cautious in her conversation with Jenny when they went to the dressmaker with the designs for the wedding.

"Being with Thady Riordan is right for you, isn't it, Anne?" Jenny pressed, her bright brown eyes dancing with pleasure. "You're positively glowing, so it has to be right."

"For the present," Anne conceded. "But since I don't know how the future will work out with Thady, I'd prefer the rest of the family to view my going to England as a career move. Nothing more, Jenny."

This warning evoked a more worried look. "I hope I didn't... He *will* marry you when he gets used to the idea, won't he, Anne?"

"Jenny, it's my life. My decision," Anne assured her gently. "Whatever happens is not your responsibility. I just don't want Mum reading something more than there is into the situation. You know how she goes on and on about getting married."

"You can't hide it forever, Anne. Besides, I bet it's only a matter of time before Thady decides he wants you as his wife," Jenny declared with all the confidence of her youth and experience. "With you doing the production design for his plays, the two of you have to be perfect for each other."

It felt that way, Anne thought, but although Thady's actions and his manner towards her spoke of a deep and compelling need for her, he hadn't once spoken of love.

Jenny, however, held to her own opinion about how matters stood. When she drove Anne to the terrace house in Paddington where Thady was organising the packing of her reference books, she made her stand on the point of family.

"I'll be dreadfully disappointed if Anne can't make it to my wedding," she informed Thady, using her big eyes to their best imploring effect. "It's just before Christmas, you know."

"Yes. Anne told me," Thady said quietly.

"You must take a break for Christmas," Jenny prompted.

"Always." For a moment there was something dark and haunted in the deep green eyes. Then he gave Jenny an indulgent smile. "Don't worry, Jenny. I'll make sure that Anne comes home for your wedding. And for Christmas."

Jenny threw Anne a triumphant grin as though that settled the family question for good and all.

Anne was not quite so certain, but she decided not to question what the brief glimpse of pain in Thady's eyes had meant. She imagined that past Christmases had been times of intense loneliness for him, and she silently vowed that this coming Christmas would be very different for him if she had anything to do with it.

The moment the front door closed on her sister, Thady swept Anne into his arms and kissed her with a storming passion that expressed an urgent need to affirm what they had together—or a need to blot out something else. They ended up making love amidst the packing cases, and the wildly erotic excitement of that coupling pushed every other thought out of Anne's mind for some considerable time. It was much later that she wondered whether it had been the talk of a wedding or Christmas that had stirred Thady into taking her as he had.

There was so much to learn about him, yet some intuitive sense warned her that she would only raise barriers between them if she tried probing into the hidden depths of Thady Riordan. Their sharing was restricted to the immediate. And the future. She could only hope that would eventually change as their relationship forged a deeper confidence between them.

Perhaps it was the coward's way out, but Anne employed the telephone to communicate her news and make her farewells to her mother and her two other sisters before departing for England. All of them complained about not having the chance to see her before she went. Anne insisted there was no time and she would see them all at Jenny's wedding.

The truth was she did not want her relationship with Thady subjected to her family's curiosity. It was far too new and private. She would write to them from London and gently lead into her real position with him. Not that she expected her mother to ever approve of an unconventional living arrangement, but the ground had to be prepared for Thady's eventual appearance at her side. She hoped that by giving her mother time to get used to the idea, Leonie Tolliver might come to accept it gracefully.

Anne realised she wasn't quite used to the idea herself, particularly when they arrived at Mascot Airport on Thursday morning and Thady went about the business of booking their luggage onto their flight to London, automatically coupling her with himself.

She had no regrets about putting her life and well-being into his hands, but she was nervously conscious of having burnt all her bridges behind her when they went through the last gate to board the Qantas Boeing jet. A steward settled them into their first-class seats and served them glasses of champagne. Thady tipped his glass to hers in a private toast, and his smile settled some of the flutters in her stomach.

This is like being married and going off on a honeymoon, Anne thought. Women throughout all of history have faced this situation. They fall in love, then go off with their men to start a different life and make a family of their own together. There was nothing new in what she was doing. It was exciting, challenging and no cause at all for the absurd well of tears that was pricking at her eyes. She sipped her champagne, determined to face her future with Thady in a happy frame of mind.

"Miss Tolliver, Mr. Riordan, can I refill your glasses?"

The steward hovered over them, not realising he had spoken the ultimate truth. Annelise Tolliver was not married. She was Thady Riordan's new live-in lover. She would never be married to him. He had made that perfectly clear. The photo of her wedding day would never appear on her mother's mantel along with her other sisters'. She would never have a family.

Anne hurriedly repressed these defeatist thoughts. She had given Thady her word that she would not try to change him, but that didn't mean he could not change himself. He had never been with her before. Not like this. Not with such wonderfully exclusive togetherness.

The jet engines began to thrum. The huge plane taxied into position on the runway for take off. Thady smiled at her and took her hand in his, squeezing it gently as they were lifted into the air en route to the other side of the world.

His eyes warmly reflected her thoughts—the start of a new life. Anne privately added another—the end of loneliness.

CHAPTER ELEVEN

LONDON SURPRISED ANNE when they arrived twenty-two hours later feeling tired and rather ragged. The city was more squat than she had imagined. She quickly realised its charm and character lay in its time-honoured and traditional architecture. Faceless skyscrapers had no historical soul.

The day was bitterly cold and grey. Soft intermittent showers followed their taxi all the way from Heathrow to Knightsbridge. If this was autumn in England, what was winter going to be like? Certainly she would need to buy much warmer clothes.

The taxi came to a halt in front of an impressive brick building, four storeys high and featuring lots of lovely bay windows. Whenever the sun did shine in London, Anne imagined it streaming through them, and she felt her heart lighten at making her home here. Their luggage was transferred to a central lift, and Thady pressed the button for the top floor.

The lift opened to what seemed like a private foyer, since only one double set of doors led off from it. Anne threw an inquiring look at Thady, who was busily emptying the lift of bags and suitcases.

"Use the key I gave you," he instructed matter-of-factly.

"This flat takes up the whole floor?" she asked.

"Yes."

Anne unlocked the door with an odd feeling of trepidation, aware that such a spacious flat had to cost the earth as it was situated in virtually the centre of London. She realised the moment she set foot inside that it was very definitely someone's home. Someone's extremely luxurious home.

Thady's possession of the key he had given her meant he had access to it. Did it belong to a friend who had gone abroad for two years? Certainly there was a great deal of trust involved, since there had been no attempt to store the personal possessions that gave the place its character.

"How did this flat come to be available to you, Thady?" Anne asked wonderingly.

She was so busy taking in the features of the huge living room that she didn't immediately notice Thady's lack of reply. Music obviously played a large part in the owner's life, she thought. A highly polished black grand piano graced one corner. At the far end of the room stood two tall black speakers for whatever sound system was stored in a massive wall unit of glassed bookcases and closed cupboards.

The carpet was a deep maroon. Black leather sofas were grouped around a large square marble coffee table. The marble had a rose hue but was strongly veined in grey and black. There were curious pieces of abstract sculpture that somehow emitted an invitation to touch and feel. The paintings on the walls were abstracts, as well, but they suggested a far more complex visual experience, layers and layers of brooding meaning.

As the mood of the room seeped into Anne, pressing an awareness of sensuality and dark passions and lonely pleasures, she had no need for Thady to answer her question. She spun around to face him and found him watching her, waiting to evaluate her response to this extension of himself.

"This is *your* home," she said quietly.

"I've lived here for some years," he subtly corrected her. His mouth took on a wry curve. "I would have removed my personal effects before you came, Anne. I can easily do so if and when you prefer not to live with me."

"Why?" she asked, her eyes challenging the apparent carelessness behind his words. She lifted her hands in helpless bewilderment. "Why give up all this to let me stay?"

He shrugged. "You need a base in London. I don't."

"But where would you have gone if I'd taken up what you offered me?"

"Away from here. Ireland. America. It wouldn't have mattered. When I'm writing there is nothing else that exists for me."

Anne felt a chill run down her spine. Would he shut her out when he began to write again? What kind of life together would they have then?

"Having you makes everything different, Anne," he said softly.

He moved forward and wrapped her in his arms. His warm hands took the chill away. His warm mouth claimed hers with a passion that suggested he was well content to lose himself in her, wanting nothing else to exist but the intense physical and emotional intimacy that came with making love together.

The unpacking was left until later.

Thady's bedroom was done in shades of green, a rich room of silk and satin and velvet with darkly gleaming rosewood furniture. The ensuite bathroom was equally luxurious, featuring a Jacuzzi set in green onyx and gold fitments adorning every other convenience. Anne became very familiar with both rooms during her first weekend in London. Thady definitely had his own unique ideas about how best to overcome jet lag. Apart from which, the weather was not conducive to sightseeing.

There was plenty of food in the well-appointed kitchen, and they made snacks for themselves whenever they felt hungry. Thady explained that a housekeeper came in weekdays to look after day-to-day maintenance.

He designated one of the spare bedrooms for Anne to use as a workroom. She could use a second bedroom, as well, if she needed more space.

He had turned another room into a study for himself. It was there that Anne secluded herself to read his new play while Thady listened to music in the living room. Somehow it did not surprise her when she heard Wagner's opera *Götterdämmerung* being played. The dark, sweeping grandeur of "The Twilight of the Gods" was very much in keeping with the mood of what Thady had written.

It was a strong drama, weaving inexorably towards a conflagration of passions that would ignite any theatre. Thady had titled it *The Long Cold Winter,* but it was far from cold. Each scene throbbed with an underlying sexual tension that gradually drew every character out of their ego-image roles, finally building to a climax of explosive power that shattered every image and revealed the people underneath in all their lonely vulnerability.

It was undoubtedly the most gripping play Thady had written so far, and it was the simmering sexual element that made it so. Anne knew that what Thady wrote reflected his own inner world. She could not help wondering if he had accepted her need for him because of his desire for the release and full expression of his strong sexuality.

She remembered that awful afternoon with Jenny when she had begged him not to go and he had bluntly told her he could not repress his physical feelings. She remembered the desire and purpose emanating from him at their initial meeting at the Park Hyatt, enfolding her, tying her to him. And from the night she had gone to him, it was as though his need for sexual expression was not only intense but wellnigh insatiable.

He had told her.

Warned her.

Shown her.

He had done his utmost, denied himself in order not to hurt her. She was not going to be hurt now because his need for her was predominantly physical.

She did not hear the music stop. She did not hear Thady enter the study or come up behind the leather armchair where she had curled up to read his play. The first she knew of his presence was the touch of his hands on her shoulders, hands that slid slowly down to caress her breasts as he leant over the backrest and grazed his lips across her hair.

"Finished?" he murmured.

Her heart thumped a painful protest at the response her body instinctively gave him. "Yes," she whispered, her breath catching in her throat as desire for him overwhelmed all other considerations.

"I was waiting for you to come and give me your opinion on it," he said questioningly. "You've been in here a long time." She heard the rueful smile in his voice as he added, "I was beginning to wonder if that meant it was good or bad."

"You know it's good, Thady. Everyone who's read it will have told you it's going to be a sensational hit."

"Mmm…" He pressed a longer, warmer kiss on the top of her head. "So what have you been thinking?"

"How glad I am to be here with you."

She turned her head to smile at him. He gave a low, sexy growl and lifted her out of the chair, swinging her into full contact with him, then teasingly rolling her body against his.

"Now tell me the truth," he insisted, his eyes feasting

off the response in hers. "Can you visualise it on stage yet?"

"Enough to start trying out ideas."

He gave her a wicked grin. "Let's go to bed and embellish them. We'll start the ball rolling tomorrow."

It wasn't all sex with Thady. They talked about aspects of the production design for his play long into the night. The mind sharing made the intimacy of their lovemaking all the more pleasurable. Anne was deeply happy to be his woman, whatever that meant to him.

On Monday morning Thady was all business, sweeping Anne off to Gray's Inn for a meeting with his solicitor, Paula Wentworth. He wanted the contract between them legally settled before taking Anne on to other important meetings.

Paula was a tall, slim woman who exuded professionalism from her neatly piled red hair to her low-heeled court shoes. Her skin was fine and very white, her eyes a sharply intelligent grey-green, her fine-boned face too long and narrow to be called pretty, yet there was a haughty elegance about her.

Thady greeted her with warmth, and it was obvious from the ensuing conversation that he had a longstanding association with Paula and her husband. Their manner to each other had the ease of close friendship, which surprised Anne. It suggested that Thady was not quite the loner she had imagined him to be.

Paula's manner to Anne conveyed a friendly interest, but there was a fast and keen measuring in her eyes that implied an intense curiosity about both Anne and the forceful impression she had apparently made on Thady Riordan. Thady's sudden and urgent insistence on such a blanket contract involving his work had obviously raised questions that had not been answered to Paula's satisfaction.

Paula went through the contract with them, altering a few details that had been on the faxed copy but that no longer applied now that Anne was in England. "Do you have an address in London yet?" she asked, raising her eyebrows at Anne in a sympathetic fashion, clearly expecting to hear the name of a stopgap hotel.

Anne gave the address of the flat in Knightsbridge.

"Oh!" Paula swiftly covered her surprise with an understanding smile. "You're staying with Thady until—"

"No, Paula," Thady cut in quietly. "That is Anne's address in London until further notice."

This firm assertion evoked a quizzical frown. "You're moving out, Thady?"

"No," he answered. "Not in the foreseeable future."

Paula kept looking at him as though she couldn't quite believe what she was hearing. Thady returned her gaze without blinking an eyelid. The naked shock on the solicitor's face remained undisguised for several seconds. Then the grey-green eyes snapped into sharp reappraisal, searching, wondering, speculating.

Paula's lips sealed into a thin line that denoted a determination to be discreet. She forced her attention to the contract. From that moment on, nothing of a personal nature was said. It was strict concentration on business.

Every time Paula lifted her eyes to Anne, however, their quizzical look was far too intense for settling a legal point.

Several times Anne felt that the question in Paula's eyes was not, *Why you?* but, *Do you know what you've taken on?*

When all the legalities were approved and signed, Paula escorted them out of her office. "You and Anne must come to dinner soon," she said to Thady, then swept a smile at Anne. "My husband, Richard, will be delighted to meet you, Anne. He loves the theatre as much as I do."

Thady slid his arm around Anne's shoulders in what felt like both a protective and possessive gesture as he replied for both of them. "If you don't mind, Paula, we'll leave socialising for a month or two. We haven't had much time to ourselves as yet, and Anne is going to be very busy on the production design for the play."

"Of course," Paula conceded with easy charm. Then with an affectionate touch on Thady's arm, she added, "I hope this will be a very happy and productive association for both of you."

The sentiment was clearly genuine, yet Anne still sensed some deep reservation, perhaps even resentment in the other woman. As soon as they were out of the building she turned to Thady, her eyes probing his for understanding.

"Why was Paula Wentworth so shocked by us and what you've done for me? It's not as though you haven't had other women associated with you."

His mouth curved with a touch of self-mockery. "None like you, Anne."

"What do you mean, like me?"

"I'm not in the habit of having live-in relationships. Paula knows that since she first met me, no woman has ever got close to me in any intimate sense."

"But you said…"

"One can have sex without intimacy, Anne. It was not something I wanted for long with any one woman."

"How long?"

"An hour or two that left me feeling empty and unsatisfied and chillingly alone," he answered, his mouth curling with contempt for the need that had driven him into the beds of women he had no feeling for beyond a passing physical desire.

He drew her into his arms, uncaring of the curious looks of passers-by. A reckless and ruthless determination flitted over his face, and once again Anne felt he was defying some private demon in taking her into his life. The green eyes glittered with intense possessiveness.

He lifted a hand to her face, gently stroked her cheek, tilted her chin. "You know it's different with you, Anne. So different that the thought of it ending makes me want to have all I can of you while I can."

His mouth claimed hers in a long, devouring kiss. The staid and respectable establishments around them ceased to exist. Only their passion for each other had any reality until Thady reluctantly withdrew his mouth from hers.

Desire still simmered in his eyes as he gave her a crooked little smile. "Business before pleasure. As much as I'd like to take you home and ravish all your senses, we have an appointment with my director, who will not be impressed by unpunctuality."

He hailed a passing taxi and helped Anne into it. His hand curled tightly around hers as they relaxed on the back seat together. It was a link of intimacy that Anne found very reassuring.

She no longer had any doubt that she was uniquely special to him compared to all the other women he had known. Paula Wentworth's shocked surprise was confirmation enough that Thady had spoken the truth in his replies to her questions. Yet there was something in Thady that didn't look for a long and lasting future for their relationship.

Was it some deep and innate pessimism that dictated it could be snatched away from him at any moment? Or did he know something she didn't, something that compelled him to live for the moment and not look too far ahead? Did he have some hereditary illness in his family, something that would claim him at a relatively early age? Or perhaps he carried some hidden defect that made having children impossible or inadvisable.

"Thady?"

He turned to her, his eyes warmly caressing. Somehow the look of happy contentment on his face made Anne swallow the impulsive question that had leapt to her tongue. Did she want to know the worst that could happen to them? Might it not be better to leave everything as it was?

She squeezed his hand and smiled. "Is everyone going to have the same reaction to us as Paula Wentworth did?"

He laughed and lifted her hand to brush his lips over her knuckles. "Will you mind if they do?" he asked teasingly.

"Why should I mind being seen as the remarkable woman who got the ungettable man?" she answered loftily.

The wicked twinkle in his eyes was swallowed by a surge of dark turbulence. "Anne... There will come a time when I can't fulfil all your needs," he warned seriously. "I want you to feel free to walk away from me when that happens. I don't want you to feel tied or obligated to a relationship that isn't satisfying you."

"Why do you think that will happen, Thady?" she asked quietly.

He shook his head, and she could see his face closing over his thoughts as he turned his head away from her. He heaved a deep sigh before tempering it with a surface smile. "I'm selfish enough to hope it won't. But I do mean that, Anne. You're free to do whatever you want. I'll never stand in your way."

Anne remembered reading somewhere that if you love someone you let them go free. She wanted to think that this was a gift of love from Thady to her, yet she could not shake off the feeling there was some other factor behind his words.

Whatever it was—if there *was* anything—Anne knew intuitively that Thady had made up his mind to keep it to himself. Whether that was to protect her, or protect what they had together as long as he could, Anne could not even guess. She told herself to be content with the one important thing that Thady had implied. *He* was not thinking of walking away from *her*. He was handing that decision to her.

Anne knew it was a decision she would never make. For better or for worse, she was tied to Thady Riordan in the deepest sense there could be between a man and a woman. She wanted to spend the rest of her life with him. As far as she was concerned, there *was* a marriage ring on her finger. She didn't need a band of gold to proclaim that truth.

CHAPTER TWELVE

FOR ANNE, the next two months were the most exciting, most challenging, most satisfying period of her life. She felt extended in a way she had never experienced before, working with people who demanded and expected the absolute best, mixing with people at a social level that took the best for granted.

At times Anne needed to be on her own to concentrate on developing her ideas for the production design of his play. Apart from that, Thady was always with her. He accompanied her to the theatre when work began there. He smoothed her path in a thousand ways, from lining up the contacts she needed to lending his strong support on any contentious issues that arose.

Thady Riordan left no-one in any doubt that he and Annelise Tolliver were in solid partnership where *The Long Cold Winter* was concerned, thereby giving Anne an acceptability, an authority and an automatic respect that would have been difficult to achieve on her own. Their personal relationship was never left in doubt, either. To many highly interested observers, they made the concept of *togetherness* a new art form.

One of those who actively displayed an intrigued curiosity was Alex Korbett, Anne's former boss. Alex had moved to England two years previously and was working on production designs for the English National Opera and the Royal Shakespeare Company. As soon as he heard of

Anne's arrival in London and how intimately she was connected to Thady Riordan, Alex got in touch with them and offered any practical help Anne might require.

Alex was the only person in the country who knew of the previous association between Anne and Thady. For all his tendency to gossip, however, he never mentioned a word about it. While Anne marvelled at his restraint, she was also relieved. Thady was such a deeply private person that Anne was quite certain he appreciated any restraint that limited the flames of speculation already leaping around them.

Alex was as good as his word at giving Anne his assistance whenever it was needed. Anne suspected he secretly enjoyed knowing more than anyone else, and he took every opportunity to increase his understanding of the situation.

When Thady and Anne accepted a dinner invitation from Paula and Richard Wentworth, Alex was a fellow guest.

He was a rotund, affable little man, much in demand at parties for his quick wit and ready store of current gossip about people of interest. He lent a sparkle to the table conversation, Anne thought, but she found his shrewd perception of people somewhat disturbing. Later in the evening when they retired to the lounge for after-dinner coffee, she became even more disturbed.

While Paula claimed Thady's attention, Alex drew Anne aside, claiming her private attention. He led her to a sofa somewhat apart from the other guests. His sharp blue eyes noted her reluctance to be parted from Thady, and his opening remark was aimed at focussing her concentration entirely on himself.

"Anne, why isn't Thady writing anymore?"

Anne was bewildered by the question. The answer was so obvious to her. "You know we're involved in the pro-

duction of *The Long Cold Winter,* Alex. Why would Thady
be writing at this time?''

''Because he always has in the past.''

Alex's reply jolted Anne, and sent an odd little shiver
down her spine. Thady had said in Sydney that he had to
get back to his writing. That he had not done so she put
down to her sharing his life and home, and his absorption
in her designs. His interest in the production she assumed
as natural.

She frowned as she tried to re-evaluate the situation.
''You mean he's never involved himself with production
before?''

''Never,'' Alex replied decisively.

''But all the problems that come up—''

''A matter of total disinterest to him. 'You've got what
I've written,' he'd say. 'Ruin it however you please. You'll
never get out of it what I put into it.' And that, my dear
Annelise, is a direct quote.''

Alex's clever mimic of Thady's voice lent a chilling au-
thenticity to the contemptuous words. This was an aspect
of Thady's character Anne had never seen. She sensed
more than knew his strength of will, recognised rather than
experienced what she suspected to be the ruthless driving
nature of the man.

He had shown her that capability within him in cutting
off their relationship when he had judged it to be in her
best interests, but apart from that, he had been good to her,
helpful, benevolent, charming. As lover, comforter, companion and friend, she could ask no more of any man.

It was hard to accept that Thady could be so dismissive
of his own work, especially since all his plays were recognised as masterpieces of the theatre. Yet according to Alex,
and Anne could not disbelieve him, Thady was now acting

entirely out of character. He had changed for her. Or she had changed him.

A heavy load of responsibility came down upon her shoulders. No wonder they were both a never-ending source of comment and speculation. *What am I doing to him? Why has he involved himself in production for the first time? Why has he involved himself with me?*

Anne looked around, needing to see him. She found him sitting with Paula at the other end of the room, but he was not looking at the other woman. He was looking directly at Anne, a heavy frown darkening his eyes. Paula said something to him, put her hand on his arm to draw his attention. He did not notice. His eyes were locked on Anne's, and the rest of the world was excluded from their contact.

Alex spoke to her in a low, urgent voice. "Anne, I can see this has come as a shock to you, but you must do something to get Thady writing again. He can't stop now. He's the genius of his generation. He probably will be, if he's not already, the greatest playwright of the twentieth century. You've got to help him."

Anne felt the flutter in her heart, felt her head swirl with dizziness. It often happened in moments of stress, and it was something she had no control over. The last time it had occurred was outside Thady's suite at the Park Hyatt, when his invitation to lunch had already turned into something else.

It was not frightening because she knew what it was. Her doctor had diagnosed it as a vaso-vagal reflex. For a split second the blood supply to her brain would be interrupted and she would feel the world spin. Then everything would right itself and the whooshing sensation was gone. Recovery was always swift. It was a minor irritation in life, no more. Anne instinctively settled herself against the backrest of the sofa, not because she had to, but because it automatically gave her a feeling of security against the sensation of falling.

Thady's head snapped up, like an animal's on alert for danger. His frown deepened. The next instant he was on his feet, totally unaware of breaking Paula's light grasp on his arm.

Anne straightened from her brief slump, the momentary attack over. Alex, whose speech had trailed off as he observed something wrong with her, quickly pushed his point before Thady came within earshot. "For God's sake, Anne! Make Thady write again!"

Then Thady was dropping to his knees beside her, his hands gripping her elbows too tightly, his face stamped with a strange mixture of fear and concern. "Are you ill, Anne?" Even his voice was a strained rasp, as though her reply was of critical importance to him.

She smiled indulgently, warmed by his deep caring. "No. I'm all right, Thady."

"I saw it, Anne. I saw it in your eyes." It was like an accusation, demanding that she not deceive him.

"Everything's fine. Truly," she assured him, beginning to feel embarrassed by the unnecessary fuss. All other conversation in the room had died. They were the focus of startled attention.

Something infinitely dangerous flared into Thady's eyes. "Has Alex said anything to upset you?" He turned towards Alex, and the look he gave him promised a deep, bloody, vengeful murder. "What have you said?" he demanded through lips that barely moved.

Alex visibly blanched under the savagery of that threatening gaze. It was shocking, a totally disproportionate reaction to what had happened.

"Nothing!" Alex and Anne cried in unison.

"I swear it, Thady. Nothing!" Alex added for good measure, a shaken note in his voice.

Thady's head turned slowly to Anne. The green eyes fastened onto hers. "Then what happened?" he asked with quiet insistence, but his fingers were biting into her flesh so hard it hurt.

"Nothing, really…"

"Tell me!"

She didn't want to. She didn't know why. Something was terribly wrong here. The tension swirled with far too much emotion. Alex was wiping his palms as though they were sweaty. The heave of Thady's chest was somehow frightening.

"Tell me!" he repeated.

Anne knew she had to. It was the only thing that might defuse this weirdly explosive situation. Paula's social occasion was definitely being spoilt by Thady's self-absorbed behaviour. It was up to Anne to do something about it.

"A silly medical condition…" she started, shaking her head over the trivial nature of the problem.

"Go on!"

"For a tiny fraction of a second…"

"Yes?"

"I get a tiny interruption in the blood supply to my brain. It means nothing—"

"God… God… *God!*"

It was a beat of despair and desperation such as Anne had never heard before. Thady bowed his head as though fate had dealt him too many blows and he could not sustain any more. It made her go cold all over. She shivered violently.

This brought another wild surge of reaction from Thady. He moved with lightning speed, his arms going around her shoulders, under her thighs. He lifted her effortlessly to his chest as though she were weightless. He straightened up, standing erect and tall. She could feel the mad pumping of his heart, saw the deathlike pallor of his face, and understood nothing.

He turned towards the remaining guests, all of whom were staring at them with expressions that ranged from puzzlement and surprise to curiosity and anticipation. All, that was, except Paula Wentworth. Her hand covered her mouth in a gesture of absolute horror.

That reaction also seemed grossly out of proportion to Anne. Admittedly Thady's behaviour had disrupted any comfortable and congenial conclusion to Paula's dinner party, but surely such a sophisticated and clever woman knew how to smooth such awkwardness without being horrified.

Anne closed her eyes on the whole scene, feeling too helpless to cope with it. Nothing made sense to her.

"Anne is sick. I'm taking her home," Thady announced in a voice that brooked no opposition.

Anne could have truthfully said she had never been so well in her life, but she was not about to contradict Thady's statement. The last thing she wanted was another outburst of violent feeling from him. The sooner they were alone together, the sooner she might be able to sort this whole madness out.

"I can walk, Thady," she murmured to him, half-opening her eyes to assure him of that point.

"I'm carrying you," he said grimly.

Richard Wentworth escorted them to the door.

"I'm so sorry," Anne whispered to him, painfully conscious of the scene they were making.

"We're all sorry to see you...stricken," Richard answered courteously.

Brisk good evenings were exchanged.

Thady walked rapidly to their car, his breath coming in short, harsh gasps.

"I'm all right, Thady. Truly I am," Anne pleaded. "You can put me down."

He didn't seem to hear. When he had her safely settled in the front passenger seat, his only reply was, "I'm taking you home."

He was still panting from his exertions when he seated himself in the driver's seat. The journey home was a nightmare. Thady insisted on hearing every detail of what had happened to her physically, and then her whole medical history from the time she was born. He was so doubting about the vaso-vagal reflex that Anne offered to get a medical certificate from her doctor in Sydney to prove what she said was true. To her further discomfort, Thady accepted her offer.

He doesn't trust me, Anne thought.

Or perhaps it was doctors he didn't trust, she amended, remembering her concerns about his health. She wished she had the courage to ask Thady about *his* medical history, but she couldn't bring herself to open up any area of jeopardy or disharmony on their future together. She knew there wasn't anything seriously wrong with her. She didn't want there to be anything seriously wrong with Thady, either.

A tense silence pervaded the atmosphere in the car by the time they reached Knightsbridge. Before Thady switched off the ignition, he turned to Anne with hard-bitten resolve etched on his face.

"I don't want you to meet, speak to or see Alex Korbett again," he said.

That extraordinary demand left Anne speechless for a moment. That Thady was capable of ruthlessly cutting off people she knew only too well, yet Alex had done nothing to deserve such treatment. With Alex's love of the theatre, it was only natural that he be concerned about Thady's future as a playwright.

"Why?" she asked.

"What was Alex speaking to you about tonight?"

"Does it matter?"

"Yes."

He was deadly serious, his eyes searing hers with intensity. Anne wondered if she should bring up the subject of his writing. But surely what Thady did or did not do was *his* choice. She had promised not to try to change him.

"Nothing really," she dismissed as casually as she could.

"Was he talking about me?" Thady persisted.

"No," she lied, and instantly felt uncomfortable with the lie.

"What was it about then?"

"Old times in Sydney."

Why had she started this untruth? The answer was frighteningly obvious. She didn't want to hurt Thady. Nor did she want their relationship changed in any way. Whether Thady sensed or saw the lie she did not know. Her heart leapt erratically as his eyes searched hers with acute suspicion.

"Give me your promise not to have anything more to do with Alex Korbett," he commanded harshly.

"He's an old friend, Thady," she cried in protest. "Why should I cut him dead?"

The green eyes glittered with a ferocity that was entirely ruthless. "Because I'm insanely jealous of him," Thady bit out, each word reinforced by the violent emotion he was clearly feeling.

Anne stared at him incredulously, knowing that now Thady was lying. He had no reason to be jealous of anyone, let alone Alex Korbett. Apart from which, she was certain that Thady was not the kind of man to be jealous without more than sufficient cause. He was essentially a fair man, a giving man.

What has become of us? she thought. *How have we come to this?* They were both lying over what should have been a trivial matter. Everything seemed to have been blown all out of proportion, mountains being made out of molehills.

"Give me your promise, Anne."

She shook her head. It was all wrong. Unreasonable. "I can't do that, Thady," she said quietly.

"Why not?"

"Because it's unfair to Alex."

"Unfair!" He snarled the word, then jerked his head aside, looking out at the night that surrounded them with its darkness. He gave a low bitter laugh, then fell into a silent brooding that grated more on Anne's nerves than the laugh had.

She could feel him separating himself from her, withdrawing. Panic seized her. The need to fight for what she wanted forced a wild spill of words.

"You said I was free to do whatever I wanted, Thady. Why are you putting restrictions on me now? I'm with you because I want to be. I worked with Alex for three years. You know there's nothing between him and me but friendship. What possible harm can there be to us if Alex and I—"

"Let me be the judge of that, Anne!" he whipped back at her, his eyes ablaze with fierce determination.

"Like you were the judge of walking out of my life for seven years?" she retorted.

His face tightened. A muscle in his cheek contracted. He spoke slowly but with forceful deliberation. "Whether you believe me or not, Alex Korbett can change things between us. If you *need* me in your life, Anne, I *need* that promise from you. Now. Without equivocation.''

He meant it. Resolution rang in his voice. It was stamped on his face. It burned in his eyes, challenging the need for him that he had answered when she had asked.

Anne didn't like it. She didn't understand it. But *need* was a powerful word. Thady would not use it lightly. She knew there was far more to his demand than he was telling her. It was not jealousy. It was not possessiveness either. Nor did she believe it had anything to do with whether he was writing or not.

Something was being kept hidden from her, something that he would not reveal under any circumstance. Nor would he allow anyone else, like Alex or Paula, to reveal whatever it was that was so intensely private to him, whatever it was that could change things between them.

The threat of change was enough to sway her. She had to answer his need, no matter what the reason behind it. He was far more important to her than Alex Korbett, and what they shared was far too precious to risk on some point of friendship with another man.

"I promise," she said dully, wishing that they'd never gone to Paula Wentworth's dinner party.

Thady gave a deep sigh of relief, then leaned forward and switched off the ignition. They were home, but the thought gave Anne no comfort. A shadow of mistrust had entered their lives, tarnishing what had seemed perfect before tonight.

When Thady opened the passenger door for her and she stepped out, the darkness of the night seemed to pulse with secrets. Whatever had transpired at Paula's party was shut behind them, just as Thady shut the car door behind her. But the secrets were still there...waiting for another time and place.

Anne took a deep breath. Suddenly it seemed very important to live for the present. She simply didn't know what tomorrow might bring. She could no longer trust it to bring unshadowed happiness.

CHAPTER THIRTEEN

THADY WAS EVEN MORE attentive to Anne and her needs in the days that followed Paula Wentworth's dinner party. Anne could not help wondering if *he* thought time was running out for them. He seemed obsessed with keeping her in sight when he wasn't actually by her side.

The fax came from her medical practitioner in Sydney, reinforcing what she had told Thady about the vaso-vagal reflex and her general state of health. His constant vigilance eased off. While Thady continued to be with her more often than not, he was far more relaxed about their togetherness. Anne realised he had simply been on guard in case something happened to her. Not possessive. Protective.

If Anne had needed any proof that Thady was not of a jealous nature, it came unequivocally when Tom Colby was suddenly cast in the lead male role of *The Long Cold Winter*. The play had already been in rehearsal for three weeks when the actor originally cast for the part, a well-known star of the London stage, was seriously injured in a falling elevator. The naming of a relatively unknown Australian actor as his replacement caused a flurry of publicity.

It also came as a shock to Anne. She had lost touch with Tom years ago and had no idea that he was in England. When Thady broke the news to her, she couldn't take it in at first.

"How? Why?" she floundered, anxiously searching

Thady's eyes for his reaction to having her former lover in the lead role in his play.

"He has the ability to do it as it should be done," Thady answered with calm authority. Then his eyes were searching hers. "Do you mind, Anne?"

"No...no, I'm glad for him. It's a big break for Tom. Maybe it will make up for..." She hastily swallowed the words she had been going to say, suddenly sensitive of speaking about the hurt she had given to another man.

"That's over for him, Anne," Thady said softly. "He's married to an English girl he met while playing repertory in the provinces."

Anne shook her head in bewilderment. "How do you know?"

"I met him six months ago. I went to Birmingham to see him act in my last play."

"Why?"

"I wanted to know how good he was." Thady's mouth curved with dry irony. "I also wanted to know if there was any chance of you joining him in England."

"What if you'd found there was a chance?" Anne asked curiously.

"Then there would have been no chance for me," he answered simply.

It gave Anne an eerie feeling that so much had been decided about her without her knowledge, without her having anything to do with it. She had a mental image of a set of scales being tipped this way and that, influencing the course of her life without any choosing by her. It was unnerving to think the balance she had achieved with Thady could be tipped again by secret factors that had unknown and immeasurable weight.

Like her health. Which was now cleared. But Thady's extreme concern about it had not been answered to her satisfaction. Even Paula Wentworth's excuse did not ring completely true. When Anne had called her to thank her for the dinner and apologise for the somewhat melodramatic scene, Paula had smoothed away any awkwardness.

"Everyone understands, Anne," she had lightly assured her. "Thady has been alone for so long, naturally the thought of losing you horrified him. You did look deathly pale, you know. I'm awfully glad, for both of you, that it's nothing serious."

Anne felt there was more to it than that. The question still remained. Why wouldn't Thady marry her? They were so happy together, made for each other, yet it was obvious that if there'd been any chance of Tom Colby marrying her, Thady would have stayed out of her life.

At least that issue was settled, Anne thought with considerable relief. It was even more thoroughly settled the next day when she and Thady met Tom Colby at rehearsal. There could be no doubt Tom knew of Anne's relationship with Thady, but it was clear from the first moment that Tom considered his own affair with Anne completely dead and buried.

He greeted them both with obvious pleasure, congratulating Anne on the huge step up in her career and thanking Thady profusely for the chance he had been given. This deep and sincere gratitude seemed to extend to Anne, as though she had something to do with his luck in being chosen. His whole manner stirred Anne's curiosity enough to ask Thady about it as soon as the director called Tom away.

"Why was Tom thanking you, Thady?"

"I used my influence to get him the part over the other actors who were being considered."

For a moment Anne saw the gleam of ruthlessness in the green eyes, the drive that had made him what he was in the theatrical world. He had wanted Tom Colby to play the lead, and he had asserted his will and used his power to enforce it, regardless of what others thought. Yet, if what Alex Korbett had told her was true, Thady had never involved himself in anything like this before.

"Why?" she asked, wondering if Thady was testing her love in some way by bringing Tom in.

"To enhance your work, Anne," he answered quietly. "I've seen Tom Colby act. I know what he can do. I wanted the best for you."

She felt shamed by doubting his trust in her and deeply moved by his commitment to her success. Thady might not have given a damn about how his other plays had been presented to the public, but he cared about this one because it could make or break her name in production design. He had been with her all this time, overseeing everything entirely for *her* sake. He had even given up his writing to ensure *her* success.

Although Thady had never said he loved her, Anne was convinced that all he had given her *was* a gift of love. Their relationship was all she had dreamed of, yet still there was the spectre of impermanence hanging over it.

The invitation to Jenny's wedding arrived. They were going through the mail while they sipped pre-dinner drinks. Anne passed the card to Thady, smiling over Jenny's choice of bells and bows etched in gold. Thady's responding smile suddenly died as he glanced through the formal invitation. His gaze lifted slowly to Anne's, his eyes dark green and oddly opaque.

"I'm sorry if there's been some misunderstanding, Anne. I never go to weddings. And that includes Jenny's."

"But you said..." Anne's mouth dried at the flat rejection written on his face.

"I said I'd make sure you were there, Anne. And for

Christmas with your family, as well. I've already booked your ticket home. Everything is in order, as I promised.''

Anne's mind spun with shock. He had only bought *her* airline ticket! He meant her to go home on her own!

''I thought…'' She felt as though an iron fist was closing around her heart. She had to force herself to continue speaking. ''I thought you'd want to be with me, Thady.''

''Anne…'' A conflict of interests warred across his face as he saw the pain of his decision clearly written on hers. The next instant he was on his feet and drawing her into his embrace, soothing her hurt with a trail of warm kisses around her temples.

''Being with you is a happiness I never expected or hoped to have,'' he murmured huskily. ''I'm sorry you're disappointed that I won't be going to Australia with you. It's impossible anyway. I have business in America.''

''Then I'll come with you,'' she pressed, her eyes searching his for reassurance that this separation need not be.

His face closed against her appeal. ''No. You promised your sister.''

''Jenny will understand,'' she pleaded.

He dragged in a deep breath. His eyes darkened. He spoke in a tight, flat voice. ''No. The answer can only be no. It must always be no whenever I go to America. I can only give you so much, Anne. There are things for which I need to be alone. I did warn you there would come a time when I couldn't fulfil all your needs. This is one of those times. I'll be with you until you fly out to Australia. My business in America is for me to do by myself. Please accept that.''

Anne didn't want to, but Thady was leaving her no choice. Any argument about it would be futile. She could either accept what he did give her, or walk away. Walking away from Thady was unthinkable to Anne. Her mind frantically searched for some reason why he needed to be alone.

"Is it to do with your writing?"

His mouth twisted into a grimace. "Perhaps."

Anne didn't know what to think. Certainly he had not written anything since she had been with him. If she was a distracting influence, it wasn't fair of her to expect him to stay with her all the time.

"How long will you be away?" she asked anxiously.

His eyes took on a dull, faraway look. "There are no certainties in this life, Anne. Who knows what will happen in the meantime? But I plan to be back in London by the middle of January."

It was not the complete assurance Anne craved, but she instinctively hid her own uncertainties under a bright smile as she curled her arms around his neck and pressed her body to his. "Then I guess I'd better make the most of this time with you," she said invitingly.

She saw the flicker of relief in his eyes before his mouth came down on hers, demonstrably wanting all she gave him. Yet it wasn't enough. If he needed to be free of her in order to write, then this would be the first of many separations.

Later that night, when Thady lay asleep beside her, Anne fretted over the separation he was insisting upon. Thady had a bad habit of deciding for himself what was best for her. What if he didn't really mean to come back from America?

Her mind flitted back and forth over all they had shared together. Thady *was* happy with her. Happier than he had ever expected to be. He had acknowledged that. Yet there were those dark hidden areas inside him that he kept from her.

Maybe he had been suppressing his needs for her sake.

He could be thinking that after the opening night of *The Long Cold Winter,* she would be assured of a long and successful career without him at her side. He might consider he had done all he could for her.

Perhaps it was his nature to give himself completely to whatever he was doing, shutting out everything else. He had undoubtedly chosen to give himself entirely to her until he went to America. When he gave the same kind of total intensity to his work, would that be like an exorcism of her from his life?

Thady had cut her out of his life before without a moment's notice. Why should it be different this time? She had spent most of the past seven years alone. She did not want to spend the rest of her life alone. There were so many uncertainties about the future with Thady that Anne could see only one solution to her problem. She agonised over it until the first light of morning was filtering through the bay window curtains. She remembered watching the sunrise on her first morning with Thady. *A new day,* she had murmured then. *A new life,* he had answered.

Ironically, it was that recollection that finally brought Anne to a firm decision. A new life it would be. If something happened so she could not be with the man she loved in the years ahead of her, she would have his child to love.

Which meant no more contraception. With any luck at all, she should become pregnant before she and Thady went their separate ways. It was almost three weeks to the opening night of the play, another four days after that before she flew out of London. There was time for her to conceive.

Then she remembered her concern that Thady might have some hereditary illness that precluded him from having healthy children. Should she risk it? He was in his thirties with no sign of anything wrong with his health. It was worth risking, Anne decided. Thady had already made too many choices for her. This was going to be *her* choice, without any consultation with him. Whatever the consequences, she would live with them.

The decision gave Anne a peace of mind that allowed her to live through the next few weeks without worrying about the future. She had a heady sense of recklessness, of freedom from all fear. For the first time in her life she felt in control of what was to happen to her, and her secret excitement about conceiving Thady's child enhanced the pleasure and happiness of being with him.

She loved him more dearly when they made love, her emotions more deeply involved with thinking of him as the father of the child she wanted. Afterwards she held on to him for a long time, wondering if this was the night that had seeded a new life.

She made no mention of their coming separation, or the future beyond that, but the intensity of her feeling was such that it led Thady into trying to reassure her that he would be coming back to her in the new year. A mellow tenderness crept into his lovemaking, a soft caring for her pleasure that was more like absolute loving.

It was a time of wonderful harmony between them, and Anne stored every moment of it in her memory. She told herself it was better to have a taste of perfection than never to have known it. When it ended, it ended. There was nothing she could do about that except what she was already doing.

Her only disagreement with Thady occurred on the opening night of the play. The premiere was to be a glittering affair, attended by the Princess of Wales and a list of other celebrities that would have awed Anne three months ago. As it was, she kept nervously checking her appearance in the mirror prior to leaving for the theatre.

"You look stunningly beautiful," Thady assured her.

Anne laughed self-consciously. "You're only saying that because you chose the dress."

It was a fabulous evening dress in deep red velvet. Anne would never have paid the price Thady had paid for it, but she had to admit she was glad he had insisted. The amber beading on the tight bodice gave the dress a rich medieval look that somehow suited her extremely well, emphasising the gold in her eyes and the honey colour of her hair, which had been looped into a confection of tiny braids and loose curls.

She was satisfied that she looked suitably elegant for the occasion, yet as Thady's partner, she was aware there would be many critical eyes on her. He, of course, looked stunningly handsome in formal dress, and was totally assured of his reception by everyone.

"You're dithering for no good purpose," Thady gently chided. "The only thing that would add perfection to perfection is if you change those garnet earrings for the diamonds I gave you when we were in Sydney."

"I don't think the diamonds would go with this dress, Thady," Anne quickly excused. "I wouldn't feel right in them."

The latter statement was the real truth. Perhaps it was some stupid form of superstition, but in her mind she equated the diamonds with being married to him, and somehow she felt if she ever wore them prematurely, Thady would never marry her. He might never marry her anyway. He was so much against marriage he wouldn't even go to weddings. But Anne could not stop herself from hoping that one day he might change his mind.

Thady frowned at her. "Why aren't they right, Anne? I thought diamonds went with anything, yet you always say they're not right. You haven't worn them since I gave them to you."

"I'd rather keep them for a special occasion," she rushed out unthinkingly.

"Isn't this a special occasion?"

He looked hurt at her refusal, and Anne inwardly squirmed in the hole she had dug for herself. "I meant a special time that was only for you and me," she said weakly. "Not for show to other people."

Thady looked as though he wanted to pursue the point, but then changed his mind and shrugged it away, much to Anne's relief. He glanced at his watch and declared that her dithering time was up.

As she accompanied Thady to the limousine, Anne surreptitiously slid her hand over her stomach. Her period had been due yesterday. Of course, it might simply be delayed because of all the hectic activity leading up to opening night, but it gave her a wonderful glow of inner happiness to think it might be due to another cause. It was possible that Thady might consider marriage if she bore him a child.

She wouldn't ask him to.

But he might.

The premiere of *The Long Cold Winter* was a triumphant night for everyone. From the opening scene to the final curtain, the audience was enthralled. Tom Colby was utterly riveting in the main role. Passion simmered through the rest of the cast. The sets Anne had designed captured each shift of mood, subtly adding more power to the climax, which, when it came, was totally electrifying.

Yet over and above anyone else's contribution, the night belonged to Thady Riordan. His genius for dramatic theatre was on spell-binding display. When the final curtain came down, the audience was still caught up in the heart-twisting emotion of the last act. The awed silence was only broken by muffled sobs, sniffs, the surreptitious blowing of noses, the rustle of handkerchiefs being hastily drawn or put away.

The applause broke slowly, gathered momentum, growing to an ovation. No matter what their usual mode of behaviour—sedate, complacent, sober, sophisticated, cynical—the whole audience rose in acclaim.

The curtain calls went on and on, but the wild response from everyone in the theatre was not really for the cast. It had been drawn from them by the creator of all they had just seen and heard and felt.

For Anne, this new insight brought the sobering realisation that Alex Korbett had spoken no more than the absolute truth. Thady Riordan was the genius of his generation, perhaps the greatest playwright of the twentieth century. If he had to be alone to write, she had no right to stop him.

There was pandemonium in the foyer afterwards. Anne caught a glimpse of Alex in the crowd. He blew her a kiss and flashed a thumbs-up sign. She was glad that their old friendship had not been harmed by her promise to Thady.

Profuse congratulations were showered on both of them as Thady steered Anne through the excited melee to the street. He could have basked in adulation if he had wanted to, but he brushed it all aside, wanting only to be alone with her. Their limousine was waiting. They were off and away before they could be caught by the people spilling out of the theatre after them.

They held each other for a long time that night, aware that the production they had shared was now behind them. The exhilaration of its success meant little compared to the sense of time running out on this phase of their lives.

The few days left to them were punctured by endless telephone calls, requests for interviews, flowers and telegrams of congratulations arriving, constant interruptions. It seemed they were hardly ever alone except at night. The time of separation grew inexorably closer, yet the thought uppermost in their minds was never spoken. They couldn't talk about it. It was in their eyes, in every touch, in the way they made love.

Thady accompanied Anne to Heathrow to see her off on her flight to Australia. The parting was too painful to prolong. There were no words to say, no promises asked or given. One fierce kiss goodbye and Anne walked away from the man she loved.

But she carried one promise for the future with her. Anne was sure she was pregnant.

CHAPTER FOURTEEN

ANNE'S WELCOME HOME was somewhat strained. To Leonie Tolliver, not even fame and success at an international level made Anne's relationship with Thady Riordan any more acceptable. He was taking advantage of Anne. The fact that he had chosen not to accompany her home condemned him as a man who was wasting Anne's time. It proved, beyond doubt, that he had no serious intentions.

Anne side-stepped the issue as much as she could, busying herself with visits to her two married sisters, Liz and Kate, minding their children while they did Christmas shopping. Yet both Liz and Kate showed a quiet concern about where their oldest sister was heading in her private life. Jenny was also disappointed that her hopes and plans for Anne had been somewhat dashed by Thady's absenting himself from her sister's side. Luckily preparations for the wedding provided some happy distraction.

The wedding was lovely. The dresses Anne had designed were pure fairytale romanticism, and all the guests remarked how absolutely right they were for Jenny and her bridesmaids. Brian looked transfixed by the sight of his bride coming down the aisle, and after the marriage ceremony, both he and Jenny radiated blissful happiness.

Anne had to blink away a rush of emotional tears. She told herself that weddings were simply superficial, sentimental shows of love, meaning little in the long run of any relationship. Nevertheless, she could not quite quell the ache of yearning for the kind of public commitment Jenny and Brian had made to each other.

It was harder to hold back the tears when Jenny gave her a farewell hug before going off on her honeymoon. "Thanks so much for everything, Anne. Without you, my wedding wouldn't have been nearly as beautiful as it was."

"Nonsense! You and Brian made it beautiful."

Jenny hesitated a moment, searching Anne's eyes. "You are happy with Thady, aren't you? You're sure it's right for you?"

"Very happy," Anne assured her. "No other man could be more right for me."

Jenny's smile was tinged with relief. "That's all right, then. He's sure to come round to marriage in the end. Don't take any notice of Mum's rantings."

Anne tried to use Jenny's unflagging optimism to bolster her confidence in Thady's love for her. Her pregnancy had been confirmed. She was going to have Thady's child, but she had no idea how Thady was going to react to the news that he was going to be a father.

She wanted him to be thrilled, as Brian would most certainly be if Jenny had such news for him. Nevertheless, Anne had no idea what Thady's response might be. If he was disapproving or censorious, the happiness they had shared together might never be recaptured. Anne did her best to dismiss such disquieting thoughts.

Nevertheless, the festive period of Christmas and New Year was a lonely time for her. Liz, Kate and Jenny had their husbands beside them, and Thady was an ocean away. Despite the kinship of family, Anne had to continually fight the sense of not belonging anymore.

Somehow she had grown past them, or their realities were no longer hers. She yearned to be back in the flat in London, waiting for Thady's return. Even if he wasn't there, she could at least feel his presence in the home they shared.

This need drove Anne to change her flight to an earlier one. She told herself she wanted the flat to be warm and welcoming for Thady's return mid-month, so she arrived in England on the eighth of January.

Thady did not come home on the fifteenth. In the following days, Anne was caught up in a churning circle of anticipation and disappointment. Any minute now, she kept thinking, but the minutes passed with taunting slowness, and still Thady did not come home. Days crept into weeks. The month of January came to an end.

The weather was bleak—wet, grey and freezing cold, adding its miserable weight to the growing bleakness in Anne's heart. There was no message from Thady to revive anticipation of their soon being together. The silence from him stretched on and on, wearing out all Anne's excuses for it.

It seemed uncharacteristic of Thady not to consider her feelings. Even if he was involved with his writing, he could have spared her a thought, couldn't he? One phone call to appease her concern?

Anne began to worry that something had happened to him. Perhaps he was in a hospital somewhere, unable to contact her for some reason. She dismissed the chilling thought that he could have died. The death of Thady Riordan would not go unreported by the media. Yet if he was alive, it seemed that she was dead to him.

As difficult as that was to accept, Anne was slowly becoming resigned to it by mid-February. She received a call from Thady's agent, who had agreed to represent her business interests, as well. Was she interested in doing the production design for an updated version of *The Pirates of Penzance?*

Anne had no idea what Thady was doing, or when she might be required to work on his next play. Common sense urged that it was better for her to get on with her life and keep busy. She had a child's future to consider. Thady might never write again, might never appear in her life again.

She called Paula Wentworth, ostensibly to check if she was legally free to accept career commitments besides those she had signed for with Thady. What she really wanted to find out was whether Paula knew anything about Thady's present situation.

"You're free to take on any work you wish, any time at all," Paula assured her.

Anne swallowed the humiliation of her own ignorance to ask, "How long do you think it will be before Thady will have more work for me, Paula?"

"I can't tell you, Anne. I simply don't know."

"Then do you know when he'll be back in London?" Anne pressed.

There was a nerve-tearing silence. Then in a soft sympathetic voice, Paula asked, "You haven't heard from him, Anne?"

"No. Not a word. Has he been in touch with you?"

Another long, agonising pause. "I hope you understand that I'm bound by confidentiality to a client, Anne," Paula said slowly.

"Can you tell me if he means to come back to London?" Anne asked in desperation.

"That's up to Thady," came the cautious reply.

"Paula, is Thady all right?" Anne pleaded, casting all pride aside in her need to know *something*.

A deep sigh. "Anne, I don't know what to say to you. I spoke to Thady yesterday. He's still in America. He sounded tired...exhausted...torn apart."

The anguish in Paula's voice sent a shiver of apprehension down Anne's spine. "Please tell me what's wrong, Paula. You're keeping something from me, you and Thady. And I think Alex must know, as well. Don't you see I've got to know? I can't go on like this."

"Anne, I've said too much already."

Anne could feel her clamming up, retreating from further disclosure. With a sense of sinking hopelessness, she said, "Then tell me what to do, Paula. You know more than I do. Give me your best advice."

"If you want my professional advice…"

"Yes, I do."

"Be independent. Lead your own life. Fulfil the wonderful talent you have. Forge a future for yourself."

"That's all?" Anne asked, pleading for some ray of hope to cling to. The advice Paula had given was totally damning of any future with Thady.

"No. That's not all," Paula answered, as though dragging the words out against her better judgement. There was a long, ragged sigh. Then in a voice that shook with emotion, "As a woman, and as a friend to you, if you love Thady Riordan, if you truly love him, Anne, be there for him when he does come back. Don't ask questions. Accept him as he is. There's no other way."

The line was instantly disconnected. Paula Wentworth had said all she was going to say, and her deep caring for Thady left an indelible impression on Anne. One message was clear. Whatever torment Thady was going through, Anne was to be kept separate from it.

Whether this was to protect her from pain, or to help Thady shut out his own pain when he was with her, Anne did not know and could not begin to guess. He had lived like a monk, a hermit, a man condemned to a world of loneliness until she had forced herself into his life, claiming a need for him.

Anne suddenly realised that Thady would never say he *needed* her. He would never put any claim on her. Whatever the reason, or impediment, he felt he had no right to tie her to him in any but a professional sense. He had neither expected nor hoped for the happiness he had known with her. But he wanted it. And needed it. That was the other message Paula had tried to put across.

Tired…exhausted…torn apart. Was it some dreadful illness that required regular treatments in America? Thady had insisted that whenever he went to America, he had to be by himself. So whatever was happening to him now was going to happen again. And again.

Her hand slid protectively over her stomach. What had she done in conceiving Thady's child? Would her pregnancy be a further torment for Thady? A torment for both of them? She had been completely and utterly selfish in wanting his baby, and wantonly reckless in not discussing it with him beforehand.

It was too late to worry about that now. In fact, worrying about what she didn't know was probably the most futile thing she could do. If she didn't make some positive decisions about her life, she would go mad in this waiting vacuum.

Best to keep her mind busy on something else, she told herself, and promptly rang her agent to say she *was* interested in the offered production design and would like to meet with the director of the show as soon as possible. Since she would be working in London, there was little likelihood of missing Thady when he came back. If she happened to be out of the flat, he would certainly know she was still living there, waiting for him.

Driven by the need for some absorbing activity, Anne

went out and bought a compact disc of Gilbert and Sullivan's *The Pirates of Penzance*. She immersed herself in the words and music so she'd be totally familiar with both when she went to the meeting where the updated concept of the show was discussed. She threw herself into work, blocking out all other concerns as she evolved her designs for the production.

The days passed relatively quickly. It was only when she went to bed that Anne was haunted by thoughts of Thady. There was little she could do about those dark hours. The night was always lonely.

On the last day of February Alex Korbett called to offer his congratulations on Anne's snagging what he called a plum job. When he invited her out for a celebratory dinner with him, Anne was sorely tempted to go, despite her promise to Thady. It was an opportunity to open Alex up, pressing on their old friendship to get the information she wanted. Yet that would be a breach of trust. She pleaded a headache and declined the invitation.

She lay awake that night, thinking of all the questions she might have asked Alex. She wondered if it would have done her any good to know the answers. Thady did not think so. Neither did Paula. Perhaps Alex would have been of the same opinion.

Sleep finally put a halt to the miserable treadmill of her thoughts, but even that was made restless by haunting dreams of phantoms forever out of reach. It was a relief to struggle free of yet another frustrating dream and wake to the brightness of morning. Anne listlessly thought there was a different quality about the light, but it took a few moments to realise what it was.

Sunshine was beaming through the bay window, sparkling sunshine without the dulling grey filter of clouds. The miseries of the night were instantly dispelled. Sunshine was definitely a good omen, she thought whimsically. It even seemed to bring the smell of spring flowers to banish the sterile bleakness of winter.

She breathed in deeply, enjoying the scent in the air. Her heart gave a funny jerk as she realised she wasn't imagining it. The smell of spring flowers *was* in the air! She sat up very abruptly, her eyes wide awake. Resting on the pillows on Thady's side of the bed was a glorious array of spring flowers!

Her heart turned over.

There was no hesitation about what to do, how to react, what she should think. Anne whirled out of bed and flew through the flat, her whole body pumping with excitement and happiness. Thady had come home to her.

She found him sprawled full length on one of the black leather sofas. The sight of him brought Anne's flying feet to a faltering halt. He was asleep, but that was not what stopped her from rushing to throw her arms around him in loving welcome. It was the shock of seeing how dreadful he looked.

He had lost so much weight that his face seemed to have no flesh on it at all. The skin was stretched tight over his cheekbones and jaw. The hollows in his cheeks had drawn deep lines on either side of his mouth. The dark shadows around his eyes made them look bruised and sunken in their deep-set sockets, a stark contrast to the glistening paleness of his forehead. Anne's heart contracted in fear and horror at what Thady must have been through to bring him to this awful state.

She wanted to take him in her arms and comfort him as one would a wounded child, cushioning his head against the softness of her breasts and tenderly stroking his hair. But he looked so tired and drained it seemed wrong to wake him. Anne contented herself with the gentlest of touches, a feather-light caress of her fingertips that assured her of the live warmth beneath the pale skin of his face.

His eyes flicked open. "I thought I felt the touch of an angel," he murmured, in the soft Irish lilt that curled her toes.

"Thady...oh, Thady." Tears swam into her eyes.

It seemed that Thady's strength had not been weakened by his loss of weight, for the next instant Anne was hauled onto the sofa with him, and he was leaning over her, his lips warmly sweeping away the moistness of her tears. "I want you so badly. Say that it's all right," he whispered, and the husky need in his voice was enough to dispel any doubts about what he felt for her.

"I'll always want you," she answered with a heart so full it felt it would burst.

A tremor ran through his body. His mouth claimed hers with a passion that hungered for the response she had promised him, and she gave it without reservation, wanting to fill him with her own life force.

She felt Thady's body harden, tighten, pulse with the wild primitive need to take all she offered. There was no fatigue in the arms that lifted her and carried her to the bedroom, no falter in the legs that strode forward with purpose. The green eyes blazed with an inner fire that demanded all-consuming attention.

"The flowers!" Anne cried as they both tumbled onto the bed.

Thady swept them aside, totally careless of where and how they might land. "*You* are spring to me," he said, and he made love to her with the ardour of a desperate man.

The intensity of his desire for her was both exciting and disturbing to Anne. It completely obliterated any possible doubt that Thady wanted her, yet the wanting seemed to be driven by a need to absorb all the warm, vital pleasures of her body. His whole being was concentrated on now. With her. In her.

There was a hungry possessiveness in the way he held her to him when he rolled onto his side. The desire to feel her around him was far from diminished by one release of sexual tension. Urgency gave way to a deep, pervasive sensuality, and every movement was piercingly sweet.

Anne could not bring herself to question anything as long as he was with her. Simply to have him again was enough. The world could end and she wouldn't care as long as she was in his arms.

She moved her head on the pillow to look at him, wanting to see her own contentment on his face. His eyes were closed, but there was a soft smile of pleasure on his lips. She reached up and lightly traced it with her fingertips, rejoicing that he looked as though he felt life was worth living.

The thick black lashes lifted to show a glimmer of deep green. He lifted a hand to her face, gently stroked her cheek, then trailed his fingers through the long, silky tresses of her hair. There was tenderness in his touch, and his smile gathered a loving indulgence.

"I've got something to tell you," she said impulsively.

"Tell me," he softly invited.

She hesitated. She knew that she had to tell him he was going to become a father, but was this the right moment? Would she lose all they had just shared? Would he leave her again? A shiver of apprehension ran down her spine.

"I've taken on the production design for *The Pirates of Penzance,*" she said weakly.

He gave her a quizzical look. "Is that good or bad for you?"

It was much simpler to pursue a side issue than to face the critical moment that might change her life. "That depends on you, Thady,'' she said slowly. "I didn't know if you'd need me. If you'd been writing.''

His smile dipped into a grimace. "I haven't done any writing. At least, none of any importance. I have no work for you, Anne,'' he stated flatly.

Whether he had some problem with inspiration, or whether he had tried and failed to put into words what he felt, Anne couldn't guess. It was all too obvious that he had been through several kinds of hell while he had been away from her, and she felt no inclination to remind him of it.

"Is *Pirates* the kind of challenge you'll enjoy?'' he asked, projecting interest in her work.

"Yes,'' she said, but she couldn't put any enthusiasm into it. There were more important things on her mind.

"That wasn't what you were going to tell me, Anne,'' he said quietly.

"How do you know that?'' she asked, her voice sharp with anxiety. Did her body feel different to him? Had he guessed?

His eyes caressed her with soft caring, inviting her trust. "I felt you tremble,'' he said, revealing his intense awareness of her every physical reaction.

Resolution battled with apprehension. The moment for truth, for trust, was now. It could not be put off any longer. Her decision had been right for her. She could only hope it was right for Thady, as well.

She dropped her hand to his chest, spreading her palm over his heart, needing to feel it beating with hers. Her legs instinctively tightened around him. Still she found the words difficult to speak. Her throat had gone dry. She swallowed.

She met the calm steadiness of his gaze, forcing herself to watch for his reaction. Her lips felt stiff as they moved to shape the fateful sentences that formed relentlessly in her mind. They came out in a taut, flat monotone, belying the seething emotion behind them.

"I'm three months pregnant, Thady. You're a father."

CHAPTER FIFTEEN

ANNE SAW THE STUNNED LOOK in Thady's eyes, felt an abrupt pause in his breathing. There was a moment of utter stillness. Then his encircling arms drew her to him, pressing her close to his chest, his chin resting against her forehead.

"Was it an accident, Anne?" he asked quietly, his voice dull, totally void of any judgement.

Fear jammed Anne's mind. Had Thady deliberately hidden his face from her so that she couldn't see his reaction? She remembered his explanation for leaving her all those years ago, that he couldn't belong in her dreams of getting married, having children, the happy ever after.

"No, it wasn't an accident," she replied, a strong sense of self-determination rising over the fear. In a firm voice that would allow her to keep her distance from him if he disapproved of what she'd done, Anne calmly stated, "It was deliberate, Thady. Quite deliberate."

His arms tightened around her. A wash of relief eased Anne's inner tension. Thady did not want to let her go. Light warm kisses touched her hair, her temples, giving more soothing balm to her anxious mind.

"You're so brave. So independent," Thady whispered huskily. "Recklessly brave and fearlessly independent. You go after life as though there's no tomorrow, and nothing and no-one to fear."

There was deep admiration—almost awe—in his voice.

While it sent a tingle of pleasure through Anne's heart, what Thady said seemed terribly ironic.

"It isn't all that easy," she demurred dryly. Then, because she ached to hear him say it, she asked, "Do you want our baby, Thady?"

He didn't answer. He rocked her in his arms. She felt a warm drop of moisture run down her forehead. Alarm bells jangled in Anne's mind. Thady was crying.

Yet if he admired her decision, didn't that mean he wanted her to have the baby? Why should he have such a reaction unless there was something to fear?

In frantic urgency, Anne pulled herself away so she could look at him. As he reluctantly released her from his embrace, she disentangled herself from him to sit up and assert her need to know all that concerned her.

"What's the matter, Thady?" she cried, her eyes sharply focussed on gathering every flicker of expression on his face.

His thick lashes were spiky from the heavy wetness of tears. Thady ruefully dashed his fingers over his cheeks. He mustered a crooked half-smile.

"I don't think I've ever felt so happy before. So much at peace with the world." His voice was a deep throb of emotion that gathered even more poignancy as he added, "I never thought I'd ever have a child."

"Why, Thady? Why did you think that?" she asked, probing his eyes for the truth.

"I never thought that anyone would do this for me," he answered simply. Then he leaned over and kissed her stomach, his lips pressing soft, adoring homage to the life within. "I'll love our baby, Anne," he whispered.

Tears pricked at her eyes as an inner voice cried, *But what about me? Why can't you say you love me?*

Anne quickly stifled it. She *knew* that in some special

unique way Thady did love her, and one day, she promised herself, she would *make* him say it, even if he never married her.

More important at this moment was the question that had been at the forefront of her mind every day for the past three months. Her fingers ran slowly through the curls of his hair, gently holding him to the child he had accepted.

"Thady..." she began hesitantly.

"Mmm?"

Anne scooped in a quick breath and poured out the critical words. "There's no reason why I shouldn't have your baby, is there?"

He kissed her stomach again. "None whatsoever, from my point of view."

"There are no hereditary factors that should be taken into account?" she persisted.

He lifted his head, his eyes still shining happily as he propped himself on his side and gave her an indulgent smile. "Anne, it's perfectly normal you should worry like this, but I promise you, to the best of my knowledge, there are no genetic problems from my family that could harm our baby."

He circled the soft roundness between her hips with reverent fingertips. "We are going to have the most perfect, most adorable, wonderful child that has ever been conceived," he declared. Then he grinned infectiously as he trailed his fingers up to her breasts and began to circle them. "You will be a perfect mother. And I'll try to be a perfect dad."

There was no doubt that he genuinely believed what he said. Anne's relief spilled into an answering grin. It was pure bliss to be assured the baby was not at risk. Not only that, Thady had just committed to being more than the biological father of their child. That must mean he saw a future of sharing their lives together.

At least, as long as he could.

A huge question mark about *his* health still remained. Anne was intensely conscious of it as he leaned over to kiss her. His collarbones had hollows above them, and despite the softening effect of his grin, his face was far too gaunt.

"I think I'll have to make love to you again," he murmured, brushing his lips seductively over hers.

"No," she said decisively.

"Why not?" He shot her a quizzical look. "Will it affect the baby?"

"No. But you're having no more sex from me until you put on ten kilos," she teased, then added more seriously, "you've lost an awful lot of weight."

He made a self-mocking grimace. "I don't feel good to you?"

"So good that I don't want you fading away on me." Her eyes searched his worriedly. "Is there something wrong, Thady?"

"I guess I need you to stir an appetite for life," he answered, dismissing her concern with casual ease. He cocked a teasing eyebrow. "Do you suppose there's enough food in the kitchen for me to put on ten kilos over breakfast?"

That was it, Anne thought with a sense of helplessness. She could almost feel the shutters going up on the past three months. But she would make the future her business, she vowed, as she swung her legs off the bed and reached for her robe.

"I'm going to cook you a whopping big breakfast, Thady Riordan, and you'd better eat every bit of it," she warned.

He did.

Within weeks Thady was looking far more like his former self, and there was no doubting his appetite for life. He exuded happiness and contentment. He fussed over Anne, insisting that she hire assistants to do all the legwork involved in getting the materials for her production design for *Pirates*. When she had to go somewhere, he accompanied her to make sure she didn't exert herself. Anne laughed over his obsessive care for her, but she was secretly glad he cared so much.

He bought books on prenatal care. He bought books on bringing up children. No father-to-be could have been more assiduous in preparing for the birth of his child.

Most of the time Anne was delighted by his attitude, yet she could not help wondering about the reasons that inspired it. Did Thady know that his future was curtailed? Was that why he was so intent on having all he could while he could? He seemed to be centring his entire world around her and the baby. He did not attempt to write. He only went into his study to check the fax machine for messages.

One thing made no sense at all to Anne. If Thady had always wanted a child, the simplest way to go about it was to marry. If he had married her seven years ago, they could have had a family by now.

But then perhaps he wouldn't have written his plays. It seemed one way of life excluded the other for him. He had to be alone to write. That was what he had told her. Maybe he had forced himself to be alone in America for those three months, but it didn't work for him anymore because she had become more important to him.

He was still not prepared to offer marriage, not even for the baby's sake. That became painfully clear when Thady handed her a copy of a long legal document setting out all the details of a trust fund to give both her and their child financial security for life.

"Thady, we haven't even had the baby yet," she protested, stunned by the generosity of the settlement.

"I want to make sure you'll both be taken care of, no matter what happens," he answered.

"Are you expecting something to happen?" she asked sharply.

He shrugged. "Who can foretell the future? If I'm run over by a bus tomorrow, I don't want you having to work to support our child, Anne. The trust fund will pay for a nanny if you want to work, but if you'd prefer to be a full-time mother, then you'll have that option open."

"Wouldn't it be simpler..." She bit down on her tongue, cutting off the treacherous words. She had promised not to try to change him.

He raised his eyebrows questioningly.

She dropped her gaze to the legal document and shrugged. "I guess you've covered all contingencies."

He nodded. "Paula is very thorough. If you ever have a problem, Anne, go to her and she'll sort it out for you."

Paula, who knew everything, Anne thought, but she forced a smile over her niggling frustration. "You didn't have to do this, Thady. It was my decision to have a baby."

"Our baby," he reminded her. "And not all the money in the world could ever repay you for such a gift to me, Anne."

She didn't want money. She wanted him. But when he wrapped her in his arms and kissed her with intense passion, Anne told herself she had to do the same as Thady and live each moment together to the fullest.

Unfortunately that concept had no appeal for Anne's mother. Leonie Tolliver had no appreciation for a man who did not offer marriage to a woman he'd made pregnant. Especially when that woman was her daughter. Ever since Anne had written to announce the baby's arrival sometime in August, her mother's letters were peppered with pointed comments.

One of these remarks, however, did give Anne pleasure. "Jenny has just learnt she is pregnant. Of course, I don't have to worry about my youngest daughter since she has a husband to take care of her. Brian might not be rich or famous, but he's a decent hardworking man whom I can trust to do the right thing by Jenny."

Anne's correspondence with Jenny was in a much happier vein. Her youngest sister was a source of loyal support for everything Anne did.

The Pirates of Penzance opened in June. The theatre critics gave fulsome praise to the innovative production design by Annelise Tolliver. The gossip columnists made comment that Annelise Tolliver looked noticeably pregnant at the premiere. She was, of course, escorted by her constant companion, the playwright Thady Riordan, who seemed to have eschewed writing in favour of approaching fatherhood.

The next month was taken up with looking at houses. Thady had decided that a city apartment was not the best environment for bringing up a child. He was determined on a place in the country, not too far from London so that Anne could easily commute if she wanted to. When they finally found a house they both liked, Thady insisted on buying it in Anne's name.

He had Paula Wentworth draw up the necessary documents. Paula was as discreet as always, carrying out Thady's instructions without so much as a questioning comment. In fact, when Anne went to her office to complete the legalities, Paula wore an approving smile throughout the whole process.

Anne felt dreadfully uncomfortable about accepting a house as well as an income, yet she knew that it was all part and parcel of Thady's determination to protect both her and their child. She had come to believe Jenny was right in her reading of Thady's motives. Right or wrong, he had been protecting her all along. The only problem was that Anne still didn't know what he was protecting her from.

She looked at Paula as she finished the last signature and ruefully remarked, "This makes me feel like a kept woman."

Paula laughed. "I don't think kept women get to keep as much as this, Anne. You're actually better off, in security terms, than most married women."

Before she could stop herself, Anne blurted out the burning question. "Why doesn't Thady marry me, Paula?"

A mask of caution instantly fell over the other woman's amusement. There was a momentary flash of sympathy in the grey-green eyes, but even that was quickly muted to a calm, impassive look. "Aren't you happy the way you are, Anne?" she asked quietly.

"It's not that I'm unhappy...."

"Then leave well enough alone," Paula advised. "You know I can't discuss any of Thady's private business with you."

"Yes, I know. I'm sorry, Paula. It's just that—" she offered an appeasing smile "—I'm getting a lot of flack from my mother."

It was a weak excuse for treading once more on Paula's ethics, but it was graciously accepted. "It's an easy trap for parents to fall into, trying to lead their children's lives for them." The sympathetic comment gathered more point as Paula softly added, "Or the lives of those we care about. Unfortunately, more often than not it drives them away from us."

The subtle warning was not wasted on Anne.

Accept or lose.

It was, more or less, the same message Paula had spelled out months ago.

Since the last thing Anne wanted was to lose Thady, she would go on accepting whatever he chose to give her, do for her, share with her.

It was a happy, exciting time leading up to the birth of their baby. They shopped for nursery things. They changed their minds a thousand times over what names they favoured for their child. Thady bought books and magazines on home decoration and gardening. They spent hours planning the furnishings for their new home in the country and working out how to make best use of the grounds surrounding it.

Then, barely two weeks before the baby was due, Anne's world with Thady suddenly started falling apart. There was no cataclysmic bolt of lightning to mark the moment. Anne had no sense of unease, no premonition at all as she went to the kitchen to cook the big breakfast she insisted Thady have every morning. As usual, he went to the study to check his fax machine before joining her in the kitchen.

The eggs and bacon were cooked, toast made, everything ready to serve, except Thady wasn't there to serve it to. Anne called for him to come. There was no answer. She set the breakfast on the table and hurried through the flat to the study, thinking that he'd been distracted by something and hadn't heard her call.

The door was open.

He stood by the fax machine, a sheet of paper in his hands, his gaze fixed on whatever was printed on the page. His face had lost all colour. His mouth was set in a grim line. His body was utterly still.

''Thady?'' Anne called sharply, feeling an urgent need

to claim his attention, to pull him back from wherever he'd gone.

His head lifted with agonising slowness and turned towards her. There was a dull, faraway look in his eyes. His gaze dropped to her bulging abdomen, and she saw pain cross his face.

"What is it?" she cried, a nameless fear clutching at her heart.

"Nothing." His mouth twisted into a savage grimace as his hands screwed up the fax transmission, compressed the sheet of paper into a tight ball, then dropped it into the wastepaper bin.

Anne did not know what to do in the face of that deliberate lie. "I called you for breakfast," she said weakly.

"I'm sorry. I didn't hear you." He forced a travesty of a smile as he walked over to her. "Let's go and eat then."

But he had no appetite. He picked at the food, swallowing a few bits of egg as though they choked him, pushing the rest around his plate, not even touching the bacon. He chomped on a piece of toast as though willing his teeth into mechanical movement. He washed the crumbs down with sips from his cup of tea.

Finally he gave up any pretence of being able to eat. "I've decided to go out for a while this morning," he stated flatly. His eyes made brief contact with hers. "Don't get up," he said as he pushed away from the table and rose to his feet. He flashed her another false smile. "I know how you enjoy sitting over your coffee."

He made no move to kiss her, as he normally did before leaving her anywhere. He strode out of the kitchen with obvious haste. Anne made no move to follow him. She felt completely paralysed, as though anything she did or said might tip some critical balance that had to be maintained if disaster was to be avoided. She heard the front door bang shut and felt the separation like a cut to the heart.

She sat over her coffee for a long time, trying to pretend that nothing important had happened. Thady would come back, and they would go on as before. Except she couldn't convince herself of that. Something in that fax had taken him away from her. The sense of sharing, the togetherness, was gone.

The image of the screwed up ball of paper plagued Anne's mind. How could she fight what she didn't know? If she was losing Thady anyway, acceptance was not going to do her any good. She had to know what she was up against.

Her whole body seemed to ache in protest as she levered herself out of the kitchen chair. For the first time throughout her pregnancy Anne felt ugly and cumbersome. She remembered the pain on his face when he had looked at her child-heavy body. Whatever else was claiming his mind and heart, he was torn by the want for the child he had never thought he would have.

Thady had shut the door to the study. Anne opened it. The time for shut doors in their relationship had been swept away this morning. She walked across the room and slowly dropped to her knees beside the wastepaper bin. Her hand shook as she reached for the fateful ball of paper. Her fingers trembled as they worked to smooth out all the twists and crinkles.

Anne felt no sense of guilt for wanting to read what had been written. There was no longer any trust to be kept for the sake of staying together in harmony. This was simply the long-delayed moment of truth that had to be faced.

CHAPTER SIXTEEN

THE MESSAGE was short and succinct.

The decision has been made.
The date is August twenty-first.
If there's anything either Richard or I can do, you have
only to ask. Our deepest sympathies go out to you at
this time.

Paula

Anne's mind whirled in confusion. She hadn't considered a legal problem. Surely that was what it had to be,
since Paula was involved. Yet what legal problem would
draw such a reaction from Thady?

Anne studied the words over and over again, trying to
find more significance in them, but there was nothing of
any real substance to work on. The decision and the date
had evoked Paula's deepest sympathies, so whatever was
happening was final, and Paula saw no way out of it.

Anne did not doubt the finality. It was what she had seen
and felt coming from Thady this morning. However, what
lay behind it still remained a mystery. Anne screwed up
the paper and dropped it in the bin. She would have to wait
for answers.

The morning dragged by. It was midafternoon when
Thady returned to the flat. Anne was lying down on one of
the black leather sofas in the lounge. She felt sick from the

ferment of uncertainties that had been stirred by Paula's message. When she heard the front door open, she instantly swung herself into a sitting position, determined to confront the situation head-on.

Whatever Thady had been doing while Anne had suffered through the wretched hours of worrying, he didn't look any the better for it. He entered the room without any awareness that Anne was there. His shoulders were slumped. His face was pale and strained from some inner torment, yet there was grim resolution etched on it.

"You've been a long time," Anne remarked as lightly as she could.

His head jerked towards her. His feet came to a halt. He stared at her as though from a great distance, as though she was a stranger who meant nothing to him. Anne's stomach churned, making her feel nauseous. It hurt to see the effort it took Thady to collect himself.

"I had a lot to do," he said quietly.

"Why don't you tell me what's wrong, Thady?" Anne accused more than asked. It was impossible to ignore what was so painfully clear.

He grimaced at her bluntness. The green eyes looked as sick as she felt as he walked down to the lounge area. He did not come directly to her. He did not sit down with her. He picked up one of the abstract sculptures from a side table and stood looking at it, his fingers idly caressing its marble curves.

"I have to go to America, Anne. I have to go." There was a driven note in his voice that denied any argument.

Rebellion stirred in Anne. Three months of America had drained Thady of any appetite for life. The effect of this morning's message on him had convinced her that nothing good was going to happen there. Another visit would be damaging not only to his well-being, but to their relationship, as well.

"When do you have to go?" she asked, trying to keep calm and clear-headed.

"Tomorrow."

"For how long, Thady?"

He slowly replaced the sculpture on the table. He met her gaze square on. "I don't know how long. It may be weeks. It may be months. I simply don't know."

Anne took a deep breath. "Then I'll come with you. Our baby can be born there as well as here," she reasoned, determined not to be separated from him no matter what the problem was.

He shook his head. "I've made arrangements for you, Anne. You may not be able to manage here alone when the baby starts coming. I thought it best if you stay with Paula and Richard. They're happy to look after you and make sure—"

"Will you stop thinking of what's best for me!" Anne burst out with fierce indignation. She struggled to her feet, ignoring the pain that shot across her lower back. "*I* know what's best for me, Thady," she insisted. "I will be much happier going to America with you. In fact, I will be extremely unhappy if you leave me behind."

His face could have been carved from stone for all the effect her words had on it. "I can't have you with me, Anne."

"But you want to be with me for the birth of our baby," Anne cried in sharp protest. "How can you leave me now, after all we've done together, and when it's almost time for our child to be born?"

He turned abruptly away from her and walked over to the bay window. She saw his shoulders heave as he dragged in a deep breath. His head bowed, as though under an unbearable burden as he spoke.

"I'm sorry. I know I led you to expect I'd be with you at the birth of our child. But I can't be, Anne."

He was not only turning his back on her, but on their baby as well. His apology was no excuse to Anne. His absence at this time was unforgivable. She seethed with so many turbulent emotions, it was almost impossible to find some saving grace for the situation he was imposing on her. Her voice shook with the intensity of her feelings as she demanded an acceptable explanation.

"Give me one good reason, just one good reason. Why can't you be with me, Thady?"

He didn't answer.

"Thady, for God's sake! We're a family now. There shouldn't be any more of these unexplained separations. We may not be married, but wherever you go, we should be together."

"Anne, I've made what provision I could for my absence," he dragged out.

"That's not good enough, Thady."

"I told you it had to be this way a long time ago," he said wearily.

In a fury of hurt and frustration Anne hurled a bitter challenge at him. "Thady, if you won't give me a damned good reason I can't come with you, then don't bother coming back to me. I won't be here. And neither will your child."

His neck arched. He swung around to face her. "You'd do that to me? After all I've done for you?"

A rush of shame burned her cheeks, yet her mind still insisted that he wasn't being fair to their relationship. "You're deserting me when I most need you, Thady."

His face worked with emotion. "For your sake, I denied

my own needs for seven years. Can't you wait a few months for me?''

"Why? Just tell me why!" she cried, unable to accept anything on blind faith anymore.

"For God's sake, Anne! Leave it alone!"

"No," she bit out vehemently. "I won't leave it alone. I don't want to be left alone again. Not for seven years, or seven months, or seven weeks, or seven days! Not without knowing why, Thady. I will not accept that anymore."

He exploded into agitated movement, pacing the floor. He threw her a tortured look. "I've tried to do the right thing by you. You wanted me, Anne. You said you needed me. You chose to have our child. I didn't ask it of you."

"You wanted me, too, Thady," she argued with feverish passion. "And you wanted the child."

"Yes. To my eternal damnation!" he rasped.

"Why do you say that?"

"Isn't it obvious?"

"No. Nothing is obvious."

"Well, it should be. It damned well should be," he muttered, angry frustration raging from him as he stormed around the room. "Why do you think I left you eight years ago?"

"I never understood that."

"I wanted you so badly. You brought me to life again, showed me joy, shared it, made me feel things that I'd thought were as good as dead. I knew it was wrong to give in to the attraction, but you were such a delight to me I couldn't resist it. Just for a while, I thought. Then you started getting serious, making plans, wanting promises I couldn't give. *Couldn't,* Anne. Doesn't that tell you something?"

She shook her head, unable to see that he was telling her anything different to what he had told her before.

"You don't want to see, do you?" he accused bitterly. "It's easier if I take the hard decisions. You still want to dream. It's up to me to face the realities that have to be faced."

"What realities are you talking about, Thady?"

"You said a career had taken the place of all your other dreams, but that wasn't true. You turned what I offered you into something else, Anne, tying me to a future that I couldn't guarantee."

His chest heaved with the turbulence of his feelings. His hands cut the air in vehement gesture as he threw more accusations at her. "Being with me, working with me...that was what you asked. But it wasn't enough for you, was it? So you decided to have a child. My child. Whom you're now using to blackmail me into staying with you when I can't."

Anne flinched. "It's not blackmail. You said you'd love our child. What kind of love is it that doesn't want to welcome a child into the world?"

"The kind of love that makes damned sure the child will never want for anything, no matter how impractical and starry-eyed its mother is!" Thady hurled at her. "We're not married, Anne. Nor are we as good as married. I never promised you marriage, nor did I leave you in any doubt about my position on that score. Why else do you think I set up a trust fund and bought you a house?"

"I haven't asked you to marry me." She fought back. "Only for us to be together. And you still haven't told me why we can't be."

"You don't want to know. If you'd wanted to know you would have worked it out by now."

"Well, I'm sorry I'm so dense!" She flung the words at him. Then, in sheer desperation, she begged, "Tell me, so I can make sense out of it, Thady."

He stopped pacing. The pain on his face, the haunted look in his eyes were terrible to see. "I've tried to protect you from this," he said harshly.

For a moment Anne wavered in her resolution. But she had to know. It had all gone too far for her not to know now.

"I'm married, Anne. I was married long before I met you. And for all that my wife and I haven't lived together for over ten years, she is still my wife. And we are still married."

If it had been a flat statement, Anne might have withstood the shock better. But the words poured from Thady with a passion that smashed any possibility that the marriage was dead for him. All the dark passions in his soul, kept hidden from her...they revolved around this marriage that was far from dead.

Her head spun as she tried to fit the pieces of what she knew together. Thady leaving her to pursue her dreams, living like a monk except when driven to ease his physical frustrations, coming back to her when he thought she might accept him on equal terms, insisting she was free...as he had to be free to go back to his wife.

Anne swallowed hard, trying to regain some equilibrium. "You should have told me. From the beginning," she choked out.

He closed his eyes, shutting out the pain between them. "I didn't *want* to remember."

"Why not tell me the second time around?" she cried.

His eyes slowly opened, revealing a bleak weariness. His mouth twisted with irony. "It wasn't relevant initially. Then, when you revealed the damage I'd done, and your need for me...would it have been better or worse for you if I'd told you I was married, Anne?"

She remembered the desperation of that night, her fear

that Thady would reject her, her joy when he had received her into his embrace. If he had told her he was married…

"You said I was the only man for you," Thady reminded her harshly. "Would you have chosen adultery, Anne? Wasn't it better for me to bear that guilt and give you all I could of what you wanted? To let you be free of any moral torment so you could have what you needed from me?"

Anne shook her head, not knowing how she would have reacted. If she had known he belonged to another woman… "Your wife," she choked out. "Why hasn't she been living with you all these years?"

It was as though her question drained him of life. His face took on a frightening death-mask as he answered her. "She does live with me. In my heart. She always has and always will. The one great passion of my life."

Anne could feel the blood draining from her own face. "You love her…that much."

"Yes."

Not for Anne his love. That had been given to the woman he had married, irrevocably and forever, despite the fact that it wasn't returned, couldn't be returned, or there would be no separation. It was so unfair, so futile, just as her love for Thady was unfair and futile. He cared about her. He desired her. But he did not love her.

"You go to her in America," Anne said dully.

"Yes."

"But she doesn't want you to stay with her."

His face twisted. "God knows what she wants! I've done everything I can think of to reach her, to bring her back to me, but I can't break the barrier between us. I've beaten my head against it for months on end. Until my own survival and sanity depended on getting away from it. Mostly I've escaped into writing."

"Until I provided a happier escape," Anne said with bitter understanding.

"You've given me a lot of happiness, Anne," he acknowledged, his eyes boring into hers as he added, "I thought I'd given you some happiness, as well."

"Yes, you have," she acknowledged in return. *With no happy ending.* She couldn't accuse Thady of deceiving her about that. He had told her straight out he didn't belong in her dream of a happy ever after. She simply hadn't wanted to believe it.

"You forced this issue, Anne," Thady reminded her in a bleak tone. "The decisions are all yours now."

Her chin lifted in proud determination. Her amber eyes glittered with a fierce resolution to rise above the pain that seemed to be racking her body. Her hands moved to hug her unborn child to herself.

"I want to know why it's so imperative for you to go to your wife now. Why can't it wait for another couple of weeks?"

His gaze dropped to her protective hold of their baby. "I have to go," he bit out, his jaw tight as he once more turned away from her and walked to the bay window. His hands were clenched at his sides as he added, "My wife comes first. The child will be born whether I'm here or not. This is the last chance I have to bring my wife back to me."

"And if you can do that, you'll stay with her?"

"Yes. I'll stay with her."

"And if you can't, you'll come back to me. And our child. Is that the plan?"

She saw his hands unclench and clench again. "Do you want me to, Anne?"

No, she thought. She couldn't bear being second best. She couldn't live with him, knowing what she now knew.

Anne had felt stabs of jealousy before, when she had seen photographs of Thady with other women, but the wave of jealousy that consumed her now was so intense she could not bear to stay in the same room with him.

Almost blind with the pain of it, she lurched her way past the furniture, down the hallway, into the bedroom where she had committed adultery countless times with a man who loved his wife. The wife who came first.

She staggered to the dressing table, opened the drawer where she kept the diamond earrings. She could not remember him kindly. Not after this. And he was never going to tell her he loved her, never going to marry her. She took out the velvet box. A pain sliced through her lower back. Liquid gushed down her legs.

Anne cried out in appalled horror as she thought she had lost all control. Then another pain hit her and she realised what had happened, realised that the pain had nothing to do with her heartbreak.

"Anne." Thady's voice called out in anxious alarm. "Anne." Running down the hallway.

Somehow she managed to turn to face him as he reached the bedroom doorway. She threw the velvet box at his feet. "Take them back! Give them to the woman you love!" she cried, then bent over, sobbing for breath as another contraction began.

"Anne, for God's sake…"

"If it's not…too much trouble, get me to the hospital…before you go."

CHAPTER SEVENTEEN

THADY WOULD NOT LEAVE HER when they got to the hospital. He remained at her side while she was being settled in a labour ward. Even after that he made no move to go.

"You don't have to stay," Anne told him, her eyes firing a fierce rejection of any further concern for her. "As you said, the baby will be born whether you're here or not. That's my responsibility. Mine alone, since having the baby was my choice."

His eyes begged her forbearance. "I want to stay, Anne."

Bitterness welled over her pain. Of course, he could stay now. His flight to America was booked for tomorrow. If her labour didn't go on for too long, he would get to see his child. The child he had never expected to have because his wife couldn't or wouldn't give him one.

"Please yourself," she said dully. "But don't expect any joy from it."

"Anne..." He took her hand, his fingers working over hers in intense agitation of spirit. "Anne, you won't transfer your...your hatred of me onto the child, will you?"

"It's *my* child. Mine," she answered with vehement possessiveness. "I don't need you anymore, Thady. And *we* don't need your trust fund, either. Nor your house. Nor the career you gave me. As soon as I'm able, I'll take my baby home to Australia with me and start a new life. Without you in it!"

She snatched her hand out of his and rolled her cumbersome body over on the bed so she was facing away from him. After several long, silent moments she heard him settle on a chair to wait out the hours with her. Anne was determined not to look at him again. Let him see his child, she thought savagely. Let him see what he was giving up for the wife who didn't deserve his love.

Oddly enough, his presence eased the loneliness of the pain she suffered through, even though they didn't talk to each other. The only words spoken were to doctors and nurses.

The baby was born just after three o'clock the next morning.

Anne was so exhausted, she did not have the strength to protest when the nurse passed the newly wrapped baby to Thady for him to bring to her. She watched him cradle it tenderly, his face softened with love and wonderment as he slowly walked to Anne's side. Very gently he placed the precious bundle next to her, then bent to kiss the soft little face.

"I wish you every blessing in life, my son," he whispered huskily. He straightened up, his hand trailing over Anne's to draw her attention. "Thank you," he said simply.

He turned away before she could make any reply. He was gone before she realised there was nothing appropriate to say, anyway. It was over. Thady had accepted her decision.

As she looked down at the tiny perfection of her baby son, the emptiness Thady had left behind was filled by a flood of maternal love. She was glad it was a boy. A boy with tight black curls. Wanting Thady's love had been hopeless from the start, but she wouldn't be the loser with this part of him. His son was hers.

Eventually she was wheeled into a private room. She relinquished her baby into the care of the nursing staff and welcomed sleep long overdue.

It was almost noon when she awoke. Thady would have left London by now, she thought, and idly wondered what *was* scheduled for the twenty-first of August. Not that it was any of her business anymore. Even if it was a divorce action, it made no difference to her future. Today was the start of a new life with her son.

Michael John, she decided. Michael John Tolliver. It was a fine name. Thady had preferred Patrick for a son, but that no longer mattered. She would call her boy Michael John.

Her bedside table was cluttered with two beautiful floral arrangements. The accompanying cards had been left in easy reach for Anne. She picked them up, certain in her mind that neither of them would hold Thady's name. One was from Paula and Richard Wentworth, the other from Alex Korbett. Of course, Thady would keep Paula informed, and Paula had probably told Alex about the birth since he was an old friend of Anne's.

A nurse made her entrance with yet another floral gift, white daisies and blue irises for a boy. "Ah, I don't have to wake you up," the nurse said cheerfully. "It's about time we fed you so you can feed your baby. My goodness, he's got a great pair of lungs when he starts bawling for his mum!"

Anne laughed with pleasure at the thought of her son wanting her, even if it was only to be fed.

"I'll put these down here, shall I?" the nurse asked, placing the new flowers on the movable tray at the end of Anne's bed. "They were ordered from Australia. How about that?" She gave Anne a big grin as she handed over the accompanying envelope.

Thady must have informed her family of the birth, Anne

thought, quickly extracting the card from the envelope. Her eyes widened in surprise as she read the message.

"Thady called. He's arranged for me to fly to England to be with you and the baby. See you both in a day or two. Keep well. Love, Jenny."

Tears swam into Anne's eyes before she could stop them.

"Hey! Not bad news, I hope," the nurse crooned sympathetically.

"No. Good news," Anne assured her with a wobbly smile. "My sister is coming to visit."

"Lovely! Now I'll just bring you a nice cup of tea, and then order up your lunch."

Anne dwelled on this last kind and generous gesture of Thady's for a long time.

One couldn't order love. It was there or it wasn't there. Perhaps it was wrong of her to deny Thady access to their child. She had made that decision out of bitter personal pain, not with any thought to the future happiness of her child. Anne had no doubt that Thady would shower love on his son, if and when he could make time to be with him.

She decided she would have to give more thought to that. At a later date. When she felt more settled, when seeing Thady wouldn't hurt so much.

Tears filled her eyes again as she thought of Jenny dropping everything to fly to her side. Never mind her husband, Brian, who was probably concerned about his wife taking off for the other side of the world. Anne could just imagine Jenny laying down the law.

"Brian, Anne *needs* me. If you called Anne and said I needed her, she would come flying to me. That's what sisters are for."

And Brian would love Jenny all the more for it, Anne decided.

At least she had her baby to love. Michael John, she

recited to herself, feeling her love for him swelling her heart with joy. She would never, never regret the decision she had made to have this child.

She thought it even more strongly when he was brought to her for feeding and she held him in her arms, watching his tiny hand curling and clutching at her breast, feeling the soft sucking motion that sent tingles right down to her stomach. Her life had been worth living simply for this wonderful experience.

Michael John was snugly nestled in the crook of Anne's arm when Paula Wentworth knocked on the door, breaking the private intimacy Anne was enjoying with her baby.

"Mind if I come in?" she asked, her smile appealing for entry.

Paula was so closely connected to Thady that Anne felt a twinge of reluctance about the visit, but she could not dismiss the friendship Paula had extended to her on any number of occasions.

"Please do. And thanks for the flowers, Paula."

"My pleasure. Is he asleep?" Paula whispered, her gaze dropping to the baby as she came forward.

"Yes."

"Oh, he's so beautiful!" Paula declared warmly. "The spitting image of Thady."

Anne's heart clenched at the comparison.

Paula reached out and pressed her hand. "I'm sorry Thady couldn't share this time with you, Anne," she said in soft sympathy.

"He had to go," Anne stated flatly.

"I know."

Anne took a deep breath as she told herself to use this opportunity to start separating herself from Thady's world. "Thady said he'd made arrangements for me to stay with you, but I won't, Paula. My sister's coming. I'll be fine with her."

"Of course. But if there's anything we can do, please don't hesitate to ask."

The concern in her voice drew a wry smile from Anne. "You don't have to be discreet anymore, Paula. Thady told me about his wife."

"Oh!" Paula looked momentarily disconcerted. She set a chair close to the bed and sat down. Her shrewd grey-green eyes registered understanding. "I guess that came as a great shock to you, Anne."

"Yes."

"The date…" Paula grimaced. "It was the worst possible timing for you."

"Yes," Anne agreed.

The grimace curved into an indulgent smile as Paula looked down at Michael John. "At least Thady was able to be with you for the birth. And to see his baby son. Such a lovely memory to take away with him."

Anne felt resentment stir. Paula had always been supportive of everything Thady did. Including adultery and deception.

Paula's gaze lifted in kindly inquiry. "Will your sister be staying in London until Thady comes back?"

"No. And neither will I. I'm not waiting for Thady this time, Paula. I'm going home to Australia. And staying there."

"You don't mean…" Paula frowned. "You can't mean you don't want him back?"

"He chose to leave me. For the wife he loves."

"But, Anne." Paula looked deeply distressed. She shook her head. "How can you be so cruel! It's only a matter of a few days and then it will all come to an end. A blessed release for both of them."

"It will never come to an end for Thady," Anne retorted sharply, angered by Paula's twisted view of who was being cruel to whom. "He loves her. He always will."

"Oh, Anne! You'd give up the reality of your love with Thady because of a remembered dream?"

It might be a memory but it was very real to Thady, Anne thought grimly. His one great passion. "His wife comes first with him," she stated bitterly.

"For God's sake, Anne! Can't you understand that at a time like this? Have you no compassion?" Paula demanded, her whole expression stamped with appalled horror.

"Why should I?"

Paula rose to her feet with frosty dignity. "I see Thady was right in wanting to keep you separate from that part of his life if this is your reaction to it. And after all Thady's done for you!" There was an icy contempt in her eyes. "You'll forgive me if I leave you to your incredible selfishness."

Paula made her exit while Anne was still swallowing the shock of that accusation. Paula's condemnation of her was so absolute it forced Anne to re-examine their conversation. The more she thought about it, the more she realised she had to be missing some important pieces of information about Thady and his wife.

As biased as Paula might be towards Thady's point of view, she was not an unreasonable person. Until now, she had been sympathetic towards Anne's position, but she had decisively insisted Thady's wife should come first at a time like this, and that Anne should have shown compassionate understanding.

The friendly nurse came in to take Michael John back to the nursery for a bath and change. Anne's mind was so busy revolving around these questions, she didn't mind giving in to hospital routine. She decided there was only one person who was likely to give her the answers she wanted. Alex Korbett. There was no reason to keep her promise to Thady anymore, and there could be very cogent reasons why she should break it.

She hitched herself up in bed and reached for the telephone on the table beside her. She breathed a sigh of relief when Alex promptly answered her call.

"It's Anne. Thank you for the lovely flowers, Alex."

"Only too delighted. Are you feeling very much the proud mother of your personal production design?"

Anne had to smile at his patter. "Very proud. But also rather lonely at the moment. Thady had to leave me to go to America. I need your company, Alex. Could you possibly…"

"Say no more. I was born to be a gallant knight to ladies in distress. I shall pop into a metal steed and gallop to your side. Now smile, dear girl, and count the minutes."

Barely half an hour later he arrived with an armful of glossy magazines. "They've got pretty pictures, if nothing else," he declared, settling on the chair Paula had vacated.

"Thanks, Alex. You're a treasure," Anne said warmly.

He preened in his extravagant manner. "Always full of goodies. But I don't open my treasure to everyone, you know. Only to special people." His bright blue eyes beamed their favour on her. "Where's the precious babe?"

"In the nursery ward. I'll show him to you later, Alex. Right now I need to talk to you about Thady and his wife."

His expression underwent an immediate change. His hands flapped in protest. "No, no, out of the question, dear girl. Can't be done. My lips are sealed on that subject. I don't want to be murdered. Thady said he'd kill me if I breathed a word. And he meant it. Very passionate about it. Can't be done."

"Alex, I know about his wife," Anne pointed out emphatically. "But I don't know enough. You've got to tell me what I don't know."

He shook his head vehemently and rose to his feet. "Sorry, Anne. Gave my solemn word. Can't help. Best if I go before I get into trouble."

"Alex, if you don't tell me, I'll leave Thady and take his son with me, and he won't be coming home to anyone because we'll be gone. Back home to Australia."

Alex sat down again, his mouth dropping open in shock. "You wouldn't do that to him, Anne."

"Yes, I would. I've already told Paula Wentworth that's what I'm going to do. And she said things to me that made me realise Thady hadn't told me everything about his wife. So if you think I should stay here for him, Alex, you'd better start telling me why."

Alex heaved a deep sigh. "Cleft stick," he muttered. "Damned if I do, and damned if I don't."

"You can start by telling me what's going to happen on the twenty-first of August," Anne bored on relentlessly.

"The machines," he said dolefully. "They're going to switch off the machines. Her family told Thady they were going to put an application to the court for that purpose when he went over there last December. Irreversible deterioration. No hope of a normal life anymore. Thady didn't feel he could fight them about it. The last ten years have been painful for them, as well. So the case went through the courts and they won the decision they wanted. And finally the date was set for the twenty-first of August."

Anne couldn't make much sense out of this information. "What machines, Alex?"

He frowned at her. "You said you knew about his wife."

"Just tell me what machines."

"I don't know. I'm not into that kind of medical technology. Whatever is involved."

"For what?"

"To keep her alive, of course. She's been in a deep coma for ten years. Can't do anything for herself. Isn't aware of anything or anyone. Just lies there in a deep coma."

"Oh, my God!" Anne clapped her hands to her face and stared at Alex in horror as all the pieces fell into place with devastating force.

"You didn't know," Alex said accusingly.

"Not about the coma," Anne choked out. "How did it happen? Was it an accident?"

"No." He shook his head. "That's the tragedy of it. They'd only been married for eighteen months. Still on their honeymoon, so to speak. Unknown to both of them she had Goodpasture's disease. One night when they were making love…"

"Go on," she urged.

Alex looked distinctly uncomfortable, but he acceded to her need to know. "She haemorrhaged severely into both lungs. Before Thady could get medical help for her, she'd virtually suffocated. She went into a coma and has never emerged from it."

He heaved a deep sigh. "Thady blamed himself for it. He found out all he could, everything that's ever been written about coma patients. Year after year he's gone and sat at her bedside, talking to her, writing his plays for her and reading them to her, doing all he can to bring her back."

And last Christmas he had been told about her family's decision to seek an end to the agony. Anne finally understood what Thady had been through while she had been waiting for him. He must have tried harder, longer, being with his wife day and night, torn apart by his inability to reach her.

It made sense now, his tears when she had told him about the baby. Having lived every minute with the imminence of a death sentence for the woman he loved, he had been granted a life to have in her place.

Alex leaned forward and took her hands. "Anne, my life is probably forfeit if Thady ever learns I've told you about this."

"How do you know it all, Alex?"

"Thady told me his circumstances when he asked me to give you a job eight years ago." He shrugged, then added, "Paula knows I know."

"I see," Anne murmured, then with puzzled curiosity asked, "how is it that there's been no publicity about any of this, Alex? What with the court case, and Thady being fairly famous…"

"His wife kept her maiden name when they married. And Thady didn't attend the court case. Besides, you must remember that Thady wasn't at all well known then. Apart from which, he keeps his visits to America very private. It would be crassly intrusive for the press to have a field day with such a painful situation."

Anne fully agreed on that. The press could be such vultures on what they euphemistically called human interest stories.

Alex squeezed her hands. His eyes filled with anxious appeal. "Anne, Thady doesn't want to lose you. He's had so little to be happy about over the years. You can't desert him now. Or rob him of his son. You must see that wouldn't be fair." His mouth made an eloquent grimace. "Besides which, he'll kill me. You mightn't think my life is important, but it is to me."

Anne managed a reassuring smile. "It's all right, Alex. You've been a good friend to both of us in telling me what you have."

He instantly brightened. "So you'll stay?"

"I don't know. I'll have to think about it. But there is one last thing you can do for me, Alex. Give me the address of the hospital."

"No." He waved his hands in truculent protest. "No. That's not a good idea, Anne."

"Give it to me, Alex," she commanded. "I don't know if I'll ever need it. Or use it. But if you don't give it to me, and things get fouled up between me and Thady, you'll be held responsible for it."

Alex turned green. "Why do I get involved in these things?" he cried despairingly.

"Because you want Thady Riordan to write more plays."

"Yes. Yes, I do. For that I would almost sacrifice my life."

"Then write down the address."

He heaved a very deep sigh, grimaced in resignation, then drew a slim notebook and a pen from the inner pocket of his suitcoat. "I hope this works out, Anne," he muttered as he wrote the address down.

"So do I," Anne agreed feelingly.

She didn't know what decision she would make. She had to look after her baby first. She had to wait until Jenny arrived from Australia. Only then would she be able to concentrate her heart and mind fully on what she was going to do about Thady.

CHAPTER EIGHTEEN

IT WAS well-nigh impossible for Anne to make a decision. To be with Thady at such a time seemed a ghoulish intrusion upon a deeply personal and private tragedy. Yet the alternative was equally unacceptable. Not to be with him at a time when he might need her strength and support to help him past such a traumatic event seemed dreadfully unfeeling.

In a way, this whole situation was his fault. He had kept his secrets right to the end, perhaps finding it unbearable to talk about what was to happen, particularly to the woman who had taken his wife's place in his life.

Guilt about infidelity, guilt about being happy with Anne while his wife's death was being decided in the courts, guilt about sharing the anticipation of having a baby instead of sticking to the task of reclaiming his wife from her coma. Anne could understand the emotional hell that had separated Thady from her when he had received that fateful fax. He would instinctively recoil from inviting Anne's pity or sympathy or compassion.

Clearly he did not want Anne with him while he strove to bring his wife back from the brink of death. He had to concentrate his entire life force on one last effort before it was too late. Anne knew he would spend every possible moment with his wife, barely sleeping, probably not eating, trying everything he knew to reach past the deep coma and touch her mind.

If the circumstances were reversed, and it was her husband under a death sentence, Anne knew she would do the same, despite the long passage of years that made their love more a remembered dream than a reality. She would not have been able to let him die without trying one last time.

But then the horror of the machines being switched off... And afterwards, the bereft emptiness, the grief for what had once been, the unchangeable finality, the cold loneliness of all the dark spaces. Thady had murmured those words to her on the night they had first made love, the night he had accepted her into his life. Anne couldn't bear the thought of Thady feeling that again, not when she could stop it by being there and assuring him he could come back to her and their baby when he was ready.

Yet how would that sound to him at such a moment? Maybe he would hate her for being alive when the wife he had loved was dead. Maybe he would see her arrival on the scene as some jealous attempt to claim him from his wife. Totally selfish.

Anne was still agonising over what she should do when Jenny arrived two days later. Despite the fatigue of the long flight from Sydney to London, Jenny did her best to be cheerful company, but Anne's emotional stress was so great she could barely respond to her sister. Nor was it doing her baby any good. Her milk dried up, and Michael John had to be bottle-fed.

Jenny grew anxious about Anne's withdrawn state. "I know you must be missing Thady, but, Anne," she pleaded, "you should be bursting with happiness about the baby, not sinking into some postnatal depression."

Somehow Jenny's plea triggered Anne's own tortured need for positive action. Right or wrong, she felt driven to go to the man she loved and show him the same kind of love and compassion he had shown her in answering her needs. She looked into the worried eyes of her youngest sister and appealed for understanding.

"Jenny, I've had to come to a decision that was very difficult to make. I need your help. I don't want to explain the whys and the wherefores."

"That's okay," Jenny encouraged. "I'll do anything you ask."

"I have to go to America to be with Thady. It's terribly important that I be there for him on the twenty-first of August. And that's only six days from now."

Jenny frowned in concern. "What about the baby?"

"Will you look after Michael John for me? I'll hire a nanny to help you. I can't take him with me. Very young babies suffer severe pain from the difference in air pressure in airplanes. One of the nurses explained it to me."

"Don't worry about it. He'll be fine with me," Jenny assured her. "I've had a lot of practice with Liz's and Kate's kids when they were babies."

"There are a couple of other matters, Jenny."

"Go on."

"An air ticket. On Concorde, if possible. I can't afford any delay."

"It's really that urgent?"

Anne projected all the inner certainty and intensity that she felt at Jenny. "This is the most important decision of my life. I'm full of fear. I have no idea what the outcome will be. It will determine what the future holds for Thady and me. And our son. Please don't make it worse by questioning."

Jenny leaned over and planted a loving kiss on her cheek. "Relax, Anne. Just tell me what you want and I'll get moving on it."

Over the next five days, Jenny was a source of indefatigable support. Somehow she managed to fulfil all Anne's requests, and never once gave into any curiosity about the situation. She was a tower of strength, particularly with caring for the baby. It tore Anne's heart to leave Michael John behind but she had no doubt about Jenny's competence to look after him.

Her inner tension virtually obliterated the lonely journey to her destination in America. Anne fiercely concentrated on blocking out any doubts about what she was doing. The decision was made. She was on her way. She would be at the hospital before the machines were switched off on Thady's wife.

If Thady had succeeded in bringing his wife out of the deep coma, then there would be nothing for Anne to do but turn around and go home. But if he had failed, she had to let him know he could share the dark, lonely spaces of his life with her again. If he wanted to.

Anne spent a restless night in her hotel room. She could not stomach the thought of breakfast the next morning. She dressed in the suit she had packed, a sage green outfit that she hoped was quietly appropriate and non-offensive should Thady see her at all. She wound her thick, long hair into a neat chignon, intensely conscious of not appearing in any way competitive for Thady's attention. Despite the paleness of fatigue and the shadows under her eyes, she eschewed make-up on the same delicate grounds.

A cab took her to the hospital. It was just nine o'clock as she walked through the entrance doors. One hour to go, she thought, her stomach churning with a thousand uncertainties. Anne wasn't sure where to go, whether she would even be able to gain admittance to the ward where Thady was undoubtedly with his wife, waiting through to the last fatal second. Her legs trembled as she approached the reception desk.

"Anne!"

The crisp British voice spun Anne around. Her eyes widened in shock as she saw Paula Wentworth rise from a table in a kiosk area adjacent to reception. Yet even as she recognised the other woman, shock faded into acceptance. It was not really surprising that Paula was here for Thady. Paula, walking smartly towards her, ready to protect Thady's interests.

She wore a black suit. Anne wondered if her clothes were terribly wrong. Perhaps it had been crazy to wear green, yet green was for spring, and hadn't Thady always associated her with spring? She had wanted to suggest to him that his long cold winter was over…if he chose it to be.

"What are you doing here?" Paula demanded, almost hissing the words at Anne as she reached her side.

"Thady's wife…she hasn't come out of the coma?" Anne asked, leaping straight to the most critical issue.

Paula shook her head. "There was never any real chance of that," she said impatiently.

"I'm neither selfish nor cruel, Paula," Anne burst out. "I didn't understand what Thady was telling me. I thought his wife was divorcing him and he didn't want to let her go. I had no idea of what was really happening until I forced Alex Korbett to tell me."

"Dear God!" Paula ran a shaky hand over her brow, then dropped it to clasp Anne's hand. Her eyes were grey with fatigue. "I came because I thought he needed someone. But you, Anne… Didn't he ask you to wait?"

"But I said I wouldn't. Don't you see?" she pleaded. "I can't let him think he's lost everyone, Paula. He has to know that there is a future with me and his son. If he wants it."

"I could tell him after it's over," Paula suggested, clearly doubtful about Anne's presence on the scene.

"Don't you think Thady might need to hear it from me?

Wouldn't it save him pain if I told him now?'' The agony of Anne's decision was in her strained voice.

"I don't know. I doubt if even Thady would know. I can't advise you on this, Anne."

"I don't know, either. But I swear to you I'm only thinking of Thady. It's not for me. Only for him, Paula."

Paula dragged in a deep breath. "Then you must do what you think is best."

"I've thought and thought about it. It's the only way I can see. I have to go to him."

Paula squeezed her hand sympathetically. "Has all this come about because of the words I said to you?"

Tears filmed Anne's eyes. "Yes. It was a turning point. I knew there had to be more that I didn't know. But really, it should never have been necessary. When you love someone, truly love someone, there's no room for secrets. This should have all come out a long time ago."

"I'll pray for both of you," Paula said huskily.

"Where do I go?"

"I'll walk with you to the door."

Anne struggled to regain composure as Paula steered her to an elevator. Once they had reached the right floor, Paula quietly indicated a sitting room where she would wait while Anne was with Thady. Then they walked along a wide corridor to the room at the end of it.

"Do you know what you're going to say?" Paula whispered, gesturing towards the closed door.

"I think so." The words trembled from Anne's lips. Her heart seemed to be slamming against her chest. "I feel terribly frightened."

"I'm frightened, too." Paula gave her shoulder a light squeeze. "Good luck, Anne."

"Thank you."

As Paula moved off down the corridor, Anne closed her

eyes, took a deep breath and gathered her courage to the sticking point. This was right. It had to be.

She opened the door, stepped into the room, every nerve in her body wire-taut. It was a severely stark place, all white except for the banks of monitors grouped around the bed and attached in some fashion to the woman who lay there. Thady sat on the other side of her, his elbows on the bed, one of his wife's hands clasped between his and pressed to his lips. His eyes were closed, his head bowed as though in deep prayer.

Anne's resolution wavered. It seemed like sacrilege to break into such intense concentration. She glanced nervously at the woman Thady had loved and married, and her heart sank at the pure beauty of her face, a young, seemingly unmarked face, its smooth perfection framed by soft, red-gold curls.

Anne wrenched her gaze away, painfully conscious now of the dream that haunted Thady. It was not the past that had brought her here, she reminded herself. It was the future.

Yet the past lived in this room, Anne suddenly realised. At the foot of the bed was propped a framed photograph, Thady with his bride, a bride with a glorious wild halo of red-gold hair. In front of it lay a red rose, its rich scent dispelling the antiseptic atmosphere of the room.

Anne did not look any further. She did not want to see other mementos. They would make her feel even more of an intruder.

She quietly closed the door behind her, then forced herself to walk around the bed to where Thady was sitting. He did not stir. There was not the slightest reaction to anyone having entered the room. His absorption with his inner world was utterly complete.

Anne stood beside him, not daring to force her presence

into this deep and private grief. After long silent, torturous minutes, she decided she couldn't. Her decision had been wrong. There had to be some other way to the future.

Tears blinded her eyes as she stepped back and turned. She carefully skirted the end of the bed, terrified of making any noise to draw attention to herself. She had to leave fast, yet she couldn't afford to hurry.

"Anne!"

The harsh rasp of her name froze her in mid-step. Panic churned through her as she darted a frantic look at Thady. His head was up. He had half risen from his chair, shock adding its ravages to the haggard lines of his face.

"I'm sorry. I'm sorry." The words spilled from her lips in a desperate rush. Tears raced uncontrollably down her cheeks.

"Why are you here?"

"So you wouldn't be alone. In case you needed me. To retract the terrible words I said to you in London when I didn't know what was happening. To help you in any way I can. To show you that your pain is my pain, Thady."

"No," he groaned. "I never meant to give you pain."

"There is no life without pain, Thady. Or love. I wanted you to know that all I have is yours to have. Or any part of it you choose. If you want it. Because I love you. Because I always will love you."

Thady sucked in a deep breath, but his face was impassive. A flicker of movement seemed to catch Anne's eye. She turned her head quickly, looked once more upon the figure in the bed and the bank of monitors. She was wrong. Nothing had moved. Nothing had changed.

"There's a waiting room just down the corridor," she said, her voice shaking with her inner misery. "I'll be there with Paula. If there's anything you want or need…" She shot one last pleading look at Thady.

His gaze was fastened on his wife's face. "Pray for her, if you will." His voice was strangely gentle.

"I will," she whispered, her voice choked with emotion.

She left as quickly and as quietly as she could. Paula looked inquiringly at her as she entered the waiting room. Anne sank gratefully into the armchair next to her.

"Bad?" Paula asked softly.

Tears swam into Anne's eyes again. "I failed. I should have respected his wishes. I should never have come. But I did learn something. Something very beautiful. I saw the pure face of love. The total giving of one person to another."

"Yes, I know," Paula murmured. "It's at the heart of his plays, isn't it?"

They lapsed into silence. Anne grieved over the thought that she could never take the place of Thady's wife. Then she found herself offering up a prayer for her. And another. And another.

Time dragged so slowly, the seconds seeming like minutes, the minutes like hours. A middle-aged couple walked past. They were sombrely dressed. The man's face was drawn with pained resignation. The woman was softly weeping.

"Her parents," Paula murmured discreetly.

Anne's thoughts returned to what was about to happen in the room at the end of the corridor, the pain and distress Thady must be feeling. She couldn't bear to look at her watch. She didn't want to know the exact moment of life giving way to death. She prayed a half-remembered litany for the dying.

The sound of sobbing broke the awful silence. The parents walked by again, heading back the way they had come, their heads bowed, the husband trying desperately to comfort his wife through his own tears of grief.

It had been done, Anne thought numbly, and nothing now could undo it. She wondered if the pain they had sought to end would ever be ended for them or for Thady. A blessed release, Paula had called it. But was it truly a release?

Anne stood up. She didn't want to be sitting down when Thady finally took his leave of the woman he had loved so much. She didn't know if he would come to the waiting room or pass by, as wrapped in grief as his parents-in-law had been. Paula stood beside Anne, silently lending her support. They waited, conscious of every second that passed. Finally there was the sound of slow footsteps in the corridor.

Thady appeared in the open doorway. His lips were bloodless, his face a ghastly grey. "It's over," he said, his voice as brittle as glass scraping over gravel.

Words were clearly inadequate. There was nothing that Anne could think of that would be adequate. She tried to show the sorrow she felt through her eyes.

Paula choked and took a half-step forward, her arms out-raised. Thady moved to meet her, wrapping her in a tight hug. "Thank you, old friend," he said gruffly. "It was good of you to come, but there's nothing you can do for me."

"Take care, Thady," Paula begged. After a brief pause, she looked up and fervently added, "We all need you." Then she returned his hug and said, "If you don't want anything from me, I'll go now."

"You can do me a favour, if you would."

"Anything at all."

"Look after Anne for me."

"I'll do everything I can."

"I'm sure you will."

Anne could feel the blood draining from her face at the

implication of that requested favour. Thady was not coming back to her.

Thady released Paula and turned towards Anne. He made no move to draw her into an embrace. He took her two hands and placed them over his heart. Anne bravely lifted her chin to face whatever had to be faced. There was a pained plea for understanding in his eyes.

"I have to be alone, Anne."

"Of course," she agreed, biting her lip to hold back the tears.

"I need to come to terms with what has happened…with many things. I've got to start afresh. When I find the words I want to say, I'll write to you."

"I'll wait for that."

"Have you named our son?"

"Yes. Michael John."

"It's a beautiful name."

"I think so."

"You are beautiful, too." He bent his head and brushed his lips over hers in the gentlest of kisses, warm, tender, kind, but without the slightest shred of desire.

He drew back, released her hands, turned away.

"Thady…"

He paused, glanced back reluctantly.

Anne flushed, ashamed of wanting more than he could give right now. "How long do you think it might be?"

The weary hopelessness on his face was answer enough. "I don't know, Anne. I truly don't know. But I won't keep you waiting any longer than is absolutely necessary. When I can resolve it all in my mind and my heart, then you'll know."

He had said all he was going to say. Anne asked for no more. She stood there transfixed by a dread feeling of inevitability as she watched him go, each step away from her taking him on his solitary journey.

Paula moved to her side and curled her arm around Anne's. "New mothers need to be looked after," she said with caring kindness. "I promised Thady to look after you. I'm taking you home."

CHAPTER NINETEEN

It was nearly three months before Anne heard from Thady. Although he had been perpetually on her mind, Anne had found a calm resignation within herself to carry her through whatever time Thady needed to come to a decision. Besides, she had Michael John to keep her busy and give her joy.

Jenny had long since gone home to Brian. Anne wrote to her regularly, giving news of the baby. Alex Korbett had appointed himself an honorary uncle and often visited them or took them out to some special event. Anne had become close friends with Paula Wentworth, who was always on hand to ensure Anne was well looked after. Taking everything into consideration, the three months had not been bad at all.

Until the parcel arrived in the mail from Thady.

A parcel, not a letter.

Anne stared at the postmark. It had been sent from Ireland, not America. Paula had told her he had family in Ireland. An elderly mother who refused to move from her home. A few cousins.

Anne opened the parcel with acute trepidation. The thick wad of pages bound in rubber bands had to be a manuscript. A new play. It was the first time, since she and Thady had come together, that he had written anything. There was a note attached to the front page.

Dear Anne,

I'm sorry it took so long to write this. I had great difficulty finding the words. There was so much to express. I hope you'll understand everything when you read it. I'll be with you and Michael John tomorrow.

                                                              Thady.

Anne lifted the note. The title of the play leapt up at her—*The Last Grand Passion*. Instantly a coil of revulsion tightened around her heart. She didn't want to read it. She had no doubt that it revolved around Thady's love for his wife and the loneliness and despair and grief that he had felt after her death.

Anne had lived through that. The last thing she wanted was to experience it again through Thady's play. Writing it all down might represent some kind of catharsis for him, but Anne was quite certain it could only give her more haunting memories of what he had felt for his wife. She wanted the past over. She wanted the future to begin.

Tomorrow, she thought, with a burgeoning of wild hope. Thady would be with her and Michael John tomorrow. Somehow, one way or another, Anne resolved to keep Thady with them. For the future.

She took the manuscript into his study and laid it on his desk. Then she went to the room she had turned into a nursery and smiled down at her baby, still sleeping peacefully from his mid-morning bottle. He was so beautiful. No way in the world could Thady resist loving him.

Later on in the afternoon, she took Michael John shopping and bought new outfits for both of them, a gorgeous red playsuit for Thady's son and a dark brown velvet pants-suit for herself.

Anne found it impossible to sleep that night. Her mind was full of nervous anticipation. Apart from which, she could not keep Thady's play out of her thoughts. He expected her to read it. He wanted her to know all he had thought and felt. She kept remembering her own words. *When you love someone, truly love someone, there's no room for secrets.*

Sharing was what love was all about. Sharing the good and the bad. *Your pain is my pain,* she had told him, and if she didn't live up to that, what would Thady think of her tomorrow? No matter how much pain it gave her, Anne decided, she had to read what Thady had written.

She pushed herself out of bed, went to his study and settled herself in the leather chair behind the desk, determined to read every word of Thady's play. Her hands trembled a little as she removed the rubber bands and lifted the title page aside.

The opening scene horrified her. There could be no doubt that *she* was Joanna, receiving a telephone call from the man she had loved seven years before. The words held her mesmerised, compelling her to read on and on, the complex passion between the two main characters reflecting so closely what had happened between her and Thady. *Her.* Not his wife.

It revealed many dimensions of feeling on Thady's side, the deep conflicts that had raged through him, the enormous swings from joy to despair and back again. It evoked memories that Anne had put aside, his horror at the thought that she might have some terrible medical problem that would rob him of her as he had been robbed of his wife. So many things gathered poignant meaning.

Anne wept and smiled in turn as his love for her took so many turnings. And always the passion, growing and deepening through every scene, winding around them, pulling them apart. Thady's words evoked every nuance of every emotion. Anne read to the last line, then sat there transfixed.

It was brilliant. More absorbing and compelling than *The Long Cold Winter*. Nothing Thady had ever written matched the grand sweep of this perception of the human heart. Yet the play was unfinished, the ending unresolved.

Anne felt it could go either of two ways. It could finish with the dark, stark tragedy that was Thady's hallmark. But for the first time in his life, he had written a glimmering of hope, a yearning for happiness, a tentative promise that this last grand passion would be fulfilled.

Tomorrow, Anne thought, her heart pumping its urgent hope for the ending she wanted. And surely Thady wanted it, too. Surely he did, or he would not be coming.

She could not believe he had written this play to commercialise what they had felt for each other. He had written it solely for her, to share with her, to banish forever the loneliness of secrets. It was an invitation to join her life with his, indissolubly, forever. That was what Thady had wanted her to understand before he came.

Anne hugged herself tightly as she realised her dreams might come true. All her dreams. She took herself to bed, willing tomorrow to come quickly, not wanting the dreams of yesterday but the reality that Thady would bring with him.

She was up early. She fed Michael John and dressed him in his new playsuit. She left him playing happily with an assortment of baby toys while she dressed herself for Thady, eager to look as beautiful as he thought her.

She had only just finished fussing over her appearance when she heard a knock at the front door. She raced to answer it. The door was already opening as she reached the living room. It had to be Thady, using his key.

He stepped into the room.

His arms opened to her as she flung herself against him. "You're home," she cried, her eyes sparkling with golden happiness as she looked up at his beloved face.

"Yes. I'm home at last," he said, his voice throbbing with the deep warmth of his happiness that it should be so.

He looked good. He felt good. Anne breathed a contented sigh. Thady had not come back to her for any healing this time. He had healed himself and had come to her a whole man, no longer torn apart by anything.

"Did you read the play?" he asked softly, his green eyes searching hers with hope and love.

"Yes. But it's not finished, Thady," she answered, her eyes mirroring the same feelings.

"That's for you to write, Anne. Any way you want."

"You tell me, Thady. What you've written is brilliant. The greatest play I've ever read. Only you can write the ending."

"It's not to be produced, Anne. Not unless you want it to be. It's my gift of love to you."

"Love in a play is one thing, Thady," she said a little sadly. "But I know the reality. I saw it between you and your wife."

He withdrew his arms to take her hands in his. He pressed a warm kiss in each palm then pressed them to his heart. His eyes were darkly serious as he answered her deepest concern, the memory that still had the power to haunt their future.

"Anne, the reason I was away so long was not just to write the play. I doubt that you'll believe what I have to tell you, but it's not the product of a distraught mind or a fevered imagination. It's a certainty that came with cool and calm reflection. Until I understood what it meant, only then could I be at peace with what I felt."

Anne's breath caught in her throat. This was what he had

held back from the play, his last secret. This was the final moment of truth for her, the resolution that could go either way. "Go on," she pressed.

"You remember when you came to the hospital."

Anne nodded, not trusting herself to speak calmly about those traumatic moments.

"Just before you left, I asked you to pray for her...."

"I did, Thady. I did," Anne assured him solemnly.

"I was looking directly at my wife then. She smiled her approval at you, Anne."

"Not at me, Thady. Surely at you."

He shook his head. "It was just after you spoke of loving me."

A queer little shiver ran down Anne's spine. She remembered. Had she imagined movement, or had it been what Thady said it was?

"Afterwards, I had the monitors checked again and again and again. They all registered the same thing. Nothing happened. Yet, to my dying day, I'll swear she smiled at you."

"No. No, Thady." That couldn't be right, Anne reasoned to herself. Why would his wife smile at her? "I thought I saw it, too," she offered tentatively. "But when I looked there was nothing. Yet if she did smile, Thady, I'm sure it was at you."

"You saw it, too?"

Anne frowned over the memory, trying to recapture it. "There was something. It caught my eye. Then I thought I had to be wrong."

"The monitors registered no change. Not the slightest deviation. Yet I'm certain in my mind that I didn't imagine it."

"Then you didn't," Anne softly agreed.

He lifted a hand to her face, lightly stroking her cheek as though she was infinitely precious to him. "For ten years

I tried to reach her. If you hadn't come that day, if you hadn't said what you did, Anne, I would have been left with nothing. I think somehow she knew.'' He paused, his eyes roving slowly, adoringly over her features.

''What do you think she knew, Thady?'' Anne prompted, needing to know what it meant to him.

''I've thought about it every day since then. I'm certain I know now. For the first time in all those years, she felt at peace, knowing that my life could go on, that I should share with you what I had once shared with her, that I should have my children with you and they'd be brought up with all the happy security of a love that lives through anything…anything at all.''

His voice dropped to a low throb. ''When we first met, Anne, you were like her in so many ways. You are now. I tried to keep you separate. Yet in some ways you are inseparable. In both nature and character. Fiercely independent. But generous in giving love and compassion. Braver than any man. Intensely loyal. Always committed to doing your best. Giving your utmost to what you believe in.''

He drew her into his embrace again, and the look on his face was the look Anne had seen there once before and thought she would never see again. But it was there for her, and he said the words she had yearned to hear for so long.

''I love you, Anne. I always did. The difference now is that you have all my love. And I can, at long last, ask you to marry me. Will you be my wife?''

Her smile was illuminated by the unshadowed fulfilment of all she had ever wanted. ''Yes, Thady. I want very much to be your wife, and for us to share the rest of our lives together.''

His smile mirrored hers. ''May I suggest we set the wedding date for the first day of spring?''

''What a lovely idea!''

"I promise I'll never leave you again, Anne. The rest of our lives we *will* be together. In everything."

Then he kissed her with all the passion Anne had been waiting for. A grand, wonderful passion, so deep it would last a lifetime.

A high-pitched shriek from the nursery broke into their absorption with each other. "The joys of parenthood." Anne laughed. Her eyes twinkled with happy teasing. "I believe that's your son calling for you, Thady."

"Mmm… Has quite an extraordinary voice box, hasn't he?"

"That is the sound of frustration. He has undoubtedly thrown his favourite toy out of the bassinette by accident and he wants you to hand it back to him."

Thady's laugh was a ripple of delight. His eyes sparkled with joyful anticipation as he hugged Anne to his side and set off to meet his son's needs.

His arms and legs were punching the air with furious energy, and his little face was screwed up ready to produce another yell when the faces of his mother and father suddenly hovered above him. This most satisfactory situation brought about a change of mind. He unscrewed his face, widened his eyes in limpid innocence and blew bubbles.

"You little rascal." Thady chuckled, hoisting the baby out of the bassinette and giving him all the indulgent attention that Michael John had been waiting for from his father.

The bonding between them was instant and complete, ratified by approving gurgles, absolutely absurd baby talk from a highly literate man and the possessive claim of tightly curled tiny fingers around a gently tickling thumb.

THE FIRST OF SPRING was a glorious day. In a little church on the outskirts of the village closest to Anne and Thady's new home in the country, Annelise Tolliver and Thady Riordan were married.

Alex Korbett gave the bride away.

Paula and Richard Wentworth served as matron of honour and best man.

All three sisters of the bride were present, accompanied by their husbands. Thady had flown the entire family to England for the occasion. Jenny's new baby daughter was being minded by Brian's parents in Australia, but she had dozens of photographs to match against Michael John, who watched the whole proceedings from the lap of his Australian grandmother.

Leonie Tolliver wept with sentimental joy as her oldest daughter walked triumphantly from the altar, a married woman at last. And what a photograph it would make to take pride of place on her mantelpiece! Not only did Anne look as beautiful as every bride should look, but on her earlobes glittered the most fabulous diamond earrings. They were a perfect match for Anne's engagement ring, which had been made by De Mestres in Brussels.

Of course, the wedding ring was the most important. But those diamonds would certainly show up in any photograph and demonstrate to all of Leonie's friends what a wonderfully generous man Anne had married. Handsome, famous, rich and generous. Really, when Anne finally set her mind on something, she certainly excelled. Even with marriage.

As the bride and groom posed on the front steps of the church to oblige the photographer, Thady smiled at his new wife and gently touched the diamond earrings that Anne was wearing for the first time in public. His eyes danced with pleasure.

"I take it this is a special occasion," he murmured.

"They feel right on me today," Anne replied, her face radiant with love for him.

"Everything is right today," Thady declared.

Without any prompting from the photographer, Thady Riordan took his wife in his arms and kissed her with all the passionate rightness he felt, and Annelise Riordan responded in the same way.

Everybody there could see how deeply in love they were. Michael John Patrick Riordan celebrated the moment by reciting the two words he had learnt, "Dada" and "Muma." Then he pulled off his shoes and played with his toes. He laughed and he gurgled and he burbled. He knew with absolute certainty that not only was everything right today, but everything would be right forever more.

POSTSCRIPT

Thady Riordan went on to write some of the most magical plays to ever touch the human heart. Annelise Riordan did the production design for all of them. *The Last Grand Passion* was never produced.

Leigh Michaels has always loved happy endings. Even when she was a child, if a book's conclusion didn't please her, she'd make up her own. And, though she always wanted to write fiction, she very sensibly planned to earn her living as a newspaper reporter. That career didn't work out, however, and she found herself writing for Mills & Boon® instead—in the kind of happy ending only a romance novelist could dream up!

Leigh likes to hear from readers; you can write to her at PO Box 935, Ottumwa, Iowa, 52501-0935, USA.

SAFE IN MY HEART
by
LEIGH MICHAELS

CHAPTER ONE

THE ROOM WAS midnight-dark except for the burglar's small flashlight flicking on at random intervals.

At the side of the room, Katherine Whitman sat stiffly upright in her straight, uncomfortable chair, fingers clenched on the edges of the seat. She was staring, eyes wide, toward the center of the room, straining to hear the occasional whisper of sound that told her where the burglar was. There was nothing to see between those irregular flashes of light, but she stared anyway in a futile effort to make out the image of what she knew was there.

Total darkness could do strange things to a person, Katherine reminded herself. It interfered with one's balance, since there was no landmark to relate to. It was almost smothering, like a blanket of warm fog. And it played games with the mind. Deprived of external stimuli, her brain insisted on making up its own data, so she actually believed that she could see a flicker of movement and shape and color as the burglar drew nearer.

The instantaneous, ludicrous urge to run had passed, but that didn't eliminate Katherine's longing to move, to cross one slim knee over the other, to scratch her nose, even to take a deep breath. Her orders, however, had been very clear. And any minute now—no, any *second* it would be over, anyway....

A tiny red light blinked once, up in the corner of the room, seeming as bright in the blackness as if it had been the sun rising, and a millisecond later a siren began to shriek above her head. Instinctively, Katherine closed her eyes just as spotlights—so powerful that she could hear the pop of the filaments as they flared into life—illuminated the burglar where he crouched in the center of the room.

He flung himself facedown and pounded a frustrated fist on the floor. "Dammit, would you shut that thing off?" he yelled, and the siren died into blessed silence. The room lights came on, the powerful spots flicked off, and Katherine took her hands away from her ears and blinked as her eyes readjusted to normal light.

The claustrophobic feel of the room had faded away along with the total darkness. This was not the small, cramped office it had seemed during the exercise, but an enormous, warehouselike space. The model room the burglar had been attempting to invade was just one of a half dozen sets in HomeSafe's test laboratory. And Katherine hadn't been alone in the dark, either; every chair in the observers' gallery was occupied.

The man sitting beside her finished the notation he was writing in his leather-bound notebook, capped his fountain pen and put it away in the breast pocket of his jacket, then strode over to the black-clad figure on the floor.

"Well, Jake," Stephen Osborne asked politely, "what do you think of our new motion detector now?"

The burglar rolled onto his back and stared up at the man standing over him. "You told me you'd built a pet alley into the damned thing, Steve," he accused. "You said the dead space was big enough so the guard dogs could wander around without setting the alarms off. You lied to me—"

"Lied? Not at all. Of course there's a pet alley, exactly where I told you it was. But you, my friend, are slightly larger than a German shepherd. More importantly, your profile's different."

The burglar sat up and tugged off his gloves. "Do you mean to say your new system recognized, in the dark, that I don't have a tail?"

"Something like that." Stephen held a hand out.

The burglar grabbed it and leapt lightly to his feet. "And I suppose that's all you're going to tell me."

Stephen's dark eyebrows lifted. "Of course. It's a trade secret. All you need to know is that it'll protect your customers even if they don't understand exactly how it works."

The burglar pulled the black stocking mask off his head and ran his fingers through his disheveled hair. They were a study in contrasts as they stood there shoulder-to-shoulder—Stephen Osborne, just a shade over six feet, impeccably tailored in silver-gray with a silk shirt and a hand-sewn tie, every dark brown hair in place. And Jake Holland, an inch shorter and a bit slighter in frame, in his black turtleneck and slacks, ruffled and dusty and every inch the cat burglar.

They were a strange pair of friends, Katherine found herself thinking.

A young woman standing nearby, one of a half dozen sales representatives who'd attended the test, turned to Katherine with a shiver. "Jake Holland really gets into this stuff, doesn't he? He could run these tests just as well with the lights on, but he insists on the darkness and the black clothes and all. The man gives me the creeps."

Katherine shrugged. "Any good security consultant wants test conditions to be as much like the real situation as possible. I wouldn't want to run into Jake in a dark alley when he's in costume, but he's harmless, really."

Stephen Osborne put a casual hand on Katherine's shoulder. "Of course he's harmless. Jake's a frustrated cloak-and-dagger type, that's all. He ended up in the security business only because the CIA wouldn't take him."

"Come on, Osborne," Jake protested. "You're just saying rude things because I beat the sensors on your windows this time."

Stephen frowned. "I know. We'll have to work on that. Katherine, if you're going back to the office, would you put this on my desk?" He handed her the leather-bound notebook. "I'm taking Jake to lunch so I can pick his brains. Oh, and would you ask Irene to reserve a table for two at The Pinnacle tonight? Ten o'clock should be safe."

Katherine frowned a little. "Safe?"

Stephen nodded. "In case the play runs long. We're seeing *Henry* the some-number-or-other."

And he obviously didn't care what number it was, Katherine thought. That meant his companion tonight would probably be Hilary Clayton, for she, not Stephen, was the Shakespeare fan. Which meant his table had better be ready the moment the play was over, because the gorgeous and self-assured Hilary did not like to be kept waiting. And *that* meant Katherine had better explain it all very carefully to the sometimes hapless Irene—or else go ahead and make the reservation herself. "I'll look after it, Stephen."

Stephen put his index finger under Katherine's chin

and tipped her face up. "You don't have to. Remember? You're not a secretary anymore—Irene is."

"Getting a table at The Pinnacle on a Friday night isn't a matter to leave to the average secretary," she pointed out.

He smiled down at her, his dark brown eyes dancing with golden lights. "What's the matter, Katherine? Are you aiming for another promotion by offering to take on even more executive responsibility? You might as well not bother—there's nothing for you to move up to except my job, and I'm not ready to retire." He and Jake Holland left the security lab and vanished down the hall.

The sales representative shook her head. "Honestly, Katherine, I don't know how you stand working for him."

"Stephen?" She was startled. "He's a great boss."

"I don't doubt that. But how do you manage to keep from exploding in flames every time he looks at you? Take the way he smiles, for instance."

Katherine's jaw dropped. "Are you feeling all right, Diane? Exposure to total darkness affects some people strangely. Stephen has a very pleasant smile, yes. It's one of the nicest things about him, but—"

Diane was staring over the tops of her half-glasses. "All right," she said abruptly. "Who is he?"

"What on earth do you mean?"

"The man who can keep you from noticing that Stephen Osborne exudes sex appeal."

Katherine shrugged. "I don't have any idea what you're talking about." The fact that she wasn't quite telling the truth tugged at her conscience. No one knew about her and Travis, and he insisted that was the way it had to remain for the present. It wouldn't be much longer, though. If the sales figures for last month ended up as Travis expected they would, and he was once again HomeSafe's top salesman…

Diane was watching her doubtfully.

"Look," Katherine said, "you wouldn't think in terms of sex appeal if you had to work with the man all the time. Don't you know the office law that says no man is a hero to his secretary?"

Diane mulled that one over. "But you're not anymore. You're his personal assistant."

"Technically, I never was his secretary. But the same principle applies." Katherine knelt beside her chair to gather up the folders she'd tucked safely underneath, in case Stephen had wanted information on any of the sensors or circuitry they'd been testing that morning. "Why wasn't Travis Baker here, Diane?" she asked carelessly. "I thought he wanted to see this demonstration."

"He's got a problem with one of his accounts in Boulder, I guess. He won't be back till late this afternoon."

Katherine tried not to let herself feel disappointed. His absence really made no difference; even if Travis had attended, they couldn't have gone out for lunch. She sighed. All this caution seemed so unnecessary. What harm was there in being seen together now and then? But Travis was being especially careful these days.

"Is he married?" Diane asked.

Katherine bit her tongue. She'd almost replied that of course Travis wasn't married. "Who do you mean?"

"Who do you think? The man in your life you're

being so secretive about. Don't worry, I won't tell anyone.''

Katherine put Stephen's notebook on top of the folders. ''If I was to get involved with a man, I certainly wouldn't choose one who was married. Any man who'd mess around behind his wife's back wouldn't stop for long even if he happened to change wives, and I want better than that for myself.'' She smiled at the quizzical look on Diane's face. ''And no, that doesn't mean I've been burned by a married man, either. So why don't you stop speculating about my romantic history and go sell security systems? There's a lot more profit in that for both of us.''

Diane shook her head in disbelief, but she went away.

Katherine stayed to talk to the head of the testing division about the next system to be installed in the model room. By the time she got back to the suite of executive offices in the front wing of the sprawling complex, it was well into the lunch hour; Irene had left her desk and locked the office door. Katherine's arms were aching from the weight of the file folders, and as she balanced them and tried to manage her key, her hand slipped and the folders scattered over the carpet.

Muttering a couple of words under her breath, she stooped to retrieve them. Stephen's leather-bound notebook had landed at her feet, open to the notes he'd been taking earlier. It was incredible, Katherine thought, that even in total darkness his writing was so neat it looked as if he'd had a desk lamp beside him.

Not only does he set female employees on fire, she mused, *but he can see in the dark, too. I should rush right down and tell Diane that bit of news!*

She left the stack of folders for Irene to file and went

on into Stephen's office, which was large and luxurious and so quiet that the sound of her own breathing seemed intrusive. It smelled good, too—a mix of leather and coffee and after-shave and the barest hint of cigar tobacco, no doubt still lingering from the chairman of the board's most recent visit.

She put Stephen's notebook squarely on the center of his desk and wasted a couple of minutes gazing out at the Denver skyline. Today it looked particularly wonderful; last night's thunderstorm had cleared the summer air, and the skyline was crisp and clear and distinct in the distance. A rare sight in mid-July, when there was usually a humid haze over the city.

The big leather chair was turned toward the window, as if Stephen had also been gazing out over the city just before he went down to the lab. Katherine didn't blame him. She, too, could think more clearly while looking at that glorious view.

Oh, well, back to business. She turned and walked the short distance to her own office, settled at her desk, and called The Pinnacle for Stephen's dinner reservation. The mere mention of his name won a warm response from the maître d' and a promise that Mr. Osborne's table would be ready no matter when he wanted it.

Obviously, Stephen tipped very well indeed. Or else that charm Diane had been talking of worked on waiters, too.

Katherine smiled. Diane had made it sound as if Stephen Osborne possessed a magnetism that drew women irresistibly into his power. And it was true that there was no lack of women in his life. Irene might be the one who had to keep his calendar straight, but Katherine certainly saw it often enough to know how frequently he was dating and who he was seeing. It wasn't a short list.

Not that there was much variety there. They all seemed to be the cool and glamorous type, like Hilary Clayton—elegant and fashionable and suspiciously perfect.

In fact, the mere thought of Hilary Clayton as Stephen's love slave was enough to cause whoops of laughter, once Katherine let her imagination slip the leash and roam free. It simply wasn't possible to picture Hilary's perfectly coiffed blond hair rumpled in the aftermath of lovemaking. But Stephen seemed to appreciate that icy perfection, so who was Katherine to question the attraction?

There was certainly no question about what Hilary saw in him; she was the kind who would have been attracted to Stephen Osborne even if he'd been two feet tall with warts on his nose, just because he was Rafe Osborne's son and he owned a good chunk of HomeSafe. For Hilary, the fact that he was undeniably good-looking, generous, and had a smile that could melt the North Pole would be frosting on the cake....

"Cut it out," Katherine told herself. Diane's flight of fancy might be silly, but it was proving to be infectious.

Katherine went to get herself a cup of coffee, wrinkled her nose at the muddy-looking brew, and started a fresh pot. While she waited, she flipped idly through the morning mail that lay stacked on the corner of Irene's desk.

She wasn't exactly surprised that Diane's question had come up, though. She supposed talk was inevitable; when a young, attractive and, to all appearances, unattached woman went to work for a young, attrac-

tive, play-the-field man, few people would believe
there was nothing more than business in the wind.

She'd considered the possibility of gossip a full year
ago, when Rafe Osborne had announced his retirement
and Stephen had taken over his father's position as
president of HomeSafe, offering Katherine the job as
his personal assistant.

But she'd never discussed it with Stephen, of course;
it would have been ridiculous, and even insulting, to
imply that the two of them might not be able to work
together without sex interfering. And of course she'd
been correct not to worry; in the entire year since she'd
become his assistant there had never been an off-color
comment or a too personal question or—heaven forbid—a pass to be deflected. They were professionals,
after all, and work came first.

She'd attempted to explain that principle to Travis—
without success. It didn't matter whether or not people
knew about them, she'd argued. As long as they continued to do their jobs well, no one cared about their
personal lives.

But most people didn't think that way, he had told
her. His fellow salesmen would assume he was trying
to use his connections to improve himself, if they knew
he was dating the president's assistant. It might even
put Katherine's own job at risk if Stephen didn't like
the idea. And even though Katherine thought he was
mad to suspect that Stephen would care one way or the
other, she'd reluctantly agreed to say nothing until
Travis got his hoped-for promotion.

They'd keep their relationship quiet until the new
sales director was named. It was bound to be Travis.
And then…

But it was difficult, Katherine admitted as she took

her coffee back to her office. Sometimes she just wanted to fling open her window and shout to the world that she loved Travis Baker. It was stupid, she told herself, to wonder sometimes if he was being so secretive because down deep he was ashamed of her....

The door of her office opened. She started guiltily, and coffee splashed over the side of the mug and onto the papers spread on her desk blotter. She grabbed a tissue and began mopping up the mess.

"Daydreaming?" Rafe Osborne said pleasantly. "I didn't know you had it in you, Katherine."

She shot an aggrieved look at the chairman of the board and founder of HomeSafe, then turned her attention back to wiping coffee off the schematics of their opposition's newest security system.

Rafe tugged a chair forward, sat down and propped his feet up on the corner of her desk, ankles crossed. He was, as usual, chewing on an unlit cigar.

Katherine thought, rather irritably, that no one could possibly look less like the stereotyped chairman of a major corporation than Rafe Osborne. He was a husky bear of a man, well into his sixties, with no inclination to try to hide the marks left by a life that hadn't always been easy. He was more comfortable in Polo shirts than in suits, in bars rather than in exclusive clubs, and now that he was retired, no longer saw any reason to play by corporate rules. His hair hadn't been cut lately and his eyebrows were threateningly bushy. Certainly few people would have guessed that this abrupt, brusque man and the sophisticated new president of HomeSafe were father and son.

Rafe Osborne's style left most people in awe of him, but Katherine sometimes suspected that underneath all the sharp edges he was a marshmallow, and the bluster was simply his way to keep the rest of the world from finding out. He had, for instance, never raised his voice to her in the two years since she'd gone to work as his secretary.

He removed the cigar from his mouth. "I'm proud of you, Katherine. Most of the world's best ideas have come from someone's thoughts wandering."

She patted the last page dry and laid it aside, hoping the coffee stains wouldn't interfere with the small print. "And, of course, you're including yourself?"

"Absolutely. Being a security guard gives a man a lot of time to think between making his rounds. Sooner or later, he starts to dream up ways to make the job easier, and before he knows it he's sitting at a desk telling other people what to do. But that's old news. What's going on around this place?"

"You missed the tests of the new motion detector this morning."

Rafe shook his head. "Didn't miss it a bit—I just didn't come. With Steve and Jake Holland, it's not really product testing, you know. They're caught up in a life-size video game."

Katherine smiled. "You're right. They're just like little boys, laying traps for each other and trying to prove who's got more skill."

Rafe nodded. "That's why I went fishing instead. At least it's a civilized pastime. So how *did* the test go?"

"That's why you're here, isn't it? You expect me to give you the condensed version."

Rafe grinned. "Of course. You're my favorite spy."

She told him briefly about the test. He listened in silence, chewing on the cigar, and for a couple of long minutes afterward he stared thoughtfully at the ceiling—thinking, she was fairly certain, of the window sensors that had failed to perform as expected in this morning's trial.

Katherine had learned long ago not to disturb him at times like these, so she sat quietly, drinking her coffee and wondering what was going on behind those half-hooded brown eyes. She was not surprised when he didn't enlighten her. Instead, he took his feet off the corner of her desk and said, "Come on, I'll buy you lunch."

"As a reward for a good espionage job?" She shook her head reluctantly. "I can't. I've got loads of work to do."

"It can't be that busy around here. I just poked my head into Steve's office, and not only is Steve not there, but his desk is so clear you could land airplanes on it."

"He took Jake to lunch. Besides, heavy thinking is his job. Mine is doing the paperwork after he finishes thinking."

"Then he ought to give you the big desk. Anyway, he can't force you to stop eating. Or playing, either— *he* certainly fits in enough time for it."

Katherine smiled. "You're being contradictory, Rafe. If truly great ideas come from idle thought…"

"Doesn't mean he can't be sitting down in his office encouraging it." Rafe sounded a bit disgruntled. "Or he could go fishing—that at least gives a man a chance to think. But not Steve. If it isn't handball and tennis, it's weekends at Winter Park. Skiing is one thing. I think it's a crazy sport myself, and I haven't any idea how both my kids developed a love for it, but—"

Katherine decided that he probably hadn't thought it through, or he would have understood. Stephen's fondness for the slopes sprang from his unquenchable energy. For Rafe's daughter, Sherry, however, the attraction was another matter altogether. Katherine suspected that Sherry was more interested in the dozens of eligible young men to be found at the après-ski parties than she was in the snow.

Sherry's young, Katherine thought charitably. She'll settle down someday.

"You know, I've always wondered what Steve finds to do up there when there's no snow." Rafe sounded honestly puzzled.

Katherine looked at him in surprise and opened her mouth to answer, then decided that she'd rather not be the one who explained the facts of life to Rafe. It wasn't as if she actually knew anything, anyway, because Stephen was very discreet about his private affairs. And if his father hadn't already guessed that Stephen wasn't always alone when he used the family condo at Winter Park, Katherine wasn't about to share her speculations on the matter.

Instead, she reached into the top desk drawer for her calendar. "He hasn't said anything about going up this weekend," she murmured. "I wonder if I should call the condo office just in case, or wait till he gets back to ask him." He wouldn't be going till tomorrow anyway, she reminded herself. Unless, of course, he was planning to take Hilary along after dinner at The Pinnacle. The drive was only an hour or so; it would be a perfectly reasonable thing to do on a July night.

Rafe was shaking his head. "Not this weekend. Sherry's having a party at the penthouse tomorrow."

"And Stephen's actually going? That's a twist." She let the calendar slide back into the drawer.

"It's a different sort of party than Sherry's usual. You're coming, aren't you?"

Katherine said carefully, "I didn't know I was invited. In fact, this is the first I've heard about a party."

Rafe frowned. "Is that so? I'm sure I put your name on the guest list."

"It's not a company party, surely?"

"Oh, no—just friends and a few HomeSafe people who had to be included."

Katherine wondered in which of those categories Rafe placed her.

He flashed her a smile. "Actually," he confided, "I'm the one who's technically giving the party this time. And I had hidden reasons for asking you."

"More espionage?" Katherine asked dryly.

"Not exactly. I was hoping you'd help keep an eye on the waiters. You know the kind of thing caterers do if they think nobody's watching. So if I could just count on you to keep them honest...."

Katherine forced back a smile. For a man who'd built a brilliant brainstorm into a multimillion-dollar company, Rafe could be incredibly cheap sometimes. "All right. I'm not doing anything else, so I'll come and supervise. But you should feel extremely guilty, Rafe."

"Oh, I do," he said earnestly. "But I'll make it up to you. If you can prevent the bartenders from drinking every third bottle of champagne, I'll—"

"Champagne?" It wasn't an idle question; in Katherine's experience, any party Rafe was hosting was far more likely to include fifteen-year-old Scotch whisky.

"Crates of champagne," he said. "Not the cheap stuff, either, but then what choice do I have? Fortunately for me, a party like this only comes once in a girl's lifetime."

Katherine raised an eyebrow.

''You know better than to ask, don't you? Oh, what the hell, I'll tell you. Sherry would kill me because it's supposed to be a surprise, but I know you can keep a secret. It's her engagement party.''

Katherine blinked, and then told herself she was being unfair. Sherry was old enough to know her own mind; she'd finished college last spring. It was her behavior that made her seem so much younger than her actual years.

''How lovely for her,'' she said sincerely. ''I had no idea she was serious about anyone.''

''Well, you're not the only one who didn't. That's how I know she means it this time. She wasn't blathering on about this one every minute, not till he'd asked the question. You know him, too, of course.''

Katherine tried to remember the last time she'd encountered Sherry. The girl popped into the office now and then to see Stephen, but she was always alone. And Katherine didn't move in the same social circles, so it was hardly likely that she knew any of Sherry's young men.

''He works for HomeSafe,'' Rafe went on.

Katherine shook her head. ''Sorry to disappoint you, Rafe, but I don't know every one of your employees.''

HomeSafe had a thousand workers at the four factories in Colorado, and dozens more sales and service representatives scattered halfway across the country. Katherine might be the president's personal assistant, but there were people in this very building she'd never met. Sherry's fiancé could be any one of them.

There was certainly no reason for the prickle of dread that was running with painful slowness along Katherine's nerves.

"Oh, you know this one, I'm sure. He's the best salesman we've got at the moment," Rafe assured her.

And then she knew. She wanted to shut Rafe out, to put her hands over her ears and deny what he was going to say. But she couldn't. She had no defense against the blow that was about to descend on her.

"He's going to be our new sales manager, too," Rafe said with satisfaction. "So, at least my little girl hasn't chosen some fly-by-night. Travis Baker—you know him, don't you, Katherine?"

CHAPTER TWO

IT WAS SHOCK, Katherine supposed, but it was as if she were standing across the room, watching herself absorb the blow instead of feeling it firsthand. She could almost see the color drain out of her face, leaving the sprinkling of freckles across her nose looking like muddy pools. Her body shrank back into the chair under the impact of Rafe's words.

It's a good thing she'd been sitting down when the blow hit, an inner voice observed with icy detachment. If she'd been standing, she would probably have fallen as hard as a logged tree.

Rafe walked over to the window. "I suppose people will think Steve gave him the job because of Sherry," he mused. "He didn't, of course."

No, Katherine thought. Of course he hadn't. The only thing that mattered to Stephen was how the job was done; she'd known that all along, deep inside her heart. Why had she let Travis convince her otherwise? He'd seemed so certain that dating him openly would put her job at risk...but all it had really endangered was his pursuit of bigger game. Travis would be a capable sales manager, Katherine was convinced of that. But why had it never occurred to her that his ambition went far beyond that relatively minor job?

Because you're a patsy, Katherine Whitman, she told herself bluntly.

"I'll say this for the young man," Rafe went on. "He asked Sherry to hold off announcing anything until it was certain he'd be the one to get the sales job. He's unusually modest for someone in that end of the business, that's sure."

And he's a viper in your bosom, Katherine wanted to tell Rafe. *Get rid of him before it's too late—*

But she bit her tongue and said nothing. If she told Rafe anything of the sort, he would want the details, and despite that easygoing manner of his where Katherine was concerned, he was capable of squeezing her like a sponge until he got them. And what could Katherine say that would sound like anything other than an outraged, jealous female, overreacting to the fact that the man she wanted preferred another woman?

She could show Rafe no proof of promises made and broken. Travis had never given her a ring. They'd never set a wedding date. Soon, he'd said, they would be free to talk about all that, but until then it would be wasted effort. He'd never even suggested that he move into her apartment; he'd kept his own and let her talk of the day when they would look for a larger one, together. Oh, how careful he had been!

Rafe seemed to shake himself out of a mood. "Well, I'll see you at the party, then. Eight o'clock tomorrow, the penthouse. Unless you've changed your mind about having lunch."

She tapped her coffee cup. "This is lunch." Mercifully, her hand was steady, and her voice didn't shake.

Rafe rolled his eyes heavenward. "Women. Sherry's dieting to get into a size smaller wedding gown, and you're working yourself to death. Bad judgment, both of you."

Katherine watched him leave. "You can say that again, Rafe," she muttered. "Both of us are fools—and over the same man."

She wanted to put her head down on her desk and huddle there like an ostrich retreating from the world. But at any moment Irene would be back, or Stephen—and she didn't want to explain what had made her so suddenly ill. On the other hand, if she could make her story convincing enough, not even Rafe would be expecting her to show up at Sherry's party tomorrow.

But if her story wasn't unshakable, people might begin asking questions. And whether the attitude behind those questions was compassionate, or simply idle, or downright nosy, it really didn't matter; once attention was focused on her, her folly would become common gossip.

A wave of nausea threatened to choke her, and she realized that in order to prevent talk, she was going to have to attend the engagement party. She would have to smile and congratulate the lucky couple. She would have to wish Travis the best—or have her own idiocy exposed, discussed, and enjoyed in the company lunchroom.

She was no longer such a fool as to think it wouldn't happen, either. She might have been innocent enough last week to believe that no one at HomeSafe cared what she did, but not after Diane's speculations this morning. If there was the slightest hint of scandal—and being the other woman in Sherry Osborne's romance was just about as scandalous as one could get at HomeSafe—there'd be no end to the gossip.

By midafternoon, she'd managed to pull herself together somewhat, and she even dared leave her office for the ladies' room down the hall so she could check out the damage. She still looked as if she'd picked up the wrong bottle of makeup that morning, one that was three shades darker than usual. "In fact," she told herself dispassionately, "you look as if you belong in a drawer at the morgue." She tried to practice her smile; her face felt like corrugated cardboard.

Stephen Osborne was leaning over her desk when she finally returned, rummaging through the papers she'd scattered there. "I don't know how you ever manage to keep things straight," he muttered.

Katherine brushed past him and slid into her chair so that the sunlight would be at her back rather than spotlighting her face. "I can't, when you insist on coming in to houseclean." Her voice was a bit on the husky side, but she congratulated herself that it sounded normal enough to get by. Certainly there was nothing unusual about Stephen's complaint; at least once a week he stirred up the contents of her desk, usually searching for something that was in plain view right on top.

He grinned at her, but he didn't stop riffling through her papers.

Katherine stared for a long moment at the gold sparkle in his eyes, the white gleam of perfect teeth. Ordinarily enough, she would smile back, forgiving him even if he had messed up her entire afternoon's work. Today, however, with her sense of humor gone AWOL, she was in no mood for his little foibles.

She fiddled with a pen and looked down at the nearest sheet of paper, not even registering what it was. Her hair swung forward in a golden brown mass, shielding her face.

Stephen pulled out a paper-clipped set of pages and thumbed through them. Katherine glanced up and saw the coffee stains on the top sheet.

"If you're looking for the schematics for the competition's new security system," she said crisply, "that's my set. Irene made a photocopy for you. And I told the lab to install the whole package so we can start testing it in the middle of next week."

"Great. What would I do without you, Katherine?" But he didn't, as she had hoped, go away. "That's not what I was looking for, though. I made some notes on a new twist in our premiere system, and I've mislaid them." He put the pages back in the pile on the corner of her desk.

She shook her head, interested in spite of herself. "Stephen, there are never more than three pieces of paper on your desk at any time. How could you lose one of them?"

"I thought perhaps you'd picked it up by accident, or it might have got mixed in with something else. It was just a sketch—it wouldn't make much sense if you didn't know what it was supposed to be." He flung himself down in a chair, his long legs sprawled across the carpet, and rested a lean cheek against one sun-browned hand.

She gave up on the idea of getting rid of him. He did this fairly often when an idea was taking shape; Katherine had long ago figured out that kicking his heels beside her desk and talking about it helped him test the usefulness of a new concept. And though Stephen's style was completely different from Rafe's habit of keeping everything to himself until he had the details worked out, in the last year she'd certainly grown accustomed to it. It was rather nice, in a way; it made her feel like a valuable part of the team.

But why did you have to pick today? she wailed silently. All she wanted right now was to be alone with her grief and her anger.

"The best part of the premiere system is its ability to call for help," Stephen said, almost as if he were beginning a lecture. "But that's also its Achilles' heel. If an intruder can stop the computer from telephoning the authorities, he can circumvent the whole system, at least for long enough to accomplish his goal." He looked at her expectantly.

Katherine sighed and played along. "Then we bury the telephone lines. Or install a dummy line, so our intruder thinks he's prevented the call by cutting the wires, but he really hasn't. Wait a minute. What about conduit? If we surround everything with metal so it can't be cut—"

Stephen was shaking his head. "You're thinking too small. Who needs lines? We can go cellular."

"As in telephone? A satellite telephone?"

"You've got it."

"Too expensive."

"We don't know that. Check on it, Katherine. It wouldn't take an elaborate telephone setup, you see— just a basic one. Also, it would be a dedicated system, used only in short bursts now and then, not to call Grandma every Saturday night, so—"

"So we might be able to get a break on the cost of access to the satellite network."

"Now you're thinking. First, let me know if it's possible, no matter what the price. Jake's working out security for an estate up in the mountains, and I want to offer him the option." He pushed his chair back and stood. "I'd also like to have some rough figures by next week on what it would cost to incorporate it into our packages. Can you do that?"

"Of course." But only if she could put aside her heartbreak and concentrate. And yet, that might be the best medicine of all....

She was still writing furiously when Stephen left her office. And when he poked his head in later, she was startled to see that two hours had passed. But Irene's personal computer was hooded and her office dim, and the busy hum of the day's business had mellowed as the weekend approached.

"Do you need anything else before I go home?" Stephen asked, leaning around the door frame as if he half expected a paperweight to come flying at him. His tie was loose, he'd slung his jacket over one shoulder, and the sleeves of his white shirt were rolled up to the elbow.

Katherine shook her head. "Enjoy the play." She thought he looked a little doubtful about the possibility. "Oh, and the maître d' deserves something extra tonight. He was very helpful."

"I'll keep him in mind." He paused. "Don't work too late, all right? Rafe will have my head if he catches you here after hours."

"Then I'll have to make sure he doesn't catch me," Katherine said lightly, and turned back to her figures.

But the interruption had broken her tightly imposed self-control and allowed the pain to sweep over her again. She clenched her teeth, managing to smile, but the moment Stephen was gone she pushed her chair back from the desk and slumped down in it. She wanted with all her heart to let go and cry. But the wrenching sobs that seemed to be chasing around inside her were too threatening to release here. Someone might see, or hear, and wonder...

A tap on the door brought her upright, and another

wave of agony washed over her as a lean young man with curly blond hair and an easy smile stepped across the threshold.

"Kathy? You wouldn't happen to have the proofs for the new ad campaign, would you?"

She closed her eyes against the pain. How many times he'd come in like this, she thought, always with a perfectly legitimate reason, in case someone was listening. "It's all right, Travis," she said finally. "Stephen's gone. Everybody is. You don't need an excuse to be here."

Travis Baker came across the office with a spring in his step. "As it happens, that wasn't an excuse. I really need to see those proofs. But since the coast is clear—"

He doesn't realize I know. He still believes he's managed to pull it off. She wondered just how long he thought that state of affairs could go on.

She propped her elbow on the edge of her desk and leaned her cheek against her hand, her arm forming what was almost a barricade. She made meaningless marks on the ledger sheet in front of her. "Company gossip says you've got the sales manager's post," she observed.

"It's not just gossip. Great, isn't it?" When she didn't respond, he looked at her quizzically. "I wasn't keeping it secret, Kathy. I was saving the news till I could tell you privately. What about it? Shall we celebrate tonight?"

The sour taste of bile rose in her throat. "Can't," she said, waving a hand at the papers strewn across her desk. A hateful little impulse prompted her to say, "How about tomorrow? We could have dinner, maybe take in a show."

He shifted uneasily from one foot to the other. "I've got a business commitment, I'm afraid. I'll be tied up till late."

"If it's HomeSafe business, why not take me along?" Katherine suggested, and wondered how far she would have to push before he broke and confessed. "Now that you've got the promotion, surely we can do that. Or do you think it would be better to wait till you get settled in the job before we're seen together?"

He looked relieved. "You're so understanding, Kathy. It would be foolish to rush things now."

"I thought you might see it that way."

He frowned. "Kathy, you don't sound like yourself."

"Hurray for you." She reached blindly for another ledger sheet. "It's just as well that you don't want to take me along on your company business tomorrow, Travis, because I couldn't go, after all. I'll be at a party instead. An engagement party."

He bit his lip. "Oh."

"You took my name off the invitation list, didn't you? What reason did you give your fiancée for that? I wonder. No, don't bother to explain. I'd rather not hear it." She pushed her chair back and stood up, her hands braced on the desk. "Damn it, Travis, what kind of stupid jerk are you? Did you honestly think you could get away with it? That no one would tell me?"

"I was going to talk to you."

"And explain? Oh, I'd like to hear how you planned to do that."

"What's to explain?" he snapped. "I never promised you anything, Kathy. I sure as hell never said anything about marrying you."

He was probably telling the truth, she reflected. It

had all seemed so clear at the time—so apparent they wanted the same things. Now that she thought about it, however, she realized that she'd been the one doing the planning. Travis had simply smiled. It had been an encouraging smile, or so she'd believed, but now she wondered if he had been thinking what a fool she was.

"You never said anything to discourage me," she replied sharply. "What was really going on, Travis? If Sherry lost interest in you, would you have married me after all? Is that it? I suppose you thought any connections would be better than none, so you kept leading me on, just in case you needed a backup plan."

"It isn't a crime for a man to keep his options open, Kathy."

"Is that what you call it? I call it lying, myself. So what options do you have in mind now? What do you want to be when you grow up, Travis? Vice president of customer service? Of research and development? Or are you aiming higher—Stephen's job, perhaps?"

"You'd better not try to undermine me, Kathy. Not if you like working here."

She almost laughed. "Oh, that's funny—threatening my job, when last week you were so busy safeguarding it. Somehow, I don't think it was me you were trying to protect by keeping Stephen from finding out about us, was it?"

"I suppose you're going to run to tell him?"

"Maybe I already have."

His eyes narrowed, and then he shook his head. "No. You're too cold-blooded to act on impulse—you'd make sure of the facts first."

Katherine's jaw dropped. He dared to call *her* cold-blooded?

"And before you do anything, make sure you understand all the facts,'' he warned. ''Sherry might not be active in this company, but she's a stockholder. That gives her certain powers.''

''Don't threaten me, Travis. And you might remember that Sherry's stock won't get you a job you're not qualified for, either. Being part of the family might speed your rise up the ladder, but it won't get you an extra rung.''

He smiled, smugly. ''That's enough. I'm impatient, I'll admit it. But I'd have gotten there someday, even if I'd settled for marrying you.''

It was like a whip landing on raw flesh. ''Don't worry about me,'' she said, very deliberately. ''I'm not planning to talk. I'm too sick from embarrassment and humiliation to share my shame with anyone.''

His blue eyes turned to ice. ''That's the most anyone would want to share with you, Kathy.''

She knew he was baiting her, and she didn't answer.

But he went straight on anyway. ''You're the coldest woman I've ever known. Even Osborne has never made a move on you, has he, Kathy?''

She had to bite her lip but stayed silent.

''You're not exactly his type, of course, though I'm sure he strays from his usual path once in a while. The truth is, you're not anybody's type. Oh, you could be fun, I suppose, if you'd lighten up and stop being so damned frigid—''

''Don't sneer at my standards, Travis.''

''If you had warmed up even a little, I might not have started looking around, you know. But the fact is, you never did. And you never will. Think about that when you start wondering why you aren't getting a whole lot of offers.''

He gave her a long, coldly appraising look, and turned away as if he'd washed his hands of her.

Katherine kept her spine straight. Not for anything would she risk letting him see her sag into her chair. She would not allow him to see the wounds his words had made.

You're lucky, Katherine, she told herself, *you've finally seen what he's really like.* She could have married him first and then found out...

A little voice in the back of her brain whispered, "No, you couldn't. Because even a jerk like Travis wasn't willing to marry you, Katherine Whitman. What's wrong with you, anyway?"

She tried to drown out the voice. There was nothing wrong with her! Except for being dumb enough to believe him, to get involved with him in the first place—

And that alone, she reflected, was reason to believe there was, indeed, something seriously wrong with her.

She sat there, unwilling to move, unable to see what she could possibly do next.

The only thing she knew for certain was that the young woman who had come to work this morning, head high, confident about herself, her job, her future, her place in the world, had died this afternoon.

SHE WENT HOME eventually, mostly because there was nowhere else to go.

It was almost midnight by then, but despite the hour, the three lonely blocks she had to walk between the parking lot and her apartment building didn't bother her. She was numb; she had absorbed all the blows she could, and if a mugger would have appeared Katherine probably would have handed him her purse before he even asked for it and trudged stoically on.

But the shadows stayed in their proper places. A couple of bars along her path belched out nothing more threatening than cigarette smoke and country-and-western music. Above the dark roofs of her neighborhood, the skyline of Denver was alight. In all those brilliant buildings, people were dancing, laughing, eating, making love. Somewhere up there, in a revolving restaurant called The Pinnacle, the maître d' was probably just now presenting an obscenely large bill....

"Give it time," Katherine told herself. "Of course it's not fair. But you'll feel better tomorrow." She thought about that, and added, "Or someday."

In the apartment across the hall from her own, a voice murmured softly, and she almost knocked on the door, so deep was her longing for some human contact. But the tenants—a woman and a little girl—had just moved in a month ago, and though they'd seemed eager to be friendly, it would hardly be fair to take advantage of them. So Katherine went on into her own apartment.

It was small, but adequate—a tiny living room with a fake fireplace in the corner, a bedroom, a bath, a kitchen. As she'd told herself when she rented it, she spent so little time at home, really. Her job was demanding and her hours were often long. She seldom entertained. She didn't need more room.

And, she reminded herself coldly, she'd believed that someday soon she and Travis would be looking for a larger place, one to share.

Tonight, the apartment looked almost foreign, as if she'd wandered unknowingly into the identical building next door and gone into some stranger's home. It looked tired, too, and a bit neglected. There was a bare wall above the couch; the framed print she'd always intended to hang there remained propped in a corner. She remembered, almost guiltily, how she'd concluded that it was pointless to make the effort. It was too much trouble to find a hanger and the hammer and the measuring tape and the precise spot to drive the nail. Besides, someday soon she'd be moving....

Well, *someday soon* wasn't going to come, and the quicker she faced that reality the better. Katherine flung her handbag halfway across the room and started for the kitchen to dig through the tool drawer. Only when she had the hammer out did it occur to her that one could not drive nails in an apartment at midnight. So she set it aside and sank into a chair.

Dawn found her there. She had dozed uneasily, wakening from time to time knowing that she should at least go to bed. But her intermittent dreams were bad enough as it was; to release all hold on her subconscious would be to invite worse, and so she stayed in the chair until the sun crept over the horizon, bringing the knowledge that before the day was over she must face Sherry's party.

"Why call it Sherry's party?" she asked herself bluntly. "Why not face facts and call it Travis's party? It's certainly a celebration for *him*. Or, if you must hide behind something, call it Rafe's party. He's the host—"

And Rafe was expecting her to be there tonight.

Suddenly, the apartment felt unbearably stuffy. Katherine opened the door onto the tiny balcony and took what felt like her first full breath of the last twenty-four hours.

Travis hadn't turned into a jerk overnight, she told herself. At some level, she must have known all along that something was wrong. Perhaps that explained why she'd always held back whenever he'd wanted to stay the night.

But if she *had* known, why on earth had she continued to see him? To plan to marry him? To let her life revolve around him?

Because, she reflected with painful honesty, despite what she'd just told herself, she had not, on any level, actually seen through him. The truth was that she had been taken in completely. She had been blinded by love....

Maybe there *was* something seriously wrong with her. Maybe she *was* cold, as Travis had said. Perhaps it *had* been unnatural of her not to have wanted to sleep with him. After all, she'd planned to live with him....

The continual, quicksand shift between blaming herself and blaming him—of not quite knowing who she was angrier at—was exhausting, and ultimately she tried to drive it out of her mind by planning various schemes of revenge.

It would be fitting, even possibly fun, to create a scene at the party tonight. Or perhaps it would be more effective just to have a quiet talk with Rafe. Or she could sabotage the sales figures somehow, making it seem that Travis wasn't the supersalesman he appeared.

Eventually, however, she concluded that plotting retaliation was a waste of time. What could she realistically do, after all? No matter how much Rafe thought of Katherine, an accusation without evidence to back it up could only cause problems. It would be her word against Travis's, and Rafe seemed to like Travis just fine, too.

She and Sherry were acquaintances, they weren't friends, and no doubt Travis had already planted the seeds of distrust in his fiancée, just in case. No, Sherry wouldn't end her engagement simply because Katherine said, "Trust me. It's the right thing to do."

Stephen would believe her, she was fairly sure of that; but her accusation wasn't sufficient cause for firing Travis. And anything short of his departure would only create more trouble in the future.

Indeed, if anyone got fired, it was likely to be herself.

She filled her day with busywork. It didn't take many projects to swallow the hours, of course, because it required a tremendous effort of will to move at all. She had to muster every ounce of energy she possessed simply to make herself choose a task and stay with it. But by dusk she had managed to hang the print over the couch, she'd dusted and straightened up the rooms, she'd even fixed herself lunch. Actually, Katherine wasn't sure if she should really take credit for that; it was only a sandwich and she'd ended up tossing all but two bites of it down the garbage disposal.

Still, she had tried, and wasn't that the important thing? If she could keep taking tiny steps like this, surely someday the hurt would be less. And eventually Travis would be only a nagging memory.

But that hoped-for time showed no sign of coming soon, and it was with reluctance that Katherine dug a party dress out of the back of her closet. It was the least favorite garment she owned, and she seldom put it on. She chose it tonight merely because it held no memories.

At least no one could accuse her of dressing to make a scene. The dress certainly wasn't flamboyant; it was a muted shade of peach, with simple lines, a plain neck, no sleeves—minimal style. "In fact," Katherine mut-

tered as she stared at herself in the mirror, "it wouldn't
be bad at all—if I *wanted* to look like a teenage boy
wearing a wig."

But that wasn't the fault of the dress, she reminded
herself. Her figure looked pretty much as it had when
she was fourteen—slender and basically flat. No deep-
cut necklines for Katherine; she had nothing to flaunt,
and she'd long ago accepted that.

She supposed that Sherry's wedding gown would be
very low-cut indeed....

"Stop it!" she warned. "Don't even begin to com-
pare yourself to her, because it will only lead to more
pain."

Besides, it hadn't been Sherry's chest measurement
that had attracted Travis, but the size of her stock portfolio. If she could remember that, it would help her
through this evening.

Katherine was waiting in the foyer for her cab when
the woman who lived in the apartment across the hall
from hers came in. The little girl beside her danced
along until she saw Katherine; then she stopped and
stared, wide-eyed, before looking up at her mother with
a gesture.

"Yes," the woman said, gesturing back. "She's
very pretty." She turned to Katherine. "That must
sound terribly rude, I'm afraid—"

"She's deaf," Katherine said, not taking her eyes
off the child.

The woman nodded. "I try to respond verbally to
whatever Alison says, so she'll associate the sign with
the movement of lips. I'm sorry...."

Katherine's heart went out to her. "Oh, please, don't
apologize. I didn't realize, when I saw her before." She
rummaged in her memory and turned to face the child

directly. "Thank you, Alison," she said, and brushed her fingers against her lips, then extended her hand as if she was blowing a kiss.

The little girl's face lighted, and her hands began to fly in an incomprehensible silent babble.

"Oh dear," Katherine said helplessly. "That's absolutely the only sign I know. It's sort of like being dumped into the middle of China only knowing how to say 'How are you?' I'd have been better off claiming total ignorance."

The child's mother laughed. "She's going into detail about how lovely you are," she explained. "She especially likes your hair."

Katherine's fingers went to the smooth roll of glossy brown hair at the nape of her neck. She'd simply given it a twist and started jabbing hairpins in, adding a spray of flowers, not because she liked the effect, but to keep from looking as if she were in mourning or something.

"It's nice to meet you. I'm Molly Day." The woman held out her hand, only to draw it back quickly. "And since we've been in the park for the last two hours, you probably won't want to shake hands with either of us." She glanced at her palm and made a face.

Katherine laughed. "Of course I do. I hope—oh, there's my cab." She hurried out, and not until the driver asked for an address did she realize, almost with wonderment, that for a few short moments she'd forgotten Travis, Sherry, the party—and the heartbreak. In the exchange with that small child, all her normal enthusiasm had briefly flickered back to life. It gave her hope.

If I can only get through this night, she told herself, *I will be all right.*

CHAPTER THREE

RAFE'S PENTHOUSE occupied the entire top floor of one of the newest of Denver's downtown towers. Katherine had been there before, naturally, for Christmas parties and the like, but she'd never seen the place display quite the elegant patina it carried tonight.

Of course, the Christmas parties were mostly for HomeSafe's employees. Tonight, with only Sherry's friends in attendance, she'd probably brought out the really good stuff—cut crystal goblets, fine silver, delicate linens.

With a stiff bow, the butler directed Katherine toward the drawing room. She was startled by his tailcoated magnificence, and part of her desperately wanted to ask whether he had been provided by the caterer or if he was one of Sherry's new toys. But his impassive countenance didn't encourage conversation, so she straightened her shoulders and turned toward the drawing room, where the muted strains of a string quartet formed a soft counterpoint for the murmur of voices.

Get through the party, she reminded herself. That's all you have to do.

The penthouse was surrounded by a wide terrace, and on this mild July evening all the french doors had been opened to bring the outdoors in. The weather was perfect; the long, ivory silk hangings stirred in the slight breeze, and the candle flames wavered, but that was all. From her vantage point in the arched doorway between foyer and drawing room, Katherine could observe the sheen of silver, the gemlike brilliance of crystal chandeliers, and the soft luxury of deep carpets and hangings. The penthouse looked like a palace.

Katherine had always wondered why Rafe had bought it. Because of Sherry, probably; Rafe would be more comfortable in a log cabin in the woods, wearing flannel shirts and smoking his cigars in the open air, where no one could complain about the smell.

But not even the most fastidious of society matrons could have complained about Rafe's appearance tonight, she realized, spotting him across the room. His dinner clothes had been cut to perfectly fit his stocky frame, and his bushy silver hair had been given a new trim and a good brushing. Katherine was willing to bet there was a cigar hidden in his breast pocket—but at least it wasn't smoldering in his hand.

He grinned at her, stopped a waiter who was passing through with a tray, and came across the room with two glasses of champagne.

It will choke me to drink to Travis's engagement, Katherine thought. But she couldn't throw it in Rafe's face, could she? She'd just take a sip, for appearances' sake.

"Good stuff, isn't it?" Rafe said.

Katherine nodded. "Too much of this and I'll forget why I'm supposed to be here."

"Oh, I've changed my mind. You just have a good time and enjoy the party."

Katherine raised her eyebrows.

"I read the caterer's contract again," Rafe admitted. "I've already paid for a tanker load of this stuff, no matter what happens to it. Frankly, I decided I'd rather not know if the waiters are passing it out to my friends or washing dishes with it.'' He smiled placidly. ''Sherry's in the dining room, by the way, if you want to say hello. Last time I saw Travis he was on the terrace.''

''Not together?''

''Sherry's determined to surprise everybody.'' His gaze slid toward the entrance, where a group of guests had just appeared. ''Excuse me, Katherine—duty calls.''

So she hadn't succeeded in avoiding the worst moment by being late, Katherine reflected. The announcement was yet to come. It would be interesting to see how Sherry broke the news—surely it would be nothing so mundane as simply rolling out a cake in the shape of two wedding rings.

Though if the cake was decorated like a giant stock certificate...

Katherine warned herself not to be catty. That would only increase her bitterness and the chance of someone noticing how upset she was, and wondering why.

There were very few HomeSafe people, she realized. She'd be cheated of even the comfort of retreating to a corner for a business chat. And she hadn't caught so much as a glimpse of Stephen yet—but that was no surprise, when she thought about it. This was a command appearance, not the sort of party he'd really enjoy; he'd probably turn up mere minutes before the highlight of the evening.

If Stephen had been there, he would have been in the thick of things. Hilary Clayton—or whichever of her sisters-in-spirit he'd asked to accompany him— would not have been attracted to private corners of the terrace if there were people around to be impressed.

And Travis thinks I'm *cold-blooded,* she reflected.

As if the mere thought of the man had been a magical incantation, Travis appeared at the open french doors and started across the drawing room, almost directly toward Katherine.

Her breathing quickened, and she could feel the beat of blood in her eardrums. But she stood her ground; what reason was there for her to scuttle out of his way, after all? She had a right to be there. And surely he had nothing left to say to her—nothing, at least, that he would choose to say before an audience.

He didn't break step as he passed, but he watched her warily. Why had she never noticed how calculating those ice blue eyes could be?

She swapped her empty glass for a full one when a waiter came by, then wandered toward the terrace. She wasn't looking for a place to hide, exactly, but surely it was foolish to stay right in the center of things. A dim, quiet corner sounded much more inviting, given the circumstances. No one would miss her, that was sure.

She paused for just a second in the french doors. The drawing room faced northwest, and by day Rafe had a glorious and ever-changing view of the Rockies. But now, after dark on an almost moonless night, the mountain range was no more than a line of deeper shadows on the horizon.

Light spilled from the drawing room across the rough-surfaced concrete terrace, highlighting groups of people here and there. Quietly, Katherine slipped around the corner. Not as many people would come back here, on the narrower terrace outside the bedroom wing.

She leaned against the railing, her champagne glass

between her hands, and looked down twenty stories to the avenue. The noise of traffic wafted up to her, muted by distance until the shriek and clatter became only a pleasant background rhythm.

The concrete barricade was cool, despite the warmth of the night. It was a solid half wall, waist high and wide enough to sit on, if anyone chose to be so foolish.

She could almost picture it—climbing onto that uncertain perch, losing one's hold, falling. The champagne flute tipped in her hands at the picture, and she clutched wildly at it. From this height, even a crystal glass, if dropped, could become a deadly missile; the thought of a human body tumbling twenty stories made her head swim so badly that for a moment she didn't know if she should pull back from the edge or just close her eyes and hold on to the railing for all she was worth.

"Katherine!" Strong hands closed on her shoulders and gave her a shake. "Are you all right?"

She looked up into a pair of concerned brown eyes. "Stupid question," Stephen muttered. "Of course you're not. Come and sit down."

Katherine shook her head. "I'm fine, really," she managed. "Just a bit dizzy. The height bothered me for a moment."

The corner of his mouth twitched a little. "Then don't stand at the edge and stare straight down," he recommended.

She had to laugh at that. It was so like Stephen— cool and matter-of-fact and straight to the point.

His hold on her shoulders loosened until it was a mere touch, not a grip to hold her upright. "Well, it is only common sense," he pointed out. "If you're nervous about heights…"

"But I'm not. Not in general, I mean. Ski lifts don't bother me, or ladders." But then, she usually hadn't been drinking champagne when she tackled them. She looked down at the glass—she was clutching it so tightly she was surprised it hadn't smashed between her hands—and then up at Stephen again.

"You don't have to stay and guard me, you know," she said gently. "I'll be perfectly fine—really."

He let her go, his hands hovering above her shoulders for a few seconds, as if he expected her to sway again. But Katherine had one hip pressed firmly against the concrete rail to steady herself, and after a moment Stephen stepped away. Instead of leaving her there, however, he leaned against the railing beside her, palms braced flat against the rough surface, looking down at the city.

She glanced around cautiously, half expecting Hilary to burst through the french doors in search of her escort. Though, when she thought about it, she realized that Stephen couldn't have been coming from the penthouse when he saw her; she would have heard him. He must already have been sitting in the shadows when she came around the corner. And though there was a patio table nearby with several chairs drawn up invitingly, there was no sign of Hilary.

"What were you doing out here, anyway?" she asked, not that it was any of her business.

"Just thinking." He sounded almost sad.

Sad? Stephen, who never lost his sense of humor, whatever the circumstances? "About what?" she said softly. "Whoever's waiting for you inside?"

Stephen turned his head quickly and smiled a little. "No. I was thinking what a shame it is the Denver art museum looks like a storage facility for nuclear waste.''

Katherine choked on a giggle. He was so incredibly, wonderfully sane—an anchor to hold on to in a crazy world. ''Really? I always thought they must have got the plans mixed up with a federal prison.''

''Just in case the paintings ever band together and try to escape?'' His dark eyes were warm and laughing—and yet, she saw a sadness there, whatever he said.

Suddenly she couldn't bear the idea that he, too, was in pain, and she impulsively put her hand on his arm. ''Really, Stephen. What's bothering you? Is it Sherry's engagement?''

He looked down at her hand as if he'd never seen one before. ''Why? Do you think it should be giving me second thoughts?'' His tone was curious, not challenging.

Katherine caught herself up short. Not only had the question been a bit on the personal side, but it might imply that she had reservations of her own about this engagement. She managed a casual shrug. ''Sherry's very young.''

''She's twenty-three.'' He looked at her appraisingly. ''Not all that much younger than you are, Katherine.''

Sherry's age was a lame excuse for her doubts; she should have known Stephen would instantly see the flaw there. She studied the dark horizon as if she were trying to memorize the vague contours of the Rockies. ''Three years. And there's a lot of difference.''

''You mean, you haven't been spoiled and catered to, as Sherry has been all her life.''

"I didn't say that." She bit her lip and added stiffly, "I certainly have no right to comment about Sherry."

"Oh, don't apologize, I happen to agree with you. Sherry *is* immature and naive. But as she's utterly and childishly determined to have her own way, there's not much point in worrying about it, is there? Katherine—" He stopped, and then said, "I've never heard anyone call you anything but Katherine. Do they?"

Her breath froze. Only Travis, she thought miserably.

"You're shivering," he said. "Let's go in."

Katherine shook her head. "No. I'd rather stay out here." Where it was dim, and where she wouldn't have to face so many people. "My father used to call me Katie." She turned, almost surprised by her own words. "You know, I'd forgotten that."

"Forgotten it? How on earth could you forget what your father called you?"

"I was only a toddler when he died, you see." She chewed thoughtfully on a fingertip. "I don't even know if I honestly remember, or if I just recall being told. Though I'm sure my mother wouldn't have made any big deal about mentioning it."

He let the silence drag on for a moment, before saying incredulously, "Your mother wouldn't have told you things like that, to help you remember him?"

But Katherine was lost in the fog of memory, and for a moment she hardly knew he was there. "She married again," she said finally. "It—it wasn't a good second try." She looked up at him before she realized that her eyes were brimmed with tears. She turned away quickly. How stupid; just because she was hurting, she was dragging out every other old injury to study as well! "Ancient history," she murmured. "I shouldn't keep you, Stephen."

"If you're worrying about Hilary swooping out here and accusing you of trying to steal me, don't." His voice was dry.

Katherine forced herself to laugh. "She'd be very foolish to think I'd considered anything of the sort, wouldn't she?"

"Yes," he said coolly. "But at any rate, there's no reason for concern, since I didn't ask her to the party."

Katherine fumbled in her tiny bag for a handkerchief, surreptitiously removing any traces of tears. Then, try as she might, she couldn't help asking, "Why on earth not?"

He slanted a disbelieving look at her. "Use your head, Katherine. A man who invites a woman to his sister's engagement party is asking for trouble."

"I see. You think she might conclude that just because Sherry and Travis are settling down you should be starting to think the same way."

"Something like that."

She tucked the handkerchief back in her bag. "Oh, I think you're safe. Hilary isn't a fool." She wasn't looking at him.

"I certainly hope not."

An instant later the rustle of formal clothes alerted her to another presence on the terrace, just as Travis said, irritably, "So here you are—discussing business, no doubt."

Katherine shrugged. "Actually, I wasn't planning to put the last hour down on my time sheet." She turned with a saccharine smile to face him and finished off the flat champagne in her glass.

Travis's jaw tightened, but he merely said, "Sherry wants you, Stephen. It's time for the announcement."

Stephen didn't even glance at him. "We'll be along in a minute. I'm sure there will be plenty of room for us."

Travis said something under his breath and went back inside.

Katherine's voice caught in her throat. "Stephen, I'd really rather not—" She stopped herself at the last possible second. She could hardly refuse to show up for the focal point of the evening without causing comment. "I mean, I don't belong right up front," she went on, almost desperately. "I'm not family...."

"And just who said that I was planning to hover next to the happy pair? I'm going to stay on the fringes of the crowd, so I don't have to look excited for the sake of the photographs." He took her elbow, rather firmly, and guided her toward the french doors. "Come on. You have to stand somewhere."

In the dining room, Stephen disposed of her empty champagne glass and handed her a brimming one; Katherine took it meekly and cautiously looked around, trying to anticipate any trouble that might be waiting.

Next to the loaded buffet table, Sherry was standing with her father. It was the first glimpse Katherine had had of her, and her expectations were satisfied; Sherry's dress was dark magenta, with beaded trim that shimmered under the lights, and a deeply cut neckline meant to draw all eyes to her abundant curves.

I can't exactly blame her for making the most of her natural assets, Katherine thought. *If I was built like that I'd probably do the same thing.*

Rafe raised his glass, and the noise in the room died to a murmur as he started to speak. Katherine heard only a word here and there; she was concentrating on keeping her face calm, her head tipped as if she were interested.

"And now the shouting begins," Stephen murmured in her ear, as Rafe reached the end of his toast and summoned Travis from the back of the room. The young man put his arms around his intended bride and gave her an enthusiastic kiss. The crowd exploded in excited noise and rushed toward Sherry and Travis, who broke into happy grins as they were surrounded.

"We really fooled everyone, didn't we?" Sherry said, almost giggling with delight, and Travis gave her a fond pat on the cheek.

Katherine told herself that she, of all people, should not be surprised at the convincing nature of that display; after all, she had plenty of evidence of Travis's qualifications as an actor.

There was nothing she could do but to join in the toasts. At least there was one saving grace, she thought. The champagne was a very good vintage, indeed. And now that the big event of the evening was fast becoming history, surely she could just fade away.

As Sherry and Travis moved off toward the dance floor, trailed by most of the crowd, Katherine stepped out of the line of traffic, and manufactured a yawn.

Stephen looked down at her quizzically.

"I *did* work too late last night, after all," she murmured. "Sherry wouldn't notice if I just vanished, would she?"

"Sherry wouldn't notice if half the world disappeared, as long as it wasn't the half with Neiman Marcus in it." He asked bluntly, "How much champagne have you had?"

Katherine's spine stiffened. "If you're worried about

me driving, you can call a cab for me. That's how I'd planned to get home, anyway.''

He finished off his own champagne. "I'm going, too, now that the excitement is over. I'll take you.''

She opened her mouth to refuse, and closed it again. She wasn't dragging him away from the party, that was certain, and as long as he was grasping for an excuse to escape, she might as well benefit. She shrugged. "Fine with me. Anytime a woman has an offer of a ride in a brand-new Porsche, she'd be a fool to insist on a cab.''

It was several miles from the luxurious tower to Katherine's more modest neighborhood. She leaned back into the soft leather seat and watched Stephen's hands, one resting easily on the wheel, the other on the gearshift. It was a quiet ride; the Porsche's engine purred so softly she could hardly hear it, and he made no effort to start a conversation.

His silence bothered her a little, until she realized that she'd never really answered his question, and he might have reached the wrong conclusions.

"I haven't had too much to drink, you know,'' she said, with a hint of sulkiness in her voice. "And I didn't set out to get smashed, either. I only took a cab because I don't like walking all the way from the parking lot to my apartment after dark.''

There was an empty parking spot directly in front of the building. Katherine muttered, "Great. So now I look like a liar, too.'' She gathered up her shawl and evening bag.

Stephen grinned at her and put the Porsche neatly into the space. He caught her surprised look and said firmly, "I'll walk you in. It's late.''

She almost told him that it was nearly always late

when she came home, that she was used to it and didn't need a protector. Then she looked at the dark building and thought, *I do not want to go in there alone.*

Uncomfortable as she had been at the party tonight, at least there had been some comfort in human company. She didn't want to walk into that apartment by herself, knowing another long night and another long day stretched ahead of her before she would have even the minimal solace of going back to work.

Her head was swimming a little. Perhaps Stephen was right after all, and she had drunk too much champagne. But surely three glasses wasn't enough to cause a reaction like this. Unless—suddenly she remembered the lunch she had fixed but hadn't eaten, and the laden buffet table she hadn't even touched. It would be no wonder if the alcohol was hitting her more than usual.

She let him take her key, and over the click of the dead bolt she said hesitantly, "Would you like coffee?"

She wasn't looking at him, but she could sense his surprise.

"Just coffee," she pointed out. "I mean—" She took a deep breath and tried to stop herself from turning red. She didn't want him to get the wrong idea; how perfectly embarrassing that would be!

But he said quietly, "I could use a cup," and Katherine relaxed.

He stayed in the small living room while she puttered about the kitchen, boiling water and spooning coffee into mugs. She felt vaguely dissatisfied that it was only instant, and so she rummaged around and found cheese and crackers and hard salami, and arranged them on a plate. For all she knew, Stephen hadn't felt like eating at that party, either.

He was looking at the photographs propped on the mantel when she came in with the tray and set it down on the coffee table. "Family pictures?" he asked.

She shook her head. "Mostly friends."

"That's why I didn't see a resemblance, then." He reached for a gold frame, a bit larger than most of the others. "Except for this one."

Katherine glanced at it. The photograph was a rather fuzzy representation of a young man in a military uniform. "That was my father."

"I could tell by the chin," Stephen said with what sounded like satisfaction.

"I'm surprised you can see any likeness at all. That was the best the restorers could do, considering what they had to work with." She could read the question in his eyes, and something pushed her to answer that unspoken inquiry. "I found the original in pieces in my mother's things, after she died."

"Oh, Katherine." He sank down beside her on the couch and sat there restlessly, as if ready to jump up and be off.

What a stupid thing to say, she told herself. Even Travis had never known that; why was she suddenly blurting it all out now?

You are one boring coffee companion, Katherine Whitman, she thought bitterly.

"I'm sorry," she said. "I don't normally inflict that story on my guests. It certainly doesn't matter any more." She reached for her coffee mug and turned on a smile—a meaningless, social smile that tried to say all was well and it was time for a new subject.

She might have succeeded, too, if she hadn't looked directly into his eyes and seen the empathy, the compassion, the sensitivity that lay in the brown depths. And something else, as well...

Her hand clenched, her fingernails cutting into her palm. "Please," she whispered.

He didn't ask what she meant; it was just as well, for she couldn't have told him. But the moment that his mouth touched hers—gently, softly, with tender understanding—she knew. This was a healing touch. This was what she needed to make her whole again....

Her hand relaxed and opened, then lifted hesitantly toward his face. Stephen's arm slipped around her shoulders and eased her back against the soft cushions of the couch.

He seemed to understand how desperately she needed to be held, caressed, desired, and he answered her plea. She didn't know how much time passed; it could have been mere moments, or forever. All she knew was that each touch, each kiss fed the next, like sticks tossed one by one onto a snapping blaze. Comfort turned to hunger, and hunger to a strange, all-enveloping desperation that ought to have frightened her—but did not.

He cupped her face between his hands and held her a little ways from him, saying in a voice she hardly recognized, "I'd better go."

"No," she whispered. "Don't."

"You know what will happen if I stay."

She wet her lips with the tip of her tongue. "I know."

He kissed her again. "You said—just coffee."

"A woman has a right to change her mind, doesn't she?"

"As long as she doesn't lose it entirely in the process."

There didn't seem to be any answer to that, so she merely pulled him down to her.

"Do you honestly understand what the hell you're doing, Katherine?" His voice had a rough edge to it, like a half-worn-out file.

"Yes!" It was a reckless lie, and she knew it, but she was past caring. Travis had said she was too cold-blooded to act on impulse, but she wasn't, after all.

And sometimes, she was beginning to understand, acting on impulse felt very good indeed....

IT WAS BARELY DAWN when she woke, and she was cold. Of course, she thought muzzily; what do you expect if you throw off the covers in the middle of the night?

She reached for a blanket and came fully awake with a start. There was an arm draped across her body. A well-muscled arm, browned by the sun and hardened by tennis and racquetball and skiing. And it belonged to a man who was still sound asleep.

That was one blessing. But at the moment, it was absolutely the only one Katherine could think of.

Eyes wide, she stared at him, as he lay half-curled around her and obviously not cold at all. Color climbed faintly into her face as she remembered the madness of the night. She had been out of control, yes—but had she really made love to him like a desperate wanton?

Yes, she thought. She most certainly had. And she didn't even have the excuse of having had too much to drink; if it had been the champagne at fault, her memories would be fuzzy. But she remembered every kiss—every touch—every whisper of sensation.... And she would never forget how completely her desires had been fulfilled.

Katherine sank back against her pillow. *Only you could take a situation that was already messy and make it ten times worse,* she told herself. *And you thought you had problems before!*

What on earth was she going to do when Stephen woke up? When they both had to face the fact that last night she—Katherine Whitman—had efficiently, cold-bloodedly, and very competently seduced her boss?

CHAPTER FOUR

STEPHEN MUTTERED something unintelligible, and Katherine's breathing froze until he was still again.

Horrible possibilities began to chase each other through her head. What if he woke right now to find her there, and in the first instant of consciousness she saw confusion in his face as he tried to remember why he was in her bed? Or worse yet, what if there was shock in his eyes—or disbelief at the memories of last night?

Or pity? That, she thought, would be the worst of all. He had felt real compassion for her when she'd told him about her father, there was no denying that. But was that the reason he had stayed with her?

He should go, he had said, but she'd practically begged him not to leave her. And he hadn't gone. Had his actions been motivated by some kind of charitable impulse—because he felt sorry for her?

The longer Katherine considered it, the less she was able to find any other reason that made sense. She wasn't—as Travis had so bluntly, rudely, but accurately pronounced—the kind of woman Stephen generally found appealing.

I think I am going to be sick, she told herself.

Stephen turned over with his back to her, and nestled his cheek into the pillow. Without the warm weight of his arm holding her fast, Katherine suddenly felt even

colder. It wasn't the chill of the mountain air pouring
in through the open windows and brushing her skin that
was causing her discomfort, but a paralyzing cold that
rose from within. What would he say when the inevitable moment came? Would he try to let her down tactfully?

With the last bit of self-control she possessed, Katherine slid over the edge of the bed. She wasn't running
away, she told herself firmly. She was simply buying
herself a little time to think.

She found yesterday's jeans and a cotton sweater and
tiptoed out into the living room before she stopped to
pull them on. The snack tray was still on the coffee
table, untouched. The cheese looked dark and dry, the
hard salami shriveled and curled. She left it there; what
difference did it make if it aged a few hours more?

She shoved her feet into espadrilles, found her handbag and fumbled for her keys, which were not in the
accustomed pocket. She lost a precious couple of
minutes locating the tiny evening bag she had carried
last night. Beside it on the mantel was her apartment
key, where Stephen had put it. She grabbed it and
turned to leave.

From the bedroom door, a husky, sleep-raveled voice
said, "Hello. Or should I say goodbye?"

Katherine wheeled around.

He was wearing trousers, and not another solitary
thing. He ought to have looked ridiculous, she thought,
with his tousled hair, bare feet, and the formal satin-
striped trousers. Instead, he looked terrific.

His mussed-up hair reminded her of how she had
buried her fingers in its softness last night. Her gaze
dropped as she tried not to stare. At the lean, narrow
hips. At his chest, covered with soft, dark curls that did

nothing to mask the ridged muscle underneath. And his face...

She reached for the doorknob.

"You're not going out after doughnuts, are you?" he asked, very quietly.

She wasn't certain what he meant, but the cynical edge to his voice made her quite sure that she didn't want an explanation. "Last night was enough of a mistake," she managed to say. "Please, Stephen. Don't make it worse."

"One massive mistake," he said, in a murmur she was obviously not intended to hear.

But Katherine's ears had always been keen, and that was the final blow. Fighting back a shudder, she slipped out and closed the door behind her with a click of finality. She didn't manage a full breath or a complete thought until she was three blocks away, in the parking lot, and then she slumped behind the wheel of her car and cursed herself for being such a fool.

She should have stayed and gotten it over with. She should have let him make whatever explanations he wanted, issue whatever warnings he felt were needed, no matter how badly it would have shredded the little self-esteem she had left. She would have to face him sometime; it would have been easier, in the long run, to have had it out with him this morning than to worry about what he was likely to say tomorrow, in that silent paneled office.

If she'd only had the sense to stay, it could have been settled now, and it wouldn't have seeped into their work...

What an idiot you are, she told herself. As if there was the slightest hope that this could remain a private matter, separate from HomeSafe! There was no way to put this mess aside and forget it, to simply go back to the way things had been before.

"Talk about going from the frying pan into the fire! If you wanted to commit suicide, Katherine Whitman, you ought to have just jumped over that railing last night. Twenty stories straight down and it would have been over with. This way—"

As it was, the consequences of her self-destructive instincts were only beginning.

She drove around the city for a long time, hardly aware of her actions. There was nowhere to go, nothing to do. And since it was Sunday, there wasn't even work to take her mind off her problems—

Would she ever again be able to do that, she wondered. Would it be possible to bury herself in paperwork and forget everything else? Could she ever again concentrate on HomeSafe, with this hanging over her head?

The enjoyment of her job was shattered. The easy working relationship she had always treasured was gone—sacrificed in a thoughtless moment of loneliness and despair.

She ordered breakfast at a greasy little diner in an anonymous suburb, and pushed soggy scrambled eggs around her plate for a while as she drank acid-strong coffee and wondered what else she might have thrown away last night.

She found herself wishing that she could go and talk to Rafe Osborne. She had done that a few times before and Rafe always listened carefully, asked thoughtful questions and ended by giving good, solid advice. But talking to Rafe was out of the question this time. For one thing, she couldn't quite envision herself telling Rafe what had happened last night. And if she did confess, her job would be at stake. No matter how fond of her Rafe happened to be, she was an employee—and seducing the boss certainly wasn't on the list of approved behavior.

But wasn't her job even now on the line? she wondered. Stephen was every bit as adamant about proper employee conduct as Rafe had ever been. If she couldn't pull herself together soon, it would be too late. In fact, he might already have decided to get rid of her, and prevent any risk of a repetition of...

No, she told herself firmly. She bore the brunt of the responsibility for what had happened last night, but she hadn't exactly dragged him into her bedroom; Stephen was too fair-minded to blame her entirely. Still, if they could no longer work together it would be Katherine who'd be asked to leave, not Stephen.

"Time to cut the losses," Rafe used to say, when some apparently promising line of research hadn't produced the expected results. And when she'd sympathized, Rafe would only shrug. "No sense in throwing good money after bad," he'd tell her. "We'll just give something else a whirl."

Would that be his advice this time? Should she muster her courage to talk to him? Or should she wait and try to ride it out, walking a tightrope every time she saw Stephen? Perhaps the problem would fade, and eventually everything would return to normal—or to some approximation of it—if only she could keep her head long enough.

And perhaps pigs would learn to fly, too.

Maybe she should quit, while she had a chance of going with dignity and salvaging something from the experience.

Was it time to cut her losses?

She hadn't decided anything by the time she paid her bill, and it certainly wasn't a conscious decision that brought her to the guard shack at the main entrance of HomeSafe; in fact, she was almost surprised to find herself there.

"Working on Sundays, Miss Whitman?" the guard asked. "Must be an important job going on."

"Just clearing up some details, Jed." The gate opened and Katherine drove through. As long as she was here, she might as well put in a couple of hours at her desk. Getting a start on that report for Stephen on the use of cellular telephones might help; it would certainly distract her for a while and stop the wild, pointless spinning of her thoughts. By the time she was finished, she might have a better idea of what she wanted—needed—to do.

She felt a little odd, walking through the quiet building. It wasn't the empty halls and the silent labs and workrooms that bothered her; she was often at HomeSafe after most of the workers had gone for the night. But walking through in the daytime, wearing such casual clothes, felt very strange. She was usually so careful of how she looked at work.

She was well inside the executive suite before she saw that the lights were on and that someone was bent over the bottom drawer of Irene's desk. Her first thought was of the elaborate security net, and how incredible it was that anyone could have circumvented all of it and gotten in. Then the figure straightened, and her panic settled into an uncomfortable lump in the pit of her stomach.

"Stephen," she said. It was no more than a choked whisper. "I didn't expect—"

"Sorry to shock you." He closed the drawer and

slapped the folder he held against the palm of his hand, as if he were trying to make up his mind about something. "But since you're here—come into my office."

It was more order than request, and automatically Katherine responded to it. As she slipped past him, Stephen made a move as if to take her arm, and she instinctively sidestepped, almost shuddering away from his touch. He stopped as abruptly as if she'd struck him.

You shouldn't have done that, she told herself. If she had only acted as she always used to... It had never bothered her before when he touched her. She'd certainly never pulled away from him as if she'd been burned.

Her instinct had been right, she thought sadly. Becoming lovers changed everything. There could be no putting this aside and ignoring it.

She bypassed the deep, comfortable chairs grouped invitingly at the end of the room and chose instead the almost straight-backed one beside his desk. Unconsciously she assumed a defensive posture—feet firmly planted on the carpet, shoulders hunched protectively...

Stephen followed her in and leaned against the corner of his desk. Katherine thought he looked almost like a bird, perching for a moment to watch for danger, with no intention of staying there for long. But the moment stretched out painfully, and neither of them moved.

Finally he broke the silence. "I'm sorry about last night. It should not have happened." His voice—even his words—was abrupt, to the point, almost flat.

It was no more than she'd expected. Katherine studied the grain along the edge of the desktop and said, "It wasn't your fault. I was out of my mind, I suppose.'' She didn't look at him; she couldn't. What on earth must he think of her? What kind of woman behaved as she had last night? Did he think she pulled that sort of stunt frequently, with any man who happened to be handy? ''At least, I think I must have been crazy,'' she muttered. ''I don't—do that kind of thing.''

He shifted his position restlessly. ''You certainly had all the moves down last night.''

She closed her eyes tightly against the prickle of tears.

Cut your losses, she told herself. You don't really have a choice; it's only a matter of time.

''I'm sorry,'' he said. ''That was uncalled for.''

Still, the harsh words had been spoken, and there was no taking their sting away. Katherine swallowed hard. ''I'm leaving HomeSafe,'' she said huskily. ''Effective immediately. I'll finish up what I can today, but I'm sure you'll understand why I'm not coming back.''

He moved again, not very gracefully. ''Katherine—''

She looked up at him then, eyes bright with unshed tears. ''Do you really think we could work together like this?''

He didn't answer.

She stood. It took all the self-control she had to walk slowly toward the door. ''I'll leave my resignation on your desk before I go, and my keys at the guard shack.''

Stephen rubbed the back of his hand across his eyes. ''I can't exactly give you a recommendation to take to the competition.'' He sounded very tired.

After all her work, after all her time and loyalty— to be refused a reference was a harsh blow. And yet, if he had written her a recommendation, Katherine knew it could only have been a guarded one, the kind that experienced personnel officers could see through in a minute. The kind she'd composed once or twice herself, at Stephen's request, when a doubtful employee left HomeSafe....

"I didn't expect that you would," she said quietly.

She made certain he was gone before she ventured out of her office to leave the carefully typed resignation letter on his desk, along with the rough draft of her report on the cellular telephones, incomplete though it was. It took just a few minutes to pack up the personal items that had collected in her office. When she left the building it wasn't yet noon.

She was putting the box in her car when she heard Travis's voice. "What's up? Stealing company secrets?"

Despite herself, her hands jerked and the box tumbled into the back of her car. She closed the trunk and turned to face him. "It's a surprise to see you here at this hour."

He grinned, breezily. "I can't say the same for you. Any normal woman who left the party with Stephen last night would still be curled up with him now. But you, of course, wouldn't even have recognized the opportunity." He paused. "Or does this mean you've decided to wait for me?"

"Wait for you to do what? Get rid of Sherry?"

"Oh, no—I wouldn't be that stupid. But after a while, I'll manage a little free time...."

"I don't doubt it," Katherine said dryly.

"Once you get loosened up, Kathy, you might be fun."

Katherine unlocked her car and got in. "Have you

ever been down to Royal Gorge, Travis?'' she asked
politely.

"Sure. What's that got to do with—"

"Next time, jump off the suspension bridge. And
don't bother with a bungee cord.'' She started the engine with a roar and backed the car out, heedless of
how close the wheels might be to his toes.

There was one good thing about the situation, she
told herself. She certainly didn't need to worry about
Travis any more. She'd created more trouble and grief
for herself than he could have caused her in a million
years.

THE PHOTOCOPY MACHINE was broken, so Katherine
had to walk two blocks to the nearest working model.
The late August heat wave was so intense that the
pavement seemed to be melting, and by the time she'd
carried her stacks of paper back to the office, her once
crisp salmon-colored shirtdress felt as limp as if she'd
put it on two weeks ago. There was a new batch of
survey forms piled haphazardly on the table in the corner beside the personal computer, and the vice president's secretary was impatiently waiting for her return.

"It's past time for my lunch break, Miss Whitman,''
she pointed out. "You might have hurried back. Mr.
Cole has a client in his office with him—hold all his
calls until further notice. I might add that he asked me
what on earth you were doing with all your time, since
those surveys don't seem to be moving. If I were you,
I'd make a dent in them this afternoon or the agency
is apt to get a complaint about your work.'' With a last
helpful nod, she vanished down the hall.

Katherine put the stack of fresh copies on the corner

of the secretary's desk and counted to ten, and then to twenty-five.

"My head aches," she muttered. "It's so hot it's impossible to sleep at night. I've picked up a nasty bug that I just can't shake, and it looks as if I'm doomed to enter stupid answers to a stupid survey into a stupid computer for all time. What else, dear heaven, can possibly go wrong?"

Venting her spleen made her feel a little better, except for the headache, and she sat down at the computer again with determination. However, it—like the photocopy machine and most of the other equipment she'd encountered around this office—had been a budget model, and the screen oscillated a bit, making the letters vibrate slightly and her head ache even more. She gritted her teeth and tried to increase her pace, but within twenty minutes the motion of the screen was making her feel faint and almost sick to her stomach.

She had just pushed her chair back from the desk and let her head drop forward to fight off the dizzy spell when the door of the inner office opened and Bill Cole and his client appeared.

Katherine jerked upright, so fast that the blood drained to her toes, and she would have pitched onto her face on the carpet if it hadn't been for the prompt response of Mr. Cole's client. Hands caught at her shoulders, easing her head down to her knees. "There—sit still a minute, you'll be all right," a gruff voice said.

Rafe? She tried to say it, but her voice wasn't working, and the mass of hair that had fallen over her face, along with the pressure of his hand on the back of her neck, kept her from looking up to make sure.

"What's wrong with the girl?" Mr. Cole asked querulously.

"She's obviously ill, that's what's wrong."

It was definitely Rafe, at his driest and most dangerous. Katherine knew that edge in his voice.

Rafe went on, "Does she have epilepsy or something?"

"How should I know? She's only a temporary, from one of those agencies. I don't know anything about her." The tone of Mr. Cole's voice indicated that, furthermore, he was washing his hands of this troublesome employee.

The grip at the back of her neck tightened momentarily. Katherine thought Rafe was probably unaware of his action, but she couldn't keep herself from moaning in protest.

He dropped to one knee beside her. "Are you in pain—Katherine!"

She wet her lips. "Hi, Rafe. Not pain, exactly, I'm just dizzy. And I've had flu. You know how that hangs on. I'm just not very lively yet."

"Well, you don't belong here." He helped her sit up, and kept a steadying hand on her shoulder.

"My very thought," Mr. Cole chimed in. "My secretary will call the agency and have them send someone else—someone who wants to work. I don't believe we'll be needing you in the future, Miss Whitman."

Rafe gave him a look that should have turned him into a charcoal briquette and bent over Katherine again. "Whenever you feel able to get up, I'll take you home."

"How about right now?" Her head was still throbbing from eyestrain, but she really was feeling better.

And certainly some air would improve things—air uncontaminated by Bill Cole's presence.

I was just fired, she thought. Wouldn't that be the perfect finishing touch on her record? Oh, well, it was too late to worry about it now; Mr. Cole wouldn't take her back even if she begged. And if she tried to get down on her knees, she'd probably never be able to get back up.

Rafe saw the unsteadiness in her step and put his arm around her. "Damn fool shoes," he complained. "It's a wonder you women aren't all cripples. Do you have a car?"

She shook her head, and wished she hadn't. "Parking is so bad here that I've just been using the bus."

"Parking and a lot of other things—like management, I'd say. Charming sort, your Mr. Cole." He broke into song as they crossed the parking lot. "'Old Bill Cole, *not* a merry old soul…'"

"That's not tactful, Rafe." But she had to smile at his enthusiastic and off-key tenor.

"You're feeling better, if you're reminding me of my manners."

"A bit. What were you doing there, anyway? I don't remember ever hearing of any connection between HomeSafe and Bill Cole's outfit."

"And if you had, you wouldn't have been working for him, I suspect," Rafe said blandly. "I was inviting him to submit a bid for some HomeSafe components. But don't worry. He's not likely to get the job." He opened the door of his Jeep so Katherine could climb in.

"It's not exactly Cinderella's carriage, I'm afraid," he said with a sideways look at her. "If I'd known, I'd have borrowed Stephen's car. Now, tell me why the hell you were working there, Katherine Whitman.'' His voice was stern.

"It's only for a week or so," she said, before she remembered that she wasn't expected to return at all. "Anyway, it was supposed to last that long—this was my third day. I'm a temp for the Mayfly Agency. You know—I fill in when businesses need an extra pair of hands."

"I know what a temp is. I just find it hard to believe that you're working as one."

She bristled a little at the incredulity in his voice. "It's not a bad job. Every now and then there's a Bill Cole, but most people are decent. And without a reference—" She bit her tongue, but it was too late to stop. "It was the best I could do."

Rafe's bushy eyebrows looked fiercer than she had ever seen them before. "What in the hell happened, Katherine?"

She stared out the window and tried to pick her words carefully. He was the chairman of HomeSafe, after all; she didn't want him to misunderstand, or think she was accusing Stephen. "Stephen and I had a disagreement," she said unsteadily. "It was entirely my fault."

"Are you telling me that he fired you? And wouldn't give you a reference?"

"Not exactly. I quit. There's my apartment house, Rafe."

He pulled into the fire zone in front of the building without a second's hesitation. Katherine opened the door and turned to put her hand out to him. "Thank you so much for bringing me home—"

A high-pitched squeal from the sidewalk drew her attention. Alison Day burst away from her mother's grasp and came running to the Jeep. She tugged excitedly at Katherine's skirt and began making frantic gestures.

Molly, half a step behind, bodily picked up her daughter and started to carry her back to the sidewalk. Then she stopped in midstride. "Katherine! What—you're feeling sick again, aren't you? Come along. I'll help you upstairs."

Grateful for the excuse, Katherine turned back to Rafe. "I'll be fine now. Thanks again."

But as she slid out of the Jeep, his hand closed on her arm. "Just one thing, Katherine. Stephen doesn't seem to have got the message. Your office still has your name on the door, and the official response to questions is that you're taking a leave of absence."

She was standing on the sidewalk, frowning, when he drove off.

Did he mean—could he mean—that her job was still there, if she wanted to try again? It had been more than six weeks since she'd left that letter on Stephen's desk. If he hadn't even told Rafe about it…

Alison was patting her arm. Absently, Katherine looked down to see the little girl rub her right hand over her heart.

"You're sorry?" she said. "For what, Alison?"

"For squealing like that," Molly explained. "And for interrupting. She was excited to see you, of course, but that's no excuse for bad behavior. Let's get you upstairs, Katherine. What happened, anyway?"

"I tried to faint."

"Did you succeed?"

"No." Katherine sighed. "I couldn't even finish a simple task like that and do it right."

Molly made soothing noises while she opened Katherine's door and settled her on the couch. "It's no wonder. You're so tired, dear."

"I know. I'll get over it if I can only keep going." She started to sit up, but Molly pushed her gently back against the cushions.

"Don't move."

Katherine subsided. She didn't have the energy to argue about it, that was sure.

"Did you eat breakfast this morning?"

"No. I didn't feel like it. I'm sorry to be such a nuisance, Molly. I was going to baby-sit tonight while you go to class, and here you are taking care of me instead—"

"Don't worry about it. You'll probably be feeling just fine by then."

"Is that a promise?" Katherine asked wearily.

Molly grinned, patted Katherine's shoulder, and stood up. "I'll get you some toast right now, and I'll come in to check on you later. Oh, and you might try soda crackers first thing in the morning. It sounds stupid, I know, but it really works. That's how I got through morning sickness."

She smiled briskly and headed for Katherine's kitchen. Alison pulled up a small stool, plopped down on it and began patiently asking questions one after another.

Katherine wasn't watching her. She was reeling under the worst attack of nausea, headache and dizziness that she'd ever experienced in her life.

"Morning sickness?" she managed to croak.

Molly's head appeared around the door frame. "That's what I— Oh, dear heaven, Katherine, don't tell me you didn't realize? No strain of flu produces symptoms like the ones you're having."

Katherine's voice was lifeless. "I thought maybe I was just depressed about losing my job, and that was making everything worse."

My job, she thought, and let herself remember what Rafe had said—that her name was still on her office door, and officially she was simply taking a leave of absence. He'd implied that if she wanted to walk back into HomeSafe tomorrow, she could do it. There would be questions, perhaps, and she would still have to deal with the problems that had led her to quit in the first place—but if she could put her memories behind her she might have a second chance.

A second chance. It was a beautiful phrase, full of hope.

She'd long ago admitted that she missed her job. But until Rafe had held out the possibility of returning, she'd never really allowed herself to think about how much she regretted her decision to leave HomeSafe. Since there was no going back, there was no point in dwelling on what could have been.

But she knew, now, that no matter how uncomfortable it might have been around the office for a time, it would have been better than the Mayfly Agency. She missed HomeSafe. She missed the feeling of being a valued, important part of the business. She missed Stephen, so much that she was afraid to let herself think about it....

But barely a moment after she had begun to hope, to wonder if things might work out after all if she and Stephen could only manage to ignore their one colossal mistake, the hope had been ripped away from her. It wouldn't be possible to put that night behind her and forget that it had ever happened. It would never be possible, now.

It had been six weeks and five days since Sherry Osborne's engagement party. And in slightly over seven months more—sometime around the middle of April—Katherine would be giving birth to Stephen's child, conceived on that incredible, insane night.

Hot, bitter tears flooded Katherine's eyes. She turned her head into her pillow and sobbed.

Molly perched on the edge of the couch and began to stroke Katherine's hair. "I assumed you just didn't want to discuss it," she said softly, "that you were keeping it to yourself while you considered what you want to do."

"What I want to do?" Katherine repeated, weakly, almost as if Molly was speaking some foreign language. She sighed. "I don't know, Molly. I don't know."

CHAPTER FIVE

MOLLY STAYED a while longer, murmuring reassurance, but there was really nothing she could say that would make things better, and both of them knew it. The hard choices were Katherine's to make, and it was almost a relief to her when Molly and Alison tiptoed out and left her alone.

She sank back against her pillow and closed her eyes. Her head still ached, but the rhythmic throbbing was nothing compared to the stony ache in her heart. The shock had passed, but it had left her in the lowest, most defeated mood of her life.

She hadn't known such despair was possible. But this was worse than the shattering moments in her childhood—still so clear in her mind—when she had been told she wasn't any good. This was worse than the day she'd rebelled against that abuse and left home—for then, though she was terrified at being entirely on her own, she'd known that if she worked hard enough, anything was possible. This was even worse than the day she'd walked out of HomeSafe, sacrificing the career she'd struggled to build.

But that had been the right decision after all, she reflected. Things were bad enough as it was; she would have to tell Stephen, of course, but she simply couldn't imagine herself standing beside the coffee cart some morning and announcing, as he refilled his cup, ''Remember the night you stayed over at my place? Well, guess what!''

Telling Stephen would not be the average fun day at the beach, that was sure, but at least this way no one at HomeSafe would need to know. Thank heaven she'd told Rafe she had the flu. And thank heaven, as well, that she didn't have to do anything right away. She had time to consider, before she ever picked up the telephone, precisely what it was she *wanted* to do.

Which brought her back to exactly where she'd started.

She was listlessly stirring the contents of a saucepan when Molly came to check on her that evening. Molly took one look at the macaroni bubbling in the pan and the shredded cheese ready to be stirred in, and said approvingly, ''It's not exactly a balanced meal, but it's hot, and that's a start.''

''I thought Alison might like it.'' Katherine shrugged. ''Besides, it's one of my comfort foods.''

''Like Mom's chicken soup when you have a cold? I see. I can leave Alison at the child-care center if you're not up to coping with her tonight.''

''I'm fine. Actually, I'd like the distraction.''

''Well, she's certainly that. I'll remind her that you're not feeling up to playing.''

''I'm all right—physically. Emotionally, I'm a wreck. If only this wasn't happening now...''

''Oh, honey, I know. But think about the baby. Of course you're not thrilled with the circumstances, but it's still a miracle. A new life always is.''

''This one is more like a disaster.''

Molly's mouth tightened. After a moment, she said quietly, ''Poor child. With that kind of attitude surrounding it even in the womb...''

"You're right. I really am a terrible person, aren't I? I suppose if I'm going to be like that, maybe I should be thinking about having an abortion." And then she wouldn't have to face Stephen, either....

"You cannot possibly be serious." Molly's voice was crisp. "Thousands of people would give everything they possess to be able to have a baby."

Katherine sighed. "No, I don't suppose I could go through with it. Adoption, then. That's all that's left, Molly. Heaven knows I can't make ends meet now, let alone if I'm trying to raise a child." But the sudden pang of loss shooting through her was startling. Was she actually feeling the stir of maternal instinct? Surely not; it must just be Molly's talk of babies and miracles that was causing this pain. And yet, could she bear to give up her baby? Sacrifice her own child, the only human being in the world who would ever belong to her?

"What about your old job? Didn't the man who brought you home today say that it was available again?"

"Not under these circumstances—believe me." Katherine drained the macaroni and stirred in the cheese. "This will be ready in a minute, and Alison and I will let you go off early to class for a change."

Molly smiled wryly. "And get rid of the nosy friend? I'm sorry, Katherine. It's just that I know what being a single parent is like. It's not always easy, but it's not so bad, either, and I hate to see you making choices without thinking them all the way through. I care about you, honey...."

Tears crept into Katherine's eyes, and she had to bite her lip to hold them back. "You're the first person in a long time who *has* cared. I guess it's just hard for me to accept.''

''That you're worth caring about?'' Molly gave her a hug. ''We'll have to work on that.''

She turned to Alison and explained patiently where she was going, and when she would be back. ''And take it easy on Katherine,'' she finished.

Katherine smiled a little. It had sounded more like a prayer than an instruction.

Yes, she thought, Molly certainly knew the downside of being a single mother. A profoundly deaf child would be a challenge for two parents. Katherine shivered at the idea of having to cope with such a handicap entirely alone. But was the responsibility honestly that much less if the child wasn't physically handicapped, she wondered.

As soon as her mother was gone, Alison dived into her macaroni and cheese with enthusiasm, managing to sign animatedly even with a fork in her hand. Katherine thought that Molly probably frowned on that sort of behavior, but she didn't really know how to explain to Alison that it wasn't mannerly. *Don't talk with your mouth full* didn't quite fit the circumstances. So she ignored it and tried to follow what Alison was telling her.

Despite her best efforts over the last few weeks, Katherine could still manage to catch only about one sign in three, just enough to guess at the context of Alison's conversation. Whenever the child paused, Katherine simply put her own fork down and employed the very first sign Molly had taught her. ''Slow down,'' she said gently, and stroked the fingers of her right hand slowly over the back of the left.

Alison frowned, and heaved a gusty sigh. For a few

moments she made her signs larger and more deliberate, but before long she was off at top speed again.

Katherine gave up on trying to follow, and found herself wondering just who was the handicapped one, after all. Alison's lack of hearing didn't bother the child; she didn't even seem to realize that her own way was the unusual one. Apparently she'd accepted Katherine as a slow learner whose disabilities must simply be endured.

"And you might be right," Katherine muttered.

Molly was raising a beautiful daughter. Alison was bright, happy, unspoiled. And though she was profoundly deaf, she was, in fact, less handicapped than many children Katherine had run into—children who didn't know the limits of discipline, or the sunshine of love.

"I wonder if I could do as well," she said to herself.

"What?" Alison signed politely. "Repeat?"

"Never mind. Would you like ice cream?" Her pidgin signing obviously got the point across, for Alison nodded eagerly, carried her plate over to the sink, then patiently waited beside the refrigerator with her spoon until Katherine got the carton out. And before she took her dish back to the table, the child gave her a bear hug, as if to say that she understood and sympathized with Katherine's disabilities, and liked her in spite of them.

The gesture touched Katherine's heart. Some things were the same in all languages, she thought. The unselfconscious hug of a child…

For the first time she found herself thinking of the baby not as an interference in her life, but as a person-in-waiting. Boy or girl, she wondered. With Stephen's dark eyes, or her own hazel ones, or something in between? More important, would this child be as happy as Alison was, or as haunted as Katherine herself had been?

She wandered into the living room and picked up the picture of her father, wondering if someday in her child's face she would see something of him—and if she would be able to recognize it. She searched the blurred image intently, finally putting the picture aside with a sigh. It was hard to make out what he had really looked like. The original had been so small, so faded, and so heavily damaged that the reproduction, poor as it was, was something of a miracle.

Katherine had never known whether her mother had torn up the original in a fit of rage and then regretted her action, or if her stepfather had been the one who destroyed it.

It didn't matter, she supposed, except as a lesson. The baby she carried would never suffer that way. She would make certain of it. No matter what she had to do...

She sat there for a long time, watching as Alison played with a fashion doll, and considered her next move. She was so absorbed that she jumped six inches when the telephone rang. Alison, of course, didn't even twitch in response.

"Katherine?" Rafe's voice was gruff. "I thought I should check on you. Are you still holding together?"

She shifted her grip on the telephone and dried her suddenly damp palms on the seat of her jeans. "Of course. It's very kind of you to call."

"Well, I'm glad you're feeling better. Listen, I'll be talking to Stephen tomorrow. If you want me to ask him about that job of yours—"

"No, please," she said, too hastily. There was a suspicious silence on the other end of the line. "Rafe, please don't say anything to him about me."

"Katherine, don't be silly."

"I'm not. But it will be better if I talk to him myself. I'll call him soon, Rafe—I promise."

There was a brief pause. "You're certain you're feeling better?"

"Absolutely. I'm fine, Rafe."

At least, she would be eventually, she told herself. She would work things out somehow—just as she always had before.

ARMED WITH MOLLY'S all-purpose soda crackers, Katherine was able to work the rest of the week, though the Mayfly Agency agreed that she shouldn't go back to Bill Cole's office.

On Saturday she managed to get to the supermarket, the laundry, and the pharmacy, and was bemused to find that everywhere she went she saw babies—in strollers and in backpacks, in ones and twos and even threes. Were there suddenly more of them, she found herself wondering, or had she simply never noticed before?

In the afternoon she wandered down the block to the ice-cream shop to buy a sundae, then carried it across the street to the park to watch the children play. It wasn't the first time this week that she'd gone there, to sit and watch and ask herself questions as if she were preparing for some sort of test.

What if she was the mother of the toddler in the sandbox who had just bonked his playmate over the head with a truck; how would she handle it? *Could* she handle it? Or what if hers was the injured child? Would she react correctly? How did a mother know whether to kiss the wound or rush the child to the emergency room, anyway? And what about the sand—or mud, or snow? Did she honestly have the patience to sit here accomplishing nothing while her child played, and enough stamina left over to clean up the mess afterward?

Because it's not just a baby you need to think about, she reminded herself. It was a person—a toddler, a child, an adolescent, a teenager—for whom she would be taking responsibility. And if she couldn't handle that challenge, with only herself to rely on, then she had better admit it before long—while there was still time to arrange an alternative.

The thought of adoption left her cold. Had she made a decision, then, without even realizing it?

A shadow fell across the bench and she automatically moved to one end to leave a place for the newcomer.

"You told Rafe you were going to call me," Stephen said.

Every muscle in her body tensed. It took an effort of will to turn her head to look at him.

He looked different, she thought. Perhaps it was the casual clothes—jeans and an open-neck Polo shirt that left his arms almost bare. Or was it simply that she'd never seen him without at least a glint of humor in his eyes before?

She finished the last bite of her ice cream and set the plastic container beside her on the bench. "And I meant that. I just didn't say when," she said coolly. "How did you know where I was, anyway?"

He shifted his weight, propping his elbow on the back of the bench, and looked out across the park. His eyes were hidden behind the dark lenses of his sunglasses, but she could see the fine lines at the corners of them, deeper now than she remembered—or was it only that the sunlight was so strong?

"I ran into your next-door neighbor," he said. "Don't blame her—she was very cautious. She looked me over for a full five minutes before concluding that I was probably not a serial killer."

Even without his usual executive garb, Stephen could convince anyone to trust him, Katherine thought. It really wouldn't be fair of her to blame Molly for not holding out. "So she sent you here?"

"To be precise, she said you'd gone to the park to play your own masochistic version of Let's Pretend. Whatever that means."

Katherine smiled despite herself. Molly thought she was crazy even to be considering the question of whether she would be a good and capable mother. Of course she would, Molly had announced, and now would Katherine kindly get on with more important matters, like deciding how she was going to manage everything. The idea of adoption Molly refused to discuss at all.

Katherine frowned. Had Molly sensed her decision, before it had even been made?

"How are you feeling?" Stephen asked. "Rafe told me you haven't been well, and I can see it for myself." His fingertip went out as if to touch the hollow in her cheek, and then dropped away before it brushed her skin.

She could see herself reflected in the shiny dark lenses of his glasses—her face thinner, her hair caught up in a careless knot at the top of her head, her eyes shadowed. "I'm feeling fine," she said, and steeled herself for what had to follow. But she couldn't look at him while she said it, so she picked out a small boy on the lawn and watched him toddle uncertainly across the grass while she added, in an undertone, "For a pregnant lady, that is."

She didn't know what she had expected—that he would shriek and jump up and run off across the park, perhaps, or go wild-eyed and start tearing out his hair by the handful—but she'd underestimated his style. The president of a major corporation doesn't show surprise, she reminded herself, no matter what the calamity.

And if, despite that code of self-control, Stephen's jaw had tightened a fraction or his mouth had shown the merest hint of distaste—well, that was the main reason she hadn't been looking at him as she broke the news. If that was what he felt, she didn't want to know it just now.

His voice was quiet. "Have you seen a doctor?"

"Not really. But I managed a quick visit to a clinic. There is, unfortunately, no chance that it's only my imagination."

"Have you thought about—options?"

She looked at him, but trying to read the expression behind the dark lenses was fruitless, and she couldn't see even a hint of what he might be feeling.

I was wrong, she thought. *Any expression—any emotion—would be better than indifference.* She found herself wanting to kick him in the kneecap just to see if that might break his calm.

"You know, Stephen," she said earnestly, "sometimes you'd be a lot more likable if you'd react like a human being instead of a chief executive officer. What the hell do you mean, have I thought about options? I haven't thought of another damned thing in the last three days!''

He rubbed his knuckles along his jaw. The action made Katherine feel better; at least it was some sign that he might actually be agitated. ''What have you decided?''

The little boy she'd been watching toddled uncertainly over to a woman sitting on the grass. His wet, toothy smile showed his obvious pride in his new skill, and his mother enfolded him in her arms with apparent joy.

I want that, Katherine thought. *And telling myself that I can accept anything else is just another version of Let's Pretend.*

Making the decision didn't take the fear away. But there was a little nugget of peace in her heart as she admitted how strongly she'd already come to feel about the baby.

''I can't give up my child,'' she whispered. ''I can't live with wondering if he's all right, if he's happy, if someday he'll hate me for giving him away. I couldn't stand wondering if, accidentally, I gave him up to parents like mine were. So I'll keep him safe in my heart, and I'll do the best I can to love him and provide for him—'' Her voice broke. ''Oh, dammit, I don't want to cry, but I always planned it to be so different! I wanted a pink-and-blue nursery in a house in the suburbs for my baby—''

And a dog, and a sandbox and a little brother or sister. And most of all, a father who would arrive home at the end of the day, eager to see the child who waited patiently for him to come—

Well, all that was out of her reach, wasn't it? So she

might as well accept what was, and do the best she could.

She fumbled for her paper napkin and blew her nose. "Stephen, will you give me a reference so at least I can get a decent job again?"

He was obviously startled; his arm jerked against the rough back of the bench and he swore. "That's what you want? A job?"

"I'm certainly not asking for a handout." She couldn't look at him. "I take full responsibility for this."

"Money wasn't quite what I had in mind."

His voice was very quiet, and her brows drew together in puzzlement as she turned to study him. "Then—what do you mean? What are you suggesting I do?"

He leaned forward with his elbows propped against his knees, and looked directly into her eyes. "What people have always done when there's an unexpected baby on the way, Katherine. They get married."

As soon as her dizzy spell passed, Katherine leaned back against the hard slats of the bench, fanned herself with the newspaper Stephen had dug out of the nearest trash container, and said, "What are you, anyway? Temporarily insane? You don't want to get married."

For just an instant he looked as if he were about to nod in agreement, but he said, mildly, "That's beside the point. This changes lots of things."

"Not necessarily. Having a baby is a terrible reason to get married, Stephen."

"Is it really?"

"Yes. You don't want to marry me any more than I want to marry you."

"Nevertheless, you're going to have to be practical,

Katherine. You know bloody well you can't make it on your own.''

"Yes, I can. If you'll give me a reference—"

He said, almost brutally, "You could go to work for the competition any day, without one. They'd love to have you—and what you know about HomeSafe.''

"I wouldn't do that to you, Stephen.''

"Well, you'd better learn to give up your scruples fast, because unless you're selling HomeSafe secrets, you can't make enough money to support yourself and a child. You're good, Katherine, but jobs of the caliber you're used to don't turn up in every corporation. And even if they do, they require total dedication. How in hell do you expect to work sixteen-hour days if you're coping with a baby?''

She hadn't considered that. "Then I'll get a job I can handle.''

"It won't pay enough. Katherine, don't you understand that you'll have to let me help?''

She turned her wristwatch round and round, and said wistfully, "I could come back to work for you. If my hours could be just a trifle more flexible…''

His voice was gentle. "You aren't thinking very clearly, are you? Can't you imagine the consequences? The questions?''

She could. Her bottom lip was quivering a little.

His hands, warm and strong, came to rest on her wrists. "Do you know what it costs just to have a baby, Katherine? I don't mean raise it and sent it to college, I'm just talking about the medical expenses before the kid is six weeks old. Pink-and-blue nurseries don't come cheap—"

"Don't laugh at me, Stephen! I have a right to my dreams!'' Her voice was muffled; she pulled her hand away and bit her knuckle to keep from crumbling into tears again.

"Of course you have a right to dream," he said softly. "You have every right to want the best for this baby." He brushed a loose tendril of hair behind her ear. His fingers were trembling. "That's what I want, too, don't you see?"

She swallowed hard and tried to blow her nose again. There wasn't a dry patch left on her paper napkin. Stephen dug a handkerchief out of his pocket and handed it to her. It was soft and pristine white, and it smelled like him—like spice and musk and summertime.

"There's nothing abnormal about having only one parent these days," she said stubbornly.

"Maybe there isn't," he conceded. "But are you willing to tell him someday that you settled for that—when he could have had more?"

"That's not fair, Stephen." There was a tinge of warning in her tone.

He pressed on anyway. "He can have the pink-and-blue nursery in the suburbs, and everything that goes with it."

For a long, tempting moment, she allowed herself to consider his offer. Was it fair to her child to turn it down? It wasn't the idea of lacy cribs and elephant-decked wallpaper that was the real lure, of course, but everything else Stephen was implying: private schools and violin lessons and ballet shoes and all the things that she would never be able to afford on her own, no matter how hard she tried.

She knew her temptation showed, and she steeled her heart. "Material things aren't as valuable as a parent's love," she insisted, but her voice sounded hollow.

"It's hardly a case of giving up one to get the other. Quite the contrary, in fact."

He was right. If she accepted this offer, her child would have Stephen's concern, his caring, as well as hers. The love of two parents. Exactly what she had told herself a few minutes ago that she wanted—or, at any rate, almost exactly that. If he actually wanted to know his child...

He can't, she thought. He's only feeling sorry for me.

Stephen was watching the struggle written in her face. "You wouldn't have to hold a job at all, if you didn't feel like it," he said quietly.

"It's the quality of the time that counts for a child, not the quantity."

"I don't think you really believe that. And in any case, what kind of quality time can it be if you're exhausted, worried and overworked?"

"That's my problem, not yours." She swallowed hard. "I don't want to ruin your life, Stephen."

"Dammit, would you stop being holier-than-thou for one minute?" He sounded furious, and it startled her; she tried to pull away. Stephen cupped her hands between his, and said very gently, "There really is only one question left, you know. It's the only one that matters."

She frowned uncertainly.

"What is best for the baby? If you truly want what's best for the baby, Katherine—"

She swallowed the lump in her throat. "All right," she whispered. "I'll think about it. And you should, too. No hard feelings if you change your mind." Before he could answer, she freed her hands and pushed herself up from the bench. "I'll let you know next week, Stephen."

"No." He glanced at his wristwatch. "Go home and have a nap. I'll pick you up at seven for dinner. We'll decide it tonight."

She stared at him. "But that's only two hours. I need some time to think about this."

"No, you don't." His voice was firm. "Time won't make it any easier to decide, because two days or two months won't make the facts any different, Katherine."

And she couldn't argue about that, could she?

HE TOOK HER to a sleepy little restaurant in Denver's oldest hotel, where business was very quiet. She wasn't surprised that he hadn't chosen The Pinnacle; there, they might run into anyone from Hilary Clayton on down, and she was certain Stephen would much rather avoid the questions that would bring.

Still, if she did what he was suggesting, questions would be inevitable, and the possibility that he was uncomfortable about facing them made her a bit uneasy. Some small imp of annoyance made her say, "I didn't know this was one of your usual haunts, Stephen."

He outmaneuvered the maître d' and held her chair himself. "I considered The Pinnacle," he said, "but I thought a revolving restaurant might make you feel seasick. Besides, the tables here are far enough apart to allow truly private conversation."

It was a perfectly reasonable answer, and Katherine's gaze dropped in embarrassment to the pale pink napkin the maître d' had just spread across her lap. Of course he didn't want to create interest before they'd even decided what to do!

"Shall I send the wine steward over, Mr. Osborne?" the maître d' asked, and looked surprised when Stephen declined.

"Not tonight. I think we'll have some sparkling water, instead. Any particular kind, Katherine?"

She shook her head. "You needn't try so very hard to take care of me," she murmured.

Stephen gave her an appraising look. "It appears to me as if somebody needs to do a better job of it."

She stared down at her menu. It was completely illogical to take that comment as a put-down. He knew she hadn't been well, and when a person was ill, it was a great comfort to have someone helping out.

So why did she feel that what he was really saying was that she looked awful?

It wasn't fair, she thought. She had taken great pains to appear at her best tonight. She was wearing her favorite dress, of a deep red fabric that made her eyes look darker and threw reflected color onto her cheeks. She had also done her best to cover up the dark circles under her eyes—at any rate, if those shadows were what he was talking about, he shouldn't blame her for their existence. Take a nap, indeed! Had he really expected her to go blithely off to sleep with everything she had on her mind this afternoon?

The wine steward brought them a bottle of sparkling water, opened it and poured it, managing all the while to maintain an air of disapproval over his customers' plebeian tastes.

Stephen lifted his glass. "Shall we have a toast?"

"To what?"

"To the baby. To the future."

Katherine left her glass sitting precisely where the

wine steward had placed it. "Stephen, I just don't know…"

Stephen sighed and set his glass down.

"What you've suggested is a pretty drastic solution to a problem."

He shrugged. "It's a pretty drastic problem. And what's so crazy about my solution?"

"Why marriage? All right, I admit I probably can't make it on my own. I'll probably need some financial help. But—"

He frowned at the bubbles in his glass. "If I'm going to be the financial support for this, I think I should have a say in the rules. Don't you?"

She looked at him. "It will cause a lot of talk, you know. The man who was never going to limit his options, suddenly turning up with not only a wife but a baby—"

"So maybe I started listening to Rafe. He's certainly been telling me for long enough that a wife would be an advantage. Maybe he's right. I admit it's not the romantic match of the season, but—"

"You can say that again," Katherine muttered. She wondered if he realized that he was nervously toying with his flatware in a way that Emily Post would never have approved.

He didn't seem to hear her. "—getting married is not the end of the world, either. And it's the only thing I can think of that solves all the problems." He gave his soup spoon a push and realigned his fork. "This way you can even have your job again, if you want it."

She blinked a little. "You really do want me back?" she said, uncertainly. "I thought—"

"Want you?" Stephen's smile glinted in the candlelight. He leaned across the table to take her hand and said, "All right, you've caught me. I admit it. I'm only doing this because the piles of paper are threatening to bury me. I can't live without you, Katherine. I'll do anything to get you to come back to HomeSafe."

She tried to pull her hand away; he held onto it. "Working well together is not exactly a good foundation for a marriage," she protested.

The teasing note died out of his voice. "It's not a bad one, either. Who knows what we might be able to build on it?"

She closed her eyes and whispered, "What do you want from this marriage, Stephen?"

He hesitated, and when he finally spoke his voice was level and matter-of-fact—and she knew he meant every syllable. "I want this child to be safe and secure and cared for. That's all."

She looked down at their linked hands resting on the linen cloth and thought, *We liked each other enough to get into this mess. Perhaps he's right in thinking that we can build something together. Something for our baby...*

"All right." Her voice was very soft. "I'll try."

His was truly a beautiful smile, she acknowledged. Reflections of the candlelight danced in his eyes, and what seemed to be a wave of warmth swirled around her, comforting her and soothing her doubts.

And it was a beautiful thing he was doing, as well. She knew that many men, under similar circumstances, would have questioned, hesitated, perhaps denied responsibility altogether. Many more would have had to be pushed into giving even minimal aid to the child. But not Stephen....

So why should she suddenly feel suspicious? Why

did she have a nagging feeling that Stephen was following some hidden agenda—a script she couldn't comprehend or even see?

Why did she feel as if, when she wasn't looking, she'd been turned into a marionette—with an invisible someone pulling the strings?

Don't be silly, she told herself. No one had the power to manipulate her. And no one would even think of trying.

CHAPTER SIX

THE CAR AHEAD of Katherine's passed through the security gate into the HomeSafe complex, and she took her foot off the brake, letting her car ease up to the guard shack. "Hello, Jed," she said pleasantly. "New uniform?"

The security guard grinned and looked admiringly at his dark blue coat sleeve. "Right—everybody's got them. Aren't they nice? Mr. Osborne said you'd be along to ask for your keys." He leaned out of the shack to drop them in her hand, and Katherine went on through the gate.

It felt strange to be there. It seemed almost as if nothing had changed—that the last seven weeks had been only a crazy dream, and that this was like any other Monday morning at HomeSafe. And yet, little things *were* different. Jed's new uniform, the fact that there was a car occupying the parking spot she had habitually used—and those things formed a nagging reminder of what a strange turn her life had taken.

She was very late, and the hallways of the office wing were already bustling. That, too, was a reminder of how different things were now. She had always been one of the first to get to work.

Inside the executive suite, Irene looked up with a smile. "Boy, am I glad you're back. How was the vacation? Did you go somewhere exotic?"

To Katherine's relief, the door of Stephen's office opened. He stopped on the threshold and stayed very still for a moment, looking at her with something in his eyes.... Concern, of course.

He had called her on Sunday, to check on how she was feeling. But she hadn't seen him since Saturday night when he'd taken her home after dinner. Suddenly, she felt almost shy under that intense gaze. She tried to cover her discomfort by studying the paisley pattern of his tie instead of looking at his face.

Stephen gave what sounded almost like a sigh of relief. "I was worried about you." His voice had a husky edge.

Aware that Irene was listening with interest, Katherine said carefully, "I got a slow start this morning, that's all."

His eyes lit with understanding. "Come on in. Irene, call the lab and tell them I'll be a couple of minutes late." He ushered Katherine into his office, his hand merely brushing her arm, and tossed his leather notebook on his desk.

Rafe would approve of the desk, Katherine thought. It was no longer pristine and uncluttered. She eyed the haphazard stacks of papers and folders littering the office. "Well, I can see what I'll be doing all week," she muttered. "Funny—I hadn't heard about a hurricane hitting Denver, but obviously it came through here."

Stephen gave her a rueful smile. "It's not as bad as it looks, really," he protested. "And I didn't bring you in here to dump a load of work on you. I just wanted to tell you that the wedding will be Wednesday afternoon."

Her hand clenched on the report she'd picked up.

"Wednesday?" she said blankly. "Do you mean the day after tomorrow?"

"Yes. That's really the earliest it can be managed. Just a small ceremony, in the chambers of a judge who happens to be a friend of Rafe's. I hope that's all right?"

She nodded. "Yes, of course. But—"

"You'll need to go down to the company clinic this morning and have a blood sample drawn, by the way."

"But Wednesday, that's so soon. Won't Rafe think it's a bit odd?" Her hazel eyes were wide with worry. "Unless—you didn't tell him about the baby, did you, Stephen?"

There was a momentary silence. Then, very gently, Stephen said, "It's not going to be any big secret for long, Katherine."

"But to be in such a rush..."

"The middle of April will be here before you know it, and people can count."

She was silent. She could feel her cheeks growing red with embarrassment, not only for herself but for him as well.

Stephen had turned back to his desk, to take something from a bottom drawer. It was a flat square package, a couple of inches thick, wrapped in glossy silver paper. He handed it to her. "I thought you might like this."

She took it reluctantly, but it obviously wasn't jewelry or masses of flowers. She'd feel even more of a counterfeit if he was to present her with things like that, and she was grateful that he was sensitive enough to realize it.

She cautiously pulled the paper back and opened the

box. Under a thick layer of tissue was a square white volume, its leather cover smooth and plain...

No, not plain, she realized. Down in the corner, in gold type, was a name. Baby Osborne.

She couldn't read the bits of type on the vellum pages because of the tears in her eyes. She clutched the book to her breast and put one hand to her face.

He's being so damned decent about everything, she thought, trying to swallow a sob. He deserves better than this....

Stephen's index fingertip stroked the upswept curve of hair above her ear, so gently that she scarcely felt his touch. "Look, don't worry about it," he said softly. "People will talk. There's no way around it. But by the time we get back, they'll have most of the gossip out of the way and we can all get on with life."

"By the time we get back?" Katherine repeated unsteadily. "Where are we going?"

"I thought we'd spend a few days at Winter Park, at the condo."

A honeymoon. At a ski resort that didn't even have snow at this time of year! A twinge of pain shot through her as she realized how different things should have been—planning her wedding trip, the first few days alone with her new husband.

"At this season, it's practically deserted up there," Stephen said. "I thought perhaps it would be better than—" He stopped abruptly.

Of course, Katherine nodded, following his reasoning. Better the condo, quiet and private and isolated, than some honeymoon resort where everyone would expect them to behave like all the other newlyweds.

"But if you'd prefer something else, Katherine..."

She'd always dreamed of a lazy honeymoon full of

sun and sand and tides—Hawaii, or Bermuda, or Jamaica, or the south of France.... But those dreams would only hurt her now, so she pushed them away and shook her head. "No, the condo will be fine. I'll make the arrangements." She turned her attention back to the stack of papers. "Would you like me to go through these here, or take them to my office?"

There was a note in his voice that sounded like relief, as if he was happy to have the subject changed. "Stay here if you like. I'll be in the lab all morning."

She looked up from a balance sheet. "Do you need me there?"

"Well, yes, I'd like to have your impressions. But are you sure it's safe for you? The noise..."

"Stephen, I'm pregnant, not handicapped," she said crisply. "I can still do everything I did before." She put the report down.

He smiled. "All right. This paperwork has been here for a while, already. It can wait a little longer."

The moment they reached the lab, however, Katherine began wishing that she'd hidden out in her office instead. The big room was buzzing with talk, and there were far more observers than usual. "What are we testing, anyway?" she murmured to Stephen. "Defense for the White House?"

Across the room she saw Rafe, cigar in hand, wandering around the set and studying the installation. Anticipation trickled uncomfortably down her spine. She hadn't expected him to be there; he so seldom showed up for product testing. And she had absolutely no idea what he might do or say when he saw her.

Why didn't I ask Stephen precisely what his father's reaction was? she asked herself. He'd said the judge was a friend of Rafe's, but did that mean Rafe had made the arrangements for the ceremony? And if he had, did that imply approval, or merely unwilling acceptance?

Rafe liked her; he'd always liked her. Even if he wasn't thrilled about the upcoming wedding, he surely wouldn't make a scene—would he?

Yes, she thought. He would, if he felt like it. She'd seen it happen dozens of times.

The moment Rafe saw her, his scrub brush eyebrows soared, and he excused himself from the sales representative he'd been talking to and made his way across the room toward Katherine. It took an excruciating amount of time for him to get through the crowd, and when he finally came up to her Katherine's body was so rigid that she could have doubled for the bronze statue in the lobby.

Rafe's eyebrows had drawn together in what was almost a scowl. "So you're going to marry my son, is that it?"

The question was like a rock dropped in a pond; shocked silence spread out in ripples across the room and all around them people turned to hear the answer.

Katherine braced herself for worse to follow, but instead of continuing the attack, Rafe grinned and gave her an awkward hug. "Welcome to the family, Katherine."

She stopped holding her breath, releasing it with a soft whoosh.

Rafe heard. He held her off a little and added, "Did you think I was going to forbid the banns or something?"

No, Katherine thought. *Not exactly. But I'm still not certain that you wouldn't like to.*

For there was something behind the smile that she

didn't quite understand, and a shadow in his eyes that looked suspiciously like doubt—or distrust—or misgivings.

And who could blame him for that?

IT WAS, as Stephen had promised, a very small group of people who gathered in the judge's chambers for a brief and unpretentious ceremony late on Wednesday afternoon. Molly fussed over Katherine's plain nutmeg-colored suit, muttered about her lack of veil or ornament, and glowed when Stephen turned up with a nosegay of chrysanthemums and daisies for his bride. Jake Holland was Stephen's best man; he kept nervously checking his pockets and moving Katherine's ring from one to another. Rafe and Sherry came in together; to Katherine's surprise and relief Travis wasn't with them. Before she had a chance to think about whether she should ask about him, the judge came in, and it was time.

During the ceremony Alison, taking advantage of her mother's distraction, wormed her way to the front of the room, turned around to face the action, and leaned against the judge with her nose almost buried in Katherine's flowers. From the corner of her eye, Katherine could see mortification rising in Molly's face as her daughter craned her neck to stare up at bride and groom, entirely oblivious to the silent lecture she was getting from the sidelines.

Katherine wasn't mortified; she was having a hard time keeping her face straight. Her only concern was what Stephen might think of this solemn little person who was studying them both so critically. When she turned to face him in order to repeat her vows, and saw that the corner of his mouth was twitching and his eyes were alight with unholy enjoyment of the situation, she almost burst into giggles. She managed to control herself, but her voice was warm with laughter as she pledged herself to him. His voice was low, intense. Katherine wasn't surprised; of course he was feeling solemn, under the circumstances.

Afterwards, the guests gathered around them. Sherry brushed cool lips against Katherine's cheek and murmured congratulations. "Who would have thought Stephen would make it to the altar before I did?" she said. "Of course, if you're content to have no frills whatsoever, I suppose it doesn't take long."

Beside her, Jake slapped Stephen on the back. "Well, I guess I don't have to worry any more about Hilary Clayton setting traps for you, right?"

Katherine didn't think she wanted to hear the answer to that. "Have you chosen your wedding date, Sherry?" she asked, rather desperately.

"June, of course." With distaste, Sherry glanced down at Alison, who was tugging at Katherine's hand. "There will be no children at my wedding. Travis and I feel they don't belong at solemn occasions."

If that was a warning, Katherine thought, it was an unnecessary one. In June, her baby would be two months old, and the mere idea of a child that age crying throughout an elaborate ceremony sent shudders down her spine. She tried to keep her voice casual. "Where is Travis, by the way?"

Sherry shrugged irritably. "Business. Isn't that what it always is? He's been gone more in the last few weeks than he's been here."

"It will quiet down when he gets settled in his new job, no doubt."

"It had better," Sherry muttered.

Jake Holland seized Katherine for a bear hug. "Keep an eye on that ring," he warned. "I've been guarding it with my life, so don't you let it vanish." He grinned and gave her a warm kiss on the cheek. "And take good care of my buddy, you hear? You're a lucky girl. It isn't just any woman he'd tie himself down for."

Katherine's good humor vanished in one of the sudden, blinding changes of mood that she was quickly becoming accustomed to.

He isn't doing it for me, Jake, she thought. *And he'd rather not be doing it at all.*

THE AFTERNOON was fading as they drove over Berthoud Pass, and by the time they reached Winter Park dusk was settling in earnest. Light still sparkled on the ski slopes, but it seemed to Katherine that in the depths of some of these narrow mountain valleys, the sunlight never struck at all, much less stayed around long enough to warm things up.

She had been to Winter Park, of course; it was within easy range of Denver, so she'd often gone out for a day of skiing. But she'd never been there in the off-season before. Even though Stephen had told her it was very quiet at this time of year, she was a bit surprised to see that in the fall, Winter Park was a sleepy little mountain town with every third business closed up altogether.

It would begin to stir, he said, as November closed in. By Thanksgiving, the snow machines would be running and the slopes would be open, and at Christmas the place would be wall-to-wall people.

He sounded as if he found that prospect less than inviting, and Katherine was wondering about it as the

Porsche turned into a long private drive that curved around the base of the mountain.

She'd never seen the Osborne condo, but she knew it was in the most elite of Winter Park's many resort developments. The service for people who owned units there, or rented them for a week or two, was said to be superb, and Katherine had always found the staff to be perfectly pleasant when she'd called to make arrangements for Stephen's weekends—

She gasped and clapped her hand to her mouth.

Stephen jammed on the brakes. "What's the matter?"

"I forgot to call and tell the manager we were coming."

"That's all? From your reaction I figured there must be a ten-ton truck bearing down on us, at the least."

"Did I shriek? I'm sorry. But what if they've rented the place out for the weekend?"

"Who do you think would want it, this time of year?"

Katherine shrugged. "I don't know. Somebody who doesn't ski and can't afford the rates during the season, maybe."

"I suppose you're right. But it's not for rent."

"Ever?"

He shook his head. "It's bad enough trying to avoid Sherry's parties at the best of times, without coordinating schedules with the reservations desk."

"I thought that was part of the deal—when the owner isn't using the place, it can be rented."

"A lot of people do that, yes. It helps with the expenses. But it's a bloody nuisance because you can't leave valuables lying around, and you have to make an appointment to stay in your own place."

She shook her head a little. "Then why do you always call to let them know you're coming?"

"That's just so there will be food in the refrigerator."

"Oh. They take care of grocery shopping, too?"

"When asked." There was a smile in his voice.

Katherine wasn't so easy on herself. "No food," she muttered. "Well, that's just great. Some personal assistant I am. I think my brain's gone soft."

He reached over to muss her hair. "What's the matter, Katie? Are you hungry?"

Katherine sighed. "I'm generally hungry these days," she admitted. "Until I see something edible, and then all urge to eat promptly goes away."

"Well, don't worry. Not everything in Winter Park closes in September." He stopped the car at the main entrance and left the engine running. "I'd better go in and let them know we're here, so no one reports us as burglars."

"Good idea," Katherine said, but he was already gone. The air that had swirled into the car was colder than she'd expected, and she edged her feet closer to warmth from the heater. At this elevation, winter always came earlier than it did down in Denver, and from the feel of the air, this year it was just around the corner.

Stephen was soon back, and in a couple of minutes he was ushering her up a covered ramp on the side of the building with the best mountain view. He set down their luggage and unlocked the door, a cedar-covered slab so rough that Katherine hoped she never had to push on it with her bare hands.

"I think the style is called rustic contemporary," Stephen said, noting her expression. "I believe the architect chose it because it's too rugged for teenagers to carve their initials in.'' He left the luggage sitting in the hallway and started turning on lights.

Katherine followed, trying to look around discreetly and not stare. This place was *huge*—as big as the average house, and a whole lot nicer. And everything was so sleek and modern and well put together...

Stephen caught her eyeing a closed door and said, ''Go ahead and explore. But there's one thing I want you to know—''

His tone set off warning bells in her head.

''Anything embarrassing that you might happen to find belongs to Sherry.''

Katherine managed to smile. ''That's certainly a nice blanket statement.'' She sounded faintly cynical, just as she had intended. He didn't need to pretend that he was some kind of saint.

But there seemed to be nothing out of place. She glanced into the bedroom wing and counted three rooms, each with its own attached bath. There was a big living room with deeply cushioned couches and a fieldstone fireplace that occupied most of one wall. There was a small terrace that looked out over a wildly wooded hillside, creating the illusion that the condo sat alone in an untouched landscape. The dining area could seat twelve with ease, and the kitchen—well, it took Katherine's breath away.

It was open and airy and efficient, with a breakfast bar along one side, an electric barbecue grill built into the range, an elaborate microwave, and a row of cabinets that might hide any number of exciting things. ''This is wonderful,'' she said, and poked her head into the refrigerator. It was empty, of course, except for a row of seasonings and sauces. ''I have this sudden urge

to tie on an apron and start kneading bread or something.''

Stephen pulled a stool up to the breakfast bar. ''The
manager promised to call in a grocery order first thing
tomorrow.''

''Not till then?''

He smiled at the woebegone look on her face. ''We
won't starve, Katherine—there are restaurants. Unless
you'd rather have pizza delivered.''

''I'd rather have a steak, and cook it myself.'' She
caught the sulky sound of her voice and smiled ruefully. ''Sorry. I don't have temper tantrums often, I
promise. What kind of restaurants do we have to
choose from?''

He folded his arms on the edge of the breakfast bar.
''You're serious, aren't you? About wanting to cook?''

She nodded. ''It would be like playing house. This
is nicer than any kitchen I've ever had.''

He smiled slowly. ''Get your coat, we'll go buy a
steak. And heaven help you if you char it. You might
not be eating much these days, but I'm starved.''

They ended up in the next town before they found
a supermarket open, and from the instant they walked
inside, Katherine should have realized what would happen. But she was absently assembling her mental shopping list—a nice sirloin, two big potatoes for baking,
a carton of sour cream, a head of lettuce—and so she
didn't notice that Stephen had disappeared until he returned with a cart.

''We don't need that,'' she said.

He shrugged. ''It will be easier than juggling
things.''

They were only halfway down the first aisle when
she realized that shopping with Alison—or, for that

matter, any five assorted preschoolers—was probably nothing compared to the challenge of shopping with Stephen Osborne. If he saw something he liked, he put it in the cart.

Besides the steak, he tossed in chops and chicken breasts and half a ham. "For sandwiches," he told Katherine earnestly. "In case we want to go on a picnic."

Then he added a carton of eggs, a bag of apples, huge slabs of two kinds of cheese, a gallon container of popcorn…

Katherine protested when he took a three-pound can of coffee off the shelf. "Just how long are we planning to stay, Stephen?"

"Oh, through Monday or so. Why?"

"You couldn't consume this much coffee by Monday if you ate the grounds raw."

He shrugged and put it in the cart. "So, we'll leave the rest for next time. How about herbal tea? Do you like that stuff? And raisins—it's always nice to have raisins on hand."

"Stephen, this is ridiculous."

"It's in case you start craving things."

"I don't think it's me you're worried about," Katherine muttered.

He flashed a smile. "You're at least partly right," he admitted. "I don't want to drive up here in the middle of the night when you get a longing for peanuts or something." He snapped his fingers. "I almost forgot the peanuts."

"I don't like peanuts," she said firmly.

"That's all right. I do, and we can feed the rest to the chipmunks." He wandered off to look for the nut section.

Katherine sighed and pushed the cart on down the aisle. She found herself in the middle of the infant section, studying rows of baby foods and juices and cereals. There was also a well-stocked section of toys, aimed at the tourist traffic, she supposed. She noticed a particularly adorable stuffed elephant, wearing a floppy bow tie with Winter Park printed on it. Katherine picked it up. She had never seen a stuffed animal with quite so much personality....

Stephen took the elephant out of her hand and inspected it with raised eyebrows.

"I thought it would be perfect for the nursery," Katherine said diffidently. "I think I've got enough cash to buy it. I wouldn't expect—"

He dropped a casual kiss on the tip of her nose and carefully put the elephant in the cart with his bag of peanuts. "That's what the household account is for," he said cheerfully. "Necessities like elephants and ice cream...how did I manage to forget the ice cream?" He headed for the freezer cases.

"Now I know why you have the manager stock the place," Katherine muttered as she watched the grand total appear on the checkout monitor. "It's less expensive."

"Not really. He knows what I like." Stephen wrote out a check and handed it over to the clerk, then flourished the leather folder at Katherine. "Don't let me forget to put your name on the household account."

"Only if you promise to let me shop by myself."

"Why?" He sounded injured. "I didn't object to the elephant."

"Because I'll take what's left over, invest it in the stock market and get rich."

He let her carry one small bag up the stairs, but he

brought the rest up himself. The steak was already scenting the whole kitchen by the time he'd unpacked their purchases. "You weren't kidding about wanting to knead bread, were you?" he asked when he found the packets of yeast she'd included. "Three of them? Talk about me overbuying..."

She took the package from his hand. "It's the smallest size they make. Go and build a fire."

"Yes, Kate," he said solemnly.

She was smiling as she turned back to the lettuce she was tearing into bite-size pieces. It startled her when she realized how much at ease she felt, and she wondered if that had been the purpose of Stephen's joking around at the supermarket—to break the ice and make them both more comfortable, to let them pretend for a while that they really were just playing house instead of entering into this solemn, scary contract. To get them through the evening, at least—

And after that? What happened after that?

They'd never talked about what came next, or about the extent of intimacy they would share. She'd avoided even thinking about that; it had seemed silly, somehow, to worry about it, considering their reason for getting married. And yet...tonight...

Stephen was lying on the hearth rug when she brought their dinner into the living room. For a moment she thought he was asleep; then she saw that he was staring into the crackling flames.

"Thinking heavy thoughts?" she asked, before it occurred to her that perhaps she didn't want to be told what was occupying his mind. She hurried on, "One steak. Definitely not charred."

Stephen sat up. "We do have a real table and chairs."

"I know." She put the plates down on the coffee table and settled herself cross-legged on the carpet. "I didn't want to miss out on the fire."

"Then I'll take care of the mess afterward, and you may lie here and luxuriate in the warmth." He cut his steak, sampled it, and nodded approvingly.

Katherine managed to eat half her dinner, then lay beside the fire while he cleaned up the kitchen. She was lulled almost to sleep by the soft irregular crackle of the embers as she watched the red flames reflected in the glass fireplace doors, in the high polish of the coffee table, in the stones that lined her wedding ring.

It was the first chance she had had to really look at the ring; she'd never seen it before this afternoon when Jake, after a moment's panic about which pocket he had ultimately stored it in, had handed it to Stephen. It was a wide gold band, very simple, with a deep groove etched all the way round. In the groove was a row of baguette diamonds, set so close together that they looked almost like a single endless stone. It was classic; it was simple; it was perfect.

She yawned, and found herself wondering sleepily if Stephen had realized that an elaborate engagement ring would have made her uncomfortable. Probably he hadn't given the matter any thought at all, other than to decide that a three-day long engagement didn't really need a ring to be official.

The kitchen lights went off, leaving the fire and a couple of dim lamps as the only source of illumination. Stephen came into the living room and quietly dropped to the floor beside her.

Katherine deliberately kept her breathing even and steady.

Stephen's fingers stroked the silky length of a loose

lock of hair. "It's late," he said. "A good night's sleep will make you feel much better."

In a different tone of voice, it might have sounded like a prelude to seduction. As it was, it was plain and matter-of-fact and logical. *Go to bed,* he was saying. *Nothing else is going to happen here.*

It was thoughtful of him, she told herself. He was very sensitive to understand what a strain all of this had been.

But there was a little lump of confusion in the precise center of her chest.

She sat up slowly. "I am tired," she said. She hardly recognized her own voice.

He rose, of course, and helped her to her feet. "I put your bag in the back bedroom," he said. "It's the quietest—not that there's much noise here at this time of year."

She remembered the room. It overlooked the terrace and the wooded hillside. And it held twin beds.

"I'll be across the hall from you," Stephen added. "Call me if you need anything. Otherwise I won't disturb you. Sleep well."

It was only then that Katherine realized that despite her earlier misgivings, her uneasiness, her apprehension, the one thing she had never anticipated was this flat rejection. She had not expected to be sent off to bed like a child—on her wedding night.

She managed to mutter, "Good night," but she wasn't sure if he heard her. He was poking at the fire, turning the remaining logs and adding a new one, when she left the room.

Her bag was already laid out at the foot of one of the twin beds. She tugged at the straps; her fingers were shaking.

"You can't say you weren't warned," she told herself. "You just weren't listening very well."

I want this child to be safe and secure and cared for, Stephen had said. That was all. He'd said nothing about Katherine, nothing about the two of them, except in connection with the baby. How could she have been so stupid as to have let herself forget for a moment what all this was about?

She unpacked her robe and slippers, telling herself that she was glad he was such a perfect gentleman. She was grateful that he was so thoughtful of her comfort, and so understanding of her state of exhaustion.

But she was not glad. She was not grateful.

Instead she felt shunned and rejected, and more alone than she had ever felt in her life.

CHAPTER SEVEN

MOLLY MUST HAVE MADE her coffee awfully strong this morning, Katherine thought. The scent had not only seeped across the hall and through her apartment, it had even permeated Katherine's pillow. She lifted her face, sniffed deeply and appreciatively, and turned over so she could truly savor the smell. In a little while, she'd get up and make some for herself....

"Wake up, lazybones."

The sound of a male voice in her bedroom brought her fully awake, aware that she wasn't in her apartment after all and that it wasn't Molly's coffee she was smelling. She opened her eyes to a rather hazy view of a bright yellow mug—hazy because the mug was suspended less than two inches from her nose, and to properly focus on it would have required her to cross her eyes.

Behind the mug was a moss green sweater. Stephen was sitting on the edge of her mattress. "Well, now I know that an automatic coffeemaker plugged in next to your bed works better than an alarm clock. I thought you were never going to wake up."

"You said to sleep well," Katherine reminded him. She stretched and started to push herself up from the pillow.

"I didn't say to sleep all day. It's halfway to noon. No, don't sit up—dry toast first." He reached for a plate on the bedside table and popped a bite-size piece in her mouth.

"Who ordered that?" Katherine said, through the crumbs. "Molly?"

Stephen shook his head. "A friend of mine who's an obstetrician. If you don't have a preference for a doctor, by the way—"

"I don't."

"Then I'd like you to see Julie."

A woman? Well, that wasn't any big surprise, Katherine reflected. He had a lot of female friends, and most of them were high-powered in one way or another. "Is she good?"

"Well, I don't know from firsthand experience, you understand," he drawled, "but I've been told that she's very good indeed." He took a long pull from the mug.

Katherine looked at it longingly. "Isn't that my coffee you're drinking?"

"Eat your toast and I'll get you some that's hot— the way this was when I first brought it in."

She obeyed, and he vanished for a bit. While he was out of sight, Katherine punched at her pillow and ran her fingers through her hair. She couldn't tell what it looked like, but it felt as tangled as a ball of yarn after a whole litter of kittens had chased it around the house. She was wearing no makeup, of course, and her mouth felt as if the army had marched through.

It didn't matter, she told herself stoutly. He'd seen her at her worst—sound asleep, face smashed against a pillow, probably snoring. She couldn't hope to repair that sort of impression, no matter what she did to herself.

Not that it would make any difference. He'd made

it entirely too plain last night that any attraction she'd ever held for him had been the fleeting sort.

He came back with a second mug, bright blue this time. Katherine sat up cautiously and reached for it.

Stephen perched on the side of the other twin bed. "Feeling all right?"

"I'm not marathon material, but I'm better than usual. I must look a fright."

His gaze moved slowly over her face. What was he doing, she wondered. Counting her freckles?

"Yes, you're feeling better," he said, and reached out to tuck the blanket around her.

Katherine hadn't realized until then that it had slipped. Not that it mattered, really; she was wearing an ordinary old flannel nightshirt, not some sexy negligee. Still, she felt a bit uncomfortable all of a sudden about making a display of herself. "I'd better get up," she said quickly. "I shouldn't keep you sitting here all day."

"Take your time. Julie said to stay still for half an hour before you stand up." He rose. "I'm going down to the lobby to get a newspaper."

The door clicked shut behind him, and Katherine lay back against her pillows, aggravated at herself. She faced half an hour of lying in bed, with nothing to do or think about, and like a fool she'd practically told Stephen to leave. She could at least have had company. Not that she blamed him for going; what an utter, boring nuisance she was. And they were facing days of this—

"I want to go home," she said.

The sound of her words, small and hopeless, reminded her that there really was no home left to go to; the movers would be packing up her things by now, under Molly's watchful eyes. She was committed. She had chosen this course of her own free will; she couldn't even accuse Stephen of misleading her.

So the only thing she *could* do was make an honest effort—as she had promised yesterday in the judge's chambers. She'd made a vow to do her best to make this marriage work. Presenting a cheerful face and not complaining certainly couldn't hurt. They had agreed to try to build something between them for the sake of their child. If the most they could manage was friendship—well, compared to what some couples ended up with, that wasn't such a bad deal, was it?

She reinforced her decision with a pep talk in the shower, greeting Stephen with a genuine smile when she reached the kitchen. "Anyone for a walk?"

He laid his newspaper aside. "Are you sure?"

"Well, I'm not prepared for a hike straight up the mountain. But if you know where there's a flat trail…"

He grinned. "Yes, I do. Relatively speaking, of course."

The trail was not flat, but they meandered up and down through the pine trees at a gentle pace, and Katherine found the exercise and the crisp air stimulating. When they came back, she tackled her lunch with gusto.

Stephen, watching with raised eyebrows as she demolished her salad and sandwich, said, "Same time tomorrow?" and Katherine nodded.

They made a habit of it after that, and over the next few days they explored a number of trails. Sometimes they packed a picnic, once they rented bicycles, but usually they simply strolled along. They talked of the scenery, or of business—there were enough safe subjects, Katherine found, that it was relatively easy to stay away from the threatening ones.

On the last walk of their long weekend, almost at dusk on Monday evening, Katherine was climbing over a fallen tree when her foot slipped on a patch of frost. She grabbed for support, arms flailing, and lunged into Stephen.

He had just crossed the log himself and was turning to help her down when she fell. He staggered a little as he unexpectedly took her weight full against his body, but he managed to keep his footing. Katherine clutched at him, eyes shut tight, feeling dizzy and expecting any moment to feel the harsh scrape of pine bark, for it seemed impossible that she had fallen clear of the log.

Instead, all she felt was the scratch of wool against her cheek, and when she finally dared open her eyes, it was to see the muted tweed of Stephen's jacket in almost microscopic detail. She moved her head just enough that her nose was no longer smashed into his collarbone and closed her eyes again. It was warm here in his arms. She hadn't realized until now how chilly the evening had become. And she was a bit short of breath, too, from the shock as well as the exertion, so she might as well be comfortable while she got her second wind.

His fingertips felt chilly as they slid under the mass of glossy brown hair to rest at the nape of her neck. And his lips were cold—but comforting, nonetheless—against her temple.

Katherine sighed and turned her face a little.

Stephen chuckled. "Playing possum, are you?" he said huskily. "A little more of that, and I'll think you engineered that fall on purpose."

Stung by the accusation, she pulled back, and realized that she was standing squarely on the toe of his boot. Remorse swept over her and she hastily stepped aside. "I've hurt you, haven't I, landing on you like this?"

"If something had to be ground into the gravel, better my foot than your face." He sank down onto the fallen tree, raising his foot and twisting it experimentally.

Katherine stood still. "Now you're lame."

"It's all right, I'm sure, just a little bruised."

Katherine went straight on. "I suppose we can build a fire to hold the grizzly bears off for a while, but eventually it won't matter anymore. We'll starve to death out here in the wilderness, won't we?"

Stephen put his foot down and tested his weight. "Hardly. We're only a hundred yards from civilization. The resort is right around that corner."

Katherine heaved an enormous sigh. "Have you no spirit of adventure, Stephen Osborne? I was just getting fired up for a fit of melodramatic hysterics in order to take your mind off the pain in your foot."

"Next time, if you'd like, I'll sneak up behind you and do my imitation of a howling wolf."

"That would certainly make it easier to have hysterics."

"What happened to your enthusiasm for the wilderness?" He grinned at her and reached for her hand.

It wasn't the first time they'd held hands as they walked along, but somehow in the dusk, on their last night in Winter Park, it just seemed natural for their fingers to be interlocked, sharing warmth and strength.

And Katherine found herself wondering what would have happened back there beside the fallen tree if she had said, "Yes, Stephen. You're quite right. I engineered that fall on purpose."

But she hadn't, of course, so it would have been a lie to say she had.

SHE'D LEFT THE terrace door open when she went out, and she could hear the soft rustling from inside the condo as Stephen gathered up another armload of possessions to take down to the car.

It was early; the valley was light, but the sun had not yet made its appearance above the line of mountaintops. She'd set her alarm clock last night, and when Stephen brought in her coffee and toast this morning she'd already had the half hour of still meditation that his doctor friend recommended. It seemed to help; Katherine found herself looking forward to meeting Julie and finding out if she had any other magic formulas.

Stephen had been surprised to find her already awake, and he was obviously worried that she hadn't slept well. Katherine had shrugged off his concern. This way, they could be back in Denver with most of the morning still ahead. He'd smiled at her eagerness and gone off to finish packing.

But the truth was, she was no longer as anxious to get back to the city as she once had been.

A chipmunk came out of his burrow just yards from the terrace. Only his rapid, jerky movements drew Katherine's eyes to him; when he was still, his striped coat camouflaged him until he almost disappeared against the rocky soil. She tossed a couple of peanuts in his direction. He watched the nuts land and warily made his way over, nose twitching, to survey the gift.

"See?" Stephen said from the terrace door. "I told

you wc'd use up the peanuts. In fact, we don't have much food left at all, except for the yeast.''

Katherine wrinkled her nose in mock annoyance. ''It takes time to bake bread, you know. If you hadn't kept me outside for hours every day—''

He flicked her cheek with his hand. ''I'm glad I did, because you look better than you did last week. You've got some color in your face now.''

She was obscurely pleased that he'd noticed—and it wasn't just her imagination that the image in her mirror looked healthier these days. ''It must be the frostbite.'' She shivered dramatically.

''I think you've got that backward, doesn't frostbite make you paler? Everything's in the car. Are you ready to go?''

Her hands tightened on the steel rail of the terrace. *No,* she thought. *I'm not ready. Despite everything, we've actually started to be friends, but when we return to the real world...*

But there was no choice, so she nodded and dropped the last handful of peanuts over the rail to become a feast for the small striped animal, and she turned her back on Winter Park.

They got caught in the morning rush hour on Denver's west side and traffic slowed to little more than a crawl, but still the time flew too fast for Katherine's comfort. She deliberately steered the talk to business, feeling that it might make the transition easier, and she didn't notice that they had missed the freeway exit leading to the HomeSafe offices until they were well past it.

''I thought you'd like to get settled at home first,'' he said, when she asked him where they were going. ''The movers should have delivered your things by now, and as the housekeeper's there today, she can help you unpack.''

His apartment was in a tower not far from Rafe's. The building was older and slightly less luxurious, and the apartment itself wasn't as large as she'd expected. To her surprise, it wasn't much bigger than her own small place had been, and it was far tinier than the condo in Winter Park. It looked almost cramped with the wall of boxes that the movers had stacked in the foyer.

''I see what you mean about getting settled,'' Katherine muttered. ''I didn't realize I had so much stuff.'' She looked around in growing dismay. Obviously Stephen already had everything he needed, and there simply wasn't room for more. ''What on earth am I going to do with it all?''

''If you aren't going to want it right away, call the building supervisor. He'll put it in the storage room downstairs with your furniture.''

''Oh, dear, I'd forgotten about the furniture.'' She looked around unhappily. If she couldn't have any of her own possessions out she'd feel like a guest in a hotel somewhere. Yet it wouldn't be fair to displace Stephen's things, and there simply wasn't room for both. ''Stacking it in a storage room isn't exactly a long-term solution. It might be better if I bought a big garbage can.''

''Don't be in such a hurry. We'll be looking for a house soon anyway, and you'll want your things then.''

It was a perfectly sensible plan, and it should have delighted her. But Katherine found herself swallowing hard at his matter-of-fact tone. She had upended Stephen's life, and he was taking it so calmly that it made her nervous.

"I'll go find Mrs. Atkins," he said, and started down the hallway.

Katherine stood her ground. "Stephen, what I said about a house in the suburbs and a pink-and-blue nursery wasn't a demand, you know."

He stopped in the doorway. "Of course it wasn't. But we really don't have a choice. This place only has two bedrooms." He vanished toward the back of the apartment.

And with the baby, they would need three. Obviously, Stephen was quite content with things just as they were.

Katherine folded her arms on top of the nearest stack of boxes. Her fingers clutched at her forearms until her knuckles were white with the strain.

This was a mistake, she told herself. Why had she ever agreed to this? She should have known it would only make more trouble in the end. What was she, anyway—some kind of shrinking violet, afraid to be on her own? Why hadn't she realized that one dreadful blunder couldn't be wiped out by making a second one?

A tear dropped onto the surface of the uppermost box and turned black as it struck the ink left by her felt-tipped marker. Valuable, she had written across the top of it. Handle with Care.

She ripped the tape off the box with her nails and rummaged until she found the most precious thing she owned. It was silly to think that having it in her hands would make any difference, but somehow right now there was comfort in holding her father's picture.

She cradled it between her hands. The glass was smudged with fingerprints, so she breathed on the surface and rubbed it clean with her handkerchief.

Stephen came back in so quietly that she didn't hear him at first. "Katherine, this is Mrs. Atkins, who takes care of the place. Mrs. Atkins—" He looked over Katherine's shoulder at the picture she held and said, "You're crying. Was that damaged in the move?"

"No. Not at all. It's just a bit dirty, that's all." She finished polishing the glass and set the frame aside. "There. That's better."

"You've put the original somewhere safe, haven't you?"

"It's in here, at the moment." She gestured at the box.

"Why haven't you put it in the vault at HomeSafe?"

"Because I never thought of that." She flipped through the contents of the box and took out a small, plain white envelope. "Will you do it for me?" The envelope fluttered out of her hand, floating to the floor, and she picked it up, automatically checking the contents to be sure nothing had escaped. It had been a very small photograph. Now it was only a dozen slivers of paper.

Stephen tucked the envelope into the breast pocket of his blazer. "I'd better get out of your way, hadn't I?"

His mouth brushed Katherine's softly, and he was gone.

She pressed her fingertip against her lips. *Don't fool yourself,* she thought. *That was a demonstration for Mrs. Atkins's benefit—nothing more.*

KATHERINE LIKED Stephen's obstetrician friend on sight, and her first examination confirmed the intuition. Julie Quinn was quietly efficient, but she managed to leave the impression of having all the time in the world if a patient should need it. And though she was a young woman, she had a comforting air about her that reminded Katherine of what grandmothers were supposed to be like.

After she'd finished the exam, the doctor took Katherine back to her office. "I've got a diet for you to follow, of course, and an exercise plan, but it's basically common sense. No alcohol, avoid caffeine, stay away from smokers—" She pushed the office door open. "Hello, Stephen. I'm not surprised to see you here."

He put a magazine aside. "I stopped in to see Katherine, and your office staff didn't want me contaminating the waiting room."

"The truth is that he couldn't wait for you to give him the results," Julie said to Katherine, without bothering to lower her voice. "You know how the bossy sort operates. Everything's fine, Stephen. There are no apparent problems and no risk factors, so we're expecting a perfectly normal pregnancy and a healthy baby. Somewhere between April second and the sixth, if you want to plan to take the week off. I'm sure your child wouldn't dare be anything but punctual." She gave him a mischievous grin and turned to the filing cabinet behind her desk. "Here's the basic information you'll need, Katherine, and I'll see you in about a month. If you have any doubts or problems, call me— anytime."

"I like her," Katherine said as they left the clinic. "Very much. Thanks, Stephen."

"My pleasure." He sounded a bit preoccupied. "I'm going out to the plant in Boulder."

She tried to summon up a mental picture of his calendar, and could only remember vague entries. "I think you've got appointments this afternoon."

"I'll be back by then." He walked her to her car. "I'm glad everything's all right, Katherine."

She sat behind the wheel of her car for a couple of minutes, telling herself that it was unfair to be disappointed by a muted response. What had she hoped for, anyway—a passionate embrace in the parking lot? It wasn't as if there had been any reason to think there was a problem—so why should there be a celebration when things turned out as expected? Wasn't it enough that he had broken up the morning's business to come to the doctor's office? She ought to be pleased by that, at least—

She might as well be honest with herself. If he hadn't been on his way to Boulder, he probably wouldn't have come at all.

It was fortunate, she reflected, that things were so busy at HomeSafe these days. She had too much time to think, as it was.

RAFE WAS OCCUPYING his favorite spot in her office when she returned. His feet, in worn-out sneakers, were propped on the corner of her desk, and the ever-present cigar, unlit, was in his hand. In his jeans and pullover shirt, he looked like a handyman, and she would swear there was grease lodged under his fingernails, as if he'd been tearing apart a car engine in the parking lot.

"Well?" he demanded as soon as she came in. "How's the little one?"

It was the first time he'd admitted to knowing about her pregnancy. The directness of the question, and the fact that Rafe had sounded as if he was gritting his teeth as he asked it, sent shivers up Katherine's spine.

She didn't answer; she walked around her desk, sat down and said, "You aren't very happy about the baby, are you, Rafe?"

His gaze dropped to the cigar between his fingers. "It's not the way I'd have planned it, no. But that's beside the point. Kids get a certain age, they do what they please. Sometimes they make mistakes."

"Rafe, I'm sorry."

He didn't seem to hear. "Take Sherry, now—miserable, and won't admit it."

What a dear he was, Katherine thought, making a valiant attempt to cover up his slip by turning the conversation to Sherry!

"I ruined that girl, Katherine. Now she expects to be able to shop her way through life." He chewed thoughtfully on the cigar. "I've got some advice for you, by the way. Or maybe it's more like a favor. I don't know."

Katherine braced herself.

"You make sure Stephen is there when the baby's born. Don't let him miss out, and regret it."

His words touched her heart. "Is that the voice of experience, Rafe?"

"It certainly is. I was there when both my kids were born. That wasn't quite the thing to do in those days. The doctors didn't know how to cope with me. But they survived the shock. Take my word, Katherine— it's very important for both of you. And for the baby, of course."

There was a tap on the door.

Rafe let his feet drop to the carpet with a thud. "I'll get out of your way," he said. "Maybe I'll wander down to engineering and offer them the advantage of my experience." He gave her a slightly crooked grin.

As Rafe went out, Diane, the sales representative, came in. "Travis sent me up to ask about the brochure on the new system. When is it going to be back from the printers?"

"Not till next week, but I've got a mock-up here." Katherine turned to the credenza behind her desk to look for it.

Diane was watching the glitter of diamonds on Katherine's left hand. "I knew it didn't make sense."

"What? The new brochure?"

"No. The fact that you denied all attraction to Stephen. Nobody could work with him for a year and not feel that magnetism of his. I should have known something was in the wind. And now—it's like a Cinderella story, isn't it?"

Not quite, Katherine almost said. She found the mock-up and passed it across the desk. She was glad Travis hadn't come for it himself, but something made her ask after him anyway. "Are things so busy down there that Travis can't get out of his office?"

Diane rolled her eyes. "Out of it? He's hardly ever in it. He seems to be trying to visit every sales rep west of the Mississippi in the shortest possible time."

Katherine remembered that Sherry had said something of the sort at the wedding. "He's off inspiring his new troops, perhaps. If he succeeds, we might all get a bonus at the end of the fiscal year."

Diane snorted and eyed Katherine's wedding ring. "Some of us need it more than others, of course."

As Diane left the office, Katherine reached for her coffee cup, realized it was empty, and made a mental note to ask Irene to buy some decaffeinated. She wasn't going to be successful at following Julie Quinn's suggestion and eliminating coffee from her diet altogether, not if she kept working.

The hormone imbalances of early pregnancy caused strange reactions, she mused. Like this sudden self-centeredness. It was almost funny, but right now de-caffeinated coffee was of far more concern to her than whether Travis Baker made a success of his new job or not.

SHE'D ONLY BEEN BACK from lunch for a short while when Stephen came in, and his afternoon appointment, a supplier of the hard plastic cases that protected HomeSafe's sensors, was already waiting. But before he met with the man, Stephen poked his head into Katherine's office. "I'll be tied up for awhile," he said. "Is there anything going on that I need to know about?"

"Jake was in and wants to talk to you. Nothing critical."

"I'll call him as soon as I'm free. When Irene gets back, would you ask her to make reservations for two at The Pinnacle for tonight?"

She was startled, and then she remembered that the supplier was from out of town. "Of course. What time?"

"Early. Seven should be okay."

She made a note.

"You're writing things down now?" he asked curiously.

"After the fiasco over groceries at the condo? My brain seems to have ceased functioning when it comes to food."

"Nonsense, our shopping expedition turned out just fine."

"I know—all except for the yeast."

Stephen grinned. "I wasn't going to mention that."

"Oh, and here's the report on the system we were testing last week." She handed it to him.

Stephen flipped the pages idly. "You've finished it already?"

Katherine shrugged. "You were anxious to get the results."

"I thought I told you to take things easy."

"I'm being careful."

She grinned as he studied the stack of papers on the corner of her desk. Less than a week back at work, and she'd managed to make a considerable dent in the mess that had cluttered his office. His eyes narrowed. "Did you have lunch?"

"Yes," she said sweetly. "Jake took me to Jolly's. Would you like me to file a report on what I ate?"

The corner of his mouth twitched in the prelude to a smile. "No. But when you have time, Katherine, check into putting a day-care center somewhere in the plant."

Katherine stared at him. "Why?"

"Because if we have a day-care center, maybe you'll come back to work after the baby's born. It's obvious I can't do without you." He collected the supplier and vanished into his office.

Katherine put her pen down and rubbed her temples. It was nice to be appreciated, she thought. Even if it was only her work that seemed to get his approval. So why didn't she feel happier?

Perhaps she simply needed a break. She could take off a bit early tonight and see the new show at the art museum. If Stephen was going to be occupied with a business dinner anyway, he certainly wouldn't miss her.

She worked steadily for the better part of an hour, then went to get a snack from the machines down the hall; when she came back she was startled to see Hilary Clayton sitting in Irene's office.

It was just like the old days. Every blond hair on the woman's head was precisely in place. The blue of her designer dress made her huge eyes look like still water. And her gaze was as cool—and as dismissing, when she glanced at Katherine and then turned away—as it had ever been before.

If the woman was an ice-cream cone she wouldn't even get slick around the edges, Katherine thought cattily.

The door of Stephen's office opened and the supplier came out. He stopped on the threshold to shake hands. "Thanks, Stephen," he said. "I'll see you on my next trip, then."

The man said goodbye to Katherine, and to Irene. His eyes widened a little when he spotted Hilary, but he didn't say a word, because just then Stephen said, "Come in, Hilary," and stepped aside to hold the door for her.

He wasn't surprised to see her waiting there, Katherine realized. And yet, Irene's orders were strict, and she didn't interrupt his conferences to announce any casual caller, no matter who it was.

So that meant he had known she was coming. And if he wasn't having dinner with the supplier, after all, then was it Hilary he was planning to take to The Pinnacle tonight?

Katherine's breathing had become fast and shallow, and there was a sharp pain deep inside her chest. What

was almost more agonizing was that she knew—
knew—why she was reacting like this.

She was jealous.

For no good reason, she told herself. She was his
wife, if only in name; she was the mother of his child.
What did it matter if he took a woman to dinner? He
had his reasons, and no doubt they were good ones.
And he had made promises to Katherine—important
promises. He was a man of his word. He wouldn't
break those promises, any more than she would break
the vows she had made to him.

But the fact was, Katherine admitted painfully, those
promises were no longer enough to satisfy her. She
wanted more than what he had pledged—much more
than to be just his wife in name, just the mother of his
child.

She wanted to be his love, the most important element of his life—as he had become the most important
part of hers.

When had she crossed the line from liking him, re-
specting him, enjoying the time she spent with him—
and let her feelings become something more?

Just when, she asked herself miserably, had she
fallen in love with Stephen Osborne?

CHAPTER EIGHT

KATHERINE CERTAINLY didn't ignore Irene's question about signing her outgoing mail; she simply didn't hear it. She went back into her office, shut the door, turned her chair toward the window and stared blindly out at the skyline.

When had she grown to love him?

The reverberation of that question was not like the blast of a single explosion, but more like the rapid-fire beat of a snare drum against her nerves, each beat driving the certainty deeper.

It hadn't been love at first sight, or anything of the sort, that was sure. She barely remembered the first time they had met, but it must have been soon after she'd come to work for Rafe. Stephen had been just another face, one of the almost-nameless hundreds she was trying to keep straight in her first week on the job. And in a company where everyone used first names— even referring to the big boss as Rafe—who would suspect that a Stephen might be any more important than a John or a Scott or a Travis?

But she'd never forget their second meeting. She'd had Irene's job then, and Stephen had come in from his own office, down in research and development, to see his father. She'd kept him waiting, kicking his heels in the outer office, because he didn't have an appointment, and it was only when Rafe greeted him that she realized how seriously flawed her judgment had been.

A little later, after Stephen had left Rafe's office, Katherine had tiptoed in to defend herself. She hadn't been as insubordinate as Stephen must have made her sound, she told Rafe. He hadn't given her his last name; he'd merely instructed her to tell the boss that Stephen wanted to see him. But she'd been acting on Rafe's orders not to disturb him until he'd finished his telephone calls, so of course she hadn't let Stephen go straight in, and if Rafe wanted to fire her for not reading minds, he could go right ahead.

Rafe had shouted with laughter at the whole misunderstanding—and then he obviously put the entire episode out of his mind and went straight on with the letters he'd been dictating.

The next day, when Katherine sought Stephen out and rather stiffly apologized, he'd presented her with his business card—so she would never forget him again, he had said—and the first of those devastatingly warm smiles....

How could anyone not like the man? And it was impossible not to respect him, because no matter how frustrating things got, he didn't take his feelings out on others. He didn't demand good work; instead, he somehow made everyone want to give him their best. And he was always there to back up his people when things got rough.

That was exactly what he had done—almost automatically, and without even knowing the cause—when Travis had dumped her, Katherine realized. She'd felt worthless and battered and rejected, and Stephen had been kind to her. His actions, and his very attitude, had been soothing and reassuring and healing.

It was certainly no wonder that she had responded to that sort of treatment.

But had it been quite normal for her to react so strongly? she asked herself. Wasn't it a bit bizarre to recover from a lost love so quickly, to transfer feelings so easily to another man, no matter how kindly he'd treated her?

She was forced to look at another possibility. Maybe that transfer of affection hadn't been so sudden after all. Maybe the change had been going on even before the actual break with Travis. Could she honestly say that it had been her heart that Travis had injured? Or only her ego?

She found herself frowning as she thought it over. In the last few months she had seen little of Travis; he'd been immersed in business, trying hard to keep his sales figures high in order to win his coveted promotion—or, as Katherine now realized, avoiding her so he could pay court to Sherry instead. She'd told herself at the time that she understood the need and accepted it, that soon the pressure would be off and they could make up for the lost opportunities. But had it really bothered her all that much? Was it possible that her feelings for Travis had lessened as time went by? Had the love she thought she felt for him gradually become little more than habit? When she found out about his engagement, had the only real blow been the one dealt to her pride?

Had she been in love with Stephen even before Travis had dumped her?

I was lucky, she told herself. But the admission did not come easily. How could she have been such a fool not to realize what was happening?

She had let herself be deceived by professionalism,

perhaps. Because so many of the things she shared with
Stephen were job-related, she hadn't even looked at the
personal side, or let herself wonder about him as a
man—consciously, at least. To do so would have vio-
lated the unspoken rules of the office, the code that had
worked so well for so many months.

And perhaps she had been blinded by familiarity, as
well. She was with Stephen so much of the time that
it was easy to ignore the changes in her feelings—
they'd come about so slowly.

But now, looking back with a new and clearer vision,
she could see that with every passing day she had
grown to care more about him. And sometime in these
last few months, she had crossed the line from liking
to loving, from respect to desire.

There had been such comfort for her, at Rafe's apartment on the night of Sherry's engagement party, just
in being beside him. She'd thought at the time that
almost anyone would have done; it was simply reassuring to have human company. But that hadn't been
it at all. Only Stephen could have made her feel that
way. Only Stephen—because she had already wanted
him.

And so when he'd taken her home that night—

"I set it up," she whispered. It had been subconscious, but that didn't make the facts less real, or her
responsibility less oppressive. She hadn't planned it out
on paper, but she had orchestrated it nonetheless.

She hadn't anticipated all the results, of course. She
hadn't planned on the baby.

But this sudden burst of honest appraisal of her motives forced her to admit that she hadn't done anything
to prevent that outcome, either. She had no excuse for

her carelessness; she was an intelligent woman who certainly knew better than to play Russian roulette.

And once again it had been Stephen who had stepped in to rescue her from the disastrous consequences—Stephen who had offered marriage…

Why had he done it?

His sense of responsibility, she told herself. He wasn't the sort of man who could walk away from a child.

But was there something else that had prompted him? More than once she had found herself thinking that there must be some other motive behind his actions, but she'd pushed that thought away. And though on the surface she, herself, had hesitated and expressed doubts, even encouraging him to think it over, the truth was that she'd leapt at his offer of marriage—because she'd desperately wanted to be his wife.

A perfunctory knock on the door was the only warning she had. Stephen was inside her office and standing beside her chair before Katherine could do much more than pull herself up straight.

"Are you all right?" he demanded. "Irene was worried."

"So she ran to you?" The question was almost nasty, and she instantly regretted it.

"It's not like you to be this way, Katherine. Do you think we should call Julie?"

"To diagnose a mood swing? I can do that myself." She swiveled her chair around so her back would be to the light. "I'm all right, just dead tired. I need to take a break."

He studied her face, and nodded. "Why don't you go home for a nap?"

And stay there alone all evening? Katherine thought. Wondering where he was, and what he was doing?

"No," she said. "I mean I need a change, not a rest." She was putting folders away without looking at him. "I think I'll go to the art museum to see the new show."

He moved then; she thought for a moment that he was leaving, but instead he circled her desk and dropped into a chair. "What's the show?"

"French impressionists." She closed the file drawer and turned to get her handbag.

"Mind if I tag along?"

She almost bumped her head on the credenza. "Why? Are you afraid I'm going to pass out?"

Stephen raised an eyebrow and countered coolly, "Is there any particular reason you don't want my company?"

"I wasn't saying that, exactly. From your opinion of the museum, I didn't think you were likely to be interested in impressionist paintings."

"I said I didn't like the building, not that I didn't appreciate what was inside. Did you make that reservation at The Pinnacle?"

"Yes." She found herself wishing she could cancel it.

He rose, lazily. "I'll have Irene change the time. After an hour of art, you may need that nap before dinner."

"You're—" Her voice was no more than a squeak. She cleared her throat and tried again. "You wanted the reservation for us?"

Stephen's eyes narrowed. "Yes, why shouldn't I? We did get good news today, remember?"

You didn't seem to want to celebrate then, she

thought rebelliously. "I thought you were taking—"
She stopped, and then finished lamely. "Someone
else."

"The supplier is the beer-and-cheeseburger type, I'm
afraid. I don't think he'd be comfortable at— Oh, I
see." He smiled a little. "You ran into Hilary, and
jumped to conclusions."

Katherine bit her lip miserably. Perhaps it *had* been
a foolish assumption, born of her own jealousy and fed
by her lack of self-confidence, and by the distant way
he'd been acting earlier. Now that she thought it over,
she realized that he surely wouldn't have flaunted Hilary in front of her at the office. If she had been thinking
clearly, Katherine would have seen how silly the whole
thing was—at least in time to keep her mouth shut
instead of sharing her idiocy with him!

"She came to beg a donation for her favorite char-
ity," Stephen said. "That's all. I'm beginning to think
Rafe was right about the advantages of being a married
man." He sounded rather self-satisfied.

Of course, Katherine told herself. That was the missing piece.

Stephen had indicated at Sherry's party that Hilary
was growing more serious than he liked. Jake Holland
had said much the same thing at the wedding, when he
had mentioned Hilary laying matrimonial traps.

But now Stephen didn't need to worry about that any
more, did he?

That was the hidden motive Katherine had sensed all
along. She should have realized that one of the biggest
advantages for Stephen in this whole affair was that no
other woman could make demands on him, now that
he was not only a married man but soon to be a father.

And at the same time, Katherine herself was in no

position to ask for anything more than he'd already given her. She couldn't become a troublemaker, because she owed him too much.

What he'd offered, of course, was largely material; a house, a pink-and-blue nursery. He had no shortage of money, so that kind of gift cost him little in real terms. What he hadn't promised her was the personal side—things like understanding, shared hopes and dreams, and fidelity. He would spend enough time with her, she was certain, to maintain his image as a family man. He had as much as told her he would. But beyond that, if he was inclined to wander, Katherine could hardly make a fuss no matter what he did, even if she was actually to catch him with another woman.

The truth was, she wouldn't dare challenge him— not because she feared losing out materially, but because having *any* of his time, his attention, his concern, was better than having none at all.

Once she had said, severely, that she would never get involved with a married man, that she wanted better than that for herself. Now she knew why women sometimes gave up their freedom for relationships like that—and why they stayed.

It was ironic, of course, though no less painful, that the married man for whom she was giving up her freedom was her own husband. Her love for him would force her to be satisfied with whatever she could have, no matter how little it was.

Meanwhile, and more ironic yet, by giving up his freedom in order to marry Katherine, Stephen was actually freer than he'd ever been before.

SHE HAD TO FORCE herself to study the paintings. They were gorgeous, and it was impressive to see the glorious colors and the intricate brush work from mere inches away. But on this afternoon Katherine would have been just as intrigued by a comic book.

Stephen seemed to have no such problem. He strolled from gallery to gallery, hands in his trouser pockets, inspecting each painting with infinite care. "Look at this," he said once, pointing. "Van Gogh put the paint on his canvas so thickly I'll bet it's still wet underneath. That's what gives it that luminous glow."

Katherine dutifully admired the technique, then wandered off to stand almost unseeing before a bunch of tiny dots that, from a distance, formed a soft and hazy vine-covered cottage.

It wasn't fair. She was supposed to be enjoying this show, while Stephen should be floundering in the unfamiliar; as far as she knew, he set foot in the art museum no more than once a year.

But then, she reflected wryly, Stephen had an advantage in this case. He didn't have the same reaction to Katherine that she did to him—the almost suffocating sense of his presence and the sonarlike quiver that ran through her whenever he came close. He was free to concentrate on the art, while the only thing she really wanted to look at was him....

Damn, she thought. *Things were a lot more comfortable this afternoon before I realized that I've fallen in love with him.*

So what could she do about it now? Not much, she admitted. She couldn't force him to return her feelings, or to change his attitude. Confronting him certainly wouldn't alter anything. Sulking, pouting or crying about her misfortune would only make matters worse. Then what was left? Accepting the reality of the situation and making the best of it, that was all. She could be pleasant, and decent, and keep her mood swings under control as much as possible—that was about it. But if she hoped for the best, rather than anticipating the worst, starting with the fact that she, not Hilary, was the one he was taking to dinner tonight—

She turned around, seeking him out, and was startled to find that he wasn't paying attention to the paintings anymore. He was sitting on a low wooden bench in the middle of the room, arms crossed, leaning forward and intently watching a baby in a stroller a few feet away. The baby, a girl Katherine guessed at about a year old, was just as somberly staring back at him.

Katherine wondered what he was thinking. Was it anticipation that was running through his mind just now? Uneasiness? Fear? Regret? Some mixture of all of them, most likely. She knew what that felt like, and a little swell of sympathy touched her heart. This couldn't be an easy adjustment for him, either.

She settled onto the bench beside him, at a careful distance. "It's not your imagination," she said. "There are more babies and pregnant women around this city than there ever were before. I've decided there must be a convention in town."

Katherine was astonished to see him turn just a little red around the ears. "You too?" he said. "I thought I was seeing things." He laid a hand over hers on the bench. His fingers were warm, contrasting sharply with the chilly wood surface under her palm. She hesitated for a moment, then turned her hand under his until their palms met and their fingers interlocked.

Was it sheer foolishness to think that reaching out to him could cause anything more than increased pain in the long run? She slowly lifted her gaze to meet his, and saw the smile coming to life in his eyes.

I don't care, she thought. *For right now, this is enough. And later, when it hurts—I'll worry about that then.*

THE MAÎTRE D' at The Pinnacle was a professional, that was certain; though he greeted Stephen by name, he didn't by the flicker of an eyelash betray that he had ever seen him in the company of a woman other than Katherine. The waiter, however, was not as well disciplined. He blinked—twice—when Stephen told him that Mrs. Osborne wished to have the tournedos of beef, and had to ask a second time about her salad.

"You've given the poor man heart failure," Katherine accused, as soon as he was gone.

"The waiter?" Stephen didn't seem interested. "I'm sure it's not the first time he's had a surprise like that. Are you sure you don't want an appetizer?"

Katherine considered, and shook her head. "I'm starving, yes," she admitted. "But I want to enjoy my tournedos."

"I thought you said Jake gave you lunch."

"He did, but I wasn't very hungry then. And in any case, we got so involved in talking about your cellular telephone idea that I forgot to eat. Did you call him this afternoon?"

"I tried. He was out. What's the verdict on my idea?"

She propped her elbows on the edge of the table and rested her chin on her clasped hands. "Didn't you know? He's got the unit installed up at the estate he was working on in the mountains, and it seems to be fine. But he said the wiring is an additional nuisance."

Stephen frowned. "Not all that much worse than an ordinary connection."

"Still, it's one more unit to be hooked into the central computer. So I thought—I mean I wondered—" She was almost breathless. "Instead of buying a regular cellular telephone, why couldn't we build a stripped-down model right into the computer that operates the whole system? Jake thought it was a great idea. It would be one less connection to install, one less to break down or be interfered with. And if the telephone needs only limited capacity anyway, why pay for a unit that can do everything?"

"It would also be a feature nobody else offers," Stephen said.

"Exactly. They can copy our product, but only by plugging the different elements together. We've got a smooth, sleek, single package—easy to market." She sat back in her chair in triumph, and promptly ruined her self-confident image by adding anxiously, "What do you think?"

He picked up his salad fork and was drawing patterns on the linen tablecloth with the handle. "You might be onto something," he said slowly. "I'll have the research and development people take a look. If it works out, Katherine, you get the honors."

A little glow suffused her whole body. "Jake deserves some of the credit, too. I had the idea, but it never would have occurred to me if it wasn't for some of the things he said. He provided the atmosphere for the brainstorm, so—"

The waiter brought their salads. "It must have been quite a lunch," Stephen said idly. "Sorry I missed it."

Katherine tackled her spinach and tomato salad with enthusiasm. "Oh, it was great fun." She would have gone on to mention some of the other things she and Jake had talked about, but before she could finish her first bite, Stephen had changed the subject.

"We need to decide some particulars about a house right away, so that as soon as you're feeling better we can start to look around."

"There's no real hurry, is there?"

"If you're going to have the pink-and-blue nursery done by the first of April, there is."

Katherine looked at the tomato wedge that was speared on her fork as if she didn't quite know what it was. She was suddenly feeling sick again. But this wasn't her usual nausea, which she was almost getting used to, but a different, soul-deep ache.

It could have all been so perfect, she thought, *if this was only real.*

"What kind of a house would you like, Katherine?"

She stopped eating. Behind her napkin, she murmured, "It doesn't matter. It doesn't even have to be a house. Anywhere that has enough room will do."

Stephen looked at her long and thoughtfully. "Of course it matters. Did you think I was only asking to be polite, before I tell you what you can't have?"

She put her napkin down and said quietly, "I'm sure you have some ideas of what *you'd* like."

"I suppose I do," he said. "I will not abide one of those long rows of town houses, or any development, in which all the houses look identical. I absolutely refuse to count driveways in order to know which one to park my car in."

Katherine tried to smile. "You could put up a flagpole. Or plant a rosebush. Or paint the front door red."

"I could, but I don't plan to. Other than that restriction the choice is yours. Is there something wrong with your salad?''

Katherine shook her head and picked up her fork to make another try at eating.

''So, what does your ideal house look like, Katherine?''

She gave in. There was no reason on earth not to tell him, was there? ''I've always wanted a red brick Colonial with white pillars and green shutters and a sun room and an attic. The kind of place that looks like it's been in the family for three hundred years and just grew slowly over time because no one ever threw anything good away. Is that different enough to please you? There are probably thousands of them.''

''As long as they're not all on the same street, it's fine with me.''

The waiter sighed over Katherine's uneaten salad and replaced it with the tournedos, small medallions of tender beef in a delicate sauce.

Stephen cut into his lamb chops. ''I'm not surprised at your tastes, but I am curious. Is that the kind of house you grew up in?''

''Me?'' Katherine said crisply. ''Try a tract house in Fort Collins. Not only the house but the neighborhood had seen better days. A couple of men down the street had a car they raced, and they were always tinkering with the engine—generally after they worked the swing shift.'' And Stephen probably couldn't be less interested in her childhood, she reminded herself.

He smiled a little. ''So you want a quiet neighborhood where the houses are far apart.''

''At least where there's enough room to breathe— and so if a child gets noisy or defiant not everyone in the block can hear.''

"Thick walls," Stephen added. "Ivy-covered, for extra soundproofing when we're beating the kid."

Katherine stared at him in astonishment, and caught the whimsical gleam in his eyes.

She was still laughing when she looked up and saw Travis and Sherry coming in. They were part of a small group following the maître d' toward a private party room at the back of the restaurant. It was the first time she had seen Travis since before her wedding, and catching sight of him was like being reminded of an old nightmare—one that was half-forgotten but still uncomfortable to think about.

Stephen followed her gaze just as Sherry saw them and broke away from the group to come over. Travis was two steps behind her; Katherine thought he looked a bit reluctant.

"The way you two have disappeared," Sherry said, without bothering to lower her voice, "it makes everyone wonder what you're hiding."

Stephen pushed his chair back and rose. "Some of us have work to do."

"Surely you don't need to keep Travis in perpetual motion, do you?" Sherry sounded sulky.

"I wasn't aware that I was," Stephen said mildly.

"I hardly see him anymore."

Travis spoke up. "I've told you, Sherry, I have a lot of new responsibilities."

Sherry shrugged and turned to Katherine. "I'll be chairing a designer showcase house next spring," she announced. "I'll tell the coordinators that you'll be helping me, if you'd like."

What sounded like a generous offer to share the limelight actually translated to a demand for free secretarial assistance, Katherine realized. "Thank you, Sherry, but I'm afraid I'll be too busy next spring."

Sherry's delicately arched eyebrows soared. "Surely you understand that chances like this don't come along often. In your position, Katherine, I should think you'd want to make your way in society."

"In Katherine's position," Stephen interrupted, "she may choose to do whatever she likes."

Sherry fussed with the ruffle that pretended to conceal the deep-slashed neckline of her glittery dress. "Well, if you want her to be a fuddy-duddy, Stephen…"

Travis eyed the gleam of diamonds on Katherine's left hand and said, under his breath, "I guess I was wrong. You do recognize your opportunities, don't you, Kathy?"

"Don't let us keep your friends waiting," Stephen said coolly. He sank back into his chair as soon as they were gone. "Sorry. Sometimes I think she was switched as a baby with the real Sherry Osborne."

"I'm sure the showcase house is a good cause."

"That's beside the point. Sherry has never learned the difference between asserting herself and being downright bossy."

Katherine pushed a bite of food around on her plate. "She doesn't know about the baby yet, does she?"

"I didn't see any particular reason to tell her."

"But you told Rafe."

"Rafe was a different case altogether."

Katherine thought that over for a minute. "Sherry wasn't very old when your mother died, was she?"

"About six. Why?"

"She must have been very hurt. When my mother

died... But of course, I was old enough to be on my own then.''

He picked up his wineglass. ''You didn't have any family left?''

''Not really. My stepfather had a couple of sons from his previous marriage, but I didn't see them often. We never were much of a family.''

''He never adopted you?''

''No. I suppose it was because my mother was getting a pension from the government for me. That isn't a very pretty picture, is it?''

''It happens. Was your father on active duty?''

''He wasn't killed in combat, no. He was on his way to his station in the Far East when his plane crashed. It was a big thing at the time—it wiped out his whole unit.'' She fidgeted a bit. ''Not that I remember, actually. I was only three.''

His hand covered hers, warmly.

Please, she thought, *don't offer me sympathy right now. I'll start to cry.*

He seemed to read the plea in her big hazel eyes. He picked up her hand and began stroking the back of it with the tip of his index finger. ''Tell me,'' he said lazily, ''in this pink-and-blue nursery, you aren't planning to drape the bassinet with rivers of white lace, are you?''

She smiled in relief. ''Why?'' she challenged. ''Do you have a problem with white lace? It won't make a baby boy into a sissy, you know, any more than teaching a little girl the proper way to throw a baseball makes her a tomboy.''

His eyes lit up. ''I suppose you're going to teach her?''

''I certainly could.''

With their momentary seriousness forgotten, they wrangled quite companionably over their after-dinner drinks—Stephen had coffee; Katherine, to the waiter's horror, asked for milk—and it was getting late when they went home.

She smothered a yawn in the elevator. She was relaxed and almost happy; it had been such a lovely evening. Surely she couldn't be alone in feeling that way, could she?

He took her coat to hang it up, and Katherine wandered into the living room and stood by the windows in the dark looking out at the golden lights of the city.

If attraction and affection and love had sneaked up on her, she thought, maybe it could happen to him as well. If she watched her moods, tried to keep things pleasant for him, made a home that he wanted to come to, then perhaps sooner or later—

He followed her into the room. She didn't turn, but she knew he was there, and her breathing quickened as he came to stand behind her, resting his hands on her shoulders and gently drawing her back against him.

Sooner or later—

"You sound as if you're ready to cry," he whispered.

Katherine shook her head.

His lips touched her temple, then traveled down across her cheekbone. He slowly pulled her hair away from her face and draped it over her ear so he could kiss the lobe, with its tiny golden topaz earring. She rested her head on his shoulder.

"Katherine," he murmured, almost against her lips. His hands slipped down over her shoulders until his arms were around her, cradling her to his chest.

She closed her eyes tightly against what promised to

be an overwhelming assault on her senses—caused not only by his kiss but by her own longings. The expectation was correct; the soft brush of his mouth against hers sent quivers all the way to her toes.

How, she wondered, could a kiss that was so gentle—hardly more than a touch—cause such powerful reactions? She felt like a chocolate-dipped ice-cream cone on a hot afternoon; from the outside, she looked just the same, but if there was a single break in the delicate shell there would be no controlling the results.

And deep down inside her, that was precisely what Katherine wanted to happen.

Stephen raised his head, and she gasped a little, trying to refill her lungs. Her fingers clutched at his arms in an attempt to keep herself from sliding helplessly through his grasp—for her knees had no more strength to support her than would a life raft with no air in it.

Stephen shifted his grip, his arms tightening around her—not holding her captive, but keeping her safe, she thought. Relieved of the effort of holding herself upright, she sagged against him.

He kissed her temple again, and her hair, and said softly, "You look so tired, Katherine. Perhaps you should have had that nap after all."

She almost staggered with the surprise of it. Surely this was a beginning, not an end. If she told him now that she was not tired at all—

He released her slowly, balancing her with his hands on her shoulders. "I'm going to try calling Jake. He should be home by now. Good night, Katherine. Sleep well."

And as easily as that, she was dismissed.

She retreated to her room, trying to hold on to what dignity she still possessed, and as she brushed her hair she told herself that she had been a fool to pretend. Games like that were for children, and she was certainly not a child. She had only one option—to accept what she had been offered, and not to pin her hopes on more. She would only break her heart if she tried to fool herself into thinking that if she was sweet and nice, Stephen would eventually fall as much in love with her as she was with him.

That sort of thing only happened in fairy tales.

CHAPTER NINE

THE REAL ESTATE saleswoman looked rather sulky as she pulled the front door shut. While she dealt with putting the keys back in the security box attached to the doorknob, Katherine walked down the steps from portico to sidewalk and turned to stare at the house.

From the outside, it was a perfect red brick Colonial—so perfect that when they'd driven past it last night, she'd immediately told Stephen that she wanted to take the whole afternoon off to inspect it. It had white pillars, green shutters, a sun porch, an attic, a fenced back lawn—and it was one of only a half dozen houses on a quiet block.

But the inside was a different story. The rooms were tiny, cramped and dark. The kitchen was antique, the bathrooms primitive, and the second floor bedrooms were interconnected instead of having a hallway between. While Katherine agreed with the real estate saleswoman that all those things could indeed be fixed, she knew they couldn't be done by April, or for any reasonable budget.

Katherine was becoming discouraged. She'd looked at a dozen houses in the last couple of weeks, and not one of them came close to what she needed. "What's next?" she asked the saleswoman, who'd followed her to the front walk. "I have the rest of the afternoon."

The saleswoman dusted her hands together emphatically. "The truth is, I don't know what else to show you, Mrs. Osborne. You insisted on a Colonial, and you've looked at every one we've got and rejected them all."

"I never said that I would only buy a Colonial. You asked me what I liked, and I told you." Then she bit her tongue; it wasn't the woman's fault that the house Katherine wanted didn't seem to be on the market. "Maybe if I was to look through the listing books again—"

The saleswoman checked her watch. "I am sorry, but I have another appointment. Perhaps some other day."

Katherine studied her with a level gaze. And perhaps with some other sales representative as well, she thought. This one didn't seem to be taking her seriously.

Katherine walked down the peaceful little street, shuffling her feet through the crisp red and gold leaves that blanketed the sidewalk. It was a quiet neighborhood, though she'd seen evidence of children at several of the houses, and it was just the kind of street she would like to live on. But she knew she'd made the only possible decision. It was the middle of October already. By the time they got possession of the house, found an architect, finalized the plans, and hired a contractor to gut the place and start over, it would be Christmas—and not a stitch of actual work would have yet been done.

She got into her car and considered what to do with her unexpectedly free afternoon. She could go back to HomeSafe, of course, where there were plenty of details to keep her mind occupied, but she really didn't want to go back to work. She was feeling gloomy and disappointed and in need of consolation. Stephen was in Boulder in the midst of a conference about a new addition to the factory there, so she couldn't even tell him about this obstacle. Not that she would bother him with it during business hours, anyway. She was trying to be very careful about keeping personal things out of the office.

And that was not the only thing she was being cautious about these days, Katherine reflected. Despite the fact that she knew it was stupid and foolish and pointless, something deep inside her would not let go of the hope that she could in some measure control her own fate. And so she continued to play a desperate, superstitious variation of the old child's game. "Don't step on the crack," said the sidewalk chant, "or you'll break your mother's back!" Katherine's version was only slightly different. If just once she was less than kind and nice and pleasant, then Stephen would never love her at all. On the other hand, if she could only avoid all the cracks that loomed in her path…

But it wasn't easy to be cheerful all the time, to be pleasant no matter what went on, to be always deferential to Stephen's wishes, not to upset the situation, not to impose her own wishes—and she was tired of trying. Almighty tired, to tell the truth, of being cautious about everything she said and did.

She pounded her fist on the steering wheel in frustration; the violent action helped a little. It also shook down, from above the sun visor, the blurry ultrasound photograph of something that looked vaguely like an overgrown shrimp. She held the picture out at arms' length and squinted at it. She could see the baby's head, of course, but to her untrained eyes the rest was a blur, even though the technician had tried to point out the proper number of arms and legs. A very snub nose was the only facial feature she could make out, and she could see that much only because the baby had obligingly presented a profile view. There was certainly no telling whether her baby was a boy or a girl.

She smiled a little at the warm glow she felt at even this fuzzy image of the baby. She tucked the picture back up for safekeeping and turned her car toward her old neighborhood. Molly would like to see that photograph, and she would probably sympathize about the house, too. A cup of tea and a little gossip with Molly, and Katherine would feel a whole lot better.

She had hardly rung the bell when the door swung open a few inches. Alison's face lighted with delight, and she started to talk with one hand while she tried desperately to undo the security chain with the other. Katherine laughed and told her to slow down, but it was a futile effort. Once the door was fully open, Alison flung herself against Katherine for a bear hug and then led her triumphantly into the kitchen.

Molly looked up from a recipe book and smiled. "You're a nice surprise. With all the noise from my mixer, I didn't even hear the bell."

Puzzled, Katherine gave her a hug and said, "Then how did Alison know I rang it?"

"Oh, we've rigged up a light to flash when it rings. Want a bite of cookie dough?"

Absently, Katherine helped herself to a spoonful. "I never thought of problems like that."

"Few people do, as long as they have normal hearing. There are so many obstacles to a deaf person being entirely independent that it boggles the mind to think of them all."

Alison pulled up a chair and climbed onto it, wielding the biggest serving spoon Katherine had ever seen.

"I've never heard you sound so gloomy before," Katherine said.

Molly took Alison's big spoon away and handed her an ordinary one. "I'm not gloomy, really, just facing facts. Think about emergencies—there are telephones for the deaf, of course, but they only work if there's special equipment at both ends. And what if there's a community-wide disaster—a tornado or an earthquake or a chemical spill? Warning sirens won't do Alison any good, and neither will the radio."

Katherine shivered.

"I'm sorry," Molly said. "It's certainly not your fault, and here I'm letting you have it with my political routine. Being deaf isn't the worst thing that can happen, though I do think sometimes that almost any other disability would be easier to handle."

"That's not a lot of comfort, Molly. I already have nightmares about something being wrong with the baby."

"And I'm not helping matters, am I? How are you doing? You look great—your hair is so shiny and your face just glows."

Katherine's fingers plucked self-consciously at the lower edge of her loose sweater. "Do you think so? I'm beginning to get disdainful looks from people who suspect I'm letting myself go."

"Don't worry about it. They'll know the truth, soon enough."

Katherine found that comment less than encouraging. She held out the ultrasound blur. "First baby picture," she announced. "But baby did not want to cooperate, I'm afraid."

Molly studied it carefully, eyes narrowed. "It's a boy," she said, finally.

Katherine snatched it back. "Now how can you tell that? I've looked and looked. Even the technician said he couldn't tell for certain, and if he could, he wasn't allowed to say."

Molly grinned. "Wait and see."

"You guessed, I'll bet. That means you've got a fifty-fifty chance of being right."

"Maybe I guessed. And maybe I know." Molly removed Alison's spoon from the cookie dough once more, covered the bowl with plastic wrap, and set it into the refrigerator. "I promised Alison we'd walk down the street for ice cream this afternoon," she said. "Want to come along?"

Katherine nodded, and watched as Alison's eyes brightened in expectation. "She may not hear," she said, "but it looks to me as if she reads minds."

They strolled down the sidewalk, with Alison impatiently dancing along a few yards ahead of them, and talked about Katherine's so-far futile search for a house.

"I've got nursery furniture picked out, and nowhere to put it," she confided. "But if we buy a place that needs work, I'm afraid that just when I want to settle into my nest and not be bothered, I'm going to have a contractor demanding total involvement. And the prices are horrible, Molly."

Molly shrugged. "What does Stephen say?"

"He's not worried." *Sometimes I think that as long as we look like a happily married couple, he doesn't care what it costs him.*

The admission caused a hollow sort of feeling in the pit of her stomach. It was three weeks now since she had faced the truth of how much she loved him. Three weeks since that enchanted evening at The Pinnacle. Three weeks since that gently explosive kiss, which to him had obviously been nothing more than a good-night gesture—because since then, nothing had changed.

He still brought coffee to her room each morning, though the worst of the morning sickness had faded away with the passing time. He still looked after her with care, and sent her home if he thought she was growing tired. He still took her out for dinner, or brought home take-out food, or complimented her efforts when she did the cooking. And he still kissed her good-night—but they weren't the kind of kisses she longed for. They were nothing like that embrace three weeks ago....

To tell the truth, he was being so nice that it was driving her crazy. If she could just work up a healthy anger—but there was nothing to be angry about, really. It was hardly fair to be furious with the man because he didn't love her!

"I bet he's getting excited about the baby," Molly said.

Excited was too dramatic a term, Katherine thought. He had sat patiently through the ultrasound test, holding her hand and watching the monitor—interested, certainly, at what it showed. And concerned about her, and about the baby. But excited? She shook her head.

Molly's voice was soft and compassionate. "What's the matter, Katherine?"

Katherine stared straight ahead, fighting to keep the blur of tears out of her eyes. She'd never told Molly the whole truth, and she sure didn't want to break down and do it now.

It wasn't a good idea to come here after all, she thought.

A few yards in front of them, Alison had stopped near where a half dozen children were kicking a big rubber ball. As Katherine watched, the ball escaped, bouncing past Alison's outstretched hands and toward the street. Alison turned to go after it, single-minded, heedless of anything but her quarry.

Katherine started to scream, then realized it wouldn't do any good. Alison couldn't hear the warning. Molly broke into a run, but her action was as futile as Katherine's; she was too far away to stop her daughter before she reached the street.

Katherine closed her eyes when she heard the tortured shriek of brakes, but a few seconds later she realized that her imagination was worse than any reality could be, and in any case, Molly needed her right now.

She cautiously stole a look. The car had stopped, skewed in the center of the street. Past it, the ball still rolled, its motion slowing.

Alison stood on the curb, her body thrust forward and her toes over the edge, as if in the very act of stepping into the street she had remembered that she was never, never to do so—and had stopped.

The driver of the car came running. "Is she all right? That ball flew at me and then I saw her out of the corner of my eye—" He got a glimpse of Alison's face, brightly interested in the commotion, and oblivious to the extent of the danger she had been in, and swore. "Damn kids," he said. "Somebody ought to teach them a few things."

Molly turned Alison gently around and picked her up. Her face was white and her hands were shaking, but her voice was firm. "Somebody has," she pointed out quietly. "She stopped, didn't she?"

They walked on. Alison fidgeted a little, wanting down, but Molly held her securely. Outside the ice-cream shop, she sat on a picnic bench and patiently explained to the child what had happened, the danger she'd been in, and how happy Molly was that Alison had remembered what she'd been told and had not gone into the street.

Katherine watched in awe and shook her head. "I can't do it," she said. "I would have killed her. No explanations, no discussions—"

Molly gave her a slightly crooked smile. "No, you won't," she said. "What kind of ice cream would you like?"

And that, Katherine thought, was yet another example of Molly-style discipline: state the facts and move on to a distraction.

The whole incident left her shaken, and she was quieter than usual a couple of hours later when she left Molly and Alison and headed for home. Could she actually carry through with this? Could she honestly be a good parent? Was she only fooling herself to think she could handle it all?

But you don't have to handle it all, she reminded herself. She would have Stephen....

But the fear of failure lingered, and it was a relief to run into Jake Holland in the lobby of the apartment tower. "Katherine!" he called, coming toward her. "I was just up to your door, trying to find Steve."

She glanced at her wristwatch. "He should be on his way home from Boulder now. Come and wait for him, if you like."

"You wouldn't mind? I really do need to talk to him."

"Not at all. I'm just going to make myself a snack."

Jake settled at the breakfast bar in the tiny kitchen and drank coffee while Katherine built herself a tremendous salad that included every fresh vegetable she could find in the refrigerator. It almost filled a small mixing bowl by the time she paused, and pouring herself a glass of orange juice she studied her handiwork. "Shredded cheese," she decided. "And slivered almonds on top."

Jake gazed at the bowl doubtfully. "Don't you think you're getting a little carried away?"

"Not as much as usual. I didn't feel like adding olives and turkey today." She found the almonds at the back of a cabinet and was starting to sprinkle them atop the salad greens when she saw a fleeting, puzzled look cross Jake's face.

Apparently, his befuddlement meant that Stephen hadn't shared the news about the baby with him yet. Katherine wasn't entirely surprised; considering what Jake had said about Hilary Clayton's attempts to trap Stephen into matrimony, she suspected he wouldn't pull his punches about this episode, either—at least to Stephen. Though she didn't think he would utter an ungentlemanly word directly to her, Katherine decided she'd rather not take the chance of hearing what Jake thought firsthand. She liked him too much to tell him half the story and allow him to think that she had planned and schemed and conspired to capture his friend—but she didn't know him well enough to trust him with the whole truth. If she let him discover her hopeless love for Stephen—

She added quickly, "Oh, you mean the sheer quantity of food here. Perhaps I did overdo it a bit, but I didn't have much for lunch. Would you like to share?'' She divided the salad onto a pair of glass plates, pulled another stool up to the breakfast bar, and ladled low-calorie dressing onto her portion.

They talked about the new addition to the Boulder plant, about the progress the engineers were making with the built-in cellular telephone, and about the latest marketing campaign their competition had begun. But somewhere along the line, the conversation shifted from business to more personal matters, and Katherine found herself telling him about Alison, and the close call the child had had that afternoon.

''I saw the look on Molly's face,'' she said, with a shiver, ''in the instant when she realized what was going to happen and knew that she absolutely could not stop it—that she couldn't reach Alison in time, and she couldn't get her attention.''

Jake patted her shoulder. ''Sounds to me as if Molly has everything under control. Give the child good training, and that's what comes through in a pinch.''

Katherine was still not satisfied. ''It doesn't always work out like that. If there had only been some way to call to her— But maybe there is,'' she mused. ''If it's possible to rig up a flashing light to replace a doorbell, why couldn't something replace a warning shout?''

''I can see the poor kid now—walking around with a streetlight strapped to her back and every time she does something wrong it glares at her, just like Mom.''

''Don't be silly. Maybe a light wouldn't work, but why not a vibration? Alison can feel that, I know, because there are songs she likes better than others, and it's the pattern of vibration that lets her tell the difference.'' She sat up straight, eyes glowing. ''If computer chips can make talking wristwatches possible, Jake, why can't we make a tiny bracelet that vibrates when a transmitter is triggered from a distance?''

"Why stop at that?" Jake drawled. "Make it an electrical shock instead. That ought to stop kids in their tracks."

Katherine glared at him.

"You're serious, aren't you?" he said.

"Absolutely. Tell me why it wouldn't work! It's just about the same principle as a garage door opener. Or any of HomeSafe's sensors."

"I guess you're right. I'm not saying it *would* work," he added hastily. "But it does seem worth looking into."

Katherine beamed, and flung her arms around him. "You're magical, Jake Holland, do you know that? Whenever I'm with you, incredible things happen!"

She had been so wrapped up in her line of argument that she hadn't heard the key in the front door, or the steady step on the quarry tile in the hallway. She didn't hear the kitchen door open. But she saw, from the corner of her eye, what could only be the gleam of a snow white shirt sleeve.

She turned her head in astonishment. Stephen was standing in the doorway, his dark red tie loose, his collar unbuttoned, the jacket of his charcoal suit slung over his shoulder.

"Oops," Jake Holland said.

Katherine was so close to him that the murmured word tickled her ear. She pulled abruptly away, struggling to keep her balance on the tall stool, and held her breath, half-fearful of the explosion to come. If Stephen would only give her a chance to explain, to tell him that it wasn't Jake's fault—

Stephen came across the kitchen. His kiss was a cool brush against Katherine's cheek, just as usual. "Did the house look promising, Katherine?"

Too stunned to open her mouth, she shook her head automatically.

"That's a pity." Stephen held out a hand to Jake. "Sorry you had to wait for me, Jake. Can I get you a drink?"

Katherine's hands clenched on the edge of the breakfast bar, and she sat there for five full minutes after Stephen had taken Jake into the living room.

Her mind was spinning in helpless circles, able to comprehend only one fact: Her husband had walked in as she embraced his best friend, and he had not even cared.

Unless, she thought, Stephen had overheard what they had been talking about, and realized that there was nothing improper going on. Did his calmness mean he knew Jake posed no threat to him?

She went back over the incident, trying to figure out how long he could have been standing there. Not more than a few seconds, she thought, for it was movement that had caught her eye, and he couldn't have appeared in the doorway without her being aware of it.

She could hear the murmur of voices in the living room, but not the words. Surely if there had been anger in one of those voices, and self-defense in the other, she would have heard it.

He trusts me, she told herself. But she wasn't convinced. If Stephen had interpreted that embrace as no more than developing friendliness, wouldn't he have made some teasing comment about it? Or would he simply turn a blind eye altogether, rather than risk his friendship with Jake Holland?

"That would certainly tell you where you rank, wouldn't it, Katherine?" she muttered bitterly.

She sat there for a long time, trying almost desperately to convince herself that nothing had changed. "It doesn't matter," she told herself. "You'll have the baby. You can make that child the center of your world. And Stephen—you'll still be his wife, in name if nothing else. That's what you agreed to in the beginning. You haven't lost anything."

She could still love him. Whether he ever responded to her love or not, nothing could stop her from doing that. And what alternative did she have, anyway? To walk away from him altogether?

It was what she should do, she reflected. If she had the smallest speck of pride, she would go straight back to her room right now and pack her things.

But she knew she wouldn't—because even through her pain, she realized that being without him would be worse.

She heard Jake leave, and she listened to the friendly tones of their parting, and waited—but Stephen didn't come back to the kitchen. A few minutes later she slid off the high stool and went into the living room. Stephen was sitting in his favorite big chair with the evening paper on his knee.

He's the picture of contentment, she thought cynically. *If I'd only brought him his slippers everything would be perfect.*

He refolded the paper. "What was wrong with the house?"

"Almost everything." Her voice was clipped.

"Do you want to tell me about it?"

"The house? Not particularly."

His eyebrows rose a fraction. "If you think I'm waiting for an explanation of the scene in the kitchen, don't worry.''

"Did Jake tell you what happened?''

"Yes, he did. But even if he hadn't, you wouldn't need to be concerned about it, Katherine.''

His calm tone should have made her feel better, but it didn't. Instead, his words seemed to light a slow-burning fuse deep inside her. She moved toward the windows, where the last purple rays of sunset gleamed against the mountains. ''Does that mean you trust me? Or that you trust Jake? Or that you don't care?''

He tossed the newspaper aside. ''Katherine, if you were hugging Jake just to get a reaction out of me...''

She said bitterly, ''Of course I wasn't. I don't think it's possible to make you react to anything.''

"Would you be happier if I made a scene?'' He followed her to the windows and turned her around to face him. Then his hand slipped from her shoulder to her chin and raised her face until he could look down into the liquid hazel of her eyes. She tried desperately to blink the tears away.

He said huskily, ''Oh, dammit, Katherine. If things were only different—''

Even if she'd wanted to, she could not have side-stepped quickly enough to avoid the sweep of his arm pulling her close. But she didn't want to escape; instead, she relaxed against him, glad of the warmth of his body and the way she fitted so precisely against his solid chest, her cheek resting on his collarbone where she could feel the way his heart was pounding.

That alone was enough to give her hope.

He didn't make any move to kiss her. He just held her, so tightly that she would have protested, except that she couldn't bear it if he let her go. So she buried her face in the curve of his neck, and tried to think about what he had said, and what it might mean for their future.

It took raw effort to force herself to whisper, "What things, Stephen? And different—how?"

He rested his chin on top of her head. She couldn't see, but she imagined he must be staring out at the darkening skyline, where lights twinkled on one by one, and thinking—what? She held her breath.

And then he brushed a hand almost awkwardly down the length of her hair and let her go. "We have some things we have to talk about, Katherine."

She felt rejected, set aside, abandoned, and she was as stunned as if the floor had suddenly turned into a log raft adrift on a tumultuous sea. If whatever was bothering him was something he couldn't discuss while he was touching her, it was a heavy matter indeed, and that terrified her.

When the doorbell rang she didn't register for a moment what it was. Then Stephen said harshly, "Ignore it. Whoever it is will go away." They stood, tensely waiting to hear the sound of retreating footsteps.

But the bell rang again, longer this time, and a fist pounded against the door. "Dammit, Stephen, I know you're in there!"

"It's Sherry," Katherine said, surprised.

Stephen put a hand out to stop her, but she had already turned toward the hallway.

Sherry stalked in and flung her trench coat over the back of the nearest chair. Katherine was staggered by the change since the last time she had seen the woman; Sherry looked ten years older. Her hair was windblown and her makeup was in desperate need of touching up. She stood with her arms folded across the front of her sweater, her chin at a defiant angle, and said to Stephen, "Thank you—I suppose."

"For what?" He sounded wary.

"For telling me that whatever Travis was doing with all his time, he wasn't working."

"I told you that?" Stephen waved a hand at a chair, inviting her to sit down.

Sherry ignored the gesture. "Not directly. But when you said it wasn't on your orders that he was working overtime, I started to wonder. I found him tonight with his little cupcake—the sales rep out in Boulder."

So that was why he was spending so much time in Boulder, Katherine thought. Travis hadn't been worried about accounts; it was affairs he had on his mind. "You poor dear," she said, and gave Sherry a comforting pat on the arm.

She meant it, too. In the long run, of course, Sherry was lucky to have found him out, as Katherine herself was. But that knowledge came slowly, as she knew from experience—and it didn't eliminate the immediate pain.

Sherry's eyes flashed with fury. She picked up her trench coat and slung it over her shoulders. "Don't twist your tongue giving me sympathy, Katherine," she snapped. "From the sound of things, you don't have a lot of room to talk."

Katherine felt an uncomfortable wave of color sweep up from her toes.

Sherry turned to Stephen. "Or haven't you heard that one yet?" she cooed. "There's a lovely rumor going round HomeSafe that Katherine's pregnant—that Travis is the baby's father, and Rafe made you marry her. How much of it is true, Stephen?" She smiled at Katherine. "And just think, all this time, I thought it was Rafe you were after.'' She strode toward the front door.

Stephen caught her arm in a grip that was obviously painful. "I'll tell you what, Sherry. Let's make a deal. You don't feed that rumor, and I won't tell anyone what a fool you are—and I'm not talking about just this mess with Travis. I know a whole lot of things that you wouldn't want your society friends to hear."

Sherry winced. "All right," she said crossly, pulling away from him. "It's no problem for me to keep my mouth shut."

She tossed her head and marched out of the apartment.

In the sudden silence, Katherine thought, *It's all right. We're safe now.*

And then she realized uneasily that Stephen had reacted just a shade too quickly. There had not been even a split second of surprise or hesitation—she had sat in on too many negotiations with him to have missed it, no matter how well masked. And surely there should have been.

Unless…

If things were only different, he had said a few minutes ago. *We have to talk.…*

Sherry's accusations had not been a shock to him, Katherine realized. He'd already known about her and Travis. He'd already heard the rumors.

And worse, he believed them.

CHAPTER TEN

SHE COULD SEE that belief in his eyes. And the compassion and sympathy. He wasn't angry, or shocked, or disappointed, for Sherry's accusation hadn't come as a surprise.

"I'm sorry," he said. "I didn't expect that to happen."

Katherine bit her lip until it felt numb from the pressure, and lifted her chin a little to look directly at him. "You were in Boulder today."

"My trip didn't have anything to do with that little scene."

"But it didn't exactly surprise you, did it?"

He sighed. "I knew about Travis, yes. But I didn't expect Sherry would have caught on just yet."

"And you knew about the rumors. Is that what you wanted to talk about? Travis and me?"

She thought he looked relieved at the level tone of her voice. She wasn't surprised; why should he realize how much pain was behind that quiet voice, how much fury was boiling up inside her? The crushing weight of helplessness was masking it even from her.

All she really knew was that she had never felt so alone in her life.

"Part of it," he said quietly.

But he didn't continue, and ultimately the silence

was too much for her to bear. "How long have you known?"

"Months." He reached out as if to touch her shoulder.

Katherine jerked away from his outstretched hand. "How?"

Stephen's hand dropped to his side. "Little things, mostly."

"But that didn't stop you from taking advantage of me, did it, when the opportunity came up?" She wasn't being entirely fair, and she knew it, but the ache inside her was so great that the only way to lessen it was to strike out.

He flinched. "Katherine, you were in such pain that night...."

"And you felt sorry for me, I suppose?" Her voice was like a lash.

"Not exactly," he said quietly. "I was afraid for you. I thought for awhile on the terrace that you were going to throw yourself over the edge. So I made up my mind not to leave you—but things got out of hand, and ended up even worse."

"And then you were trapped," she said cynically.

"Trapped? No. Katherine, please give me credit for one thing. I have never tried to avoid my responsibility."

She frowned a little. "If you didn't think the baby was yours—"

"I certainly knew it could be."

She was rummaging through her memory, and coming up short. "Stephen," she accused, "you never even asked me if the baby was yours." It hadn't occurred to her before that the question, important as it was, had never come up in all their discussions of the child. She hadn't noticed the lack at the time; because there had been no uncertainty in her own mind, she had assumed that there was also none in his. But the fact remained that the question—the doubts—had never been expressed.

He shifted from one foot to the other, as if uneasy. "And I'm not asking now. It doesn't matter, Katherine."

"How generous of you," she mocked. "Of course, what that really means is that you wouldn't believe me if I told you—so why should I waste my breath?" She turned her back on him, fighting to keep what little self-control she still had.

What do I do now? she asked herself. Because, no matter what he said, it *did* matter. There were genetic tests; she could force him to admit, sooner or later, that the child she carried was indeed his—

But that, she realized, wasn't really the issue. The question of parentage was much less important than the one of trust. If he couldn't trust her, if he couldn't accept her word—*I can deal with the knowledge that he doesn't love me,* she told herself. She could even share his life, and his home, and his child, knowing that he would never love her in the way she loved him. But she couldn't live without trust. She could not share her life with a man who thought she would lie to him about such a fundamental thing.

For no matter what he said, it would make a difference. She could already see how his doubts had harmed them. The quiet way he had received Dr. Quinn's report that all was well, as if he didn't care. His lack of excitement over the ultrasound exam. The fact that he hadn't shared, even with his best friend, the news that he was to be a father.

"You haven't told anyone at all, have you?" she accused. "You've kept it to yourself, as if it's some kind of nightmare and you'll wake up soon. Except for Rafe—"

What was it he had said about his father? *Rafe is a different case,* that was it. If it hadn't been necessary to explain his action, he wouldn't even have confessed the truth to Rafe, she supposed.

Stephen sighed. "If you want pinpoint accuracy, Katherine, I might as well admit that I didn't tell Rafe, either. He told me, after he saw you at that ridiculous temporary job of yours."

"He guessed?" Color scorched her cheeks in a painful flood. "So when you came to the park that day—"

"I wasn't surprised by the news, no."

"How did he know?"

Stephen shrugged. "You'll have to ask him how he made his diagnosis. All I know is that he came into my office and sat down with his feet on the corner of my desk and lit that damned cigar of his. You've realized, haven't you, that he only fires it up when there's trouble brewing? He told me he'd seen you, and that in his opinion the last thing you were suffering from was flu."

There was a sarcastic edge to her voice. "Didn't you tell him it probably had nothing to do with you?"

"I didn't tell him anything. I wish you'd get over the idea that your attraction to Travis was any big secret."

Katherine had to fight for composure. "Rafe knew that, too?"

"Of course he did."

"Then why did he come to you?"

"He said he thought I might be interested. Since he did see us leave the party together—"

"He drew his own conclusions," Katherine whispered. Then another, even more horrible possibility occurred to her. "Or did he want you to marry me to save Sherry from humiliation?"

"Don't be ridiculous, Katherine."

She clenched her hands helplessly. "Well, I suppose Rafe's reasons don't really matter—the effect was the same, wasn't it?" No wonder Stephen had told her that she couldn't come back to work unless she married him. Rafe would have been furious....

Stephen's face had gone grim. "Rafe doesn't give me orders, Katherine."

"But he's great at making suggestions, isn't he? I wonder if that's why he's so set on you being there when the baby's born—because it will make you feel more like a real daddy?"

"Dammit, Katherine—"

She put her chin up and glared at him, eyes blazing. "I release you from all promises, all debts, and all obligations, Stephen. And I consider myself free of mine as well. Now if you'll leave me alone so I can pack, I'll be gone within an hour and you won't hear from me again."

He took two steps toward her and reached for her arms. "You can't do that."

Katherine sidestepped him. "You don't have a single thing to say about it," she snapped.

"You might be surprised. You're my wife, Katherine."

"That state of affairs can be changed."

"Nevertheless, it gives me certain rights."

"Such enthusiasm all of a sudden!" she mocked.

"Oh, I see, now—you're worried about the way Rafe will react if I walk out. Well, don't fret. I'll explain to him that it's all my fault, and I'm sure he won't take it out on you." She spun on her heel and started down the hall toward her bedroom, then paused to fling one more barb over her shoulder. "After all, I certainly have nothing to lose—my reputation is gone already. It won't cost me anything to help whitewash yours!"

Stephen's voice pursued her, harsh and cynical. "As long as you're talking to Rafe, be sure to tell him I said he was right a year ago when he told me to fire you!"

She stopped, dead still, in the center of the hallway, and felt herself swaying in shock.

It was the last direction from which she would have expected an attack, the one aspect of her life Katherine would have sworn no one could challenge. She was good at her job. Everyone said so. Even in the midst of this cool, mixed-up marriage, Stephen had always been complimentary about her work. And as for Rafe, hadn't he told her when she'd worked for him that she was nearly indispensible—to him and to HomeSafe?

She groped for the wall to help support herself.

No! Rafe would never have made such a statement, and that left only one possibility—that Stephen would say or do anything right now if he thought it would hurt her. This was a side of him she had never seen before, and that fact steeled her resolve to leave. It would be better to be truly on her own than to subject her child to this.

She stumbled, unable to see clearly because of the tears in her eyes. She was totally alone now—more alone, actually, than she would have been if she had chosen a different road from the beginning. If she'd refused Stephen's proposal, or even if she'd decided never to tell him about their child, then she would have been able to delude herself with the belief that she could have had his support if she had only chosen to ask for it. And she could have told her child about his father with confidence.

But now both she and the baby had been rejected—flatly, finally, unfairly, and without cause—and now she couldn't even pretend that things might have been different if she had chosen another way.

I can do it, she told herself fiercely. *I will do it—alone. I can survive this, too.*

She grabbed an overnight bag from the closet shelf. She would take the bare necessities and go to Molly's apartment for now. There would be time later for gathering up all the rest of her belongings—if she still wanted them at all, tainted as they were with memories.

She didn't hear Stephen until he was in the doorway of her bedroom, standing with his hands braced against the frame, blocking the opening. "Katherine, I'm sorry. That was unforgivable." His voice was hoarse.

Katherine didn't look up. "Oh, it's my fault entirely," she said tightly. "I said I wanted a reaction from you. I got one—and I don't much like what I saw. Go to hell, Stephen."

He stayed planted in the doorway. "Don't be upset. It's not good for you."

She was dumping the contents of her dressing table helter-skelter into the bag. Her hands were shaking with fury. "You have got the audacity to tell me to stay calm?" She picked up the last item on the dressing table—a gold picture frame—and slammed it as hard as she could against the door beside him. He didn't even jump.

The frame hit the doorknob, shattering the glass and punching a hole through the blurry photograph of a young man in military uniform.

For what seemed like an eon, Katherine held the ravaged remnants of the frame as fragments of glass dropped onto the carpet, staring in horrified disbelief at what just a little while ago had been the only remembrance she had of her father. Now it was nothing more than meaningless scraps of metal, glass and paper.

She dropped the pieces because her hands were shaking too badly to hold them any longer, and sagged onto the edge of the bed, arms folded tightly across her chest. Her head was bowed, and sobs of almost animal intensity tore at her throat.

Stephen stepped across the broken glass and knelt beside her. "Katherine," he whispered. "Honey, please, don't do this to yourself. It can be fixed...."

She knew he was right, in a sense. This photograph was ruined, but she could take the fragments of the original out of the vault and go through the whole process of restoration once more. But that didn't take away the pain caused by the wanton, thoughtless destruction. It was like losing her father all over again—except that this time she had done it on purpose. And mixed in was the knowledge that *her* child was losing his father, as well...

She shuddered away from Stephen's touch. He stayed there quietly for a moment longer, then he got to his feet and left the room.

It was completely unreasonable to feel she'd been abandoned, when that was precisely what she had told him she wanted. But the suddenness of his leaving made her ache even more.

She huddled there, her throat raw, her head pounding, too lifeless even to fling herself down against the pillows. She had no idea how long it was before he once again appeared in the doorway.

She didn't look up, so she didn't see the package he was holding. "I was going to save this for a couple of weeks," he said. "Till your birthday. But maybe it will make you feel better."

Nothing, she almost told him, would ever make her feel better. Certainly no mere gift had the power to salve her pain.

But he sat down beside her, at a careful distance, and thrust the package at her. It was a flat rectangle, like a candy box, but a little larger.

She might as well humor him, Katherine thought dully. What difference did it make? Her head hurt too badly to get up and pack just now, anyway.

The box wasn't wrapped, it wasn't marked in any way. It was plain brown corrugated cardboard, sturdy and solid and not at all glamorous. She lifted the lid.

And stared in disbelief at a photograph of a young man in a military uniform. A young man whose face was not blurry or indistinct. A young man whose smile seemed to reach out like a mirror image of her own—

"Where did you get this?" she whispered.

"From the studio where it was taken. They still had the files."

"How—?" Her throat was so raw that every word hurt. "There was no mark on the original, nothing to say where it came from."

"As soon as I saw that terrible copy you had, I was intrigued." He waved a hand at the remnants, scattered on the carpet. "I was convinced there should be some way to get a better one."

She shook her head. "It was the best they could do."

"I realized that when you gave me the original to put in the vault." Stephen's fingertip brushed a lock of hair back from her face, tucking it behind her ear.

Katherine scarcely noticed.

"It was such a tiny picture," he said. "But it was a formal portrait, not a snapshot, and that meant a studio, so maybe the negatives still existed. That also meant perhaps it hadn't been the only picture taken." His voice was quiet, soothing, as if he were telling a bed-time story. "But I didn't know where to start looking, or even what your father's name was, for certain. I couldn't read the name tag on his uniform, and for all I knew your mother had changed your last name when she remarried. A hopeless quest, right?"

"It would seem so." Katherine was still staring at the photograph, at the clear dark eyes of the man she had longed to know. "But obviously it wasn't."

"You were right about the crash that killed your father," he said gently. "It *was* a big event. It made front pages all over the country. So it wasn't hard to find out where and when it happened, and get a list of the victims that included his full name. I discovered where he'd been stationed, and that he'd just been pro-moted. It seemed reasonable he would have had his picture taken with his brand-new rank showing, and that he wouldn't have gone far to find a photographer—so that gave me an idea of where to look, and the approximate date of the picture."

With the edge of her fingernail, Katherine traced the insignia on the uniform collar. "But…"

"Then it came down to finding every studio around the base, hoping that the one I wanted was still in busi-ness, and praying that someone would have been too conscientious, or busy, or lazy, to clean out the old files."

"That's incredible. The odds of finding the right one…"

Stephen shrugged. "I was lucky. The owner's father started the place, and he never threw anything away. So—here you are."

"But it's so clear, so perfect." She held it up at an angle to catch the light.

"What you had was just a preliminary print. Perhaps he sent a set to your mother so she could choose the one she wanted. It was never intended to be permanent. That's why it was so faded and worn—even aside from being ripped to shreds—that the restoration didn't work very well."

She sat there in silence for a full minute, and then she whispered, "Stephen, I don't know how to thank you."

He didn't answer, but he squeezed her hand briefly, and then put it carefully back in her lap.

Tears flooded her eyes again, a mixture of self-pity and sadness and grief for what could have been if things had only been a little different…

Hadn't Stephen said that, too, somewhere in the minutes before Sherry had arrived and the world blew apart? What he had meant was clear now.

If it wasn't for his doubts about the baby, Katherine thought, *I could still fight for him.* If he could do something like this, there had to be hope that someday things could be different—if only that awful lack of trust wasn't getting in the way.

And yet—was that what he'd meant? He had seemed to be wishing they could be closer—and yet if there'd been no baby, doubts or no doubts, there would have been no marriage—nothing on which to build any kind of closeness at all.

His voice had been almost wistful, she thought. It hadn't held resentment, or anger, or bitterness....

"Stephen," she whispered. "Why didn't you ask me? About the baby, I mean."

For a moment she didn't know if he'd heard her. Then, finally, there was a sigh, and an almost inaudible response. "Because I was afraid of what you would tell me."

The silence in the room was so intense that Katherine could hear the hum of the refrigerator, down the hall and around the corner, as clearly as if she were standing next to it. If he actually meant that...

Her throat was tight and dry, and her voice was almost a croak. "You would trust me to tell you the truth?"

He didn't look at her, but at his hands. "Yes. I would."

All the blood seemed to have drained from her brain. The sensation made it even more difficult to grasp the incredible implications of that statement. For if he honestly believed that she wouldn't lie to him, even if the answer was one he didn't want to hear—then anything was possible.

"I hoped the baby was mine," he went on quietly. "And as long as I didn't know differently, then I didn't have to face the questions that knowledge would bring." He raised his head and looked at her, a quick, sidelong glance. "I won't say I didn't wrestle with it for awhile, Katherine. But then I realized that it didn't matter. It honestly didn't matter. You needed me, and I..."

The hope that had been slowly trickling into her

heart drained away in a gush. "So you married me because you felt sorry for me, having to cope all by myself. And maybe a little guilty, too, because you slept with me once."

"Of course I felt guilty." His voice was low, almost painful. "I knew how unhappy you were. I knew you were only looking for comfort that night. But when you offered me all that gloriously lovely warmth of yours—I couldn't stop myself, Katherine. When you're suddenly offered what you've wanted for months—for years—sometimes you don't think very clearly about the consequences of taking it."

Katherine thought for a moment that her heart had stopped beating. There was a painful hollow in her chest.

"Fate handed you to me that night, gift-wrapped. And I'd had just enough champagne to let myself hope that you were real, that you meant it—that perhaps you weren't so deeply involved with Travis as I'd thought. At least you were seeing me, for a change. Me, not the boss—and you seemed to want me as much right then as I wanted you."

The room was starting to spin around her. Katherine carefully put her hands out and braced them against the mattress.

"But then the morning came, and you ran from me." He turned to scowl at her, his brown eyes brilliant with anger—and perhaps something else. "Is it any wonder I feel guilty? It was obvious that you hated me for what I'd done. You couldn't wait to get away from me. You even quit a job you loved just so you wouldn't have to look at me again—"

Her voice was ragged. "You wanted me to go!"

"No. I just didn't want to hurt you any more than I

already had.'' He put his head down into his hands. ''I loved you too much to do that.''

And I, she thought humbly, *actually believed that he was capable of using me.* She had found motives where none existed, and now, finally, she understood why. All her life she'd known men who used rather than loved, and she had thought Stephen must be the same.

''But when I found out you were pregnant, I couldn't let you go through that alone.''

She tried to reach out to him, but her hands were trembling so hard that she couldn't control her movements. ''Even when you aren't sure the baby is yours?''

He raised his head. His voice was almost harsh. ''I told you it doesn't matter. As far as he will ever know, I am his father. And that's enough for me, Katherine. That—and having you. Even if you can never exactly love me…''

It was a beautiful gift—a treasure of love that she would hold always close to her heart. She put her arms around him, and he buried his face in the curve of her neck, against the spill of golden brown hair.

''I was too stupid to realize it that night,'' she whispered. ''But somewhere deep inside I must have known even then that it was you I loved.''

He raised his head, and the blazing glory in his eyes sent startled anticipation shivering along Katherine's nerves.

''I have certainly never behaved that way before,'' she continued. ''I never realized that I knew how to seduce a man…''

''I'm sure it's easier when he doesn't put up much of a fight.'' His fingers slipped slowly through her hair, pulling it back away from her face and cupping her head securely. "But any time you feel a need to practice, I'm available."

Katherine's stomach did flip-flops at the sultry promise. His mouth against hers took away any need for words, and by the time he let her go again, Katherine could hardly manage to say, "I thought you didn't even want to touch me."

He drew his fingers through her hair. "I was too afraid of losing control again to take a chance. And I wanted you too much to risk pushing you back into that shell of yours. I hoped if I could only wait long enough—"

"Foolish," she whispered.

"Maybe. But you're not the only one who would have liked a little human reaction now and then. Dammit, Katherine, whenever I tried to kiss you, you just got more polite. Or else you yawned in my face." He pulled her down with him against the satin. "I'd have had to be a brute to try to take you to bed when you were exhausted all the time."

That reminded her of things that were yet unsettled. The sooner they were made clear, she thought, the better.

"About the baby, Stephen," she said firmly.

His arms were around her, and she could feel the momentary tensing of his muscles.

"Do you really believe that I could have married you, carrying another man's child, and not told you?"

"No," he said. "In fact, it hadn't even occurred to me that you might, until Julie said the baby was due the first of April, not the middle."

Katherine's eyes dilated in shock. It was no wonder he hadn't been full of excited plans the day he had got that news, she thought. No wonder there had been no more baby books or stuffed elephants....

"And then once I started wondering, I remembered all kinds of little things that fit right in. You'd been dizzy at Sherry's party…"

She remembered that, now. "I hadn't eaten all day. And if there's a problem with the date, it's in Julie's charts, because I told her precisely when this baby was conceived. And believe me, I do know—" Suddenly she was once more almost on the edge of tears. "Oh, Stephen, I want so much for you to be excited—to be happy about our baby! Please, for my sake, will you try?"

He drew her closer. "I am, darling. Watching the little guy on the ultrasound monitor—I wanted to shout. I could have bought out a whole toy store, but I was afraid to—scared you felt trapped, not only with the baby but with me. When you cried over that baby book… And after all, you're the one who has morning sickness and backaches—"

She smiled mistily up at him. "And mood swings."

"Well, you're not the only one suffering from those. When I saw for myself how much you enjoyed being with Jake, and it seemed you could barely tolerate me—" His arms tightened possessively. "And when I'd bring you coffee every morning and have to look at those nightshirts of yours—"

"What's wrong with my nightshirts?"

"Nothing, love. That's the problem. Sound asleep in a flannel nightshirt you're sexier than most women in red satin."

She tipped her head up and gave her hair a shake. "And how much do you know about women in red satin?"

"Well...there were all those women I was continually parading through my office, trying to make you jealous. Or were you actually so oblivious that you didn't notice?" He sighed. "Dammit, Rafe was right. I should have fired you."

"You will never make me believe Rafe said that!"

Stephen held her a little way off from him. "He most certainly did. In fact, he offered to do it himself before he retired."

She didn't quite know whether to be hurt or offended. "If he thought I wasn't doing my job—"

"He thought you were doing it a great deal too well, and he told me if I wanted you to ever take me seriously, I'd get you out of my office. He also warned me that if I insisted on giving you that blasted promotion, I'd never get close to you, and that you'd still be distantly pleasant to me at our mutual retirement party."

"Oh," she said. "Well, I'll do my best. To be pleasant to you, I mean."

He looked down at her, eyes narrowed. "If you ever revert to the way you used to treat me, I will rip your clothes off in my office."

"Mr. Osborne," she murmured, "you do have a way with threats."

He pulled her close to him with a groan. "We've gone about everything backward, haven't we?" he mused. "I'm sorry, love. I swear you'll get the courtship you deserve, Katherine—even if it takes the rest of my life."

She smiled up at him, and rubbed her cheek against his shoulder like a contented kitten, safe in the circle of his arms—and safe, for always, in his heart.

"Oh, it will," she murmured. "You can plan on it."

EPILOGUE

RAFE'S FINGERS TIGHTENED on the arms of his chair as the doctor came across the small waiting room. It was apparent that she was coming to talk to him, for he was the only one there at the moment; fathers' lounges outside maternity wings no longer were the busy places they once had been.

But a few minutes later, after Julie Quinn had given him the news, he didn't go in to join the new little family. There would be plenty of time for that, later. Instead, he strolled outside into a soft and silent April snowstorm, and paused to light the cigar he'd been nervously chewing since well before midnight.

It hadn't come off quite the way he had designed it, that was true. But it was close enough to satisfy him. In fact, he reflected, it was one of the better deals he'd put together in a long career of negotiation and compromise and flat-out manipulation. It was just too bad he couldn't sell stock in it.

Though as far as that was concerned, a seven-pound grandson wasn't a bad profit at all. He was contented with that.

Besides, with the way Stephen and Katherine were looking at each other these days—ever since they'd gone off to Hawaii last fall, as a matter of fact—there was the promise of another baby someday. Maybe it would be a girl next time.

A lighter streak slowly grew in the eastern sky as dawn approached, and Rafe Osborne smiled as he walked through the snow.

MILLS & BOON®

*M*akes
any time
special

Enjoy a romantic novel from
Mills & Boon®

Presents...™   *Enchanted*™   TEMPTATION.

Historical Romance™   **⊣MEDICAL**
ROMANCE™

Copyright © Harlequin Enterprises Limited 1997
All rights reserved

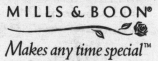

MILLS & BOON®

Makes any time special™

**Bestselling themed romances brought
back to you by popular demand**

Each month By Request brings you three full-
length novels in one beautiful volume
featuring the best of the best.

So if you missed a favourite Romance
the first time around, here is your chance
to relive the magic from some of our
most popular authors.

Look out for

Christmas
Presents

in December 1999

**featuring Penny Jordan,
Anne McAllister and Sally Wentworth**

*Available at most branches of WH Smith, Tesco,
Martins, Borders, Easons, Volume One/James Thin
and most good paperback bookshops*

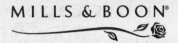

MILLS & BOON®

MISTLETOE *Magic*

Three favourite Enchanted™ authors
bring you romance at Christmas.

Three stories in one volume:

A Christmas Romance
BETTY NEELS

Outback Christmas
MARGARET WAY

Sarah's First Christmas
REBECCA WINTERS

Published 19th November 1999

*Available at most branches of WH Smith, Tesco,
Martins, Borders, Easons, Volume One/James Thin
and most good paperback bookshops*

MILLENNIUM

Celebrate the Millennium with your favourite romance authors. With so many to choose from, there's a Millennium story for everyone!

Presents...™
Morgan's Child
Anne Mather
On sale 3rd December 1999

Enchanted™
Bride 2000
Trisha David
On sale 3rd December 1999

TEMPTATION.
Once a Hero
Kate Hoffmann
On sale 3rd December 1999

Always a Hero
Kate Hoffmann
On sale 7th January 2000

MEDICAL ROMANCE™
Perfect Timing
Alison Roberts
On sale 3rd December 1999

MILLS & BOON®
Makes any time special™

THE
Regency
COLLECTION

Where rogues find romance

**Look out for the eighth volume in this limited
collection of Regency Romances from
Mills & Boon® in December.**

Featuring:

Fair Juno
by Stephanie Laurens

and

Serafina
by Sylvia Andrew

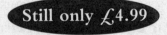

Still only £4.99

MILLS & BOON®

Makes any time special™

*Available at most branches of WH Smith, Tesco, Martins,
Borders, Easons, Volume One/James Thin
and most good paperback bookshops*

COMING NEXT MONTH

MILLS & BOON®

Presents...™

A MARRIAGE BETRAYED *by Emma Darcy*

Having been adopted, Kristy was now in search of her natural family. Armand was her only lead, but his need for revenge and the powerful attraction between them were a dangerous combination…

AN ENGAGEMENT OF CONVENIENCE *by Catherine George*

Harriet seemed to have fooled Leo Fortinari with her impersonation of her friend Rosa—he even suggested an engagement of convenience to please his grandmother. Harriet couldn't deceive the old lady further, but how could she confess the truth to Leo?

MORGAN'S CHILD *by Anne Mather*

After four years of believing her husband to be dead, Fliss learns Morgan is alive! Fliss has moved on, but will she able to resist the long-suppressed desire his return ignites?

A YULETIDE SEDUCTION *by Carole Mortimer*

When Jane meets Gabriel at a Christmas party, she fears he will recognise her. Their mutual attraction is reignited and Jane is forced to remember why she's changed her identity…

Available from 3rd December 1999

Available at most branches of WH Smith, Tesco, Martins, Borders, Easons, Volume One/James Thin and most good paperback bookshops

COMING NEXT MONTH

MILLS & BOON®
Presents...™

TERMS OF ENGAGEMENT *by Kathryn Ross*

Emma introduces Frazer McClarran as her new fiancé in order to resist her ex-husband's advances, forcing them to play the happy couple many times. But Emma knows she can never be with Frazer for real—or give him what he wants...

ZACHARY'S VIRGIN *by Catherine Spencer*

When Zachary mistakenly brands Claire a spoiled socialite, she vows that by the time Christmas is over she'll have won an apology from Zach—as well as his hand in marriage!

MALE FOR CHRISTMAS *by Lynsey Stevens*

When Rick set Tayla's pulse racing she had to remind herself she was a widow with a teenage daughter! It looked as if Tayla's quiet Christmas was turning into a steamy affair!

A DAUGHTER FOR CHRISTMAS *by Cathy Williams*

When Leigh got custody of her little niece, Amy, the child's father insisted the three of them move in together! Leigh would do anything to keep Amy—but marry a stranger...?

Available from 3rd December 1999

Available at most branches of WH Smith, Tesco, Martins, Borders, Easons, Volume One/James Thin and most good paperback bookshops

GIRL *in the* MIRROR
MARY ALICE MONROE

Charlotte Godowski and Charlotte Godfrey
are two sides to the same woman—a woman
who can trust no one with her secret. But
when fate forces Charlotte to deal with the
truth about her past, about the man she loves,
about her self—she discovers that only love
has the power to transform a scarred soul.

MIRA®

Available from 22nd October

A game of hearts.
A story of lust, greed...
and murder.

TWIST OF FATE

JAYNE ANN KRENTZ

Will Hannah have to pay
for her reckless desire?

MIRA®

Available from 22nd October